COMING OF AGE

Crystal Knight was thirteen, and she didn't mind saying so to her johns. To the police, of course, she indignantly claimed she was sixteen. She knew there wasn't going to be any argument. For some reason she couldn't fathom, she'd grown very good at persuading people to do as she wanted.

Not long after she embarked on her career she'd even talked a drunk, sadistic john out of slashing her with a knife . . . and into turning it on himself. For the rest of her life, she would be able to visualize again that squalid room, that rumpled bed, liter after liter of blood spewing out, so red, so red . . .

By John Brunner
Published by Ballantine Books:

BEDLAM PLANET

THE BEST OF JOHN BRUNNER

CATCH A FALLING STAR

CHILDREN OF THE THUNDER

THE CRUCIBLE OF TIME

DOUBLE, DOUBLE

THE DRAMATURGES OF YAN

THE INFINITIVE OF GO

THE LONG RESULT

PLAYERS AT THE GAME OF PEOPLE

THE SHEEP LOOK UP

THE SHOCKWAVE RIDER

STAND ON ZANZIBAR

THE TIDES OF TIME

TIMES WITHOUT NUMBER

THE WEBS OF EVERYWHERE

THE WHOLE MAN

CHILDREN OF THE
THUNDER

JOHN BRUNNER

A Del Rey Book
BALLANTINE BOOKS • NEW YORK

To
WENDY MINTON
for being a brick

AUTHOR'S NOTE

While researching this novel I received a great deal of helpful information from Dr. Louis Hughes of Harley Street, London, to whom I am consequently much obliged.

—JKHB

PART ONE

"Little Johnny may, like the sons of Belial, love evil for its own sake; he may hate being nice to others, but recognize it as a cost he has to incur if he is the more effectively to do them in later, and he may very accurately calculate the optimal concessions he must make to niceness for the sake of nastiness."

—From "What's Good For Us" by Alan Ryan (*New Society* 30 Jan 87)

THE SWIMMING POOL WAS EMPTY SAVE FOR WIND-blown litter. Most private pools in Silicon Valley were out of use this year, despite the heat of the California summer. Too many industrial solvents had leaked into the local water table, and the price of purifiers capable of removing them had tripled in the past three months.

Nonetheless—perhaps because they had arrived from Britain too recently not to treasure every sunny day as though tomorrow it might snow—Harry and Alice Shay had received their boring old cank of a visitor beside the pool, in canvas chairs with their names stencilled on the back.

From the refuge of his private wing of the house, David, who was nearly fourteen, spied on them between the slats of a Venetian blind. At this distance he could hear nothing, but he could make plenty of informed guesses about the conversation. Shaytronix Inc. was undergoing what was politely called a "liquidity crisis" and the caller was Herman Goldfarb, the firm's accountant, a portly, bespectacled man in his mid-fifties, and an absolutely archetypal whenzie, forever saying, "I can remember when—"

For at least two reasons he was looking extremely uncomfortable. His dark suit was doubtless okay in an office with the air-conditioning turned up high, but it was absurd for out-of-doors, even though he had been accorded a tall cold drink and the shade of a striped umbrella. So far he hadn't even doffed his jacket. And what was more . . .

The long-standing West Coast cult of the body beautiful was yielding to the risk from the ever-strengthening radiation passed by Earth's damaged ozone layer. Nonetheless both Shays still adhered to it enthusiastically. Though he was about the same age as Goldfarb, and going gray even to the hair on his chest, Harry kept in excellent shape and didn't mind who knew it. He was wearing exiguous French briefs and a pair of dark glasses. So was Alice—plus a gleaming coat of sun-cream. Harry liked her to be admired. He was inordinately proud of having married her when he was forty and she was barely twenty.

He tended to skate lightly over the fact that he had abandoned his first wife and two teen-age children in order to do so.

For a while it amused David—who was wearing nothing at all—to watch Goldfarb pretending not to stare at his mother's bosom. But that soon palled, and he went back to his computer. Coupled to a modem that accessed an international datanet, it was running a program of his own devising from which he hoped for interesting results.

This large, cool, low-ceilinged room, built on at right angles to the older main part of the house, was his private kingdom. A curtain across an alcove concealed his bed and the door to the adjacent bathroom. Shelves on all sides were crammed with books and tapes, barely leaving space for his stereo and his TV set, the latter murmuring to itself with the sound turned low. In the center of the floor stood a desk with his computer on it, its half-open drawers full of untidy papers. Most of the rest was taken up with memorials to past and current interests: along one wall a comprehensive home laboratory, including a second-hand electron microscope and a rig for genalysis and enzyme and ribozyme tailoring; elsewhere a bench with a rack of woodworking tools below it; at another place a broken-down domestic robot he was partway through repairing and modifying; in the furthest corner an easel bearing an abandoned portrait, jars nearby holding brushes on which the paint had dried six months ago . . .

The air was full of gentle music. On a whim he had set his auto-composer to generate a fugue on a theme of his own using the traditional instrumentation of a Dixieland jazz band. The effect, he thought, was rather striking.

The computer program still seemed to be quite a distance from the end of its run. When the TV said something barely distinguishable about riots in half a dozen big cities, David glanced incuriously at the screen. A mob, mainly composed of young blacks, was hurling rocks at store windows. Turning up the sound with the remote control, he caught the name of a soft drink, and curled his lip. So they were protesting about the FDA's ban on CrusAde! Foolishness on a grand scale, that! Something about the way the stuff was promoted had made him wary, and it wasn't just the claim that by buying it you would be serving the cause of the godly—half the profits, it was said, would go to some fundamentalist church already worth as much as a minor-league multinational. So he had bought a can not to drink but to analyze, and several weeks before the FDA clampdown had found out about the trace of a designer drug that it contained, not so much an additive as an addictive.

He had no trouble identifying it. It was one of his own inventions, and particularly popular with the dealers he supplied it to because it hooked its users nearly as fast as crack— nearly as fast, indeed, as the legendary (but in David's opinion also mythical) Big L.

How the makers of CrusAde had ever expected to get away with it, heaven knew. Maybe they had just hoped to take advantage of people's increasing distrust—and dislike—of government.

And/or the increasing immunity churches enjoyed from the enforcement of the law.

The computer beeped. He turned back to it.

And tugged in annoyance at his dark hair. Either there was a glitch in his program, which he doubted, or the data he was searching for were totally shellbacked. Or, of course, they simply were not available on-line. The last seemed all too likely, given their confidential nature.

Well, that settled it. Harry Shay was going to have to move his family back to Britain for as long as necessary, whether or not Shaytronix Inc. went belly-up in consequence. In fact, in David's view, it would serve the puky cank right if he lost control of the firm he had founded. He would still be a very wealthy man, for he was good at providing—well—safety nets. What he would say if he ever found out that for the past eighteen months David had been imitating him by siphoning the proceeds of his drug-designing to a bank in the Bahamas, it was impossible to guess. But if the need arose the revelation would provide leverage; being a minor, he'd had to deposit the money in his parents' name, with credit references furnished unwittingly by members of the Shaytronix board, and what he had done was so *barely* legal, relying as it did on gene-tailoring to make yeasts secrete his new drugs rather than synthesizing them, that news of it would instantly draw FBI and maybe SEC attention to the corporation. Indeed, the former had already taken notice of David, although not the company —but there would be no further trouble from that quarter, or at any rate from those particular agents . . . Faced with such a threat, Harry would have no alternative but to sell up and agree to return to England.

It probably wouldn't be necessary, though. David had considerable confidence in his powers of persuasion, especially after his brush with the FBI. Nonetheless, if push came to shove he would have no qualms about exerting that kind of pressure on his father.

He tilted back his chair and heaved a sigh, thinking: *Father—son* . . .

He had suspected since he was ten and known since he was twelve that Harry was not in fact his father. At any rate, given his and his parents' respective blood groups, the odds were entirely against it. Harry was fond of saying that biotechnology was going to recover from its current setbacks, and would indeed become the next boom industry once fifth-generation computers had been digested. Accordingly he had been delighted when David requested a biology kit for his twelfth birthday—one the boy had carefully selected because blood-typing was among the experiments listed in the instruction manual. He had, though, drawn the line at providing an actual blood sample, and David had had to sneak a tissue out of the bathroom waste-bin one morning when Harry had cut himself shaving. A tampon used by his mother had been easy to obtain, though somewhat harder to dispose of discreetly afterward.

And more than once, when he had glimpsed his father

naked, he had noticed what appeared suspiciously like a vasectomy scar...

He was a very cool, very reasonable child. He would have been quite content if Harry and Alice had levelled with him from the start, or at least from the age at which he could be expected to understand answers to the relevant questions. What made him deeply, icily angry with his parents was the fact that they had lied to him. Worse: they had gone to great lengths to reinforce their lie not only directly but indirectly. For instance, his mother, even now, was given to asking people, "Don't you think David looks like his father?"

Maybe I do. If I knew who my father was, I could say.

There came a shy tap at the door. Aware what it portended, he strode noiselessly to the window again. His parents were still arguing with Goldfarb, who had finally removed his jacket, and it looked as though the discussion was growing as heated as he was. They should be at it for another half-hour, at least.

So he waited, his face twisting into a feral grin.

After a pause the door opened and Bethsaida entered circumspectly, come to make his bed and change his towels. She was the Shays' Filipina cook and housekeeper: pretty, plump, married to a steward working on a cruise liner, a respectable Catholic mother of three—and desperately hoping her employers' son wasn't in here.

On realizing he was, and naked, she gasped and made to flee, but he was too quick. Darting past her, he pushed the door shut with his foot as he embraced her from behind, cupping her breasts in his small pale hands and nuzzling the nape of her neck. She made to resist for a moment, and then the magic took over. He unzipped her skirt and let it fall, followed by her panties, and drew her half-clad toward the rumpled bed. She moaned a little while he gratified himself, but she could not stop herself from giving in.

It had been a good two years since anyone had failed to do as David had wanted when he wanted it.

Now what he wanted most in all the world was to find out why.

You're watching TV Plus. Now for Newsframe.

A child has died in Scoutwood, County Durham, and thirteen people are in hospital, after eating vegetables grown in the garden of a house sited on a former rubbish tip. Arthur Smalley, 31, unemployed, who grew and sold them but is said to have been afraid to eat any himself, has been charged with failing to declare the income they brought in and will appear in court tomorrow.

General Sir Hampton Thrower, who resigned as deputy C-in-C of NATO in protest against the withdrawal of medium-range nuclear missiles, told a cheering crowd at Salisbury that patriotic Britons should declare their views and . . .

FREELANCE SCIENCE WRITER PETER LEVIN RE-turned to his three-roomed top-floor flat in London's Islington behind schedule and in a foul temper.

He had spent the day covering a conference on computer security. It sounded newsworthy. Two months ago a logic bomb had burst in a computer at British Gas, planted, no doubt, by an employee disgruntled about the performance of his or her shares, which resulted in each of its customers in the London area being sent the bill intended for the next person on the list—whereupon all record of the sums due had been erased. Consequently such matters were in the forefront of public attention.

However, Peter was much afraid that the editor of the *Comet*, from whom he had pried the assignment, wasn't going to be happy with the outcome. The paper, founded two years ago, was in effect a news digest, aimed at people with intellectual pretensions but whose attention span was conditioned by the brevity of radio and TV bulletins, and what the guy wanted was a string of sensational snippets about his readers' privacy being infringed, bent programmers blackmailing famous corporations, saboteurs worming their way into GCHQ and the Ministry of Defense . . . But most of what Peter had brought home consisted of a series of dry mathematical analyses, because the proceedings had been dominated by cryptographers. Worse yet, the most interesting session had been closed to the press and everyone else bar members of the sponsoring society.

Then, to add the final straw, he'd found that yet another unrepaired sewer had burst, putting his local underground line out of action, so he'd had to come back by bus, and while he was waiting at the stop it had begun to rain.

Cursing aloud, he dumped his briefcase with its load of conference documents and commercial handouts on a chair, draped his damp jacket over its back to await cleaning, and kicked off his shoes, soaked because he had trodden in one of the storm's first puddles. In socks he padded toward the doorless closet that passed for his kitchen, found a half-full bottle of whiskey, and poured a lot of it on a little ice.

After the second gulp he calmed down. There was an angle he could exploit, although it was far from ideal. One of the speakers—the only one with any sense of humor—had devoted part of his talk to the lack of comprehension still shown by lay computer users when faced with the need to invent secure passwords. Most of his listeners were serious-faced young men and women (an unexpected number of the latter, which was also a point worth mentioning) more concerned with the mathematical implications of their work than its value to companies trying to keep industrial spies from penetrating their research records, but some of his examples had made even them break into derisive laughter. In particular, his account of how that managing director—

But it was time to stop thinking and start writing! The clock on his computer showed half-past seven, and he had been sternly warned that he must file, via modem, before nine if his copy was to make the Scottish and West Country editions. Despite the fact that the *Comet*'s management boasted of possessing the most advanced technology of any newspaper in Britain, its outlying offices still wouldn't accept text direct from London without plenty of time to sub-edit it for the local readership. Maybe that explained why the paper had never achieved its target circulation, and was rumored to be on the verge of bankruptcy.

Hating to think what corruption might be introduced by scientifically illiterate meddling, Peter retrieved his pocket organizer from his jacket, downloaded its contents to the computer and set about converting rough notes into a usable story. Rain battering the roof-slates provided a dismal counterpoint to the tapping of the keys.

In the upshot he beat his deadline by a comfortable margin. He was even tolerably pleased with the way he had highlighted the joky speech and played down the mathematical side without actually ignoring it. He celebrated by pouring another drink, then paced back and forth to stretch his legs. He was stiff not only from his stint at the keyboard but also from spending so much of the day on plastic chairs apparently designed for *Australopithecus*. But there was bound to be a phone call once the editor had had a chance to read his text, so despite increasing hunger pangs he did not yet dare to go out for a bite to eat.

The wait, though, was a long one, and during it his previous mood of depression and frustration returned. In his late thirties now, he felt he deserved something better than this apartment. The politest term one could apply to such accommodation was "compact": this room that he worked in, with the computer and his reference library; a bedroom so much reduced by shoehorning in a shower and toilet that he had to walk sideways around the bed when he needed to change the sheets; and what he termed his "if-you-can-call-it-living" room which despite its electronic wall with TV, stereo/CD and radio tuner was scarcely calculated to overawe his visitors, especially female ones.

No, that was untrue—the result of a bad day and bad weather. In fact, he rarely lacked for presentable girlfriends, even though he was by no stretch of the imagination handsome. He was of average height, reasonably slim, in reasonably good health, with dark hair and brown eyes. Nothing about him was out of the ordinary, even his voice. Indeed, every time he heard himself on tape, he was struck by how much it resembled any and every British male voice on radio or TV, a common denominator, as it were . . .

Thinking of the TV, remembering it was time for a news bulletin, he switched on, and found the lead story was a subject he himself had written about a score of times, to the point where he was getting bored with it. Yet another group of famine-desperate black refugees had penetrated the *cordon sanitaire* the South Africans maintained along their northern border, and duly been shot down on the grounds that they were "biological warfare vectors" . . . There was no doubt who was going to win this particular war of attrition: the Afrikaners, like other wealthy advanced nations, had the AIDS vaccine while their opponents just had AIDS. Nowadays the incidence of "slim" in Kenya, Uganda, Angola, was estimated at fifty percent. What army could prevail against so subtle and vicious an enemy?

And the next item concerned a food colorant that had been shown to reduce intelligence in children—about ten years too late to save its millions of victims. To this one he paid serious attention, even making notes.

Stories with a medical slant were the chief kind that editors called on him to handle, because of the way he had drifted into his highly specialized field. In his early twenties he had been a student at a London teaching hospital, hoping to enter general practice. When he was at the midpoint of his course, however, and not making much headway, he met by chance a researcher for TV Plus, the maverick among Britain's television services, rarely attracting as much as ten percent of the audience yet constantly breaking major stories the competition was afraid to touch. The producer of the science series *Continuum* was planning a documentary on recent advances in medicine. Peter was able to supply useful information and prevent one gross mistake from reaching the screen—for which he received due acknowledgment in the credits.

Much to the annoyance of his professor, who did not approve of extramural activities by his students.

There followed a stand-up row and a not-too-polite suggestion that he might consider studying elsewhere. When he rang

TV Plus to complain about what had happened he met with a surprising response: the producer said he had been impressed by the lucid way Peter could talk about abstruse subjects, and the researcher he had met was quitting, so there was a vacancy. What about coming for an interview?

He got the job, and spent the next eight years with the team that every week for twenty-six weeks out of the fifty-two put *Continuum* together, graduating from researcher to writer to co-presenter. During his stint the series won two prestigious awards. Then the producer emigrated, tempted by a higher salary, and the show was cancelled.

But by then Peter Levin had a reputation, and plenty of contacts in the press as well as in broadcasting. He decided to set up as a freelance, and so far he had managed to stay afloat. Acting as a consultant here, writing a script or two there, occasionally helping to design and edit a coffee-table science book, he had in fact done very nicely to begin with. In particular he had had the chance to travel to places he could never have afforded to visit except at a publisher's or TV company's expense.

Lately, though . . .

He sighed. It wasn't simply his problem. So long as computer generated panics kept driving the stock markets crazy, so long as Britain was excluded from the Japanese economic sphere—which meant in effect as long as this damned stupid government remained in power—things could only get worse.

The phone rang. Startled, he realized he had paid no attention whatever to the rest of the news. Hastily cutting the volume with one hand, he snatched up the instrument with the other.

"Jake Lafarge for you," the phone said. That was the editor who had sent him to cover today's conference.

"Well, what did you think of my piece?" he demanded with feigned heartiness.

"It'll do," Lafarge grunted. "It'll have to."

"That's all? I thought it was rather featly, considering. Some of the jokes—"

"Peter, this paper is the *Comet*, not the *Comic*!" Lafarge interrupted. "Wasn't there supposed to be a closed session this afternoon?"

"Of course." Peter blinked. "You saw the program."

"And you weren't at it?"

"How would you expect me to manage that? Sneak in with a forged membership card? Jake, this was a conference on security, for heaven's sake!"

"You didn't pick the brains of the people who had been at it? You didn't grab hold of even one and pour him full of booze to loosen his tongue?"

"I talked to everyone I could!" Peter flared. "In fact I spent so long picking brains I didn't get home until—"

But it was obvious Lafarge was in no mood to listen to excuses. He was carrying on as though Peter hadn't spoken.

"What I wouldn't give for a decent beat on a major scandal! What the hell is the use of having the best equipment in the business if I can't afford to hire the best staff? Day after day, week after week, I see stories we ought to have broken turning up in the *Guardian* or *Observer*—the blunt end of the market for God's sake, when we're supposed to be the sharp one! We're neck-deep in bocky computers and we still can't use them to dig up the kind of dirt I'm sure must be accessible if you know how. At least I've finally managed to—"

He broke off in mid-sentence. Silently Peter wondered how long Lafarge was going to keep his job. By the sound of it the guy was bending his elbow rather too often. After a long pause, he said maliciously, "You were saying?"

"Forget it!" Lafarge snapped. "And I mean that!"

Yes, baas! But Peter kept that to himself. Instead he reverted to the most important matter in hand. "Have you authorized my fee?"

"Yes, of course. It'll be in your account tomorrow. And"—effortfully—"I'm sorry I snapped your head off. Not your fault. Just bear in mind, will you, that I'm quite serious about needing a major break? I . . . Well, we do pay competitive rates."

There speaks the voice of desperation. Maybe those rumors about the paper going under are true!

With half his mind Peter wondered where he could peddle that particular snippet of information; with the other, he uttered comforting noises and gloomily cradled the phone. The

Comet wasn't his best market, but it was a useful standby, and without it . . .

But he was ravenous, and the rain had let up. Time to go in search of food.

THIRTEEN-YEAR-OLD DYMPHNA CLANCY PAUSED outside the Mother Superior's office whither she had been bidden at the unlikely hour of bedtime. She wished there were a mirror nearby, but there were very few within the precincts of the convent school, it being held that to contemplate one's own reflection was to cultivate the sin of vanity. But there was an uncurtained window, at least, in which she could catch a glimpse of herself. So far as she could judge her uniform was acceptably neat and her dark hair acceptably tidy. If she were at fault in either regard, of course, she could expect to be told, and in no uncertain terms.

Not that it made—not that it could make—very much difference. Not nowadays. But having to face up to, then outface, the kind of tongue-lashing the nuns could bring to bear on a pupil was at best uncomfortable, making her palms sweat and her heart pound hammerwise, and all too often it was downright exhausting. Dymphna found it best to conform, at least on the surface.

She wished she were not so afraid that one of the offenses she was now accustomed to committing as it were below the surface might have come to light. But how else to account for this late summons to the Presence?

Steeling herself for a lengthy and unwelcome ordeal, she tapped on the office door. Mother Aloysia called at once, "Come in, child!"

Child? What on earth makes her say that?

More puzzled than ever, though a fraction less anxious, Dymphna opened the door.

Mother Aloysia was not alone. Present also were Sister Ursula, the nun who had general oversight of Dymphna's age-group among the pupils, Father Rogan, the school's chaplain and confessor, and a stranger in a dark suit: a ruddy-faced man with a walrus moustache, balancing a black Homburg hat awkwardly on his knee.

There was a vacant chair in the middle of the floor.

"Sit down, child," Dymphna heard. She complied, wondering at the unfamiliar expression on Mother Aloysia's face. Seldom before had she seen it otherwise than as if carved in stone, the eyes narrowed, the cheeks sucked in, the mouth a compressed slit. Nor had she ever heard the least hint of tenderness in her reedy but authoritative voice.

There was a pause. Then the Mother Superior resumed.

"I am going to have to ask you to be strong, Dymphna. We—well, we have bad news. This is Mr. Corkran, a partner in the law firm that administers the estate of your late father. He has kindly come to inform you in person, rather than simply telephoning."

So I'm not here to be hauled over the coals!

Dymphna relaxed, trying not to make the response too visible, and taking care to press her knees together in the prescribed fashion.

She scarcely recalled her father, and indeed had never been told much about him directly. But malicious gossip abounded in the school, among the teaching nuns as well as the pupils, and from hints and insults she had pieced together the most crucial truth concerning Brendan Clancy. He had killed himself. Though it had been in a fit of drunken misery, he had indubitably committed a mortal sin.

At first she had been terrified; were not the sins of the fathers visited upon the children, even to the third and fourth generation?

Oddly, though, within a relatively short time, she had begun to feel quite otherwise. Now she had come to picture her background as rather romantic, and to look down on her more respectable schoolmates as unenterprising and conform-

ist. Little by little she had taken to exploring the limits of her
potential for misbehavior, commencing with minor acts of defiance, graduating a year or so ago to offenses that in the
normal way—committed, that was to say, by any other of the
girls—would have resulted in punishment on the grand scale.
For instance, had any of them been caught by a monitor in
possession of photographs showing men and women embracing in the nude . . .

But Dymphna had lots of them, that she had bribed from
the baker's delivery boy with kisses and occasional permission
to grope inside her blouse, which she circulated among the
older pupils—for a consideration. Within the past few
months, moreover, she had started to earn some real money.
The supplier of the material was the delivery boy's older
brother, a long-distance lorry driver, able to smuggle in the
very latest magazines from France and Italy. Having nearly
been caught once by the *Gardai*, he had needed a secure place
to hide his stocks, and was willing to pay handsomely for one.
Dymphna obliged. Who would think of searching a convent
school for pornographic magazines? Not to mention condoms,
sold at a markup of several hundred per cent!

Was there no limit to what she could get away with?

I think I must take after my mother!

Of whom, equally, she knew little, for they met only once
a month, on a Saturday afternoon, when a nurse brought Mrs.
Imelda Clancy to the school in a taxi: a frail, vague woman
looking far older than her age, with a drawn face and untidy
gray hair, saying little and seeming to understand less. For
years the other girls had been accustomed to poke fun at
Dymphna after each visit, though lately they had given up,
perhaps because in some remote incomprehensible sense they
were envious of the difference between her background—redolent of sensational newspaper stories—and their own futures, as predictable as they were humdrum.

It had been explained, in roundabout terms, that when her
father ran away her mother had suffered a nervous breakdown,
which was why the nuns had taken her into care. Yet that
could only be part of the story. Further clues garnered from
general gossip found their way to her ears, and she pieced

them together. Allegedly her "father" was not indeed her father (though she lacked perfect understanding of biological parenthood despite her store of contraceptives and the pictures she possessed). In other words, her mother had been unfaithful to him with another man, and Dymphna was the fruit of an adulterous union.

More romantic than ever! She must be a love-child! And thought there was no more beautiful word in the language.

When she prayed—which she did at the times ordained, though without conviction, for she was far from satisfied about the Creator's continuing interest in His handiwork—she begged not for salvation, nor for a vocation to the Order, but for something the nuns would have had conniptions about. She pleaded to be reunited with her real father, who must surely have other children. She wanted to meet her half-sisters and above all her half-brothers. She wanted to meet boys with whom she could . . . But at that point even her fevered imagination faltered. And in any case, this was not the moment to think about such matters.

Carefully composing her small face into a mask that mingled puzzlement and apprehension—since that was obviously what they were expecting of her—she turned to Mr. Corkran and looked a mute question.

He tugged a handkerchief from the breast pocket of his jacket and mopped his forehead before answering.

"I won't beat about the bush, Miss Clancy. It is my sad duty to report that your mother won't be coming to visit you any more."

"You mean . . .?" Dymphna whispered with a show of anxiety worthy of a professional actress.

Mr. Corkran gave a solemn nod. "I do indeed. She passed away earlier this evening, after a heart attack. All that could be done was done, I promise you. And the doctor who was called said she must have suffered very little pain."

There was silence for a while. They were all gazing at her expectantly. But what sort of reaction were they looking for? Should she break down in tears? Mother Aloysia had instructed her to be brave, so that could scarcely be it—Ah! Of course!

As though repressing sobs, she forced out, "Was there time for her to see a priest?"

They relaxed. She had guessed correctly. In a tone of unprecedented gentleness Sister Ursula—normally the fiercest disciplinarian at the school—replied.

"I'm afraid, my dear, that by the time he arrived your mother was already unconscious. But we are assured that she had made confession very recently, and there can have been but little burden of sin on her poor weak mind."

"Besides," rumbled Father Rogan, "God is merciful to those who have spent long in expiating youthful faults."

He crossed himself; so did the others, and Dymphna made haste to copy them. Then silence fell again.

What was she supposed to do now? Several possibilities sprang to mind, and she settled on the one that struck her as most likely to be approved by Sister Ursula. Mother Aloysia was a comparatively remote figure, which was why the girls referred to visiting her office as "being summoned into the Presence." Leaning forward, she ventured, "May I please not go straight back to the dormitory? I"—she introduced a convincing break into her voice—"I would like to spend a while by myself. In the chapel."

Sister Ursula glanced at the Mother Superior. After a moment the latter gave a nod.

"I think in the circumstances that would be appropriate. Shall we say—ah—half an hour? We can talk about the rest in the morning: arrangements for the funeral, and the other sad necessities. Sister Ursula, please escort Dymphna to the chapel, then return to the dormitory and inform the girls of what has happened, to prevent any silly rumors breaking out. Tell them they must be especially kind to their friend during this period of trial."

"Yes, Mother Superior," said Sister Ursula, rising. "Come along, child."

On the threshold Dymphna turned back. Almost inaudibly she said, "Thank you, Mr. Corkran. For taking the trouble to come and tell me in person. I appreciate it."

When the door swung closed, the lawyer said heartily, "She seems to be taking it amazingly well. I was rather afraid she might . . . And she's most polite, too. Your standards must be very high."

Had that too not been a manifestation of pride, Mother Aloysia might almost have been said to preen at the compliment. However, she said only, "We do our best. And I think we may count Dymphna among our successes, especially in view of her background. For quite some time she was—well—troublesome, but over the past year or two I don't believe I've heard a single complaint about her. None, at least, that can't be ascribed to youthful high spirits."

She reached for a notepad and pen. "Now"—briskening—"what arrangements must we make for her to attend the funeral? Where and when is it to be held?"

The chapel was almost completely in darkness. Thanking Sister Ursula, Dymphna glanced at her watch, which had been her mother's. It was old-fashioned, pre-digital, and tended to gain, but it did have luminous hands. As soon as Sister Ursula's clumping footsteps had faded out of earshot, she made for the corner where there was least light of all and sat down, shaking her head.

Had they really expected her to weep and moan and scream on being told that that near-stranger, her mother, could no longer be brought here for those strained, boring hour-long encounters? Whatever Imelda Clancy had been like when she bore her only child, she must subsequently have altered out of recognition. It was impossible to imagine such a feeble, nearly mindless person conducting a passionate affair with a man she wasn't married to.

And that affair was the only thing about her mother that Dymphna Clancy had ever admired. Just as his suicide was all she could find to admire about her father.

She consulted her watch again. Five minutes had passed. Sister Ursula might possibly return five minutes before the promised half-hour was up, but until then . . .

She must make the most of the next twenty minutes, for such a chance might not occur again. The evening being mild, she would have liked to strip off completely, but that was far too risky; she could well become too lost in her own delight to notice Sister Ursula's thumping tread in time to dress again. She must content herself with thrusting her ugly, bulky knickers down around her ankles, sliding her left hand up inside her blouse and vest to stroke her nipples, probing with her right middle finger among the tuft of silky curls that since the onset of her menses had sprouted at the base of her belly, locating that special spot she had been taught about by "wicked" Caitlin, the monitor to whom, strictly speaking, she owed a considerable apology, as well as a debt of gratitude for enlightening her about the pleasure hidden in her body. In a phrase learned from her illicit reading, though: what the hell? Caitlin had been bright, popular, much approved; nonetheless she had been expelled last year on the day she turned sixteen, because a pornographic picture had come to light when Sister Ursula searched under her mattress, and it was far easier to believe that pretty, sexy Caitlin had sneaked it in than a mere thirteen-year-old—especially one who could lie so convincingly, and cared not a hoot for anybody's reputation save her own . . .

When Dymphna had come, she picked the lock of the ambry with one of her hairclips—something she had done before—took out the communion chalice and peed in it. Since, as usual, she had already relieved herself in expectation of bedtime, she passed only a few drops, but it was enough to make her quiver with unbearable excitement at her blasphemy. She poured the urine out of a window that stood ajar, and such was the thrill that she was able to make herself come a second time, and then a third.

Sister Ursula was calling. Pale and exhausted, Dymphna emerged into the light. Her clothing was in neat array again.

"Poor child," said Sister Ursula, laying a bony arm around her shoulders. "I heard you moaning, didn't I? Be comforted! Surely your mother has been called to join the company in heaven."

Dymphna made no reply. But it was hard for her not to chuckle as she fell asleep.

You're watching TV Plus. It's time for Newsframe.

Reports of intensely acid rain over much of northwest Europe during the afternoon led to sharp rises on the Stock Exchange, particularly in respect of wool, cotton and linen futures, and shares in companies producing synthetic fibers also showed a marked gain. However, forestry and agricultural shares fell by several points.

General Thrower's views have been condemned by a number of opposition MPs, one of whom accused him of attempting to revive the Blackshirts of the 1930's . . .

By THE TIME PETER HAD BOUGHT AND EATEN A doner kebab, washed down with a can of lager, it was after ten, but he felt restless rather than tired. He considered phoning a girl who lived nearby, to ask if he might drop in, but decided his day had taken too much out of him. Besides, though she had shown him her AIDS certificate, he wasn't sure it was valid. According to the grapevine, several of last year's batches of vaccine had proved faulty.

The television was still on, so he decided to play channel roulette. Even as he punched the first button on the remote control, however, he remembered he had checked neither his answering machine nor his email, though he should have done so by calling in from the conference hall, or at the latest when he arrived home.

Annoyed with himself, for there was always a chance that a new assignment might be in the offing, and currently he needed all the work he could get, he played back the phone

21

messages first. Someone wanted him at the launch party for a new book; he made a note of that, because there would be free food and booze and possibly some useful contacts. Someone else had invited him (and who could guess how many colleagues?) to a meeting of physicists at The Hague next month, but made no reference to expenses, let alone a fee—assuming, obviously, that he would find a paper or magazine to pay his way. It might be worth sussing out, but it didn't sound especially hopeful. And that was it.

Maybe email would be more interesting. His modem still being up, he entered his net-code and dumped the contents of his mailbox into local memory. Reviewing what appeared on screen, though, he found nothing but routine odds and ends: a friend promising to answer an inquiry when she'd done some research (blast! If he didn't get that story out quickly someone else would beat him to it); a call from a woman called Lesley Walters saying it had been too long since they interfaced (who in hell was she? Had they interfaced, as it were, in bed, and if so would it be worth renewing the acquaintance?); and—

Nuts!

The rest was junk mail. Thank goodness they'd been forced to abandon the idea of billing email users for incoming messages! Victorian values be damned—that was reverting to the past with a vengeance! There was that story in Walter Scott's memoirs about paying for a parcel containing the MS of a romance about Indian lovers by a woman who had never set foot outside the English town where she was born, and then as much again for another copy that she'd sent for fear the first might go astray...

Some day he was going to buy one of those new gadgets that wiped junk automatically unless countermanded. But demand for them was so great that the price was staying up in the stratosphere, like the cost of water purifiers in California this year.

Thinking of California: he might perhaps log on some time with Harry Shay, who was also on this net. Living in the old Silicon Valley area, he was no doubt suffering the effects of the poisoned water there. There might even be a short feature in what he had to say, provided the TV and newspaper editors weren't yet sick of being fed the same old disaster stories over and over.

I know I'm sick of writing them.

There still wasn't anything worth looking at on TV: a bunch of idiot quiz shows, darts and snooker, a series of reruns some of which were *also* quiz shows, darts and snooker . . . A Scandinavian satellite channel was carrying one of the new interactives, hailed as the latest greatest manifestation of the medium, but it had apparently been commandeered by randy adolescent males greedy for tits and bums. Lord! Among the reasons he—and other tenants—had bought a flat in this building, formerly a nurses' hostel, was that the owners promised a satellite dish on the roof. How could he or anyone have been naïve enough to imagine that extra quantity guaranteed extra quality?

Dispirited, he considered finishing his whisky, but better sense prevailed and he made a cup of tea instead. He had another job tomorrow, no more promising than today's, but better than nothing, so he must not risk a hangover. Yet after the tea he was still not ready to turn in. Some of the tantalizing hints he had picked up at the computer conference, those he would never have dared to include in his story, were itching at the back of his mind. Meeting people who were permanently high on enthusiasm for their speciality always had that effect on him. What he chiefly wanted to do was access a mathematical data-base and study up on the theory of prime numbers—

Access a data-base!

Of course. That was the best way to exploit this vacant slot in his life. It had been nearly a week since he last consulted the various bulletin boards he subscribed to. What was the point of letting money leak out of his bank account like blood from a wound if he didn't utilize the services he was paying for?

Admittedly, it would be a lot more fun to log on to Minitel —he understood French pretty well—and spend a while with AMY or AMANDINE or one of the other erotica services, the like of which had never been permitted in Britain although they thrived across the Channel. Some people admired the common sense of the French authorities; by encouraging masturbation, AIDS might be held in check until there was enough vaccine to send it the way of smallpox. He had even written a story along those lines, but it had been rejected. Offensive to the religious minority...

He began to feel a little less contemptuous about the interactive he had just switched off. He wondered how the alleged objectors would feel if they tuned into that.

But—automatically his fingers were tapping out the code that interrogated his bank, and for a moment he felt alarmed until he remembered that what Jake Lafarge was due to pay him would put him handsomely in credit for another week or two—*but* at this moment what he needed was a lead. He needed to find and file a story at top price, and Jake was in the market.

Well, then: back to basics. There was an American board called BIOSOC where he had often spotted profitable clues. Now if he could only remember how to retrieve its access code...

Oh, yes. Something that speaker said today, the one who told amusing stories. Never let anyone second-guess your thinking, even if you are afraid of forgetting what you chose for a password. Pick something you will never forget and no one else will ever guess and hide all your passwords behind it. And don't write it down in clear!

All old stuff, but no less valid for being tried and true. Here was the proof. Being reminded meant he didn't actually have to invoke his master code, which was the name of a woman he had dreamed of in his teens, fallen in love with never having met her or anybody in the slightest like her, but which was engraved in his memory—a name he never spoke nor wrote. Were he one day to meet a person with that name...

He never had. It didn't matter. He had recalled how to access BIOSOC, which specialized in three areas of great concern to him: medical drugs, biology and genetics, and the connection of both with human behavior. He keyed in his fourteen-letter password, which since this was an American data-base was THEBEERSTOOCOLD, and waited for the screen to light.

He was not, of course, expecting to find any messages

addressed to him personally. He logged on to BIOSOC only intermittently, and in any case journalists were not overly welcome on such boards. Essentially what they provided was a means of swapping data between specialists in adjacent fields in the hope of sorting out problems that were hanging them up. Now and then, however, adding two and one-and-a-half together out of hints and scraps had led him to an interesting story.

Of course, that had mainly been while he was working for *Continuum*, and could pass on what he spotted to someone else rather than strive to trace all the ramifications by himself. He did miss—he was obliged more and more to admit the fact—he *did* miss the support, the interaction, that he had enjoyed during those eight delirious years, especially after the program evolved into a co-production with German, American and Australian networks, so that one never knew who was able to dredge up what fascinating unsuspected facts at the weekly planning conferences held over a satellite link . . .

For a while he had even imagined that rationality might overcome the worldwide spread of blind religious fanaticism. Well, the chance of that seemed slimmer all the time—but he still felt doomed to carry on the fight.

Enough!

Sometimes at this late hour, especially if he had had a disappointing day, he tended to grow maudlin. He forced his attention back to the screen. Having dumped into memory in less than a heartbeat everything the board had to offer, his computer was now scrolling through the data at a leisurely pace. So far none of the keywords he had chosen for this particular configuration had made it beep and freeze. But, even as he was reaching for the wipe command because the sequence had cycled to personal messages, it did precisely that.

He blinked. What in the world—? *Oh!* All of a sudden, there among a gaggle of pseudonyms was a name that the machine had recognized. And so did he.

Vaguely, at any rate. For a moment "Claudia Morris" was as strange as the handle of the woman who wanted to interface with him again, and he was at a loss to know why he had posted it on his email list. Then recollection dawned.

Yes, of course. That conference in New York when I was still with Continuum. *I chatted with her in the bar for a bit. No doubt I picked up a lead that made me want to keep track of her. But why?*

He was on the point of punching for access to *Who's Who in American Science*, as the likeliest stimulus to memory, when he slumped back in his chair and snapped his fingers. Lord above! How could he have forgotten that Dr. Claudia Morris was the author of *Our Greatest Nuclear Danger: Crime and the Traditional Family*? She had even signed his copy!

It had caused a scandal: how long ago—three years? No, more like four. It had appeared just before *Continuum* became, as the sour joke went among its contributors, "Discontinue 'em." Had the program still been running, an hour slot would certainly have been devoted to Dr. Morris and her radical, but extensively documented, views. Boiling her argument down to fundamentals, she maintained that the runaway crime rate in the Western world was primarily due to an attempt to keep in being the structure of the nuclear family, a system for the bearing and raising of children that no longer accorded with the needs of society. Raise a generation with ten, twenty, fifty "parents" to all of whom they owed equal loyalty, she proposed, and young people would no longer feel the need to strike out randomly at an impersonal mass of anonymous authoritarian strangers.

Well, even in this age when a "sensation" is out of date within a day and forgotten after three . . .

He re-read the message she had posted:

CLAUMOR / CLAUDIA MORRIS / WILL BE IN LONDON ENGLAND UNTIL FURTHER NOTICE ON SABBATICAL TO RESEARCH A THESIS. CHECK BIOSOC FOR UK ADDRESS AND CODE. POSTED THIS BOARD ONLY!

And the date of her arrival was appended: today.
Well, well, *well!*
The chances were excellent he was the first science journalist in Britain to spot this announcement. One of the few things he remembered about Dr. Morris was that she was dis-

dainful of publicity; she had spent half their time together mocking the ignorance of those who had reviewed her book so generously that for at least one week it made the *New York Times* bestseller list.

So her publisher would be the likeliest lead to her. And he knew several people working in the same field that she was almost bound to contact. He set about collating their numbers right away.

But it took until well after midnight, despite his array of state-of-the-art-two-years-ago equipment, before he felt he could relax and turn in, satisfied that wherever in the city Claudia Morris decided to put up, the moment her name was mentioned over a phone line belonging to her publisher or any friend of hers he had a number for, he or one of the machines he paid for access to would be alerted.

Such facilities, of course, did not come cheap. As soon as possible, he must, he warned himself, find somebody to underwrite his costs.

"WILSON, WHITFIELD HOUSE!" BARKED THE HEAD prefect of Hopstanton School. Tall, suave, fair, eighteen, he was due to leave for university in three months. At the moment, however, his duty was to marshal thirteen- and fourteen-year-old new boys in a drab Victorian corridor.

These so-called "squits," waiting to meet their respective housemasters, shifted from foot to foot. The school's main intake was in September, at the beginning of the scholastic year, so those who came to it in May at the start of the summer term typically arrived with some blot on their copybooks from the preparatory boarding schools they had attended since they were eight or nine.

But none of the newcomers stepped forward in response.

"Wilson!" the head prefect barked again.

A slender boy with dark hair and brown eyes, seeming more at ease than his companions, glanced up.

"Do you by any chance mean Cray Wilson?" he offered in a clear voice that had obviously already broken.

Taken aback, the prefect looked at the list in his hand. He said after a moment, "Wilson R.C.!"

"Ah. That must be me. I'm sorry, it should read 'Cray Wilson, R.' R for Roger. That's why I didn't answer at once. I do hope the error will not be repeated."

While the prefect was still hunting for words, Roger walked past him with impeccable aplomb. The prefect called out, "Third on the right—Mr. Brock!"

"Thank you. I took notice of the signs on the doors as I came in."

And was already knocking, and being told to enter.

Later, the head prefect, who came from Tolland's House, told Flitchwood, prefect of Whitfield House, "You're going to have to watch out for that Wilson—I mean, Cray Wilson! He smells like trouble!"

"Funny!"—with a frown. "I'd have said he was settling in a sight faster than any other squit we've had this year. What makes you so concerned about him?"

"I . . . I don't know. Except he's awfully cocky!"

"We'll soon sort that out of him," Flitchwood promised.

In the meantime: "So you're Wilson, are you?"

"No, sir."

"What?"

"My surname is actually Cray Wilson, sir. I just had to explain the mistake to the prefect on duty outside."

"Hmm! All right, then: I'll get it sorted out . . . Well, take a pew!"

The boy complied, studying his new housemaster. Fat and graying, he sat behind a table rather than a desk. It was obvious that these rooms must have been assigned and reassigned to scores of new purposes since they were built a century or more ago. There were bookshelves and filing cabinets, even a computer terminal, but none of them fitted the space allotted. In the boy's view, it was high time the whole edifice was demolished to make room for something functional.

If anything in a school of this type could be honored with that epithet.

Mr. Brock was not alone. Sitting at his left was a thin fortyish woman in a green dress with blue eyes and brown hair and an inexpert smear of lipstick. The boy smiled at her, and his immediate guess was confirmed. She smiled back, whereby her face was transformed and became almost pretty. Since—well, it had to be—her husband was still riffling through a file of papers, she risked leaning forward and speaking.

"Welcome to Whitfield House, Roger! I'm Mrs. Brock. Do remember, won't you, that if you ever have any problems—"

"Not yet, please, Margaret!" Mr. Brock cut in. She subsided, blushing, while he leaned back in his chair and surveyed Roger beneath untidy gray eyebrows.

"The first thing I have to say to you, young man, is this. According to a letter I have in front of me, from the headmaster of your prep school, while your examination marks were excellent in a wide range of subjects, the moral effect you had on your fellow pupils was not what might have been wished! What do you have to say to that?"

Ah. I was wondering what line the old bastard was going to take. He could scarcely say, could he, that most of his staff were customers for the sexual services we kids provided? Especially when his bee-lov-ed daughter joined in so enthusiastically! He wouldn't wish it to be noised abroad that she adored a gang-bang!

It had been an enjoyable and highly profitable undertaking, especially after the teachers started bringing in clients from the town. Roger was only sorry that it had been cut short. However, one of his friends' parents had discovered, during the holidays and out of reach of Roger's powers of persuasion, that his son had contracted rectal gonorrhea. So the cat had finally been let out of the bag.

Of course, the scandal had been efficiently hushed up, and money had changed hands, and his old school was back to normal—though several of the staff had vanished overnight and had to be replaced. Moreover he had wrought a suitable revenge on the bastard who had shopped him. Having found out that the family was due to go abroad, since they lived not far away he had cycled over with a reel of extension cable on the back of his bike, located an electric heater, plugged it into the reel without unwinding it, and switched on. The resulting blaze had caused a gratifying amount of damage . . .

It was time, though, to react. Composing his features into the strictest possible mask of disbelief, Roger said, "I do assure you, sir, that no matter what allegations have been made against me, I can either explain or rebut them."

He borrowed both words and tone from his father Julian. For two or three years he had been aware that there was little physical resemblance between them, so he was at pains to ensure that he adopted the same mannerisms. Now and then he salted his behavior pattern with a phrase or look copied from his mother, Susan, so she would not feel neglected. Given the way Julian ignored her, she deserved no less—

But Mr. Brock was staring at him.

"You think," he said slowly—"you dare to imagine that you can contradict the judgment of your prep headmaster?"

Stupid arse! Borderline sadist! You ought to talk to Sarah about the way her father treats her and her brother! No wonder she was desperate for a bit of outside affection! And I don't suppose he gave me any credit for knowing that Coca-Cola is an efficient spermicide, and making sure she always douched with it afterward.

Or, come to that, for insisting that all our customers produce an AIDS certificate!

This, however, was no time for reasoned argument. What was called for was an exercise of charm . . . Roger donned his most winning smile, and felt the familiar, welcome, sense of cold command pervade his mind.

"Sir, it is an offense to libel an adult, is it not? How much more so, then, to libel a child my age, who cannot afford legal assistance to defend himself? If it had been in my power, I would certainly have sued my old headmaster!"

He waited. Little by little, he saw uncertainty invade Mr. Brock's expression. Eventually he shut his file and gave a shrug.

"Fair comment, I suppose," he grunted. "I hadn't thought of it that way, but—well, you have a point. I hope you'll enjoy your time in my house. Off to bed with you."

In the doorway Roger glanced back, smiling. Just as he had expected, Mrs. Brock clasped her hands on her breast and whispered, "Sweet dreams!"

Very good. Yes, *very* good indeed!

Climbing worn stone stairs on his way to a predictably uncomfortable bed, Roger had to struggle not to laugh. There were people he could twist around his little finger . . . or maybe another organ.

"Wilson!" snapped the dormitory monitor, who was sixteen and very conscious of his responsibilities. "You're late!"

"That's *Cray* Wilson, if you don't mind," Roger said with a friendly pat on the older boy's hand. "And it was Mr. and Mrs. Brock who delayed me, so you'll have to take the matter up with them. Good night. Sweet dreams!"

And made for his assigned cubicle, wondering how long it would be before he wound up in bed with Mrs. Brock.

Or the dormitory monitor. So long as he was adequately paid, he had no special preference.

Though he definitely didn't fancy Mr. Brock.

You're watching TV Plus. Time now for Newsframe.

As the summer draws to a close, more and more holiday-makers are threatening to sue manufacturers of sunscreen lotions. Perhaps we in Britain should count ourselves lucky, says a spokesman for the British Medical Association. Given that so few of us can afford to travel to the Riviera or North Africa any longer, we're escaping the worst effects of powerful ultraviolet radiation leaking in through the diminished ozone layer. More in a moment.

Response to General Thrower's appeal continues to gather momentum. In London this afternoon, a thousand people . . .

PETER STRUCK PAYDIRT SOONER THAN HE HAD DARED to hope. Having spent the following morning with an affable flack for an expensive alternative-therapy clinic, and agreed to ghost half a dozen articles emphasizing the side effects of orthodox drugs—not his usual line, and not reflecting his personal convictions, but they pay was generous and there was no shortage of material to draw on—he called his home phone from the pub where he had eaten lunch to check for messages. What he heard was better than just a message:

Click: "No, she's still asleep. Jet lag, you know."

So the machines had picked up "Claudia Morris!"

The answer had been in a woman's voice. Peter didn't recognize it, but the accent was upper-crust English.

"Tell her I rang, then. I'm on the staff of her London publishers. And say I'll try tomorrow at the same time." That was a man, a youthful baritone.

"Yes, okay. Thank you."

The circuit broke. Peter waited. A hum ensued. Then the number that had been called appeared on the display screen of the pay-phone. Hastily he noted it on his pocket organizer. Someone else was waiting, and growing impatient, but Peter ignored him. Setting the organizer down, he tapped out an access code for British Telecom's street-by-street customer listing. No one apart from BT employees was authorized to possess such codes; in fact, of course, thousands of people did, not only journalists but market researchers, telephone salespeople, credit agencies, private security firms . . . He followed it with the called number, and in moments a recorded voice relayed the name and address of the subscriber.

Perfect. It was in The Wansdyke, a riot-proofed high-security apartment complex near the Angel: only a short walk from his home.

He was whistling as he left the phone booth, and to the

scowl with which the other would-be caller favored him he
returned a sunny and infuriating smile.

There were days like yesterday when he felt the universe
was conspiring against him, and days like today when everything seemed to fall patly into place. It wasn't even raining
when he arrived opposite The Wansdyke just after seven, by
which time, he estimated, Dr. Morris would have slept off her
jet lag. He felt so cheerful, he literally did not notice the gang
of sore-exhibiting beggars whining around the bus stop where
he got off, but passed between them like a boat dividing scum
on stagnant water.

Well, they were so commonplace in London now, one had
to ignore them unless they turned violent . . .

And even as he started to cross the road toward his destination, debating what to say if challenged by one of its guards,
the building's gas-proof revolving door uttered the very person
he had come in search of. The instant he set eyes on her
memory came flooding back. Yes, of course! She'd been *that*
one! Rather stocky, only an inch shorter than himself, with a
square face framed by dark-blond hair cut in a pageboy style
that she still affected, she had reminded him of Signe Hasso in
L'Éternel Retour.

As a matter of fact, did now, in spite of the sweater and
jeans she was wearing.

Half a dozen alternative strategies chased across his mind.
He settled for trying to look as though he was on his way
somewhere else entirely, glancing around, glancing again,
checking in mid-stride and calling out.

"Dr. Morris? Dr. Claudia Morris?"

For a second he feared she was going to deny her name and
march off. But faint recognition flickered, and he seized his
advantage, closing the gap between them.

"I can't believe it! It is! I wish I'd known you were in
London—I'd have been in touch before . . . Oh, you probably
don't remember me. My name is Peter Levin. We met at a
conference at Columbia a few years ago. I used to be with
Continuum—you know, the TV science program they called
Quasar in America."

By this time he had halted squarely in front of her, blocking her progress. After surveying him in a cool detached manner, she said at length, "Yes, I do remember. The program had been cancelled just before we met. Correct?"

"I'm afraid so. If not, I'd have insisted that we give you a slot. I—well, I suspect I sounded off rather, about it being the worst possible time to kill the show because there had never been more need for rationality."

When I could slip a word in edgeways!

"You certainly did. Even when I told you I wasn't the slightest bit interested in being put under the TV microscope. Now please excuse me."

"Hang about, hang about! Are you doing anything special at the moment? I was just on my way home to face an empty evening, so if you're free—Would you perhaps be going out in search of dinner? Could I invite you? On a professional basis, of course. I must warn you straight away that what I'd like to do is pick your brains and turn the result into an article. You see, I'm a freelance now."

Gamble, gamble. But I recall her as a very direct person, almost embarrassingly so.

She spent so long making up her mind, he let his worse judgment overcome his better by adding, "I know this area pretty well. If your jet lag means you're more in the mood for brunch than dinner I know just the place."

"I suspect," Claudia said with a twist of her lip, "it's as well you write non-fiction rather than fiction."

"What?" The apparent irrelevance took Peter aback.

"You're a poor liar and a worse actor. You 'wished you'd known I was in London,' did you? How long have you been standing around in case I put in an appearance?"

"I don't understand what you—"

"Oh, fold it and stow it!"—with unfeigned annoyance. "If I'd arrived more than a day or two ago, would I still be jet-lagged enough to go out for brunch at seven in the evening? How the hell did you find out I was here? I was hoping for a couple of weeks' peace and quiet before word got around!"

For a moment Peter considered sticking to his original pretense. On balance he decided against. When dealing with a woman like this it made better sense to play the fallible, vulnerable male. Donning a sheepish grin, he spread his hands. "BIOSOC," he admitted.

"You're sharp," she conceded grudgingly. "There can't be

more than a dozen people in Britain who log on to that board. Talk about a dead zone—! Everybody over here who was doing original research in my field seems to have been driven abroad or forced to quit. I don't know whether it's because your government genuinely can't afford to fund them, or because they're afraid of what we might turn up."

Without apparent intent, they had turned together and were walking side by side toward the main road. Peter seized his chance.

"More the latter than the former. It isn't that we're too broke—can't be. Your kind of research calls more for data-analysis than expensive new equipment, and in Britain we have some of the best resources anywhere. Mass Observation's records alone are a treasure without equal. But as soon as one starts to search for the roots of our contemporary mess in decisions taken by previous governments, one's bound to turn up unpleasant truths that call for remedial action, and that action might very well entail changes that would deprive the ruling class of power on grounds of incompetence—*Watch it!*"

He checked her with a touch on her arm as she reflexively glanced the wrong way before crossing the street. A minicab driver in a hurry blasted his horn as he raced by at well above the legal limit. From a side road a police car burned rubber in pursuit, flashing and howling.

"More like New York every time I come back," Claudia muttered when they had crossed the road.

"What does bring you back?" Peter ventured. "To a country that in your view is falling so far behind?"

She halted and swung to face him. For a moment her expression was harsh. Then she relaxed.

"All right, I'll give you your due. You're a cunning cank, aren't you? I could even believe that you gave yourself away deliberately with that reference to jet lag, just to underline how much quicker off the mark you'd been than any of your colleagues . . . Okay, where do we go?"

He hesitated a moment, for in truth he didn't know the area as well as he had claimed. Within moments, though, a relay of memory closed.

"You like Greek food?"

"Right now I don't mind what the hell I eat so long as it's fit for human consumption. All I've had in the past twenty-four hours is airline puke and a bowl of porage. My hostess had to go out and when I looked at what she'd left in the refrigerator . . ." An elaborate shudder.

Better and better!

But even as he turned in the direction of the restaurant he had in mind, Peter was aware that he would be well advised not to take this particular lady's arm next time they had to cross a street.

When they reached their destination, however, it was in darkness. A sign on the door said it had been closed by the Medical Officer of Health. No reason for the order was given, but it was easy enough to guess. With the cost of pollution-certified food rising to astronomical levels, more and more restaurants were resorting, out of desperation, to supplies that had evaded official inspection, and along with it value-added tax, now at a swingeing 20 percent. The owner here must have been one of the unlucky ones.

A wordless grunt indicated Claudia's opinion of Peter's "knowledge of the area." Afraid she might change her mind and decide to risk what her hostess had in the fridge after all, he glanced around and caught sight of a bright red sign above an Indian restaurant only fifty yards away. It was indubitably open, and quite possibly the only one in the area that was, judging by the queue of dismerables outside its takeaway window, each clutching his or her one-pound daily food voucher. In passing he wondered how much a pound could buy now—a handful of scraps, at best . . .

"We could try there," he suggested uncertainly. The fact that its sign was switched on indicated that it was bound to be expensive, but he could probably risk deducting the bill from his income tax.

"Okay," Claudia sighed, and strode ahead. He followed, less accustomed than she was to outfacing the jealous glares of the urban poor.

In the upshot, Peter decided Indian cuisine would have been a sensible choice anyway. The more mass-production methods were applied to food, the less it tasted of anything. Farmed salmon, for example, or intensively raised pork, were now beyond redemption, while as for bread—! But here at least the spices made for variety, though they might of course also be employed for their traditional purpose: disguising sub-standard ingredients. He suggested lamb biriyani and curried vegetables, and an adequately rough red wine, and waited until nothing remained but a spoonful of rice and a smear of sauce before he again broached the matter of Claudia's reason for spending her sabbatical in Britain.

Looking her full in the face—and nearly being thrown off stride on realizing for the first time that her unusually colored irises, blue with green radial striations, were not in fact her own but implants—he confined himself to a single word: "Well?"

She knew precisely what he meant. Raising her glass, tilting it back and forth beneath her blunt-tipped nose, she said at length, "All right. But I'm going to impose conditions. I imagine you're wearing a recorder?"

"As a matter of fact I'm not. I own one, of course, and I thought about bringing it, but I came to the conclusion that if you spotted it I wouldn't stand a hope in hell of convincing you we met by chance and getting you to talk to me. All I have is my regular organizer." He laid it on the table. And added, "Plus one good old-fashioned spiral-bound notebook, and some ball-pens. Voilà!"

"I see. You are exactly as much of a smartass cank as I suspected." A faint but welcome smile quirked the corners of her mouth. "Okay, let's get rid of the formal bit, shall we? Use a page of that notebook to write down an assurance that you won't publish anything I tell you in whole or in part without a notarized release and a fee to be mutually agreed, and add that I'm at liberty to withhold permission regardless of how much I'm offered."

This was standard practice, especially when dealing with Americans. Peter was already writing. When he tore out and proffered the page, Claudia first nodded, then frowned.

"What's this about material attributable to other—?"

And had already cancelled the question before he had a chance to explain.

"I see. I see. You think you may be better informed about at least some of what concerns me than I am myself. I can't argue, though I wish I could. You see . . ." She took a sip more wine before continuing.

"You see, my only possible reason for telling you about the thesis I'm researching is because I hope to be repaid in kind

—with information. This puky country of yours is obsessed with secrecy! If they could, they'd make the time the sun comes up an official secret! I've been in Cuba—I've been in China, for pity's sake!—and they opened more doors for me more easily than ever in Britain!"

"I know," Peter muttered. "Like any journalist, I've bruised my knuckles on a good few of those doors . . . On the other hand, they don't seem to care how much they infringe on their citizens' privacy, do they?"

"Not so long as they're doing it. Anybody else . . ."

"Exactly"—in a bitter tone. "We aren't even allowed to correct errors in our own computer files. There's at least one file on me that's riddled with falsehoods—data relating to someone else who gave my name when he was arrested on a drunk-driving charge—but when I tried to have something done about it I was threatened with prosecution because I wasn't supposed to know it even existed!"

There was a pause. Then, gazing into her glass as though it were a crystal ball, Claudia said, "You remember the theme of my book?"

"Of course. I still have the copy you signed for me."

"I think I was wrong."

Peter blinked at her. He was about to ask why when she rushed ahead.

"Something that doesn't fit has turned up, and I'm scared. I don't want to sound alarmist. In any case I don't dare. For one thing, all the evidence isn't in yet. For another, if I overstep the mark I've been warned that the funds for my sabbatical will be withdrawn. Even so . . ."

She raised her strange artificial irises to look him squarely in the face.

"Do you remember that weird old phrase about 'boiling everything down to brass tacks'? When I was a kid, it used to worry the hell out of me. But I suspect we're about to tread barefoot on a whole *pile* of tacks! And if that's so—"

During the past few minutes, while neither of them was paying attention, a trio of musicians had taken station on a dais in the far corner of the restaurant: a sitar-player, a veena-player and a drummer. They had amplifiers. At that moment they struck up the theme from the latest hit film in Bombay, and their combined volume wiped out the rest of what Claudia had begun to say.

Reaching for his credit cards, Peter proposed at the top of his voice that they adjourn to a nearby pub. For a few seconds he thought she was inclining to agree.

Then, however, she checked her watch and shook her head.

"Sorry," she muttered. "I have to go. My hosts are due back around now. Thanks for the meal, anyway."

"Wait! You can't just—"

"Leave you in the lurch?" A repeat of her quirky smile. "Sorry again. I shouldn't have said as much as I did. I only just arrived in Europe, remember. Give me time to convince myself that I can trust my judgment."

Is this going to be yet another case where because I do the "gentlemanly thing" I lose out on a major story?

In a flash of insight, Peter realized this was the main reason why he was still living on his own in a cramped top-floor apartment. Someone with the killer instinct . . .

But he didn't possess it. He found it repugnant. He was operating on reflexes, pocketing his organizer, proffering his business card, saying, "When you feel sufficiently relaxed to talk this through with somebody, or need some information I might find for you . . ."

"Yes. Yes. I'll bear that in mind. Thank you again. I can find my own way home. I've stayed at The Wansdyke before. Good night."

She turned away, momentarily forgetting the release that he had signed for her, swinging back to reclaim it a heartbeat before he could remind her, thus depriving him of one more chance to reinforce the favorable impression he was striving to make.

The waiter seized his credit card and wiped it through the reader on the till as though afraid Peter intended to leave before paying. Fuming, he made a mental resolution to pursue this one, even if it meant pestering Claudia until she lost her temper. He felt rather as though he had been brought to the brink of orgasm, and then let down.

In an alleyway beside the restaurant, where dustbins stood, a frightened kitchen-hand had been cornered by half a dozen dismerables on his way to dump what they regarded as precious food. Just as Peter passed, he flung his burden at them and disappeared. They fell on the mess as though it were manna, cursing and beating one another.

Peter ignored them and trudged on homeward, wind-blown litter assailing his legs.

LONDON APPROACHING THE 21ST CENTURY...

Noise, dark wet night, many of the streetlights broken, dismerables trudging from dustbin to overflowing dustbin in search of anything to eat or wear or sell; those luckier, with homes to go to, glancing anxiously over-shoulder as though afraid the buildings might sprout mobile pylon legs and trample them; riders in the scarce cars and buses eager to be anywhere but here . . . In other words:

The city the humming the thrumming the drumming the city the bumming the summing it up as a MINUS—!

That, echoing between her ears from her headset stereo (the shout at the climax weakened as the batteries weakened —buy more tomorrow, if any were to be had), furnished a running commentary on what Crystal Knight could see at this much-too-ordinary moment: black sky, drifting rain, unhappy people, a few bright but hideous illuminated signs, most of the vehicles stinking on their way to a breakdown because so few could afford to keep their suit of wheels in legal repair and new ones were so scarce now Britain was excluded from the Japanese economic sphere . . . The buses stank the worst and broke down the most often. (The rich, naturally, shunned areas like this, convinced they might catch AIDS by drawing breath. Elsewhere, as for instance in Parliament, they didn't seem nearly so anxious to keep their mouths shut.)

But the normal grumble of traffic had just changed to a howl. Here came the Old Bill, and in a hurry.

On what kind of business? Obviously they weren't just hauling in beggars to keep up the arrest rate.

Crystal switched off the bad-rap tape she was allowing to occupy her mind until another customer happened along. Aside from the stereo, she was wearing what was likeliest to turn her punters on because they were mostly middle-aged whenzies and what they chiefly wanted was to screw their teener daughters in the guise their girlfriends had worn at the same age. She knew enough psychology to suspect that that sort of urge underlay the stringent discipline imposed by the uncle who had grudgingly taken her in after her parents died and from whom she had ultimately fled: the endless petty put-downs, the harsh beatings for even minor offenses, and the final insult, his dismissal of her as unfit to keep company with his own children because she was a literal bastard. For him to have implied that about her mother . . . !

She no longer recalled her parents very clearly because they had died when she was five—in that epidemic of meningitis which, so some people still claimed, had escaped from a research laboratory, only the charge had never been proved, or even investigated—but she was sure they had been loving and affectionate, and she knew they must have had something her aunt and uncle lacked: a sense of humor. If not, why had a couple whose names were Jem and Beryl decided to name their daughter Crystal?

Of course, it did mean people tended to address her as Crissie, which she hated. But they generally didn't do it twice.

In full Sixties fig—minidress and high leather boots, plus false eyelashes and an idiotic bouffant wig of the same color as her own dark hair—she was at her hard-won evening post in a shop doorway opposite St. Pancras Station. It was a featly patch, particularly since they had refurbished the huge Victorian hotel across the way. Deprived of much of their former custom—late-arriving rail travelers and those whose trains had been cancelled without warning—the smaller hotels in the area had opened up for prostitution. Yes, all things considered a very good patch, because the staff didn't mind what age their clients were, nor which sex, either. Not so long as they carried a certificate of vaccination against AIDS.

Of course, the vaccine cost a bomb. So there was a thriving trade in forgeries.

Crystal was thirteen, and she didn't mind saying so to her punters. Sometimes she even said twelve, because the younger she claimed to be the more she turned most of them on, and the sooner she got them de-spunked the sooner she could turn another trick. To the Bill, of course, she always indignantly declared that she was sixteen—legal age . . . But then added "and a half" with a disarming giggle.

What am I going to do when I really reach sixteen?

At the moment, however, she had something else to worry about. The police car had passed without stopping, but a two-member serial was working this side of the street on foot—armored, of course, as always nowadays in the rougher districts. One could only guess by their respective heights which was the man and which the woman, for they were identically clad from their heavy black boots to their round black visored helmets. Inside the latter, radios relayed everything they said, everything they heard, to the tireless computers at Scotland Yard, on alert the clock around for any programmed keyword that might indicate more trouble than two constables on foot could cope with.

A patrol like that usually posed considerable problems, though never anything Crystal couldn't handle. As she had discovered, she could handle anything—most days of the month. It might, however, mean a waste of precious working time . . .

As it turned out, luck tonight was on her side.

At this most opportune juncture, she spotted a man she had a score to settle with: directly across the street, keeping his back turned, hat pulled down, coat collar up in hopes the police wouldn't look his way. Thus far they hadn't. But there was no chance of him escaping Crystal's notice. She would have known him at ten times the distance.

"Winston Farmer," she said under her breath. "Is your shit ever going to hit the fan . . . !" And, in a vigorous stage whisper: "Officer!"

The constables glanced around.

"Come this way. Don't worry. Pretend you're checking my certificate."

Puzzled, wary of a trap, yet nonetheless tilting back his visor so she could see his face, the man approached while his companion stood aloof, poised to signal for help.

"What do you want?" he demanded, obviously surprised at being addressed by someone who would normally do her utmost to steer clear of the law.

"Got something for you. See that growser across the way, trying so hard not to attract attention? He's Winston Farmer. Name mean anything?"

The policeman frowned, then suddenly nodded. "Dealer?"

"And ponce. Manages three girls. Crackers." Crystal wasn't referring to their looks or their sanity, but to their drug habit. "Once a week he makes a trip north—to Liverpool, I think, though I'm not sure. They say that's when he picks up his supplies. A car will be here to collect him any moment, a Jaguar. It's usually on time. Nick him now and I'm pretty sure you'll find he's holding."

She was trying to speak in a controlled tone, but her utmost efforts couldn't keep the venom out of her voice.

The woman constable had drawn closer in time to hear the last few words. She said, "That sounds personal. What have you got against him?"

"He tried to slip me a horn of crack. Wanted to get me angled and force me to work for him. One of the girls who does used to be my best friend. She's likely to be dead before she's twenty."

There wasn't going to be any argument. Crystal knew that already. For some reason she couldn't fathom, she had grown very good at persuading people to do as she wanted. Not long after she embarked on her career she'd even talked a drunk sadistic punter out of slashing her with a knife . . . and into turning it against himself. For the rest of her life she would be able to close her eyes and visualize again that squalid room, that rumpled bed, liter after liter of blood spewing out so red, so red—! She'd thrown up at the sight of it, right there on his dying body! But though they arrested her, claiming she had murdered him, when she was brought to court she made even the judge believe her story. That had been the second time she ever felt the way she did now: angry, but utterly clear-headed, with a sense of inexplicable power. The moment she saved herself from her knife-wielding client was the first.

Of course, when it turned out he was one of the soldiers set to guard radioactive waste on the Isle of Jura, shunned by the natives for fear of contamination, cursed and spat at by the local girls when he and his mates passed along the street, that did rather contribute to her defense . . .

She had been so afraid her aunt and uncle would learn about the case, but luckily, because she was a minor, the media were forbidden to mention her name or show a picture of her. So, no doubt, they still didn't know.

If they ever did find out—!

"Bock!" she added, staring past the police. "There's the car now. It looks like the same as usual—yes, it is. In which case I know the number. You better call it in."

The woman constable was already reciting, "Dark blue Jaguar proceeding east along Euston Road, two men aboard, stop and search for illegal drugs, possibly crack . . ." Then to Crystal: "What was that number again?"

Crystal repeated it, and added, "Better include 'armed and dangerous'—isn't that the way you phrase it?"

"Gun?" the man demanded.

"I don't think so. But I've seen him threaten his girls with a shiv."

The woman listened to her radio a moment, then gave a satisfied nod.

"There are two patrol cars in the area. One or both of them should catch him. Any idea where he might be heading for if he manages to slip past?"

"He lives in Docklands. I'm not sure exactly where."

"Hmm!" The man cocked an eyebrow. "And he owns a new Jaguar, *and* has someone to drive it. I'm surprised he goes by train, even though it has become a classy habit now the fares are so high. I'd have expected him to fly."

"Don't they sometimes search people at airports?" Crystal countered. "That's the last thing he'd want."

"Yes, of course." The man bit his lip and glanced at his

companion. "Well, I suppose all we can do now is say thanks."

"Exactly. And good night!"

They took the hint and moved away at regulation pace.

During the last few minutes another train had discharged its passengers, and forty or fifty people were waiting for a chance to cross the road. Crystal's practiced eye identified some of them as servicemen on leave, always promising targets—and safe, too, apart from the occasional nutter like the one she had run into before, because they received free AIDS vaccinations. Despite the rain, she moved into plain sight and donned her professional smile. She had had few reasons for smiling since her parents' death, but her expression was more sincere than usual after her success in shopping Winston Farmer.

She only wished she could find a way to do the same to her aunt and uncle and all the canks like them who must have wanted this kind of world, because they had worked so hard to put and keep in power the government that made it possible.

You're watching TV Plus. Time for Newsframe.

The increasing scarcity, and the high cost, of potatoes has been officially attributed to a virus that entered Britain with imports from the Middle East, most likely from Cyprus or Egypt. Local varieties in those countries are resistant, while those grown in Britain are not. Many farmers are predicting that their land will have to be cleared and sterilized, and are demanding EEC aid on the same scale as the French sugar-beet producers whose crops were ruined by blight last year. More in a moment.

General Sir Hampton Thrower, at a rally of several thousand supporters in Birmingham, has repeated his proposal that patriots "make their views known," this time suggesting that they wear red-white-and-blue ribands . . .

IMMEDIATELY ON RETURNING HOME PETER RE-corded, as nearly verbatim as he could, the tantalizing—the infuriating—snippets Claudia had let escape. It would have been infinitely better for his peace of mind if, for instance, she had flatly stated that she didn't want to be bothered right now, because she intended a vacation before starting work. (In passing: she had, he remembered, specified that it was a thesis she planned, not another book.)

Instead . . .

And for a moment, both her voice and her expression had betrayed—he was certain of it—real fear.

Having read and re-read his notes, he leafed through her book to refresh his memory, but gleaned no clues. Her reasoning, though in his view less than conclusive, was nonetheless well documented, and it was plain that at the time of writing she had believed completely in what she had to say. What, then, could have changed her mind to the point where she now suspected she'd been wrong?

Perhaps her more recent publications might offer enlightenment. Heedless of the cost, he set about interrogating the relevant data-base. They all proved to be brief papers in journals of sociology and sociobiology, and all dealt with aspects of her original argument, qualifying or enlarging it or offering fresh supporting evidence. The latest had appeared only last year, so her new discovery, if that was what it was—

Just a moment!

He checked the date of receipt. It had been submitted seven months before it eventually appeared. Computerized publication might be fast; peer-review still took time. Not quite so up-to-date, then. But there was nothing more recent, not even an informal communication to establish priority, not even a letter in response to one of the many colleagues who disagreed with her.

Blank wall.

Growing more and more frustrated, he considered phoning

contacts in America who might have spoken with her lately. He dismissed the idea at once; he was already spending more than he could justify. Tomorrow, though, in between drafting those pieces about the alternative therapy center he must find time to ring her publishers. Claudia might not care for publicity, but they ought to be able to talk her round. He wished he knew the name of the person who had tried to phone her, so he could ask for him directly. Also there was a growser called Jim Spurman, an ex-probation officer now lecturing at one of the northern universities. He had been among the first people in Britain to promote Claudia's ideas, by publishing an article about her in *Society Now*. Perhaps he might be of help.

Having made a list of all the things he wanted to do but couldn't because it was nearly midnight, Peter went to bed, where he lay awake for over an hour. When he did doze off he had uneasy dreams.

BELOW THE SHOULDER OF A PEAK HALF GREEN WITH summer grass, half gray with rocky outcrops, slashed across by drystone walls and a tumbling beck and speckled toward its summit with a flock of sheep, stood a farmhouse built of that same stone and roofed with slates—but some were missing, and had been replaced with plastic sheet. Its window frames needed repainting, and sundry panes were blind with plywood . . . or possibly cardboard. Behind it, like the petrified skeleton of a giant ostrich, lurched the frame of an abandoned windmill. Alongside was a barn in even worse repair, patched with rusty corrugated iron.

And, just discernible against the dazzle of sunshine on the beck: could that be intended for a watermill?

If so, it wasn't turning.

Glad of her seat belt as the rusty Mini in which she was a passenger jounced along an ill-made lane, Miss Fisher was attempting to assess this place the way she would an actual school. She was an education inspector. Some said she had an ideal cast of mind for the job.

As though needing to swot up for an exam, she considered putting the same questions as before to her companion and driver, Mr. Youngman. (Miss Fisher was not the sort of person who progressed rapidly to first-name terms.) But he was biting his lip with concentration as he negotiated bumps and ruts, and she was obliged to content herself by reviewing what he had already told her. After all, he had been courteous enough to offer her a ride up here, rather than simply giving directions and leaving her to find the way by herself.

Accordingly:

"How long ago did the Crowders arrive?"

"The year Garth started school. He's thirteen now, so that must have been eight years ago. I didn't know them then— didn't meet them until Garth came to me at eleven."

"Even though Mrs. Crowder herself had been a teacher?"

"People are very reclusive around here. They don't like offcomers. Besides, Roy and Tilly were regarded as bossy, as wanting to make people give up their old ways. In fact, of course, their dream was to go back to them. To be self-sufficient and live off their own plot of land."

"But did they settle in? Was Garth accepted at school, for instance?"

"It took a while, but according to what I've heard from his teachers at the primary he adjusted fairly well. It was obvious from the start he was very bright, and that always causes problems. But on the whole . . . And of course Roy did have a fair amount of money saved up, so he could pay on the nail for everything he wanted done."

"I understand he'd been an engineer?"

"Electrical engineer. He had visions of applying what he knew to—well, for example, the waterwheel that he installed. Rewired the house so he could light it off a car-dynamo using headlight bulbs."

"Did it work out?"

"For a while, yes. They even had a black-and-white TV. All they have now, though, is a battery radio."

"What went amiss?"

"I don't know. But something did."

"When?"

"I suppose it must have been shortly after Garth moved to my school."

"Did he get on as well there as at the primary?"

"For the first couple of terms, yes. But...Oh, I don't know. Kids tend to grow quarrelsome at that age, don't they? And secretive with it. Maybe it was due to the other kids realizing just how bright he is. Hardly one in fifty of them stands a chance of higher education, and here was Garth, university material if ever I saw such, bursting with questions at a time when most of the boys I've been trying to teach since I came here are deciding they already know enough to carry them through the rest of their lives. So they just stop listening. Of course, it's the parents' fault."

Miss Fisher gave a wise nod. She knew Mr. Youngman's type. In his late thirties, he was resigned to never becoming a head teacher and on the verge of accepting he might not even make head of department.

"Had something gone wrong at home? You said it was about then you first met the Crowders. And a crisis at home just as a child enters adolescence—"

A vigorous headshake that made Mr. Youngman's already untidy fair hair even more tousled.

"No, they seem to be a devoted couple. Mark you, I'm not sure Tilly was ever as enthusiastic as Roy about going to live in the middle of nowhere, but right from our first meeting she's always insisted that she went along with the idea for Garth's sake, because back where they came from the kids she used to teach were so cut off from reality and she didn't want him to turn out the same way."

"'Where they came from' being—?"

"Spang in the middle of Birmingham. About as urban as you can get."

"By 'reality' she meant—?"

"I suppose the way crops are grown, animals are bred and slaughtered...Not that that applies; they're vegetarian."

"Did they try to—well—proselytize for their beliefs? I mean, most of the local farmers depend on sheep, don't they? They wouldn't like people who hoped to put them out of the meat business."

Another fierce headshake. "No, they always struck me as very tolerant."

"Nonetheless, I read about certain clashes . . ."

"I know what you mean"—in a bitter tone. "And I'm just as worried about what's been going on as anybody else. But I simply can't believe Garth had a hand in it!"

"There was a boundary dispute following which a sheep-dog was poisoned, a potential champion that its owner hoped might get him into the national trials."

"And on television! That was Jack Atterthwaite's Judy. He farms in the next valley."

"Wasn't it his son who was found drowned? And wasn't he one of your pupils, in the same form as Garth but older?"

"You have done your homework, haven't you?"—with a sarcastic twist of his lip. "Yes and yes. And they tried to make out that the snare Bob tripped on, so he fell in the beck and knocked himself unconscious on a rock, was made from wire in the Crowders' barn. But it's a common type! Nothing was proved at the inquest! Listen, you can judge how much store to set by these charges when I tell you that the local people are accusing the Crowders of witchcraft!"

"You can't be serious."

"Your homework wasn't quite that complete, was it? I'm talking literally!" Fire sparkled in Mr. Youngman's eyes—and voice. "Stick around here a few days, and you'll notice words being spoken that haven't been uttered in half a century at least— 'darklady,' 'hornylord'!"

Miss Fisher found herself at a loss for the first time in a long while. She said after a pause, "I'm sure that's of interest to students of folklore, but—"

With a sigh: "You're only here to find out whether the boy is receiving a decent upbringing. Right?"

"Of course." And, recovering her normal tart manner: "You seem to be distinctly *parti pris* in this affair! If you feel you can still offer an unbiased opinion, tell me your view. Are or are not Garth's parents providing him with a sound, well-rounded education?"

"I wish I knew!" An amazing shrug hoisted the shoulders of his worn tweed jacket high as his ears. "I call on the Crowders once a month, because about every four weeks I start to worry."

"And—?"

"And I stay worried until I'm indoors, and then I come away perfectly happy. I mean . . . But you're supposed to see for yourself, aren't you?"

Yes, of course. It was entirely legal for parents to educate their children at home. It was their right. But they had to demonstrate that they were doing it as well as a school could. And in a broken-down farmhouse, without TV . . . Was there even a phone?

"We'll have to walk the last bit. A Mini doesn't have enough ground-clearance."

Miss Fisher started, for not memory but reality had supplied Mr. Youngman's latest comment. He had brought them to a halt about a hundred yards below the house, where the way turned from lane to track. Releasing her safety belt by reflex, she was about to ask how the Crowders managed for transportation when she caught sight of an elderly Citroën *deux-chevaux* shadowed inside the barn.

Against the wall of which, a few logs. Also a stack of something like enormous dark-brown sandwiches.

"Is that peat?"

"Hmm? Oh, yes. They use a lot of it. For heating."

Does using peat for fuel rather than fertilizer square with the concept of relying on renewable resources?

Already prepared to deliver a hostile verdict, Miss Fisher followed in Mr. Youngman's wake, picking her awkward way between clods and puddles and wishing she had chosen a more sensible pair of shoes.

"Hello, Mr. Youngman! And I suppose you must be Miss Fisher! I'm Garth, of course! How do you do?"

It was a black-haired, brown-eyed boy—neatly enough attired in jersey, jeans and trainers—who had called from the front door of the house. Now he ran to meet the visitors at the front gate, that stood ajar on rusted hinges between tilted stone posts. Either side of his path were rows of wilting vegetables around which flies were buzzing, but the visitors' attention was wholly focused on Garth, who not only shook their hands but clasped them between both of his, and as he turned to lead them into the house put an arm companionably around Miss Fisher's waist . . . or nearly around, for she had put on a lot of weight. Such familiarity on first acquaintance was normally anathema to her, but this time she raised no objection, for the boy had such an appealing smile.

"Mother's in the kitchen!" Garth declared cheerfully. "I told her you'd be here soon so she ought to put a kettle on— you'd like a cup of tea, I'm sure. Nettle tea, of course; we can't afford the real stuff, but my parents say it's healthier anyway. And Dad . . . Yes, there he comes!"

They followed his pointing hand. Scruffy in corduroys and an ancient shirt without a collar, Roy Crowder was approaching with an armful of creosote-blackened wood.

"He's been breaking up the old chicken-run," said Garth. "You know we're vegetarian, yes? So we don't have any need for it, but we're always short of firewood . . . Come on in!"

And, within two shakes of a lamb's tail, there they were seated around a four-square farm-style kitchen table, sipping clear astringent tea, being plied with fresh-baked scones spread with home-churned butter and home-made jam sweetened with honey from the Crowders' own hives . . .

For a while Miss Fisher struggled to remember what she had been planning to ask about. She tore her gaze away from Garth with a near-physical effort. Then she caught sight of rows of books reposing on ill-planed but substantial shelves filling an alcove beside the fireplace. She recognized some of them—Mabey's *Food for Free*, Seymour's *The Forgotten Arts*—and noticed others she had never heard of: *One Acre and Security* by Bradford Angier, *The Mother Earth Book of Home-Made Power* . . .

And, underneath, the current *Encyclopedia Britannica*.

"I can well understand," Garth said, squeaking his chair closer to Miss Fisher's across the stone-flagged floor, "how concerned the authorities must be if people opt to educate their children at home. But, ma'am, you must surely have been told that Tilly—that's my mother—is a qualified teacher. How many children benefit from a one-on-one situation all day long? I ought rather to say a two-on-one, for Dad imparts his knowledge to me just as ceaselessly. With all respect to Mr. Youngman, had I remained under his tutelage would I by now be perusing the general theory of relativity along with the elements of practical design involved in buildings and operating power stations designed to feed the National Grid?"

With sudden stubbornness, Mr. Youngman said, "I see four half-burned candles over there! What about your water-powered dynamo? And the wind-powered one before it?"

Miss Fisher jerked her head around. She'd missed that!

"We're working on a better design," Roy Crowder cut in.

"That's right," his wife confirmed. "Meanwhile, using candles allows me to instruct Garth in the fundamentals of combustion. Roy and I devote ourselves unreservedly to his welfare and enlightenment. More tea?"

So completely were the visitors under Garth's spell, they departed without noticing how haggard Roy and Tilly had grown since that terrible day when he had returned from school—or rather, from avoiding school—and said:

"Roy! I don't want to call you Dad any longer! You're not really my father, are you?"

"What in the world—?"

"Shut up! And switch off that fucking radio!" It was reporting how yet another Jewish home in Tokyo had been burned down, but such matters were too far away for Garth to care about at the moment. He went on with undiminished intensity, "Tilly, I accept that you're my mother. But you lied to me as well."

"What—?" and "How—?" simultaneously from Roy.

"I was waiting for that 'how?'" was Garth's snap answer. "Until this moment I merely suspected. Now I'm sure. I'm not going back to school. I can't put up any more with—"

"We were going to tell you!" Tilly burst out. "At the proper time!"

"Which never came, did it? You've stuck me out here in

the wilds, surrounded by yobs I can't stand, at the tender mercy of teachers who are a sight more ignorant than you— even than I am at my age!—and I'm going to get my own back! You've run my life for nearly twelve years under false pretenses, and *it stops now*! Make the necessary arrangements to teach me at home. Keep me fit and fed and tell me what I want to know—start by buying a set of the *Encyclopedia Britannica*, because there's a cut-price offer from a book club this week and you can always dump the club afterward. Don't make me sweat over your damned turnips any more, or clear the ashes from the hearth! I won't do it! I've found out enough about the sort of life I should look forward to—buses and taxis and discos and concerts and computers and libraries and television and girls and all kinds of goodies! That you have robbed me of! That for the sake of a patch of barren ground you're now too goddamned *broke* to provide for me!"

His eyes were full of tears, but his voice remained level and controlled.

"So you, Roy, can get on with your farming bit. I admit you have to do that by daylight. But if you let me go hungry I promise you'll starve before I do! And whenever I want information you can supply, you drop your spade and come running, hear me? As for you, *Mother*, you can take care of your bocky household chores before I get up and after I go to bed, even if it means you never get more than five hours' sleep for the rest of your life! When I leave here, which I estimate will be in roughly four years' time, I intend to take with me all the vicarious information you can supply by teaching me non-stop all day, from cooking to quantum physics! When I finally dump you dishonest creeps I intend to be capable in the abstract sense at least of making out *fine* on my own . . . and after that I hope you have to squeal to pass for pork!"

Not only tears now, but sweat as well, were pearling down his face.

"Son—" ventured Roy.

"Whose?" came the cutting answer. And that was the last objection.

* * *

Of course, when Garth wasn't turning his full force on them—as for instance now, when much of it had been expended on sending the visitors away happy—Roy and Tilly did succeed in uttering an occasional brief question.

"Garth, what if that inspector—?"

"What what?" with unspeakable contempt. "Haven't I taken as much care of you as you of me? Didn't I get even with Jack Atterthwaite when he trained that bitch of his to drive his sheep into your cabbages? Even though I hate bocky cabbage! Didn't he shy off when his canky son wound up in the beck? And didn't I warn you not to bring in water till it ran clear again, meaning after they took away Bob's body?"

Roy's face was perfectly white; Tilly's was gray.

"So it *was* you who—!"

"Why should you care? They haven't bothered us since, have they?"

"But the police—" Tilly whimpered.

"Did they even call us as witnesses at the inquest?"

"No, but—"

"And doesn't everybody think we're untouchable now? Don't they call you 'darklady' and 'hornylord'? *Don't you find offerings at the farm gate that no one asks you to pay for? If you deny it—!*"

Roy's pallor yielded to a blush. He started to speak, but Garth erupted to his feet.

"I'm sick of your 'yes buts'! Tilly, get back to your stove! I want my dinner on time! And I want meat with it—hear me? You may want to waste away on greens and roots, but I need bocky *protein*!"

For once his mother managed to withstand the force of his anger. Instead of obeying immediately, she whispered, "If that's what they're calling us, what can they be calling you?"

The boy had no answer. He felt unsure of himself for the first time since the moment he thought of as his coming-of-age, that morning when he woke to find a wet patch in his bed. Roy and Tilly—he must grant them that much—had soothed his panic with frank and reassuring explanations about the onset of puberty. Even so . . .

Faint doubts began to stir about the justice of the course he had embarked on, as deep in his subconscious as whatever made his penis stiffen in the night and spill his seed. He knew in theory what ought to harden it in waking life, but when his mother was a drawn-faced drudge...

And anyway he'd been accustomed to watching his parents dress and undress since he could remember.

He was tired from having to make the proper impression on Miss Fisher and Mr. Youngman. Snappishly he repeated his former command, and was obeyed. As usual.

That night, however, lying in bed, he tried to recall in detail how and why he had concluded that Roy was not his father.

He could not.
He could not.
He could not...

You're watching TV Plus. Here is Newsframe.

For the third successive day students have rioted in Tokyo and other large Japanese cities, protesting against their parents' willingness to mortgage their children's future earnings as security for flats and houses. The average price of a three-room flat in central Tokyo is now one million pounds. More in a moment.

Followers of General Thrower cheered him this afternoon when he declared that the "steely spirit of Britain" must be re-tempered in the fire, even if that fire should prove to be nuclear. Opposition MPs...

PETER WAS OUT OF TOUCH. SINCE THEIR LAST CONtact, Jim Spurman had been appointed a full professor. Now he was "out of the office"—"addressing a conference"—"supervising a course"... Peter cursed the string of excuses that he found every time he checked for a response to the message he'd left to crop up twice a day on the guy's phone. In the end, because worrying about what Claudia might have meant was distracting him from paid work, he risked posting a general request for information on an American board he knew Claudia didn't log on to but several of her colleagues did—colleagues who tended to pooh-pooh her ideas.

Given the time of year, he wasn't expecting either a quick or a substantial response, but that same evening—as it happened, the day when, under the influence of Islamic expansionism, Malaysia occupied Singapore, an event that boded ill for Britain's precarious economy inasmuch as it meant the breaking of yet another Commonwealth link—returning late from the book-launch party which had evolved into dinner with a bunch of former colleagues, he found among his email a one-word message, presumably a password, addressed to a code he could have sworn he had only disclosed to a handful of particular friends. It was a warm night. Opening windows, brewing coffee that he needed to clear his head, he wondered aloud who on Earth—?

And realized the likeliest possibility in the same instant. He uttered a shrill whistle. During the conference in New York at which he had met Claudia, he had bumped into a thin tall man with graying hair, who seemed not to know anyone else present and whose sole identification consisted in a name badge reading GUEST. He was obviously bored and—fortunately for Peter—rather drunk. On spotting Peter's badge, which identified him as representing *Continuum/Quasar*, he had struck up a conversation.

After which... Peter racked his brains for further details. The gray-haired growser, who proved to be a lawyer, had made it clear how much he loathed the people who were, in his view, attempting to undermine the American Constitution by imposing a state religion—or possibly it was "religion state by state," for his argument grew more confused with each Martini he sank. At any rate he was noisily predicting that the result would be world domination by the Communist bloc because they would wind up with a monopoly of practical science while his own people would be reduced to praying,

sticking pins in chance-opened Bibles, and casting lots to decide whose eldest son should be sacrificed to stave off disaster.

And he had said . . . Yes! It was coming back! He had said,
"If you want to hear the only sound sense being talked during
this entire weekend, you must catch Claudia Morris. Has she
given her speech yet?"

Peter's answer was sharp. "Yes, this morning. Weren't you
there?"

A headshake: "She sent me the text and I read it last week.
Great stuff. We need more like Claudia . . . You going to do a
program about her? Y'ought to!"

At which point, not waiting for a reply, he turned and
waved his empty glass at the barman.

Peter was minded to slip away. Yet something made him
hesitate. A lawyer who was plainly agnostic—the ongoing
dispute between the scientists and the fundamentalists . . . And
now *Continuum* was definitely scheduled for the chop, he
needed plenty of leads if he was to stand any hope of surviving as a freelance.

*I gave him my card with that code written on the back. And
I never asked his name!*

But as far as he could recall, that was the one and only
time he had ever released that code—normally reserved for
intimate friends and very special informants—to anybody
outside Britain.

Why would he be on that board?

An answer sprang instantly to mind: it was used by people
who disagreed with Claudia. Probably the lawyer was not in
fact one of its contributors—just maintained a program to
monitor it. This could be interesting!

With exaggerated care Peter tapped out the password he
had received, then waited for the screen to light.

What it scrolled was a montage of OCR'ed news cuttings,
obviously run fast and carelessly because there were many
errors, but the gist was plain. At first they related to attempts
by fundamentalists to take over major centers of American
education, using the vast monetary leverage they had accumulated as the millennium approached and the faithful grew less
and less confident that the Rapture would save them seven

years before the onset of Armageddon. Time was running out . . .

Then the subject switched abruptly to something Peter had heard about but never taken seriously: a group nicknamed "the Strugfolk" after one Cecil Strugman, who had inherited millions of dollars from a family meat-packing business, turned vegetarian-ecologist-rationalist, and mounted a counter-campaign designed to prove that of the fundamentalists un-constitutional by emphasizing their use of un-American terms like "king" and "lord"—precisely what the Founding Fathers had striven to get rid of. With growing excitement Peter sat down at his desk, occasionally halting the display as a salient point emerged.

Until this moment he had imagined that this venture was essentially symbolic, and doomed to inevitable failure. On the contrary; if he was to believe what he was reading, the Strug-folk had been burrowing away through strata of legal prece-dents, assembling a virtually unassailable case while at the same time attracting additional funds from industrial corpora-tions whose directors were afraid that in the next generation there might not be any petroleum geologists or volunteers for lunar prospecting missions . . . at any rate, not outside Russia, Europe and Japan.

Ranged against them, naturally, were the worshippers of the Almighty Dollar who were growing far richer far quicker by manipulating the stock markets with computerized help than anyone could hope to achieve these days by actually working.

Peter whistled again. He had never seen that particular split in American society so graphically portrayed. Of course, here in Britain—

And even as he pursed his lips, the lines on the screen wiggled into illegibility for a moment, then reformed as gar-bage. He jumped to his feet, abruptly furious.

The bastards! The bastards!

He recognized the warning. Special Branch (or SIS, or whichever—there wasn't much distinction between the var-ious British police agencies any longer) had been prompt to obey Big Brother at Langley. Here were data the ordinary citizen of the UK was not supposed to access.

Fits. You wouldn't see it on TV these days. Or read it in the papers . . . Except maybe on TV Plus *or in the* Comet!

For a moment he actually thought kindly of Jake Lafarge, who of late had been stingy in providing him with assignments.

His mind darting back to what Claudia had said about the British government's obsession with secrecy, he pounded fist into palm. That gray-haired lawyer, doing him a favor (but why? Logically, because Claudia must be involved with the Strugfolk, or else her university was under threat from the bigots—*stop!* He was spiralling in three directions at once and he had to force himself back on an even keel)—

That lawyer might well have unintentionally wished on him another visit from the Bill.

Well, like everyone else in his profession, he had emergency arrangements. If only they weren't so expensive . . . !

Sighing, he dumped the text from America into a remote store supposed to be inviolate under the Data Protection Act. It was almost certainly not, given the massive computing power the government disposed of nowadays, but at least it might not be worth their while trying to break the rule by which it was enciphered. If they had really been upset, they wouldn't have left anything on his screen at all, but simply disguised the event as a system crash by engineering a block-wide power failure, and the hell with how many innocent users suffered as a result. On busy nights some areas of London could be seen flashing like trafficators—if the streetlamps were still working.

Then he set all his alarms, so as to make the police's arrival as conspicuous as possible. He belonged to a Neighborhood Watch. When such schemes had been set up in the eighties, few people had foreseen that within so short a time they would become hated rather than supported by the police and government. None of the other residents of his building belonged, but there were fifteen members within earshot of his alarms, prepared to turn out at any time of day or night with cameras, video-cameras, sound-recording equipment . . .

Christ! This is how it must have been in Russia before

*glasnost! Except the neighbors wouldn't have had so much of
the essential gear.*

His miserable train of thought was broken by the phone.
For a moment he assumed it must be the Bill ringing from
downstairs asking whether he would come quietly. Then he
spotted the calling number on the display screen. It was the
one on which he had been trying to reach Jim Spurman.

He rushed to answer, and heard a voice that was suddenly
familiar despite the passage of four years.

"Peter Levin! Jim Spurman here! I'm sorry! We had a
computer glitch and the bocky machines told me *Petra* Levin,
an ex-student of mine that I sincerely hope I'll never set eyes
on again. . . . I gather you want to talk about what Claudia
Morris has been up to lately, is that right?"

Abruptly alert again, Peter said tensely, "Yes! What can
you tell me?"

A dry chuckle. "Well, as I've so often seen, I'm afraid,
among sundry of my colleagues, she appears to be yielding to
pressure. One has to be forgiving—I'm suffering much the
same problem myself, though luckily I'm blessed with a supportive vice-chancellor. But isn't it always the fate of pioneers
to be mocked by the whenzies?"

*Oh, lord. I'd forgotten how devotedly he imitates the usage
of his students . . .*

"I'd like a scrap or two more data on that level," Peter said
aloud.

"You didn't hear that this university of hers became a
prime target for the bigots? What's the name of it—?"

"Never mind!" Peter cut in. "I know what you mean."

"What you should say nowadays"—reprovingly—"is the
inverse: 'you know what I mean.' As long ago as the mid-
eighties this had been spotted as . . . "

*What progress from probation officer to professor can do
to muddle someone's thinking!*

As politely as he could contrive, Peter intimated how little
interested he was in the fact that since their last encounter Jim
Spurman had decided to concentrate on verbal usage as an
infallible index of predictable social behavior. Sitting on the

corner of his desk, staring out of the window, watching the lights of airliners ascending and descending around Heathrow, he finally managed to insert a further question about Claudia's university.

"Ah! I'm surprised you haven't heard. Well, it seems one set of funders, the repulsive lot, are displacing another who are somewhat more welcome."

This was getting worse by the minute! Peter had one ear cocked for the arrival of Special Branch. But if they did turn up, he wanted at least to pry some sense out of *Professor* Spurman first . . .

Controlling himself with vast effort, he said, "I take it you mean religious fundamentalists are trying to buy control of the university where she works."

"Featly!"

But that's not why and how one uses that word . . . Cancel that. He's just explained why she's afraid the money for her sabbatical may be withdrawn.

"Please go on!"

"Well, obviously, as soon as she went high-profile with her book, and so many people responded positively, she was a prime target for the obscurantists. I'm not shamming when I say we get literally dozens of letters every week in my department from parents who feel she's explained why their children went to the bad. How else do you think we've managed to maintain our funding when what we're spreading the gospel about is anathema to the received wisdom? We can point to massive public support!"

Peter's mouth was growing dry; he had indulged in too much free wine at the book launch, and the coffee hadn't helped, being no doubt largely ersatz despite the label on the jar. Still staring out of the window beyond which red and white and green lights wove endless abstract patterns, he said after a pause, "Let me get this straight. You're saying her university—"

"Is due to be swung to the anti-science side by a massive injection of money. Precisely. The poor bitch is going to have to fight like hell to retain her tenure."

"Have you seen her lately? Or spoken to her?"

The next words were accompanied by an audible frown.

"Funny you should ask that. As a matter of fact, I've been rather disappointed in the lady recently, given that I worked so hard to promote her ideas over here . . . That's why I suspect she's bending under pressure. When I last tried to get in touch she didn't return my call, and a message I posted on an email board she used to log on to at least as often as I did—"

Flash.

Bright in the sky above Heathrow Airport. Peter's jaw dropped even as he realized what he was watching.

Bang.

But it was worse than a bang. It was a slap, a growl, a rumble, and then a succession of thuds. The phone was still murmuring. He disregarded it, waiting for what he was sure must follow. It did, and windows over half of London shook in their frames, as a fireball shed glowing fragments on— where would it be? Hounslow? Southall? Likely both, and even further!

And I happened actually to be watching! Camera!

Incontinently he let fall the phone, rushed to snatch up what he should have seized the moment the glare first lit the sky, aimed and shot. This was going to save him from the Bill! Here was what had been so long predicted, the fruit of the government's policy of withdrawing public funds from air traffic control on the grounds that private firms were far more cost-efficient. But in the service of Mammon they sometimes skimped the exhaustive checks needed to make sure all their computers could always talk to one another . . . And as a result, two airliners had collided and caught fire above what for a generation had been promoted as the busiest airport in the world.

Not to mention an awful lot of people's homes.

Clearing up the mess would occupy the Bill for quite a while, just as making sure the blame fell on some overworked traffic controller instead of the people who had made fortunes by cutting the necessary corners would preoccupy the government. He could relax—

Oh no I can't!

The phone was saying something. He caught it up without looking and snapped, "Thanks for what you didn't tell me! But you've been pre-empted!"

"What do you mean?"—in a frosty *academic* tone.

"Watch the TV news!"

He cut Spurman off and tapped the *Comet*'s number.

Engaged.

Well, of course. The line must be stacked umpteen deep. Hundreds of people closer to the accident must be phoning all the papers, TV stations, et cetera et cetera, hoping their amateur footage (because three out of four families now owned, etc., therefore high standard of living) might make it to the screen for a fat fee . . .

With an increasing sense of desperation, compounded by memory of the debt he had incurred by dumping those data from America into secure store, he spent a while staring toward the fires breaking out where fragments of the airliners had fallen. From here, though, he could no longer see anything but an orange glow, like old-style sodium lamps on fluctuating current.

And other planes being diverted to Luton and Gatwick.

He poured himself another shot of whisky. The bottle was nearly empty and he made a mental note to buy more tomorrow, if there was any in the shops; most, in this desperate economic climate, was earmarked for export. Even as he was raising the glass, however, the phone shrilled.

"Yes?"

"Jake Lafarge. Did you know two planes—?"

"I saw it! I even shot some pictures!"

"Pictures we got, and TV beats all of us anyhow. Give me eight hundred words explaining why it happened! Nearly ten percent of our regular readers are shareholders in British Airways—and it was two BA planes that collided!"

There was a tone of pleading in Jake's voice. But Peter had been mentally drafting just such an article for years. He drew a deep breath and reached for his modem.

"Put me on line," he said. "I can set it cold."

And brought it in at 789 by automatic count: a chilling indictment of the policies that had led to the worst midair crash in British history, long predicted, now a fact.

"Front page," Jake said when he called back. "Thanks."

And many thanks to you, sir!

For to have an article like that splashed and by-lined on page one of a national paper without being subbed was like an accolade—even though the *Comet* was not exactly in the front rank. In the morning, Peter was woken far sooner than he would have liked (since he had made the mistake of finishing the whisky to bring himself down from the high his article had engendered) by a succession of colleagues complimenting him, saying it was the best thing he'd done, how much they wished they could have had the same chance, he was a lucky growser and why didn't he—?

And most important: come and say it again on TV Plus at lunchtime, if you're prepared to confront a pro-government spokesman "to provide balance."

He had to think about that for a moment. Then he concluded he had unassailable documentation. And what the hell else was he going to do with his life?

He made mincemeat out of the bocky cank from the government. All of a sudden he was famous again. Of course, that meant he needed protection, but TV companies still had clout, and there was talk of making a documentary. . .

It was giddying. But the most important part was that he felt as though he was falling back into the context of a team. He knew in the distant parts of his mind that the airliner crash would be forgotten in a week or less, except by the bereaved and those whose homes had been burned down—and of course the lawyers suing on their behalf, who stood to make a mint—but this was the way he had . . .

Yes. This was the way he had grown up. He'd been a kid before he signed with the *Continuum* team. His years with them had constituted his true adolescence. Now, after a gap that might be termed his *Wanderjahre*, he had the chance to continue the process.

He was reminded of Claudia Morris a few days later when he received the bill for the data about the Strugfolk that he had dumped in a fit of panic. The amount was horrifying, and although he paid up for fear of incurring a bad credit rating, he filed an erase code.

When Professor Spurman left a message on his answering machine inquiring whether he could confirm a rumor that Claudia Morris was in Britain, he wiped the tape without bothering to call back.

I DON'T KNOW WHO I AM.

Oh, I know my name all right—Sheila Hubbard. At least Hubbard is what I go by, though really it's the name of my mother's second husband. The first was an artist called Doug Mackay. He and Ingrid (my mother) broke up when I was still very young. I never quite found out why, but I get the impression it was something to do with her wanting a kid and him not caring to be lumbered, though I had this attachment to him that must have been more like a fixation because when she got married again, to Joe (who's a real business whiz, a high-flyer absolutely dripping money), I got all kind of upset. I sneaked a look at a psychiatrist's report on me once. It was full of loaded terms like "disturbed" and "irrelevance of affect."

Which is how come I wound up at this "progressive" school in the back of beyond, called Mappleby House.

But I like it a lot better than any school I was at before, I must admit. Mainly here you do what you want so long as it doesn't hurt anybody else. There are some great teachers who honestly seem to love kids. Before I got here I didn't know how much fun you can have finding things out. Sometimes I get terribly angry with the teachers I used to have who didn't care about anything except forcing you to come up with the approved answer.

I'm wandering off the point.

I was going to say: I know how old I am—fourteen next birthday—and I recognize my face when I see it in the mirror, the usual black hair and brown eyes and rather olivey skin as though there's some kind of Middle Eastern ancestry in there . . . I often stare at myself for ages and ages trying to see what someone else would notice on looking at me for the first time. I can't work it out, any more than I can decide whether I'm pretty. I hope I am—I mean naturally. I hate the idea of smothering my face in gunk the way some of the older girls do, just to make a better impression on some bocky boy.

No, the reason I don't know who I am any more is because I've changed. Inside. I remember *when* it happened, but I don't know *why*. And I'm scared. It went this way.

Mappleby used to be a big country house, not exactly a stately home—it's only Victorian—but it has this huge garden and lots of nice private corners among laurel hedges and the place most of us like, especially in summer, is where one of the walks runs down to a bend in the river. It's quite shallow there, so you can bathe if you want, but the other bank doesn't belong to us and sometimes you get the local yobs coming to stare and even trying to chat us up—long range at the tops of their voices. They can't actually get across to us because there's a sort of weird thing made of wire mesh, that we call the Palisade, and anyway the water's a bit murky and we have a proper swimming pool as well. But it's great for sunbathing, and since Mappleby was founded back in the twenties when there was this terrific craze for *Freikörperkultur* (I think that's right) you don't even have to wear a thong if you don't want to.

Of course we're all encouraged to be terribly natural and healthy about our bodies and boys and girls share the same dormitory and go to the showers together and all the rest of it, but I like that, and if it wasn't for the fact that the cooking is kind of bocky I'd say the whole setup was featly, except of course it scandalizes the natives who practically make an industry out of being offended.

A moment back I said the yobs can't get over to us, only stare from the other bank beyond the wire. But that's not absolutely true. One of them did manage it.

I was exactly midway between two periods. I started young, like my mother apparently. Luckily I don't have a bad time before I bleed—no PMT or whatever they call it, and no cramps—but around the middle of the month I do get incredibly frustrated. So I was feeling in a particularly bocky mood even though it was fine and sunny, so I went off by myself to the river with a couple of books I wanted to finish. But it got so hot I had to peel off and I was still sweating so I went in for a dip. I'd noticed a gang of natives on the other bank but I didn't give a tinker's toss for them. I lost count years ago how many people have seen me in the nude. Then . . . Oh, I suppose one of them must have boasted to his mates that he could get to me, because he stripped off—not completely, he kept his underpants on—and jumped in and swam to the Palisade. It's sort of curved at the top in a way that's supposed to make it impossible to climb over, and the water's at its deepest there so there isn't any footing, and trying to support your weight on fingers and toes while you scramble up must be terribly painful. Like climbing chickenwire, see what I mean?

Except as I found out afterward this particular native, who was nineteen, was on leave from the Commandos where they'd put him through what's supposed to be the toughest assault course in NATO, and he was on my side before I knew what was happening, while his pals on the far bank clapped and cheered.

"Didn't think I could make it, did you?" he said as he found his footing and started to push through the water toward me. "Just because it was never done before! Well, for that I think I deserve a kiss, don't you? And maybe a bit more than just a kiss!"

I was absolutely stunned. I thought I was going to pass out. I mean, they say I'm well-developed for my age, but that doesn't mean I could face up to a hunk like him with muscles growing out of his muscles. I can still see his grin. He was sunburned, so there were kind of red patches on his cheeks, and he had practically no hair. I mean on his head. His chest was like a bocky doormat, and lower down—well, the word isn't even thicket!

It wasn't the idea of being kissed. I must make that clear. I mean, it happens a lot at my school. It's natural, isn't it? And lots more than just kissing, too. But we get properly taught about pregnancy and AIDS and all that kind of thing, and in any case it's no very big thing except perhaps among the oldest of the kids. One of the teachers I like best showed me this book by someone—I think he's American only he's got this German name: Bet-something, is it?—he found the same sort of situation among kids on an Israeli kibbutz, who because they grew up together acted toward each other like brothers and sisters. I know a lot of brothers and sisters do do things with each other, but—

Look, this isn't a defense of the way things are at Mappleby, okay? I was trying to explain what scared me. It was the way he took it for granted that because he'd proved he was a Big Strong Man I was instantly going to lie down and spread my legs. Pardon my crudity, but it's not half as crude as what I could read on his face like plain English.

And that was when I stopped being scared. That was when I stopped knowing who I am. Because being scared was more like the me I was used to. Only...

Only all of a sudden I wasn't afraid any more. I was angry. I was—

All right. It probably sounds too fancy, too like something I picked up from a book, but I don't know any better way to express it. I was suddenly *possessed*, by ice-cold rage that showed me precisely what I had to do. I felt myself smiling as he reached out toward me, and instead of pushing his hands away I met them with mine, locking my small fingers with his big thick ones. This surprised him long enough for me to say, "I'm a virgin, you know. I'm not even thirteen yet."

He blinked water out of his eyes; it was trickling down from what little hair he had on his scalp. Then he grinned again.

"You can't fool me like that! *I* know about this school of yours! *I* know what you get up to! Running about starkers—like you right this minute! Boys as well as girls!"

I was gradually luring him backward into the shallows, so my breasts appeared above the water, provoking another outburst of cheering from his mates. His eyes fastened on them hungrily. Next moment it would probably be his mouth, but that wasn't the idea. I said, and something made my tone cajoling and seductive, "All right. But . . ."

"But what?"

"I want you to go down on me first. Know what I mean?"

"What do you think I bloody am? A virgin like you? 'Course I know what you mean!"

"Then go ahead," I said. "And if you make me come by doing it, I'll make you come the same way."

His grin became enormous, stretching those red-blotched cheeks until I thought he'd sprain the muscles of his mouth—and he did exactly as I'd told him to.

Under a foot of water.

It was as though he simply forgot he couldn't breathe the stuff! I felt his tongue on my belly, then around my pubic hairs, and then among them. Then, when I was sure he couldn't hold his breath any longer, he simply didn't come up. He stopped moving, and all of a sudden he was drifting away, all limp, like a wet rag-doll.

After that it gets confused. The next thing I remember is stumbling out on the bank and grabbing my clothes and my books and racing toward the school. I looked back once, and there wasn't any sign of him. By the time they found him against the Palisade, carried there by the current—still underwater—he was dead.

There was an inquest, of course. I said I didn't mind being called as a witness, and stood up in front of the coroner and answered her questions as calmly as I could, saying I knew about rape and felt I was fortunate to have been spared so terrible an ordeal, though I had been very frightened. The coroner was a woman doctor. She congratulated me on my lucky escape. The surgeon who carried out the postmortem said death was due to drowning but he'd also discovered some kind of weakness in the growser's heart in spite of him being a Commando and supposed to be perfectly fit. The jury brought in a verdict of misadventure. The local paper said it served the bastard right, or words to that effect, and called for reassessment of the educational system at Mappleby on the grounds that it could produce a pupil not yet thirteen who could display such presence of mind when assaulted by a would-be rapist. I don't know if you remember, but according to the news half a dozen girls my age had been raped and killed in the previous few months.

After which, of course, my mum and dad—my dads, I suppose I mean, because Doug turned up for the inquest, too —and the staff of the school all said I was wonderful and marvelous and so did the other kids and lots of them wanted all of a sudden to be best friends with me.

But who are they making friends with? I don't know! I can't believe I'm *me* any longer! You see, *I committed a murder in public view*! All the growser's mates were watching, like I told you—five or six of them, there must have been. And I got away with it!

I don't think I *want* to be me any more!

If they go on pestering me, I'm afraid I'll do the same again. I could. I know I could.

I don't want to! Do you hear me? *I don't want to!*

Please help. Somebody. Please help . . .

You're watching TV Plus. Now for Newsframe.

A group of American terrorists, one of the so-called "Rambo squads," has claimed responsibility for the bomb that destroyed the headquarters of the West German Green Party. Eight people are known to have lost their lives, and nine others are in hospital.

Here in Britain, four self-confessed supporters of General Thrower have been remanded on bail after setting fire

to shops owned by Chinese and Pakistanis. At the hearing
the magistrate said patriotism had its limits, but shouts
from the public area of the court . . .

PETER LEVIN'S APPEARANCE ON TV PLUS WITH THE government spokesman had transformed his life.

Above all, he had a new home, in a block built on what had been the playground of a school until emigration from Inner London dramatically cut its population—and exported the problems of drugs and crime to provincial towns that hitherto had been relatively peaceful. He still had only three rooms but all were bigger, and instead of being under the leaves they were at street level in a better area. The kitchen was three times the size and the bathroom boasted a proper tub. Also there was off-street parking. He still could not afford a car, but there was a chance TV Plus might soon allot him one on the company.

Of course, the price was horrendous—but nothing compared to what people were paying in Manhattan or Tokyo. So the moment he set eyes on it, he said, "I'll take it." And moved in ASAP to forestall squatters.

After the removal crew had left he poured himself a shot of Scotch, humming a cheerful tune despite the fact that the evening was unseasonably cool and wet. Seemingly autumn had decided to visit Britain ahead of time this year. Passing his desk, to check that his gear was correctly connected, he hit an email code on his computer: that of Harry Shay out in California, whom he'd been meaning to contact for ages. Even if over there people weren't out of bed yet he could leave a message—

What?

The screen was flashing at him: *No such code.*

Had he mis-hit the number? He tried again, more slowly, with the same result.

Professional reflexes made the nape of his neck tingle. Setting aside his glass, he dropped into his working chair and tried the only other address he had for Harry, that of his company Shaytronix, which should at least have a machine on line.

No such code.

"This is ridiculous!" Peter said aloud. He remembered Harry Shay from his early days with *Continuum*. The guy had been one of the most successful British software entrepreneurs—not a programmer himself, but brilliant at putting commercial firms in touch with experts who could tailor existing systems to meet their special requirements, and a positive genius at collecting commission fees. Granted, a shadow had fallen over his last months in Britain, some suspicion that he had diverted funds belonging to his customers for his own benefit . . . But nothing had ever been proved, and he had done the accepted thing by marching off to California as it were with drums and trumpets, announcing that he was forced to emigrate because the fools in charge at home had no understanding of modern business.

True enough, in Peter's view. If any of Britain's major corporations were to be run as inefficiently as its government, they'd be bankrupt within months . . .

Half-noticed in the background, but with the sound loud enough to furnish a distraction, the TV was reporting from Chicago, where flooding was driving thousands of people from their homes. Angrily he pressed the remote control and left its images to mop and mow in silence while he searched for the reason why the code for Shaytronix wasn't valid any more.

But this time, when he entered the correct digits, he saw on his screen: *Normal routing not available.* That was a message he had never encountered before. He sat back, frowning, and took a sip of his whisky. Then, even as he poised his fingers to try again, realization dawned and he turned in dismay to the TV.

By then the report from Chicago was over, and there were scenes of Brazilian refugees, the Indians who according to their country's government did not exist in Grand Carajas, bellies bloated with pellagra under a skim of reddish-yellow dust, too listless even to brush away the flies that came to sup the moisture from their eyes.

Grief, not another bocky mess in South America!

But the glimpse he had had earlier was enough to remind him of something he already knew but had overlooked. The main clearinghouse for the email networks he was accustomed to using was at the University of Chicago . . .

Among the goodies he had awarded himself when he moved from his former home was a short-range timeshifter, a recorder that monitored sixteen pre-set TV channels on an endless-loop tape, so he could review anything of interest within twenty-four hours, whereafter the data were wiped. Now he needed that Chicago report, and in a hurry!

A few oath-ridden minutes later he got the hang of the instructions, and was able to watch exactly what he was afraid of. It was no news that the Great Lakes were returning to the level that had obtained before the city was founded; right now, however, a northerly wind was whipping water over Lake Shore Drive and into basements, cellars, underground garages . . . There were shots of drowning cars. Some that were unusually airtight with their windows closed bobbed around on the surface for a little, but then—through the exhaust pipe, maybe—the water claimed them, and they burped and sank amid a string of bubbles.

Peter had visited Chicago. He knew where the computers were housed that relayed his messages—this having become a valuable commercial service for the university when Federal subsidies grew scarce. They were in concrete rooms below ground level, designed to keep out terrorists.

But more than likely not designed to keep out water.

For the first time since his late teens when he stopped worrying about nuclear war on the prevalent grounds that it hadn't happened yet, he felt an overwhelming sense of the frailty of civilization. Chicago might be thousands of miles from London, yet a day or two ago he could have contacted a hundred friends there at the touch of a key. Now, though, thanks to a freak storm . . .

But there must be alternative routings! Why had they not been automatically invoked? He checked, and to his dismay found the machines had outguessed him. There was a nil response by any route whether surface or satellite from any of the Shays' codes. Why in the *world* . . . ?

Peter had been vaguely wondering what his new neighbors were like. Now, reminded of the insecurity of life in any great city, he decided that one of his first steps must be to join the Neighborhood Watch; he'd seen stickers in nearby windows, although not as many as around his former home. He was filing a memo to attend to the matter in the morning when the doorbell rang.

For a moment he forgot that his new affluence had also supplied a closed-circuit TV camera above his front door. Jumping up, he was halfway to the streetward window before the point struck him. When he recalled where he had sited the monitor, he was taken aback at what it showed. For, stepping back from the threshold, gazing around as though wary of a trap, there was a policewoman.

A woman? Alone? Not wearing armor?

With vast effort he cancelled his reflex responses. Of course: this was a different area. Maybe she had simply heard that a new resident had arrived in the street and wanted to make sure that everything was okay.

Except, of course, that any finger of the Bill . . .

Yes. She might have come to warn him to stop attacking the government in public, though that sort of duty would normally be entrusted to someone in plain clothes. Alternatively, she could be the area intelligence officer, following up a tip from one of her informants with a view to filing data about him on PNC, the Police National Computer.

In either case it behoved Peter to answer the door in a hurry and be terribly polite. Memory of Claudia Morris stirred for the first time in weeks as he recalled his bitter reference to the computer that under his name had stored a mass of data concerning someone else. Long ago he had striven to have it altered, only to be met with harsh rebuff: "You shouldn't know about that file—shut up or I'll nick you for a breach of the Official Secrets Act!"

Grief! Since the eighties, haven't they figured out any way of amending their data? What about when someone dies?

But governments being governments, and that of Britain being particularly loathsome, all he did on the way to the front door was check that his pro-Thrower ribbon was pinned conspicuously on the breast of his sweatshirt. There was a possibility, not yet confirmed, that he might be offered a steady job with TV Plus. However, the executive who had brought him the good news had also handed him the ribbon and advised him to wear it if he hoped to obtain the post. He concluded by saying apologetically, "Better safe than sorry, Peter! Though sorry, I admit, is what I am . . ."

Moreover, against regulations, the policewoman was wearing one, too.

She was not in fact alone. Nearby but out of range of the camera, a white car had drawn up, and its driver was keeping an eye on her. Having registered the fact, Peter said in his politest tones, "Good evening, officer. What can I do for you?"

And thought for a second he was looking at Claudia, for this woman had the same solid build, much the same color hair, and the same slightly sour expression on her square pale face. But the resemblance was fleeting.

Consulting some notes in her hand, she said brusquely, "You're Peter Andrew Levin?"

"Yes." He blinked. "If someone has reported me as a squatter, I can assure you—"

"Father of Ellen Dass, alias Gupta?"

At first he failed to take in the words. It had all been so long ago . . . A terrible sinking feeling developed in his belly and his mouth turned dry.

"Come on!" the woman snapped. "You admitted paternity, according to our records!"

And that was true. It came from one of the files about him that was not corrupt. Eventually he forced a weary nod.

"So what? I haven't seen the kid in ten years! Kamala didn't want me to! And since she took up with her new man I haven't even had to pay maintenance!"

The WPC wasn't listening. Folding her notes, she was

shouting to her companion. "We finally found the right place! Bring her over!"

Bewildered, Peter suddenly realized there was another person in the car, getting out now, clutching a canvas bag: a slim, tawny-skinned child in sweatshirt and jeans, a girl about the right age to be Ellen. The driver escorted her toward the door.

As they drew nearer, he saw she had been crying. Her lids were puffy and she kept biting her lower lip. She clung to her bag like a shipwreck survivor to a lifebelt.

Stopping in front of him, staring up with immense dark eyes, she said uncertainly, "Dad?"

"What's all this about?" Peter whispered.

"Don't you think you'd better ask us in?" riposted the policewoman.

"I . . . Oh, Christ!"—thinking what an impression this visit from the Bill must be making on his new neighbors. "Yes, I suppose so. It's a mess because I only moved in today, but— Oh, *shit*. Okay!" He stood aside, gesturing in the direction of the living room. The woman entered first; Ellen followed, and the male constable insisted on Peter preceding him.

Closing the door behind him, he said, "I'm PC Jones. My colleague is WPC Prentis."

"How do you do?" As Peter spoke the automatic words he thought they were the stupidest he had ever heard himself utter. He couldn't tear his eyes away from this stranger who must be his daughter. Nor she from him.

"Sizable place, this," said Prentis, sitting down without invitation. "Plenty of room for a kid."

"What do you mean?" Peter snapped, rounding on her. "What's all this about?"

"Mainly it's about a kid with nowhere else to go," Jones murmured. "You want to explain, Ellen? No? I suppose not. . . . All right then, Mr. Levin." He drew a deep breath.

"Remember the airliners that crashed the other day? I'm sure you do. You had a lot to say, I'm told, about the wickedness of the government in hiring private firms for air traffic control. You may be right, you may be wrong, but what it boils down to is that a chunk of one of the planes fell on your daughter's home. She was out visiting friends. When she came back it was all over. Burnt down. With her mother and father—excuse me: her *common-law stepfather*—inside. Mr. Gupta died at once. Ms. Dass died today. So when we checked the records . . ."

"Oh, my God." Peter had to grope his way to a chair, thinking: *How could I ever have guessed? I didn't even know where Kamala was living!*

"Had a hell of a time tracking you down!" Prentis said acidly. "Like you were trying to hide!"

In a milder tone Jones objected, "Maggie, Mr. Levin's a very busy man! You know that . . . Well, now we've got the kid settled, we'd best be getting back. There'll be a social worker round in the morning to sort out things like victim support and advice on clothes and such—all she's got left is in that bag, of course. The rest was burnt. Best thing in cases like this is to get back to normal ASAP, though this is a long way from her old school. Still, the social worker will explain. On our way?"

Prentis rose briskly and both constables made for the door.

"Wait!" Peter shouted. "You can't just—"

And could have bitten his tongue out. In their faces he read uniform contempt. But, as it turned out, they had different reasons.

Jones said, still in the same mild tone, but now it sounded sinister, like an inquisitor's: "In case you hadn't heard, hundreds of people were killed by the falling debris and thousands were rendered homeless. Mainly they've been camping out in schools. But term starts next week, so they've got to move. You ought to keep up with the news. Dependent children are to be cared for by their nearest able-bodied relatives. Since yesterday, that's the law. And in Ellen's case that means you."

And Prentis: "Anyway, it's your responsibility, isn't it? Serves you bocky right in any case! Same as anyone who fucks around with niggers! Traitor to your country, that's what you are, 'spite of that ribbon on your shirt!"

Slam.

And they were gone, leaving Peter to contemplate the ruin of a thousand dreams.

"Morning, Dad—morning, Mum!" cried Terry
Owens as he rushed into the kitchen accompanied by a whiff
of expensive aftershave. He wasn't of an age to shave yet,
actually, but it was the style.

"Morning, dear," his mother Renee replied over her
shoulder as she refilled the teapot after pouring the first cups.
Then, turning: "Is that a new jacket?"

"Mm-hm." The boy's mouth was already crowded with
cornflakes. "Like it?"

Renee suppressed a sigh. To her current fashions, such as
they were, looked like something bought off a second-hand
cart, but . . . "I'm sure it's very nice, dear," she said diplomati-
cally. And added, "You'll get indigestion if you gobble like
that! Do you want an egg?"

His cereal bowl nearly empty, Terry shook his head. After
swallowing, he answered, "This'll have to do. I'm late.
'Bye!"

"Will you be back for—?"

She had been going to say lunch, but her son's feet were
already clattering down the stairs.

After a pause, she said, "I'm worried about our Terry. He's
changed so much in the past few months."

Not looking up from his newspaper, her husband Brian
grunted, "'Sonly natural. It's the normal time. And I'd say the
change is for the better. He doesn't get picked on at this
school the way he did at his last one. Matter of fact he's got
more mates than I ever had at his age. Older than he is, too.
Must mean they respect him, right?"

"Yes, but . . ." Renee bit her lip, sitting down and stirring
sugar into her tea, eyes fixed on nowhere. "I do worry. Can't

help it. I mean, *another* new jacket! And all those tapes he buys! Where does he get the money?"

"Not from us!" Brian snapped. "We've been all over this a dozen times! We've never come up short on the takings, 'cept a pound or two that was probably due to Sarah giving someone the wrong change." He meant the girl who helped out in their grocery shop on Saturdays. "Reminds me—how are we doing for time?" With a glance at his watch. "Oh, that's all right. Be a love and pour me another cuppa."

Complying, she persisted, "But even so—"

"Look!" Wearily Brian laid aside his paper. "He *works* for his money! He's told us! Isn't he out all day Saturday and Sunday, and most evenings too, doing odd jobs around the neighborhood? Shows a proper sense of responsibility, to my mind. Better than having him come whining to us day in, day out, saying, 'So-and-so at school has this and that, why can't I have it too?' Isn't it?"

"Oh, I admit that, but even so—"

"All right, I know it's not strictly legal and all that, not at his age, but he hangs out with these older boys and they split the take with him. That's what mates are for. You pull your weight, they take care of you. Anyway, it's all cash-in-hand stuff. What the eye doesn't see . . ."

He drank most of his tea at a gulp and rose, wiping his lips.

"Right, time to go and let Sarah in. See you downstairs in a minute. Don't be too long—there's bound to be the usual rush."

On the other side of the street was a corner shop, formerly and for a brief while owned by a guy in videotape rental, that had been boarded up for the past six months. Its closure being a memorial of their only failure to date, Terry insisted on meeting his oppos in the recess of its doorway, to remind them where they'd be without him.

This morning, though, they were waiting for him outside.

A single glance explained the reason: some cank had bocked all over it last night, and it reeked.

"We'll put in a complaint about that," Terry muttered. "Offense to public health, or something. I'll ring up about it later, get it seen to."

He was very good at affecting an adult voice and manner on the phone. He could mimic an angry member of the upper crust to near-perfection. Also he knew more about what could be done, even nowadays, even by people at the bottom of the heap, to force official action, than almost anyone in the area. The harassed careers master at his school, whose failure rate in finding jobs for the leavers was now seventy percent, had once said quite seriously, "I shan't need to worry when it's your turn, Terry! You're practically a one-man Citizens' Advice Bureau already!"

Terry knew what he meant, but the other kids in earshot had had to ask, the CABs having been abolished as hotbeds of anti-government subversion.

His oppos—the regular ones—numbered three. Barney had not been baptized Barnabas; he'd earned his name thanks to his fondness for a fight. Built the way he was, and weighing twice as much as Terry, he generally won. Sometimes Terry worried what would happen if he started to generally lose. Taff was called Taff for the usual reason, because he came from Wales; he was much given to asking people who poked fun at his accent whether he didn't have a better right to British streets than the Packies and the Windies, and leaving his mark on those who disagreed. The third one, the oldest—nearly eighteen—was known as Rio because he affected embossed leather boots and a matador hat his father had brought back from Spain and liked to talk about fighting off the topless talent on the beach at Benidorm, regardless of the fact that owing to the slump the bottom had dropped out of the package tour trade and he had never been further from home than Whitley Bay—where he had bought the knife he carried in his right boot.

Terry had cultivated them with care, and between them they added up to a formidable force.

But today he had a bone or two to pick with them.

"All right, business!" he announced in his precociously deep voice. "Rio, what's this I hear about your not taking out Mr. Lee's dustbins? How often have I told you? We've got to be seen to be doing *something*! We've got to show legit! It's not hard graft, is it? He's good for fifteen smackers and all it takes is fifteen minutes. Or isn't a maggie a minute enough for you?"

Abashed before the younger boy's piercing stare, Rio shifted from foot to foot. "He wouldn't let me," he muttered. "Said he won't pay up this week. Or ever again."

"Why, the bocky slope!" Terry exclaimed. Mr. Lee owned the fish-and-chip shop and Chinese takeaway: a thin, perpetually worried man with a short fat wife and a platoon of interchangeable small children with flat faces and inscrutable expressions, who peeked at the customers from behind a curtain.

"Same with Mr. Lal!" Taff exclaimed. Lal was the Indian who ran the newsagent-tobacconist-confectioner's shop. Its window was covered with iron grilles because of repeated attacks by Pakistanis. The grumbling war on the subcontinent had spun off many such far-distant clashes. He spoke with the accent called "Bombay Welsh" and Taff delighted in mocking it. Doing so now, he added, "'So sorry, mister sir! It is not good enough takings any more for you carry out my unsold papers!'"

"I think they're ganging up on us," rumbled Barney, and a grin parted the punch-broadened lips beneath his twice-broken nose. "What are we going to do about it, Terry?"

By now they were strolling down the street. Early shoppers parted nervously to let them by, even if it meant pushing prams and strollers into the roadway. The boys took no notice.

"Well, I think I'd better tell Mr. Lee that I know the flashpoint of commercial frying-oil, don't you?" Terry said after a moment for thought. "And I know what burns at a higher temperature!"

Rio chuckled. Barney looked disappointed. That sort of thing was too indirect to suit his taste.

"And," Terry went on, "I'd better explain to Mr. Lal that people who don't get their papers won't pay him. We know all the kids who deliver for him, don't we? Catch?"

Taff pondered a moment, figured out the connection, and gave a double thumbs-up sign accompanied by a broad smile.

"And," Terry concluded, "I think I'll also tell them that

their weekly touch goes up to twenty in future, for acting so bocky."

At that even Barney looked pleased again, and they parted on the best of terms.

Just as Brian was closing the shop that evening, there came a tap at the door. Prepared to bellow, "Sorry, too late!", he recognized the caller through the glass and was taken aback. He knew Mr. Lee by sight, of course, but he and his family kept themselves entirely to themselves, which was the way most people in the area preferred it. Never before had he called here. And, by the expression on his face, it wasn't in the way of custom.

Opening the door, he said uncertainly, "Good evening, Mr. Lee. What is it?"

"It's about your son. May I please talk for a moment?"

Brian hesitated. Then he muttered, "All right. Come on upstairs."

"Evening, Mum! Evening, Dad!" Terry called as he rushed into the sitting room.

And stopped dead in the doorway. The TV was on, as usual, but the sound was muted. And there was a visitor.

His heart pounded. This smelt of crisis!

How long have they had by themselves?

But his mother was saying, "Would you like a cup of tea, Mr. Lee? I don't suppose it'll be like what you have in China, of course."

Relief flooded Terry's mind, and he felt a sudden sense of calm control. That was a sign that Mr. Lee could only just have arrived; offering tea to a visitor was a kneejerk reflex with his mother, the first thing she thought of after "let me take your coat" and "please sit down."

Brian was saying, "Mr. Lee said he wanted to talk about you, Terry."

"Oh, good!" The boy advanced, taking Mr. Lee's hand and shaking it warmly. "And I bet I know what he's going to say! Let me see if I'm right! He's come to say how pleased he is with the work me and my friends do for him—isn't that right, Mr. Lee? He's come to say that because he finds us so helpful he's going to up our pay—isn't that right, Mr. Lee? *Isn't it?*"

He could practically feel the man's toes curling inside his shoes. After a pause, dully:

"Yes. Yes, that is right. Thank you, missis, but I think I won't stay for tea. Now you know, I will have to get back. We open in half an hour. Excuse me."

And he headed for the stairs.

"Well!" Renee said, staring after him. "That was a funny sort of call, I must say!"

"Ah, you never know where you are with the Oriental mind," Terry declared authoritatively. "They think differently from us—says so in all the books . . . What's for tea? I'm starving!"

Later, as he was changing to go out for the evening, he reflected:

They can't think all that differently, of course. Even a slope like him knows which side his bread is buttered—No, they don't eat bread, do they? What would they say? Which side to sauce their noodles?

And that was good for a laugh with his oppos when they met up later at their usual pub, whose landlord knew better than to try and keep Terry out for being under the legal drinking age.

You're watching TV Plus. Now for Newsframe.

The inquiry into the disaster that rendered hundreds of people homeless in Carlisle last year has been told that the explosion was caused by an oversight when scaling up a chemical reaction from laboratory to commercial scale. A firm bottling mineral water, forced to cease trading by con

tamination of natural springs, is to sue the company re-
sponsible, Flixotrol, for a million pounds in damages.

In Tottenham, London, today a black youth was beaten
nearly to death for refusing to wear a Thrower ribbon.
Wilfred Holder, 17 . . .

THE FOLLOWING WEEK TURNED OUT, IN FACT, TO BE
not quite as terrible as Peter had envisaged during those awful
minutes after the police marched out and slammed the door.

Not *quite . . .*

But that was a minor consolation for having this stranger
hung around his neck. He thought of pendants strung with
millstones.

Bad was finding himself reduced to living and working in
an even smaller area than at his old home, for Ellen had to
have a room to herself. The social worker, who duly appeared
next morning, left a stack of leaflets in which, she declared,
he would find the regulations that made it obligatory. Her
attitude indicated that she suspected him of planning to rape
his daughter as soon as she left.

And of course the petty annoyances were endless—like
having to don a dressing gown on his way to and from the
bathroom. He didn't own pajamas, hadn't since he was a kid
himself, and had grown reflexively used to walking naked
round his home, for if anybody else was there, she'd likely
shared his bed the night before.

Worse, though, was having to turn down the next really
juicy assignment offered by TV Plus. According to rumor,
rabid rats had arrived in Kent through the pilot workings for
the Channel Tunnel. During its final series *Continuum* had
covered hydrophobia, which year by year was drawing closer
to the coast of France, so Peter would have been an ideal
choice to handle the story. Instead, he had to plead helplessly,
"Ellen's a victim of the Heathrow disaster—I've got to find a
school for her, can't leave her by herself because she's far too
young, and anyway after what she's been through . . ."

"I'll have to try someone else, then!"

Click.

With which, the prospect of a company car receded over the horizon.

Yet maybe worst of all was the fact that this timid, fawn-eyed creature, this fragile worse-than-orphaned plaything of malevolent chance—this not-yet person whose existence was admittedly his fault—was so desperate to please! She didn't want to be what she realized she was: a nuisance. So she begged to be allowed to keep out of his way, to do the washing-up, to launder her own pitifully few clothes which he had to supplement on much-resented shopping trips, to sit immobile in front of the TV wearing headphones so he wouldn't be disturbed by the sound . . .

No. That wasn't the worst. *The* worst was when the suspicion stole into his mind that he might have been better off had he coaxed Kamala out of her fit of fury after she found out about—well, what he'd done that made her lose all patience with him. He had been very fond of her: a slim and pretty nurse, met while he was a medical student. Then thanks to a terrible mischance . . .

He shut out the notion, or rather tried to. Against his best attempts, images leaked through of what his life might have been like by now: as a GP with an established practice and a supportive wife, a daughter at the local school—

Stop! They'd have been stoning me on the streets!

If WPC Prentis was anyone to go by . . .

Some problems evaporated with amazing swiftness. He had paid no attention at the time, but among the selling points listed by the estate agents through whom he had bought his new flat (and when was his old one going to be sold? "For Sale" signs were infecting London like measle spots, and as if he didn't have enough trouble already, one prospective buyer had been ruled ineligible for so large a mortgage, so he was the involuntary owner of two homes!) had been the fact that there was still a school within walking distance. He visited it with Ellen, told her story to the head teacher, and met with nothing but sympathy. Strings would have to be pulled, and she might have to join her class a week late, but—well, it could be arranged.

That marked the first time when he consulted his daughter's opinion directly, apart from trivia such as what to buy for dinner. There in the head teacher's office he reached out for her hand and asked, "Will it be all right if you come here?"

Her eyes were still puffy; most nights he heard her cry herself to sleep, and more than once she'd woken screaming from a nightmare full of burning houses. But she smiled and returned the squeeze he gave her fingers.

"Yes, Dad. I think I could get on here very well."

It was that evening, when he'd cobbled up a meal, that for the first time he called her to it saying, "Darling! It's ready!"

Followed the first time that she kissed him good night.

Next day she ventured the news that at her former school she had been taught how to run a computer. Was there any chance . . . ? Because having watched him at work—

He had a spare one he'd been planning to sell when he found a customer. Well, it wouldn't have fetched much more than scrap price anyhow. He plugged it in; it proved to be still functional. When he said it was hers she hugged him—for the first time—and thereafter seemed quite content to sit alone in her room and play with it. Or watch his old television, or listen to his old stereo. Sometimes, too, she asked to borrow one of his old books, saying she'd never seen so many except in a public library.

Reach-me-downs.

It wasn't right, yet the phrase rang in his head. He recalled it not from his own childhood but from what he had been told about then. It seemed to imply something he couldn't quite define.

Not, at least, until resonance from it led him to another half-forgotten term:

Latch-key kid.

In other words, a child who returned from school to an empty house because both parents were still at work. He'd been one himself, though fortunately for a very brief while after his father left his mother for another woman . . .

That put him on the phone to the head teacher again, in search of someone prepared to mind children during the late afternoon. Yes, there was such a service, owing to the high incidence of single parents in the area.

The fees were disproportionate. Recklessly he committed

himself to meeting them on the grounds that if he were not free to work he couldn't pay for a dependent, which and who so ever. And when he asked Ellen how things had gone during the first day at her new school, and whether she had been properly looked after before he returned, she gave a nod, and then a surprising grin, and hugged him again.

Maybe Kamala wasn't doing quite such a good job after all . . . Job! Mine is turning out to be a brute! Keeping me up until all hours—!

Back to it. Right now, with Ellen apparently content to turn in early and leave him to get on with it.

Apparently. That didn't mean truly. Did it?

In spite of all, however, he felt an absurd sense of achievement as he sat at his desk after dinner, sorting out his commitments for the morrow. There was a warm glow in the back of his mind, as though he had passed some particularly daunting interview for a new post.

Things were falling tidily into place in spite of all. Now Ellen was going to school, now the teachers and even apparently the pupils were showing sympathy about her loss—she was invited to a tea party on Saturday (weird, *weird* to look at his on-screen list of engagements and see another set of commitments listed alongside his own!)—now he could set aside his more ridiculous worries and get back to making plans. For instance, the *Comet* was still afloat and rumor had it that extra money was being pumped in. Before the transfusion dried up he stood a chance of—

"Dad?"

In Ellen's usual diffident tone, redolent of insecurity. He turned to her with a sigh.

"Dad, I'm dreadfully sorry, but I'm bleeding! I got undressed and went to bed, and I was half asleep when I found I'd made a dreadful mess on the sheets! Mum warned me to expect it about now, but I never thought . . . ! *I'm sorry!*"

And a wail, and tears she struggled to repress.

It was something that had never struck Peter before because he had never lived with a woman. He had only been frustrated by it during an affair. Naturally, being a nurse, Ka-

mala had taught Ellen the facts of life, but between the theory
and the reality—!

Yet of course one knew in the abstract that the onset was
sometimes precipitated by stress. What worse stress than the
disaster she had undergone?

He improvised. He felt when the task was over he had
improvised exceptionally well. The new woman was provided
with cottonwool to staunch the flow and a tight pair of panties to
hold the pad in place, albeit she must spend tonight in a tattered
sleeping-bag and he had to revise his schedule for tomorrow yet
again to take account of a long visit to the launderette . . .

But he had cuddled her, and asked if she was in pain,
which she was not, and remembered that Kamala too had
often been taken by surprise (one time in bed . . .) and made
her a cup of reassuring tea, and left her watching the TV, and
generally impressed himself with his ability to cope.

*If only it matched my ability to make a living I'd be quids
in, home and dry!*

The telephone rang.

"Oh, shit! *Yes?*"

Cool, detached, a woman with an American accent: "You
sound as though you have as many problems as I do."

Blocks of awareness clashed inside Peter's head like ice-
bergs. He blurted, "Claudia Morris!"

"Yes. Were you expecting my call? Were you sufficiently
in touch to hear before I did that another bastion of rationality
has fallen?"

"I . . ." But it was stupid to explain. Instead he parried, as
though caught up in a pointless fencing match.

"How did you trace me? I've moved!"

"Ach!" And a sound like spitting. "I was wrong on more
points than one! I thought this country was webbed with secrecy. Only your government is armored. You want to find out
about a private citizen's affairs? You grease the proper
palm—"

"Don't say such things on the phone!"

"They got you snagged along with all the rest, did they?
Then I bet you're wearing a red-white-and-blue ribbon on
your business suit these days—like a good boy!"

"Claudia, for God's sake—!"

"Stuff the paranoia." Her tone was suddenly shrill. "I need to talk to you, and analysis of intercepted calls is exponential. Listening to what our people and yours recorded last year alone would take till Doomsday. I want you to meet me at—"

"I can't!"

"Ah, they trod on you, too. Well, too bad. I'm very sorry for you."

"Wait!"—at the last moment halving his volume so as not to disturb Ellen.

"And for why?"

"You haven't told me why you want to talk to me!"

"You didn't hear? The puky funders got the better of the other funders—"

"Oh. Wait. I think I do know what you mean. But I haven't been keeping up with the news."

"It's your profession, isn't it?"—mockingly.

"I got lumbered! My daughter!"

"That doesn't sound like the most fatherly of—"

"Oh, stop it, will you? Her periods started tonight and I've been trying to comfort her."

There was a pause. Eventually Claudia said, "I'm sorry. I didn't realize you were married."

"I'm not. In fact"—he sought the antique phrase that hovered in a distant corner of his mind, and trapped it as a hawk might catch its prey—"she's a byblow. But her home was burnt out in the Heathrow disaster, so I've taken her in charge."

Next time Claudia spoke, her tone was noticeably more cordial.

"I still want to talk to you. In fact I need to talk to you. Can you meet me at—?"

"Come out this evening? You must be precessing with all your gyros! Leave on her tod a kid who's having her first period? More likely I'll be sitting up beside her bed!"

"Then can I come to your place?"

Peter thought for a long moment, torn between duties. Eventually professionalism won.

"All right," he sighed. "What time?"

"I can make it in about half an hour."

"Okay. Let me tell you how to get here—"

She cut him short.

"If I didn't know how to find you, how could I have called you up? But don't worry. All record of the circuits I used will self-erase the moment I put down this phone . . . Oh! One other thing!"

"Yes?"—impatiently, for he found Ellen's large sad eyes on him.

"What computer do you have?"

He named it.

"That's fine, then. I'll bring a disk with me. I think you'll be interested . . . See you in half an hour."

Ellen needed more cottonwool. The flow was considerable for a first time. When it was stanched she asked whether she must go back to bed immediately. Feeling as though, if he insisted, she would regard it as a rejection, he said she could wait up until his visitor arrived. At once she curled up on the couch beside him, to watch the TV news.

Who am I? Where am I? Am I caught in a trap worse than the worst my nightmare could contrive, or am I on the verge of a breakthrough that will make my name and reputation? Worst of all: am I on the track of a major story that I can't follow through because of Ellen?

She's a sweet kid. She's so nice she's made me regret not patching matters up with Kamala. But nonetheless she feels like shackles!

RENATO TESSOLARI WAS IMMENSELY PROUD OF HIS son—his only child—GianMarco. As he was fond of saying, the boy had his own black hair and his wife Constanza's brown eyes, even though there was little noticeable resemblance in other respects.

And to think he had been born after seven fruitless years! When Renato was indeed beginning to fear that the fault might lie on his side, for he had had his share of youthful escapades, and not once had any of the girls he'd lain with . . .

Well, in the end it had turned out for the best. And he owed a tremendous debt to GianMarco's uncle, his brother-in-law Fabio Bonni, who knew so much about advances in modern science and had suggested that Constanza visit England, where doctors were making amazing new discoveries in the field of infertility.

The treatment had been like a miracle! Within a month of her return she had come smiling to him to report her pregnancy, and it was as though a colossal weight receded from his mind.

For, without an heir in the direct line, what would happen to the estates the Tessolari family had owned since the seventeenth century? They would pass perhaps to cousins—but most of them were in the north, making money in ways far removed from Mother Earth. Not for them the patient cycle of the seasons, pressing oil, treading grapes, reaping maize, drying tomatoes. No, they preferred the hustle and bustle of big cities: Milan, Turin, Marghera. The ancient traditions of the *Mezzogiorno* had grown alien to them, as though they were foreigners in their own homeland, and if the estates fell to them as an inheritance they would be most concerned about how soon and for how much they could be sold.

So at least Renato felt, and loudly and vigorously Fabio concurred, occasionally winking unnoticed at Constanza.

In turn, little by little, GianMarco learned to be proud of his father. When he was eight or nine, he began to understand the workings of the adult world; by the time he was ten, he fully appreciated the fact that—because his family had been landowners here for so long—no decision was taken by the town council that might infringe Tessolari interests. Renato was of course a councillor himself, and had been mayor. So had his father, his grandfather, and countless of his uncles. And the family's influence extended to the provincial level, too, and even as far as Rome.

What was more, there were other matters he was encouraged to take pride in. The rambling house where he grew up might have patches of stucco missing from its façade—but it had once sheltered one of Garibaldi's agents on a secret mission. The cars his parents owned might be commonplace Fiats rather than spectacular Ferraris—but Great-great-grandfather Ruggiero had been the first person in the region to possess a car, and many were the amusing stories related about how the peasants panicked when a carriage with no horse to draw it rolled down their streets.

Nonetheless, he sometimes asked Renato why the family was no longer so exceptionally rich as it must have been in old Ruggiero's day, and was always rewarded by the same lecture concerning the true nature of wealth. "Suppose," his father would say sententiously, "there were another economic crisis. Money might be worthless again, as it has so often been in the past. Then you'd see our 'wealthy' relatives come crawling to us for help—to us who can grow food! *That's* the ultimate source of all riches: the land. I shan't be around for ever, you know. But I shall leave you the finest patrimony anybody could wish for. Now come along. We have to visit"—and he'd name one of the tenant farmers, perhaps because he was growing slack about his duties, perhaps because a member of his family was sick and he needed a loan to pay the doctor. With his tenants, Renato behaved as he did toward his son: strictly or leniently as the occasion called for. When the boy was twelve, and therefore of an age to be involved (and moreover he had physically entered manhood), he was permitted to sit in a corner while his father held discussions with his bailiffs, and heard him utter judgment: this man was feckless and must be turned out, but this other who had done worse yet had after all lost his wife last year and not yet found another, so he could be forgiven...

GianMarco preened, looking forward to the time when he too could assist his father in such weighty matters.

His chance came sooner than he had expected.

One day in the autumn of that same year, when the harvest was in, Renato drove him to visit relatives in a town fifty kilometers away. His mother did not go with them, allegedly because she felt unwell—yet she had shown no sign of illness. However, her brother was at home to keep her company, so... And off they went: two men together, as Renato chaffed.

Something intangible conveyed to GianMarco that for the first time he was directly involved in adult business. He waited in excitement to discover what it was.

They stayed late. It was full dark before they set out homeward—and then they took a slightly different route. At first GianMarco was puzzled. Then, little by little, he started to recognize the area they were traversing. They were on land that did not belong to the Tessolaris or any of their friends. Abandoned at the end of World War II, it had been taken over by a peasant cooperative. It was rich soil—as rich went in the hot dry south of Italy—and there were several long-established olive groves and vineyards on it. Consequently the old families whose lands abutted it had spent fortunes in lawsuits designed to dispossess those they regarded as mere squatters. But courts in distant Rome, after years of litigation, declared they had no valid claim, and authorized the former landless peasants to grow rich, put on airs, and ape their betters.

This had been taught to GianMarco, in detail and with considerable bitterness. His uncle Fabio, in particular, was contemptuous of the peasants' aspirations. Once when GianMarco had dared to ask why he was still a bachelor at forty, he had admitted that his own people, the Bonni, had lost a claim to the land now being farmed cooperatively, and had it not been for his sister's fortunate marriage he might have been poverty-stricken by now. As it was, thanks to his suggestion that Constanza visit England for treatment, he was a welcome resident in the Tessolari house.

(Behind this colorable tale there was a hint of something darker. GianMarco had occasionally overheard servants joking about certain handsome boys that Fabio took up as friends and dropped abruptly after bestowing gifts on them without avail . . . but this was nothing he could understand.)

And lately it had emerged that for some reason to do with fertilizers or other chemicals, or some such kind of modern aids to husbandry which Renato had enthusiastically adopted under Fabio's guidance, the buyer from Genoa whose firm had for half a century purchased olive oil from the Tessolari estate at an advantageous price, had this year offered more to the cooperative, on the grounds that theirs could be exported to the health-conscious USA as "organically" grown.

This was of course an affront not to be tolerated.

It began to dawn on GianMarco's drowsy mind what his father was about when the car headed down a dry bumpy track toward an isolated barn. Here was where the cooperative kept its oil-press and storage vats . . .

It must, he guessed, be after midnight. Never before had he been allowed to stay up so late, not even in the tolerant environment of Mediterranean culture. He tried to read his watch, but his father had switched off the car's lights and the sky was overcast. He concluded:

This is indeed men's business!

The realization sent a frisson down his spine and jolted him back to wakefulness.

"You wait here," Renato said curtly as he brought the car to a halt and got out. "And remember! If anybody asks you—I'm not saying who, mind, but if *anybody* asks you— we drove straight home from Anna's. Is that understood?"

"Yes!" GianMarco breathed, and stared with aching eyes as the blurred shadow of his father faded into the shadow that was the looming barn.

Two men greeted him—GianMarco heard their voices—
and then all became darkness and mystery.

Trembling, expecting he knew not what except that his
imagination kept offering pictures of an open valve at the bottom of a huge vat full of oil (would it be set on fire or simply
left to drain? He thought the latter but it was a guess), Gian-
Marco sat in the car alone for five or seven minutes.

Then there was a shot.

And a scream.

And a sense of frenzied running.

And his father was back beside him, starting the engine,
backing up, sawing his way on to the track again, and all the
while cursing in language GianMarco had never thought
would pass his lips. Amid the torrent of obscenity the boy
gathered that the stinking peasants had been so impressed by
the high price their oil was to command this year they had
arranged for members of the cooperative to sleep in the barn,
turn and turn about, and guard their treasure.

And tonight's watchman had been fool enough to wake and
intervene.

GianMarco tried not to visualize the bloody mess a shotgun
at close range would make of a human body.

"Remember!" his father was insisting as the car bounced
crazily toward the metalled road. "We drove straight home
tonight! We drove straight back from Anna's!"

"Yes, father," GianMarco said composedly. For, after all,
what mattered one blockheaded peasant more or less?

He was sent to bed immediately on arriving home, but for a
long while he was too excited to sleep. His room was above
the hallway where the main telephone was kept; by straining
his ears he could hear Renato speaking to Anna, instructing
her that he and GianMarco had in fact left twenty minutes
later than in reality.

This is like being in a gangster film!

Then, perhaps roused by the unavoidable click of the extension phone in her bedroom, his mother went downstairs
and at once divined that something was amiss. Renato tried to
convince her he was phoning Anna only to let her know they

had reached home safely, but she didn't believe his story. Within minutes she had either pried out the truth, or guessed it. After that there was no need to strain to listen, for a full-blown shouting match developed. It roused Fabio, who joined them and tried with small success to calm things down.

"Our only son!" Constanza kept shouting. "A twelve-year-old boy! And you risked his life! Suppose there had been more than one guard? Suppose they'd been armed, and fired back?"

"But there wasn't, and they weren't!" Renato bellowed. "Now will you shut up and go back to bed? I have more calls to make—urgent calls!"

In the end, Constanza let Fabio usher her away. By then she was crying. Hearing her sobs, for the first time Gian-Marco realized the seriousness of the situation. Someone had been shot and maybe killed, by one of his father's men, raiding the cooperative's barn on his orders and in his presence. In Ruggiero's time no doubt it would have been easy to arrange a cover-up. Nowadays, even though Renato was a councillor and former mayor, it might not be so simple.

In which case—he clenched his fists under the bedclothes as he heard his father's increasingly despairing voice below—what would become of him? Oh, obviously he and his mother and uncle, and Anna, would lie to protect Renato . . . but what if the truth came out some other way, say because one of the men panicked or had a fit of conscience? Or because the seal of the confessional proved less sacred than it used to be? The incumbent priest was an outsider from Foggia, allegedly assigned here as punishment for holding radical views, a suggestion borne out by his popularity with members of the cooperative. He would show scant sympathy toward the Tessolaris.

If the facts did emerge, then those who had told lies would also be criminals, wouldn't they? He himself might be sent to a reformatory! His mother and uncle might be jailed, and his father most assuredly!

Visions of the house being lost, along with the estates that were promised to him, assailed GianMarco's mind. No, it was unthinkable! It must not happen!

He fell at last into uneasy slumber.

* * *

And was roused not long after dawn by the sound of engines. Running to the window, he saw black-clad men on motorcycles escorting a police car. When it halted the first passenger to get out carried a submachine gun, and the second was the *Maresciallo*, the local chief of police, a frequent visitor to the Tessolari house—but only when off duty.

No!

The word sounded so clearly in GianMarco's mind, he imagined for an instant that he had spoken it aloud. But it was only the focus of a sudden resolve that had gripped him, like a shiver that began and never ended.

No, they are not going to arrest my family like common criminals!

Frantically he dragged on his clothes and rushed downstairs.

Getting dressed had been a mistake.

GianMarco realized that as soon as he reached the hall. The only other person in the house who was out of bed yet was his family's maid, Giuseppina, who had answered the door; she was always up first, to light the kitchen stove and prepare breakfast. If this were a perfectly normal day, as they must pretend, what was he doing with his clothes on at this hour?

Well, it was too late to do anything about it now, except act for all he was worth.

"Good morning, *Signor Maresciallo*!" he exclaimed. "The noise of the motorbikes awakened me, so I thought I'd come down and see if anything exciting is going on!"

The *Maresciallo*, a stout man growing bald, with a thick black moustache, favored him with a scowl.

"What kids your age think exciting isn't anything we grown-ups greatly care for," he rumbled. "It's a nasty business that's brought me here, a very nasty business . . . Giuseppina, I must request you to rouse Signor Tessolari and say I want to talk to him. Immediately!"

Eyes wide with dismay and alarm, Giuseppina assured him she would do so. Asking him to take a seat in the drawing room, she departed with muttered promises of coffee in a little while.

Uncertain, GianMarco remained in the hall until she came down again and retreated to the kitchen. A minute or two later Renato also descended the stairs, belting a dressing gown around him. His face was like a statue's, but there was no hint of a tremor in his voice when he called out.

"You're up early, young fellow! I'd have thought after coming home so late last night you'd sleep till noon! What's all this about the *Maresciallo* being here, and with an armed guard?"

"It's quite true," GianMarco confirmed. "He's waiting in there"—with a nod at the door, which Giuseppina had left ajar.

"Hmm! Sounds ominous! You'd better hang on while I find out what's the matter."

Shamelessly eavesdropping, GianMarco heard him greet the police chief and ask what brought him.

"There was an attack on the barn at the cooperative last night," came the answer. "A man was shot."

"You don't mean dead!"—in properly horrified tones.

"Not yet, though the doctors don't expect him to live. But he's conscious, and . . ."

A solemn pause.

"And what?"

"And he has made a deposition to the effect that he recognized the man who shot him. Luigi Renzo. One of your tenants."

"But that's ridiculous! How could he be sure? There was no moon last night, as I know very well. It so happens that I took GianMarco to visit my sister-in-law Anna—you know Anna, of course—and we didn't get back until late. That's why I was so surprised to find my son up and about. I suppose it was the noise that woke him."

"He came to ask if anything exciting was going on."

"Well, it sounds as though there is. But if the man with the gun was recognized as Renzo, why are you here instead of at his place?"

"Oh, I've sent another detachment after him," said the *Maresciallo*. "I'm here because the victim also says he overheard three men talking—that's what alerted him. And," he concluded with deliberation, "he says one of the voices was yours."

"But that's absurd!"

"When I left the hospital he was about to receive Extreme Unction. Men who know they are dying don't generally lie. In addition, we found tire-tracks in the dust near where he was shot. They match exactly those on your own car."

How different his tone and manner were from his usual joviality! GianMarco found himself starting to tremble.

"Now you said you came back late from visiting your sister-in-law. I know where she lives. Your direct route would have taken you not across the cooperative but down a road alongside it . . . Hmm! How late is 'late'?"

"I suppose we returned about half past midnight."

"And the attack took place just after twelve. You must have been within earshot when the gun—"

"Now look here!" Renato jumped to his feet. "I see what you're implying, and I don't like it! I drove directly home! GianMarco, are you still there? Come and tell the *Maresciallo* what happened on the way home last night!"

Unable to avoid a show of timidity, GianMarco entered the room.

"Nothing happened," he said flatly. "We drove straight home, just as Papa says."

And the coldness that had overtaken him increased, as though something within him had seized control of his voice, his motions, his very thoughts.

The *Maresciallo* uttered a disbelieving grunt. "Were you awake in the car?" he began, and somehow seemed to give up expecting an answer as soon as the words were out. Gian-Marco had fixed him with his gaze and laid a pleading hand on his arm as though this man were still the avuncular family friend he was used to.

"*Signor Maresciallo*, you know my father is an honorable man. He wouldn't descend to such an awful deed! I agree that men who know they are dying don't usually lie—but aren't there exceptions? Even if he has received Extreme Unction he may not be an honest believer. Aren't many of the members of the cooperative communists and even atheists? He could eas-ily be lying about hearing my father's voice because he sees it as a way of settling a grudge—after all, we old families aren't exactly popular in radical circles, are we? Besides, he could simply have been mistaken. It was certainly very dark, and if he was aroused from sleep, which I take to be the case since the hour was so late, he must have been confused. I say *must*, because my father definitely was not there. I was with him the whole time, and as he says we came straight home. As for the tire-tracks—well, we're patriotic Italians! Just as we buy Fiat cars, we buy Pirelli tires! And they're sold by the millions, aren't they?"

With mingled amazement and relief he saw the police chief's expression of certainty fade away, until at the end of the speech he was shaking his head lugubriously.

"Yes, of course, you must be right. It was dark, as you say, and indeed many of the members of the cooperative are socialists or worse, and . . . Yes, what is it?"

He was facing the door. Around it Giuseppina was peering nervously. "Excuse me, *signori*," she blurted. "But one of the policemen has a message on the radio."

"Coming!"

When he returned, the *Maresciallo* looked positively embarrassed.

"It sounds as though I owe you an apology. Luigi Renzo didn't come home last night. Must have made a bolt for it. No doubt he's the genuine culprit. Well, I'm sorry to have disturbed you. I'll let you know when there's any news."

Replacing his uniform cap on his balding head, he left the house with a distracted air.

"What was all that about?" Constanza called from the upstairs landing, in a convincingly innocent tone for the benefit of Giuseppina, who was closing the front door.

"A dreadful thing happened. Apparently Luigi Renzo and someone else shot a man at the cooperative barn, not long before we got home. So the police came to ask whether we'd seen or heard anything suspicious."

"How dreadful!"—from Fabio, who had emerged from his room in time to catch the last few sentences. "Could you be of any help?"

"Neither I nor GianMarco, I'm afraid . . . Well, Giuseppina, where's our coffee?"

Later, when they were alone and could talk in confidence, Renato murmured to his son:

"When I said you couldn't be of any help, I meant to the *Maresciallo*, of course. You were the most amazing help to me. I never saw such a job of acting in my life! You practically convinced me, do you realize that? You practically had me believing what you said!"

GianMarco could only grin by way of answer. But he felt his chest swell with pride.

Old, family pride.

You're watching TV Plus. Newsframe follows.

Last week's air crash in Tenerife has today been officially blamed on computer error, as was the recent collision over London Airport. A spokesman for the pilots' association, BALPA, criticized what he described as "greed" on the part of airline operators and "incompetence" on the part of air traffic controllers, rather than the computers.

Here in Britain, General Thrower's name seems set to become a generic term, like Hoover. A mob of youths sporting badges reading "I'm a Thrower" smashed and wrecked . . .

IN THE UPSHOT CLAUDIA ARRIVED NOT HALF AN hour but a full hour later. Waiting for her, watching the news with Ellen at his side, Peter thought a lot about his daughter. In the past, as she had admitted, she had rarely bothered with the news. However, now that she had found out what her "dad's" profession was, she made a point of paying attention and showed, indeed, a lively interest.

Nobody could accuse her of not trying!

He had gathered the impression that she had been told almost nothing about him. She had been aware, for as long as she could remember, that her mother's husband wasn't her father, but this was a commonplace among her friends at school, so she had never worried much about it. And since Kamala never mentioned her paternity...

At least I seem to be doing the right kind of thing.

Now and then he asked whether she felt okay, and each time she forced a smile and nodded.

"It's only natural," was her verdict. "It was just a shock to find it happening to me, as well."

And how many other things could one say the same of?

The news bulletin consisted of the usual chapter of accidents and disasters, interspersed with adulation of the leaders who were going to put everything right tomorrow. A tower-block had been set on fire by a former mental patient discharged from a closed-down hospital under the guise of "returning her to the community." The price had been ten lives including hers. A street of houses was collapsing because water from an unmended pipe had washed away the subsoil from the foundations. A neglected bridge had given way. Two tankers containing chemicals that combusted spontaneously when mixed had fallen into the river below along with a bus; sixty people had burned or drowned. Yet more doubt had been cast on the viability of the Chunnel by a psychiatrist who had carried out tests at the Fréjus tunnel under the Alps on a group of long-distance lorry-drivers, normally supposed to be a stolid bunch. A third of them had declined to complete the four successive runs that he had asked of them, because they developed claustrophobia. Further inquiries had established that the same proportion of their colleagues had for some while past been refusing to travel that route. How many prospective users of the Chunnel would display the same symptoms?

During the current-affairs program that followed on another channel, a cabinet minister was sleekly pointing out that the psychiatrist was Italian and therefore not to be taken seriously, when the doorbell finally rang.

Claudia entered amid a storm of mingled curses and apologies. Apparently the minicab service her hosts relied on was owned by Tamil expatriates and tonight its headquarters had been firebombed as part of their running battle with the Sinhalese, so she had had to find an alternative.

Another thread in life's rich tapestry . . .

Ellen waited long enough to be introduced, then kissed Peter and disappeared to her own room again. Dropping a laden bag on the couch, Claudia nodded after her.

"Pretty kid! How does it feel to be a single parent?"

"She's making it easy for me," Peter grunted, switching off the TV. "Goodness knows how, after all the traumata she's been through."

"Tranquilizers?"

"Won't touch 'em. Kamala's influence—her mother, that is. She was a nurse. Ellen does have bad dreams, of course, and the social worker suggested sleepers, but she won't take them either. Wakes me sometimes in the small hours so I have to go and comfort her, but—well, they do say it's best not to repress grief, don't they? Do sit down! Care for a drink?"

"I wouldn't mind." Claudia leaned back, face eloquent of weariness, and ran her fingers through her pageboy hair.

"I haven't got much to offer, I'm afraid. My—ah—circumstances have changed rather radically. Scotch and water?"

"On the rocks. I need a kick in the *kishkas*."

"Excuse me?"—thinking this was recent American slang he hadn't yet caught up with.

It was her turn to be confused. "Sorry! I took it for granted that with a name like Levin . . ."

Realization dawned. "Oh! Was that Yiddish? Did you think I was Jewish?"

"Well—uh—yes, as a matter of fact." For the first time Claudia seemed visibly embarrassed.

Does she think she's offended me? No, I don't think so. More likely she's annoyed at having made a wrong guess.

"You're not the first," he said lightly. "But in fact it's an old English name. Started out as Leofwine—'love-friend.'"

"Sorry anyway. Should have known better."

She remained silent and preoccupied while he poured the drinks. When he had delivered them and sat down in an armchair facing her, she resumed, "After our last encounter I imagine you were moderately angry with me, hm?"

"I wasn't overjoyed . . . Cheers."

"*L'chaim!* That's to make it clear that I *am* Jewish . . ." She took a sip and set the glass aside. "I can only say I had a lot on my mind. You did hear what happened at my university?"

"I haven't checked, but I can guess from what you told me. One of these fundamentalist takeovers, right?"

"One of the worst. I knew the dean and most of the senior faculty were soft in the brain, but I never expected them to cave in so quickly the moment I wasn't around."

"You were the prime target?"

"Of course. Aren't I the one who's been attacking Mom and apple pie?"

"So what exactly has happened?"

This time Claudia took a generous gulp of her whiskey before answering.

"The funders moved in with an offer of a million-dollar endowment for a department of 'creation science'"—she made the quote marks audible—"on condition that funding for my sabbatical was withdrawn and my tenure cancelled."

"Can they do that? I thought once you had tenure—"

"*Plus* whatever it might cost to contest any suit I bring against the university."

"I'd have thought it was cheaper and quicker to hire a Rambo squad," Peter muttered.

On the brink of saying something else, she checked. "You sounded almost serious!"

"Why not?"

"But I thought—"

"You thought Rambo squads were an invention of the media? That's what most Americans believe. No, they're real enough. They operate in groups of three, one firearms expert, one explosives expert, and a communications specialist . . . But I wasn't in fact being serious. Just cynical. More to the point: can't your friend Mr. Strugman help?"

"He may be rich," was the tart response, "but he's not that rich. For one thing, he's not as rich as he was—he's funded half a dozen lawsuits for us already. We won three and lost three. Win some, lose some . . . But he is prepared to underwrite my year in Britain, bless him."

"Ah, you're staying on. With the friends who are putting you up?"

"Scarcely"—with a sour smile. "'Guests and fish stink after three days.' In any case, my hosts have problems. My hostess's sister died yesterday, after cutting herself with a kitchen knife."

"Good grief! Was she a hemophiliac?"

Shaking her head, Claudia emptied her glass. "She contracted antibiotic-resistant toxemia from beef that she was cutting up for a stew. Her family can sue, of course, but would you bet on their chance of winning?" She set the empty glass down with an angry slam and Peter rose hastily to refill it. He wanted Claudia in this expansive mood, and the whiskey seemed to be having a rapid effect.

Over his shoulder he said, "So what will you do?"

"I don't know. I don't want to waste Cecil's money, and renting in this burg is horribly expensive, yet if I move out to the suburbs I'll spend so much time commuting . . ."

"I think I have the answer," Peter interjected.

"Tell me!"—in excitement as she accepted the fresh drink.

"What say you take on my old place? It isn't much, just three tiny rooms, a place to cook and sort of a bathroom. A shower, at least. It's on the top floor, but I survived there for four years."

"You'll rent it to me? How much?"

"No, that's not what I had in mind." Peter resumed his chair. "I have to sell it—absolutely have to. In fact I thought I had, only the deal fell through." He didn't go into details. "What I think you ought to do is get a bank to buy it."

"A bank?" Claudia echoed incredulously.

"Precisely. In the eighties a lot of them moved into real estate, especially in London where property prices haven't gone down in more than a generation. Pretty soon they're going to own more of this town than the Duchy of Westminster . . . With Strugman to guarantee you, you should have no trouble. Go to a bank—my own is a pretty good bet—and say you want my flat for a year. They'll buy it. When you leave, they'll sell it, or rent it again. Like you said, there's a shortage of accommodation to let. All it'll cost you will be interest on the bank's investment, plus insurance and the running costs. It's a sight cheaper than ordinary renting, I promise you."

Her face was alight with enthusiasm. It made her look almost pretty—though Peter doubted she would be pleased were he to say so.

"Banks really do this?"

"A lot. Mainly for overseas investment companies who need one of their executives to spend a year in Britain. I could kick myself for not thinking of it before." He pulled a self-consciously comical face.

"That's wonderful! I'm so glad I came!" And, with a mercurial shift of mood: "Lord, I haven't even mentioned the reason I wanted to see you, have I?"

"Just a second before you get around to it. I ought to check that Ellen is okay."

On his return:

"Fast asleep, thank goodness. Let's hope it's all night this time. Being woken up in the small hours is making me understand how parents can be driven to batter a squalling baby . . . Well, what about the reason for your visit? You said you were going to bring a disk."

"Right here." She reached for her bag. "So if you'll boot your computer . . . ?"

"No sooner said than . . ."

But, as she was about to load the data, she hesitated. "In all fairness," she muttered, "I ought to warn you. This may give you still more sleepless nights."

"Certainly that's the effect it has on me."

And at that precise moment all the lights went off.

NOT YET FOURTEEN, THOUGH SHE HAD THE LOOKS and manner of a sixteen-year-old, Tracy Coward was the youngest pupil in the top class of her school. But keeping company with her seniors had never troubled her. Nor did it seem to bother the other children, for she was extremely popular.

Well, she must be. That at any rate was the view of her adoring parents Matthew and Doreen. Was she not forever receiving presents, sometimes quite expensive ones? And not just from boyfriends, either, as might be expected, but from girls as well!

This morning was a school day. As ever Tracy rose in good time, despite a warning abdominal cramp—against which she took a painkiller after she had cleaned her teeth—donned her uniform, made herself up with a hint of blusher, a line of eyebrow pencil, the merest trace of lipstick . . . and opened her treasure chest, as she called the drawer of her bedside table, to decide what extra touches to add.

Sooner or later, and probably sooner, she was going to need something larger than this drawer to store her acquisitions. There were rings, watches, brooches, pendants, necklaces, bracelets, hair-slides—a positive Aladdin's Cave of jewelry, all carefully protected in crumpled tissue and cotton-wool.

She decided on a silver clip that drew up her dark tresses in a 1940's style, reminiscent of pictures of Veronica Lake, a quartz watch with a silver bracelet, and a silver brooch set with brilliants. Nothing so flashy as to irritate the teachers— not that they dared to reprimand her nowadays—but enough to reinforce her friends' opinion of her as a stylish person.

Few of the other pupils dared to wear jewelry with uniform, it being discouraged.

And, after breakfast, it being a fine morning, she set off as usual to walk the three blocks to her school.

As she approached, however, she realized something most unusual was going on. Waiting for the bell to call them to assembly, the younger children were as always rushing about in the playground, shouting and taunting one another. But a group of the older girls, her own classmates, were standing on the pavement outside the gate, surrounding someone she could not quite recognize at first.

A stir of annoyance arose in the back of her mind. That was what she had come to think of as her personal prerogative: being the honeypot surrounded by bees was the way she expressed it to herself . . . though of course she would never have admitted as much even to her best friend.

If she had one. Sometimes she felt she didn't. Although she was accepted, indeed sought after, although the other girls and often even boys turned to her for advice and repaid her generously with prized possessions, she seemed not to have any real *friends*—people with whom she felt wholly at ease, to whom she could confide secret fears and ambitions.

But such thoughts belonged rather to bedtime, before sleep, than to the morning. In any case she was distracted from them as, drawing closer, she suddenly realized who was the focus of the other girls' attention.

Of course!

It was Shirley Waxman, who having reached sixteen had left at the end of the last term in order—and this had caused a mild sensation, because the puritan backlash engendered by AIDS was far from over despite the existence of an effective vaccine—to live with her boyfriend. Now it looked as though . . .

Oh, no doubt of it. She was holding out her left hand, turning it this way and that, while the other girls *ooh*ed and *aah*ed. She must be, could only be, showing off an engagement ring.

Tracy had involuntarily quickened her footsteps. Slowing to a more deliberate pace, she approached quietly and was within arm's reach before anyone took notice of her.

That wasn't the way it ought to be. She had decided long ago—well, eighteen months ago, anyway—that she was always going to be the center of attention. And somehow she had found a means of achieving it.

The painkiller had fixed her cramps, but it had side effects: she wasn't thinking altogether clearly. In vain she sought for the sense of perfect calmness and clarity that had always preceded her greatest coups.

Well, not to worry. She'd worked the trick so often, she must have the hang of it by now.

"Oh, Tracy, look at my ring! Isn't it featly?"

And Shirley, beaming, was displaying it for her. It was indeed splendid. Of course the brilliant in the center was probably only zircon, but it glittered near enough like a diamond, and the setting was beautiful. A wave of greedy resentment swept through Tracy's mind.

She's fat, the bitch! She isn't even pretty! And she's got that magnificent ring, and she lives on her own—well, with her boyfriend, or I suppose now you have to say fiancé—and she doesn't have to put up with puky stupid teachers and parents so thickheaded they don't know what kind of a daughter they've got, and . . .

But none of this showed on the surface. Instead, taking Shirley's hand as though to admire the ring from closer to, Tracy said in her sweetest and most cajoling tone, "Oh, it's lovely, isn't it? I'd so much like to have it! You will give it to me, won't you . . . ?"

And abruptly realized that the magic wasn't working.

Letting the hand fall, she stepped back a pace in dismay, to meet harsh and hostile glares.

"Are you mad?" Shirley cried, clutching her left hand in her right as though afraid Tracy meant physically to rob her (but it had never been physically, only mentally, and by a means she did not understand).

"Typical!" That was Jackie, who had been a close friend of Shirley's while she was at school. "Always wants everybody else's best things!"

"And gets them, the bocky cank, though God knows

how!"—from Netta, who was on the other side of the group. "That clip in her hair! That was mine!"

"That's my watch!" exclaimed Vanessa, next to her, and grabbed Tracy's watch.

"My brooch!" shouted Jane, next to her again. And the last of the group, Marian, chimed in.

"It's not just things she takes! I was going out with Brian until she decided she wanted him!"

"She broke up me and Harry!"—from Vanessa.

"And me and Tom!" Jackie exploded. "*And* took my tickets for the Black Fire concert! Well, I'm sick of it! And I'm sick of *her*!"

"Right! Right! Right!"

Terrified, Tracy shook off Vanessa's grip and spun on her heel to flee. But Jackie adroitly tripped her so that she crashed face-down on the hard paving.

Then they fell on her, not only to reclaim their belongings but to vent their pent-up hate. By the time the playground supervisor realized what was happening, they had achieved their aim. Tracy went to hospital with countless cuts and bruises, a broken nose, a ruptured spleen, and a great raw patch on her scalp where furious Netta had ripped away not only the silver clip but a lock of hair as well.

Later, to Matthew and Doreen's horror, the police confiscated the contents of the drawer in Tracy's bedside table, calling them stolen goods. Yet, when the case came to court, it was the other girls who were reprimanded and put on probation, and ordered to return everything to the defiant Tracy, still wearing plaster on her many wounds.

That, though, was in the middle of her month.

It was her greatest triumph so far. In between wheedling her parents around to the view that she absolutely must move to a different school—which wasn't hard—she savored the discovery that her "magic" could be made to work on adults, too.

Provided, of course, the time was right.

You're watching TV Plus. It's Newsframe time.

Holiday-makers and home-owners on the French Riviera are in a state of panic. Following the price-hike imposed by the uranium-producing countries' cartel, UPAS, the French, who depend heavily on nuclear power, set about stripping the hills of Provence in search of more of the mineral. Now northerly winds are dumping radioactive dust on many popular beaches, including Cannes, Nice and St. Tropez.

Here in Britain, supporters of General Thrower held a rally in Leeds today. Police called out to control the crowds are to be disciplined, says the Chief Constable, for breaking ranks and joining in, instead of . . .

CURSING, PETER FOUND A FLASHLIGHT—POWER-cuts were so frequent nowadays, he always kept one handy—and cleared down the computer to avoid draining its battery pack.

"Maybe it's as well," Claudia said with a wry grimace. "I shouldn't throw you straight in at the deep end. Let me take the chance to supply a bit of background."

"As you like," Peter muttered. "A refill?"

"Oh, why not? This is strictly a case of going the whole hog, and for someone who was supposed to turn into a traditional Jewish momma . . . Sorry again! But—uh—you don't smoke by any chance, do you?"

"No." Peter blinked. "I didn't think you did."

"Used to." Another grimace, this one more like a scowl. "Gave up five years ago. But now and then under stress—Oh, hell, it's a disgusting habit, and if I can't learn to handle stress without a disgusting prop . . . How about that refill you suggested?"

"Coming up."

* * *

Installed again on the couch, she leaned back, crossed her legs and gazed into nowhere.

"You remember I told you I'm worried in case my original argument turns out to be wrong after all?"

"Yes."

"Did you follow that up?"

"I got in touch with Jim Spurman," Peter admitted.

"I suspected as much." She gave a bitter chuckle. "You know, that growser is terribly disappointed in me! He got his professorship on the strength of being my British protagonist, and when he discovered I was a turncoat . . ."

"In what sense?" Peter said with sudden impatience.

"This one!" Abruptly she was fixing him with her strange striped irises, and her tone and expression alike were intense. "I've established to my own satisfaction that there are cases of juvenile delinquency—hell, no! Juvenile *crime*, because some of them go 'way beyond anything you could excuse as mischief or high spirits or poor social adjustment—there *are* cases that aren't allowed for by my theory because something far more like a literal power of evil is involved."

She was breathing hard, staring at him through the dimness as though daring him to disagree.

Oh dear. This bears all the signs of a conversion.

"Know what I kept thinking of while I was doing the research?" she went on.

"No idea."

"It's a farfetched comparison, I guess, but . . . Well, it made me feel like the people who had to evaluate flying saucer sightings. Remember the UFO craze?"

"Yes, of course," Peter muttered. "But why?"

"Why was I reminded? Oh, because I was sifting through a mountain of evidence, determined to dismiss the lot, and kept getting stuck with an insoluble residue."

From one bee in the bonnet to another—is that it?

However, withdrawing his eyes from hers with difficulty and contriving to watch the ice dissolving in his glass instead, Peter said merely, "Well, now we know there's a chemical basis for schizophrenia—"

She brushed his words aside with an impatient gesture. "Flying saucer equals weather balloon! Take it as read that

I've ruled out orthodox forms of mental derangement."

"Then environmental contaminants. Extreme intolerance of things like permitted food-colors."

"There's enough in the literature about that kind of reaction to dismiss that as well. You're clutching at the same straws I did—flying saucer equals Venus or Jupiter! Which, incidentally, I never accepted . . . No, I'm perfectly serious, though I would rather not be. And before you ask, I've also allowed for the fact that I was raised to believe in the unique wickedness of the Nazis but learned enough history later on to compensate. Any more ideas?"

Peter hesitated a long while before speaking again. At length, reluctantly, he said, "Well, there was a book called *The Bad Seed* back in—was it the fifties?"

"You know it!" Claudia almost erupted from her seat. "I'd more or less given up hope of meeting anyone else who'd read it. You have read it? You remember it?"

"Oh, long ago. There were these teenage girls who committed the most appalling crimes and wrote a sort of diary about them, half fact, half fantasy . . . Are you on to something like that?"

"In a way." She sipped her drink, no longer looking at him. "I was so convinced, you see, that I'd hit on the fundamental explanation for this—this hostility of the younger generation against society. The nuclear family isn't exactly ancient, you know."

"You pointed that out in your book," Peter countered drily. "You showed how it arose in Europe in the sixteenth and seventeenth centuries and was converted into a norm after the Industrial Revolution. You said it was a suitable makeshift for its period, but in the modern age we need something closer to the tribal system we evolved with, in which every child can turn for help to ten or twenty adults, relatives or not, as easily as to its parents. You said the tradition of godparenting recognized this."

"And what did you think of my argument?"

"I have reservations, but you documented it well."

Claudia accepted that. After another swig, she went on, "Know how the puky funders got at me? Said I was advocating group marriage, i.e. promiscuity, which is against the Word of the Lord . . . You don't look surprised."

"Nothing about fundamentalists surprises me any longer," Peter grunted, and at long last helped himself to his second drink. His intention was to unlock Claudia's tongue while himself remaining comparatively sober. So far it seemed to be working, but he wished she'd get to the point.

"If they'd only *read* the Bible instead of just quoting it— Sorry *again*. I don't want to wander off into theology . . . I still believe I hit on a very important point, don't misunderstand me. But I was naïve enough to imagine it was the whole truth, a perfect solution. And also I'm scientist enough to recognize that a single exception calls a whole theory into question. Right?"

It apparently being expected, Peter gave a solemn nod.

"Right! Well, for a while my self-confidence was under-propped by all the letters I was receiving from desperate parents, mainly women but also quite a lot from men, saying they'd been given insight into the reason why Billy was abusing drugs and Nelly was on the streets and Sammy was in jail and . . . You get the picture.

"Then"—with sudden renewed intensity—"out of the blue I received quite a different letter. For one thing, it wasn't from a parent, but from a retired social worker, who had obviously read my book with great care and set out the best-reasoned case against my views that I've ever encountered." A brittle laugh. "Sometimes I wish I hadn't, you know!"

"What did she say?"

"Apart from points that other people had already made— only not so elegantly—she insisted that right at the end of a career spanning forty years she had run across a case she couldn't account for by any theory, including mine, bar the assumption of inborn wickedness."

"You took this seriously?"

"Well, I'd received a good deal of hate-mail as well as letters in support, so for a moment I was inclined to throw it away. But, as I said, it was couched in such reasonable terms that I couldn't drive it out of my mind."

"Did you get in touch with the writer?"

"I tried to. Unfortunately she had died. Young—only about sixty-five. Nonetheless, what she said went on bugging me. In the end I couldn't stand it any more. Even that single exception . . . So I started pulling strings."

She sipped her drink again and appended a sour chuckle.

"Ah, what it is to have status and renown! Before the book came out I was just another college professor. Once it had spent even a week in the bestseller lists I was famous and influential! I remember when I met you the first time I was contemptuous of publicity and the media. Back then, I didn't know what advantage I could turn them to . . .

"Never mind. The point is that I found I was able to access a whole area of data that I didn't even know existed until I started digging around. Once again I'd been naïve. I didn't know, for example, that there were police forces like yours that routinely put not just hard facts but rumor, gossip and suspicion on permanent file. Did I say the letter I was talking about came from England?"

"No." Peter was leaning forward now, hanging on every word.

"Well, it did. So, out of sheer curiosity and—what's that vivid English-English term for being ornery?"

"Bloody-mindedness?" Peter offered after a brief hesitation.

"That's it! Out of that sort of impulse, anyway, I dug around and discovered I could access some very strange records. Later on I'll tell you exactly how, but for the moment I'll just say they are police files. They're—well, I guess the term would be 'on the back burner.' But they do open them, now and then, to attested social researchers. With the appearance of my book, I'd turned into one. Bless the growser who put my name on the list!

"And that was how I found out that there were at least ten cases that to all appearances totally undermined my dogmatic assertions."

And, again, a generous gulp of whiskey. Afraid she might overdo it to the point of passing out before she finally let him in on her secret, Peter said, "Are your findings on the disk you brought?"

Claudia had been briefly brooding. Now she roused with a start.

"Yes! And a lot more. As soon as the power comes on again—"

Which it did, as though she had rubbed a magic lamp.

After a pause to make sure it wasn't a false alarm, she rose and returned to the computer. Peter made haste to follow, for fear that she might have grown clumsy. But she appeared totally in control as she booted it and tapped a succession of commands into the board. There was a security code that took a long while and considerable accuracy to enter; she got it right first time.

And for the next hour Peter could not tell whether he was being let in on the ground floor of the most important newsbreak of his life, or lured into the mazes of a deluded fanatic's dream.

IN THE COUNTRY TOWN OF MARSHMERE, WHERE many people still found it possible to maintain an illusion of prosperity despite Britain's economic decline, Richard Gall, branch manager of the County and Consolidated Building Society, was a respected figure. So was his wife Edna. He was a Mason and a member of the golf club; she was a school governor and active on charity committees. They lived in a medium-sized modern house on the outskirts of the town. He drove a Renault—distinctive but not inappropriate—and she a second-hand Mini. Their acquaintances regarded them as an ideal couple.

Mary Gall knew different. They never quarrelled in public, but she wasn't "public." That was how she had come to find out that she was not her father's natural child. During one of their recurrent rows, when she was twelve, she had heard Edna hurl the fact at Richard, reminding him of all the humiliation she had undergone—endless medical examinations, internal inspections, the final coldly clinical process that he had insisted on—and winding up with a barrage of comments about his inadequate masculinity.

At which point the doorbell rang, and instantly they were their usual affable selves.

Mary pondered that for a long time. At last she understood why her mother was so often moody, why she drank too much, why she smoked in spite of knowing how bad it was for her health. She had no clear idea of the "process" Edna had been obliged to undergo, but by making some discreet inquiries of the biology teacher at her school—which was not the one of which her mother was a governor—she contrived to assemble a fairly accurate picture.

And started to plot her revenge.

Precisely why it was so easy, she never worked out. She only knew that, quite recently, she had become able to influence her parents to the point where she could stop their quarrels in mid-spate, though they generally resumed again after she had gone to bed, where she lay listening and trembling as they traded insults.

Gradually resolve hardened in her mind. But it was two months before she put her plan into effect, and over a year before it reached its long-awaited climax. She was a patient child; she rarely took a hasty decision.

Especially in truly significant matters.

She already knew a certain amount about Richard's occupation. Her first step was to find out more, until she was sure that her idea was feasible. For a while after discovering he was not actually her father she had behaved coldly toward him, but soon enough she realized this was counterproductive, and began to play up to him. Indeed, for a time she went too far in the opposite direction, so that Edna accused her of taking sides. After a while, though, she established the proper balance.

Then, directly after the auditors had made their annual visit to the local branch of the building society, she started asking Richard to . . .

Asking?

No, that wasn't quite right. It was more like persuading, except it wasn't such hard work as persuading. It was a matter of gentling herself into the proper frame of mind, finding the right words and tone of voice, and then watching the outcome. She didn't always succeed, but she soon learned when and guessed why not, so she avoided the days when she felt her talent to be unreliable.

At the right moment, though—*wow!*

Stretching her patience to the maximum, she waited month after frustrating month before springing the trap she had set for her not-father. The temptation to hurry was atrocious, but she resisted it until three months before the auditors were due again: a gestation period.

Thereupon she "persuaded" Richard that his family ought to own a better car. That was how the Jaguar arrived. Next came the move, on short notice and a long mortgage, to a bigger house, costing twice as much as the old one, with a tennis court in the back garden. (At this point Edna grew worried—but Mary calmed and reassured her.) Then there was the booking for all three of them on a round-the-world luxury cruise. Mary was a smidgin regretful that it wasn't actually going to happen . . . Later, maybe. At the moment she was intent on her revenge.

So there followed the expensive home computer, and the TV camera, and the state-of-the-art CD player complete with a library of records to play on it, and a brand-new Citroën to take the place of Edna's Mini, and—and—and . . .

By the time the auditors arrived half the town was asking, "How does he manage it?" By the time they departed the entire town was asking, "How did he expect to get away with it?"

Because, of course, he didn't. Thanks to manipulation of the building society's financial records via his home computer, which stupidly took no account of the master records held at head office, half a million pounds of other people's money was missing from his branch, of which two hundred thousand had vanished heaven knew where.

And Mary.

To the police, and later at his trial, the only defense Richard had to offer was a whimpered excuse.

"My daughter made me do it!"

Sitting in the courtroom at her own insistence, calm and incredibly mature of manner most of the time, Mary turned to her mother and clutched her arm, demanding, "How can he say such dreadful things?"

Everybody heard her, including the judge and jury, just as she had intended. Though the judge reproved her for speaking aloud, it was clear he shared her attitude. He sentenced Richard to five years.

When they reached home Edna broke down in tears, looking at the magnificence of their new house.

"It'll all have to go!" she whimpered. "God knows where we'll wind up! We're going to be *homeless*!"

"No, we're not," Mary said composedly, dropping into one of the drawing room's splendid brocade armchairs.

"What do you mean?" Edna stared at her.

"You've got plenty to pay off the mortgage."

"Don't talk such nonsense! I've got the little bit—"

"The little bit Aunt Minnie left you," Mary interrupted. "I know! You've told me about it enough times. In fact it's not so little, is it? If we decide to stay here, it will be sufficient to survive on. We can run a car, though it'll have to be another Mini, I suppose, not a Jag—"

"Mary, you *are* talking nonsense! The interest on the mortgage alone—"

"I told you! It can be paid off!" Mary threw her head back and laughed joyously. "And at last we're free of that horrible man who put you through such torture to have me, and quarrelled with you so incessantly!"

Lately she had grown fond of unusual words, and taken to deploying them in conversation when the chance arose.

"*Mary!*" Edna was leaning over her. "I can't possibly repay our mortgage!"

"But you can," Mary sighed. "You have two hundred thousand pounds. It's in a bank in London. In your name."

"*What?*"

"One of these not-quite-respectable licensed deposit takers," Mary amplified. "But I made sure it was reliable, if not respectable, before I picked it."

"You mean that's where . . . ?" Edna's voice tailed away through a whisper to a breath.

Mary rose briskly and embraced her mother. Her power of

persuasion operated better at close quarters. She had often had to sit on Richard's lap to make it work.

"So what? He always said he wasn't being paid as much as he was worth. So we can stay here if you want to, or we can move somewhere else . . . Are you angry with me?"

And the power worked. A moment later Edna was cuddling her and crying, not from anger, but from joy.

You're watching TV Plus. In a moment, Newsframe.

Farmers marching on London from the East Anglian dustbowl, who reached the capital this afternoon, have accused the police of politically motivated brutality. Many claim they were beaten up because they weren't wearing the red-white-and-blue ribbons lately adopted by supporters of General Thrower.

The Throwers themselves . . .

"FIRST I'LL EXPLAIN HOW I ESTABLISHED MY RESIdue," Claudia said as the computer screen displayed a directory of the disk's contents. "This being a whole-hog kind of evening . . . I originally intended to start my analysis in the States, but they're a lot stricter over there about access to criminal records, and besides you have to deal with hundreds of separate police forces. A friend of mine in our criminology department suggested I try mousing into Interpol via the British police. I didn't expect it to work, but I had a stroke of luck. There was an international conference on police use of computers in New York, so I went to it and chatted up one of the British delegates, a chief superintendent. And he happened to have run across just the sort of case I had in mind.

"What's more he'd read my book. He was the right kind of cop: seriously interested in his work. I don't know how he swung the deal, but a few weeks later I got a letter to say that he'd arranged for me to access your PNC through a filter that would automatically disguise the identity of the subjects I inquired about. At that stage, I was *here*." She tapped a command and the display changed to show a table of crimes in alphabetical order. There was a number against each. Most were in the three-figure range, but a few attained four.

To demonstrate interest Peter said, "Those are the total cases of each type of crime?" And, on her nod: "Hmm! You set yourself quite a task, didn't you? How many altogether?"

"Six or seven thousand. But I didn't have to analyze them one by one. The way things had been set up, I could eliminate the cases that didn't concern me."

"Using what criteria for exclusion?"

"Oh, drug abuse, alcohol or solvent abuse, formal mental derangement—the sort of thing you already mentioned. And I set parameters for the kind of home background that conduces to violence. Want to be walked through the lot?"

"Not unless you think it's essential."

"Good. I've stared at this display so often, sometimes I feel I'm just not seeing it any more." She keyed another command. Peter noticed that any effect the whiskey had had was no longer discernible.

"One thing you've got to understand is that I didn't *want* to find anything. I was convinced that my original idea was sound, and I was only doing this out of—well, you might say a sense of duty. Like a guy in a lab running all the experiments he can think of that might disprove his favorite theory."

"The impression I gained from your book," Peter said slowly, "was that you regarded your insight not just as generally applicable, but universally. If you don't mind my saying so, I felt that was its weakest point."

She gave a harsh laugh. "If only you knew how right you are!" she muttered. "Still, you will, in just a few minutes . . . As a matter of fact, the first item that rocked me back on my heels didn't come from PNC at all. And I have a couple more that didn't, either, that I'll get around to in due time. Here's the first one—Can you see okay?"

Peter had been standing behind her. Now he drew up a chair and sat down for a better-angled view.

"I got this from my friend in the criminology department, who had it from a colleague at Stanford. There's an epidemic of designer drugs in California. You heard the funders launched a soft drink spiked with one of them?"

"CrusAde," Peter said with a nod. "Didn't they try to claim it was legal?"

"Right. Because it wasn't synthesized but secreted by a tailored yeast. That didn't cut any ice with the FDA. And some believers are claiming that yeasts imply brewing, i.e. 'strong liquor,' and so— Never mind! They're still trying to clarify the law on that point. But here's what got me interested." She gestured at the screen.

"The FBI are certain that the drug-designer is a kid. They caught one of his dealers, who confessed where he'd got the modified yeast, so they sent an agent after him. And he came back swearing the kid was the nicest guy he'd ever met, couldn't possibly have done what he's accused of, and a few days later quit the bureau. The same happened the second time, and the third, at which point the local director decided he must be barking up the wrong tree. But new drugs are still emerging. Someone's responsible, and more dealers have been caught and more of them have claimed to know the designer is only a kid."

Peter's heart was hammering. From a mouth abruptly dry he said, "Perhaps I should have asked what criteria you chose for inclusion, rather than exclusion."

Claudia marked each with an extended finger. "A major crime—committed by a child—who subsequently got away with it. That's the important bit: getting away with it."

" 'Child' meaning . . . ?"

"As it turns out: above twelve or thirteen."

Peter whistled. "And you really mean major crimes?"

She twisted around to glare at him. "Do you have any idea how many patients in American mental hospitals had to be locked away because of designer drugs?"

"I'm not disputing that definition. It's a major crime by anybody's standards. But . . . Have you found a lot of similar cases?"

"No, not a lot. Less than a dozen. Enough, though, to cast doubt on my beloved theory! Let me show you the others. First the ones I got off PNC, the British ones."

Another command, and the display changed. She gave, as before, a commentary.

"Now this one is again a boy—there's a fairly even spread between the sexes, incidentally. At age thirteen he was attending an expensive private boarding school. He turned out to be running a sex-for-sale operation among the pupils, with the assistance of the headmaster's daughter. She serviced the men whose tastes didn't include boys."

"Nothing was done about this?"

"The culprit was transferred one term ahead of schedule to another school. I wouldn't bet on that reforming him!"

"But didn't the teachers—?"

"Several of the teachers were among his customers."

Peter pondered that for a while. At length he said, "Go on."

"The next one I came up with was a girl. She ran away from an aunt and uncle who'd taken her over after her parents died. Not accident, disease. I can't be sure what kind—I told you there's a filter on my gateway to PNC, which deletes anything that might give a clue to identity. But I found an approximate date, and it coincides with that epidemic of meningitis you had here a few years ago. I think you covered it for *Continuum*, didn't you?"

"I did indeed. Though if you're hoping to trace her parents through me, it won't work. We respected the anonymity of the victims."

"I assure you I wasn't thinking along those lines."

"Good. Carry on about the girl who ran away."

"She headed for a big city, likely London, but again, of course, I can't be certain. Before her twelfth birthday she was on the streets—how else could a kid that age earn a living? One of her customers turned nasty and pulled a knife on her. He wound up cut to ribbons."

"And they didn't do anything about that, either?"

"I know what you're going to say! She ought to have been put into a foster home, at least, if not sent to reform school, right? Instead this girl was acquitted. Even the prosecution admitted there were none of her fingerprints on the handle of the knife. She wanted the court to believe the man had killed himself . . . and they did."

Peter was staring at her in unveiled dismay. "They believed that he'd cut himself to ribbons, as you put it?"

A firm nod, a grim tensing of her wide lips.

"She was discharged from custody at once and apparently was back at her usual post the same afternoon."

"They let a twelve-year-old go back to prostitution after what had happened? How the hell did I not get to hear about this?"

Claudia shrugged. "Well, the trial took place in whatever your counterpart is of Juvenile Hall, so I guess the media weren't allowed to publish the details. They sure as hell got stored on PNC, though. I warned you my findings don't make for sound sleep . . . Can you think of an explanation for what I just told you—? No, hold on. Let me show you the rest before you make up your mind.

"The next I came across was a boy again, somewhere in the north of England, far as I can make out. Sheep-farming country, at any rate, where they say beck instead of brook or creek. There was a quarrel between his family and some neighbors. A prize dog was killed. Then the rival family's son was found drowned, his foot caught in a wire noose so that he pitched headlong into a stream, hit his head, and drowned. It didn't look like an accident, more a deliberate trap.

"But the inquest found for accident, and—this'll amuse you!—now the local people speak about the family as though they're witches."

"In this day and age?"

"Yes indeed. I had to go to my theology department— where I am not exactly a regular visitor . . . *Was*, I guess I have to say now. Had to go there for explanations of some of the words I found in the report, like 'darklady' and 'hornylord.' Apparently they can be traced back to the religion of pre-Christian Britain."

"Mm-hm." Peter nodded vigorously. "Hornylord would be Cernunnos, the Wild Man of the Mountains, who had a stag's head or a pair of antlers on a human head. They still worship him at Carnac in Brittany, in the guise of a Christian saint called Cornély."

"You did a *Continuum* program about that too, did you?"

"Why else do you think I know so many peculiar facts? But you know a lot that I don't, even so . . . Go on."

"Ahh . . . yes. Next one's a girl again. Another killer. Drowned a man in plain sight of his friends. She was just a kid and he was a trained Commando, like a Marine Ranger."

Peter jolted upright on his chair. "That doesn't make sense!"

"Damned little about this makes sense," Claudia retorted caustically. "Read it for yourself."

He hunched closer to the screen. Some day soon he was going to need glasses . . .

He said eventually, "But if he was intending to rape her—"

"She personally didn't claim that. Of course no one heard what they said to one another, not at that distance. He just apparently put his head under the water and didn't come up. I wish I could get at more detail, but that puky filter has been programed to err on the side of caution, and all I know is that he drowned in a river and his body was found bobbing against some kind of barrier—presumably marking out an area as safe for swimming. But there must be hundreds such in Britain."

"Do you get the dates of these events?" Peter demanded. Claudia shook her head, her hair swooping up and down like an oscilloscope trace.

"An indication of the season is as much as the filter will let pass. This one happened in summer, obviously. But they're all comparatively recent. Indirect evidence suggests they're all within the past couple of years."

"I ought to be taking notes!" Peter realized belatedly.

"You can copy the disk if you like. I didn't realize until this evening just how badly I need a second opinion. Shall we go on?"

"Yes!"

"Okay, here's another boy, obviously living in a rundown city, again probably in the north of England. According to a report on PNC, one of the rumors they encourage their local intelligence officers to file—"

"No need to tell me about those!" Peter interrupted in a bitter tone.

"Run foul of them yourself, haven't you?" She scowled at his sidelong. "Yes, I remember your mentioning it. Your government seems to encourage paranoia in its citizens... Anyway, the report indicates, as you see, that he's the leader of a gang of older kids who operate a protection racket, blackmailing local shopkeepers into paying them ridiculous sums for doing practically nothing. Like they get ten or fifteen pounds for throwing away unsold newspapers, or carrying garbage cans from the back of a shop to the front."

"But the shopkeepers—"

"They won't testify. Won't give evidence."

"It doesn't make sense!"

"You said that before. I still agree."

"But how could they be so terrified of a few kids?"

"That's the strangest part of all. They *aren't* terrified."

"What?"

"They aren't terrified," Claudia repeated patiently. "They claim to like the kids, to be paying them willingly! By the way, this is the case my friend the chief superintendent had run across and was so annoyed about. That's why I can be so positive about it. But he didn't steer me to it. I write to him occasionally to tell him how the research is progressing, and when I came up with this one he admitted it was the example he'd had in mind."

"I need another drink," Peter said, rising. "You?"

"I'd rather have coffee."

"Can do. If you don't mind instant, that is. It's been some time since I could afford the real stuff."

When he set the steaming mug beside her, she resumed.

"Now we're getting into a borderline area. Here are a couple of cases which may not be related, but they do have certain similarities.

"The first one concerns a trial in juvenile court where some schoolgirls were charged with assaulting one of their classmates—the youngest in the class, if that has any bearing on the matter. According to what they said at the time of the offense, she had turned up wearing jewelry that had formerly belonged to them, but which she had somehow conned them out of, and then tried to do the same to a girl who had left and come back to show her friends an engagement ring she had just been given. She was quite badly hurt and had to be taken to the hospital. But when the trial came on, meek as lambs they all confirmed what the injured girl said: they had given her their belongings willingly—and some, by the way, were very expensive, so expensive that the former owners had lied to their parents about having 'lost' them and been severely scolded."

"But even if the girls themselves retracted, what about their parents, who presumably paid for the things that she had taken?"

"If they were in court, they were won over. If they called on her at home, they were won over. Now do you see what—what *obsesses* me about all this?"

"I do indeed," Peter muttered, and sipped his fresh drink. "You said there were more cases to come."

"Yes indeed. All, as I said, on the borderline, linked only by a very curious coincidence that— No, I'm running ahead of myself. I want you to see the rest of my evidence first." Fingers leapt briskly to the keyboard.

"This one concerns the manager of—do you say building society?"

"Yes."

"I had to get someone to explain that to me. They don't exist in the States. Far as I can gather, they perform the same kind of function as savings-and-loan operations, is that right?"

"I imagine it's pretty close. What happened to the guy?"

"He helped himself from the till to buy a new car, a new house, lots of goodies. As you might expect, he got caught and wound up in jail. He has a daughter. His only defense consisted in claiming, over and over, that she had put him up to it."

"I take it the court didn't believe him," Peter offered dryly.

"Of course not. But you know something? I think I do."

After digesting that, Peter said, "What else do you have for me?"

"The two items I didn't get off the British PNC. But there's still the same connection as between the others."

Assuming he had already guessed what the connection was, Peter nodded an invitation to go ahead. Claudia tapped keys again.

"Here's a girl in a convent school in Ireland. I heard about her from someone over there who knows about my work and wrote me—anonymously, so I can't tell how much credence to give the story. By the way, she was determined to prove my theory wrong."

Peter broke in. "You said anonymously. She?"

"Green ink on scented pink notepaper," Claudia sighed. "I believe the phrase you use in England is 'a dead giveaway.'"

"Granted. Sorry."

"She seemed to have an *idée fixe* about religious education, blaming it, rather than the nuclear family, for juvenile crime. Here's the case she reported: the daughter of a man who committed suicide and a woman who lost her mind as a result of the shock, alleged to be operating a porno racket from her school, the material being supplied by a delivery boy and his older brother, whom she allows to kiss and fondle her—a big deal in Ireland, apparently! My correspondent's daughter got blamed for what the other girl was doing, and was expelled."

"I thought," Peter said slowly, "you were concentrating on major crimes."

"And this hardly counts as one? Agreed. On the other hand. . . No, you'll have to wait until the last case. This crime *is* major. I got it from an Italian farmer who read the translation of my book—not popular in his country, as you can imagine, but this guy is an atheist and a radical, so he made a point of laying hands on it when he saw a review. Once again, however, it's anonymous. I know where the letter was posted, though, and I'm fairly sure I could trace the actual case. In fact that's one of the first tasks I want to tackle now I'm in Europe. There can't be too many places in Italy where the night watchman at a farm co-operative's oil-store was shot dead last fall."

"Especially by a kid of twelve!"

"In this case it wasn't the kid but his putative father who got away with it."

Momentarily distracted as he reached for his glass, Peter

missed the implications of a crucial word in the last sentence. He said, "I didn't quite follow . . . ?"

In her turn misunderstanding, Claudia said, "He talked the police out of a prosecution. Someone else got blamed, just as in the Irish case: one of the father's tenants, who disappeared the same night. But why am I reading aloud to you? Look at the screen! It's all there."

And sipped her coffee, cool enough to drink by now.

At length Peter said slowly, "You think this is reliable—or simply hearsay? It sounds to me as though someone is venting a grudge against the local landowner. Why aren't there any names in this one, incidentally? You'd think that someone with a grudge would want to be as specific as possible."

Claudia gave a harsh chuckle. "You ought to ask my husband about that!"

Peter blinked several times. "Excuse me," he said at last. "It's my turn to say I had no idea you were married."

"I'm not. Not any more. It didn't work out. Mainly because he expected me to turn into a machine for making babies . . . But he was tremendously handsome and dramatic, and I was terribly proud of him while we were engaged. It was only afterward that I found out the drawbacks of having been raised in the culture of the Italian Deep South. Oh, shit! It's over and done with, and I hope I never meet the puky cank again! The point *is*"—and she leaned earnestly toward him, as though her earlier drinks were finally taking effect—"the poor guy may have been afraid that if he named names in his letter he would find the same thing happening to him. I can assure you he had grounds."

"I'm getting a bit confused," Peter admitted after a pause for reflection. "All right, I grant that the growser from Italy may have been scared to—ah—name names. But what makes you connect this case with the others?"

"Because it was the boy who talked the police out of prosecuting his father, when they had the deathbed word of the victim to convict him on. This carries a lot of weight in Catholic countries."

"It still isn't clear," Peter insisted. "So maybe the boy is exceptionally charming! Or maybe his father wasn't anywhere near the place at the time. That's what they both said, isn't it?"—with a tap on the screen to indicate the relevant passage. "What on earth makes you connect this with all the others?"

Claudia blanked the screen before answering, then rose and returned to her former place on the couch without removing her disk. Peter swivelled his chair around to face her.

She said at length, having emptied her coffee mug, "They all have one thing in common. In the PNC cases, I don't know why the filter let it pass, because in theory at least it could be a clue to identity. In the case from Ireland and the one from Italy, I have only rumor to rely on, yet it seems improbable that it should crop up time after time in such a similar context . . .

"Not one of them is the natural child of his or her ostensible father. They were all conceived by artinsem. Or, as you may have known it before its initials clashed with a well-known disease, AID."

SMARTLY BUT NOT CONSPICUOUSLY DRESSED, CAREfully made up and with her hair styled to make her look much older than her true age, Pepita Hallam brought her supermarket trolley to a halt and glanced along the row of busy checkouts. She didn't like to leave by the same one two weeks running. Not that she had ever had any problems, but it was as well to be on the safe side.

Although it meant waiting rather longer, she chose a line that included two women whose trolleys were almost collapsing under their loads. She could, she felt sure, have cut straight in at the head of the line today, because her aura—as she thought of it—felt particularly strong, but she suspected there were limits to its efficacy. Again, she preferred not to run any risks.

Besides, later this morning she wanted to make a good few other purchases under less advantageous circumstances.

The girl at the desk was suitably tired and harassed. She barely glanced at Pepita, loading her wheeled canvas shopper, as she totted up the bill. Including two bottles of vodka and a carton of king-sized cigarettes for her mother, it came to more than forty-six pounds. Pepita handed over three twenty-pound notes. The girl made change. Pepita waited with an expectant air.

"Oh, sorry," the girl said after a moment, and handed back the twenties. Pepita favored her with a flashing smile and went her way.

There was an unusually rapid turnover of staff at this supermarket. Pepita sometimes wondered whether she had anything to do with that.

Her bill at the make-up counter of the chemist's was seven pounds something. She proffered one of the twenties and received it back plus change. Things didn't go quite so smoothly when she bought her weekly stock of tights, plus some new underwear, for the shop was a lot less crowded and the assistant not as easy to distract, but she still received a ten on top of the change she was entitled to. Not wanting to wear out her aura, she decided to go to only one more shop, to pick up some tapes by her favorite group, and then head for home.

Where the rest of the aura would have to be used up, as it were, on her mother. Cynthia Hallam was in a miserable state today...

But then, she generally was.

She and Pepita lived in a block of council flats where the lifts kept breaking down, surrounded by what had been intended as gardens and playgrounds but had turned instead into a giant rubbish-heap. It was a rough area, seething with constant suppressed violence—not that that bothered Pepita much, for she had ways of coping. In this instance she had decided to acquire a large and muscular boyfriend, whose threats would stave off unwanted attentions. His name was Kevin and he was seventeen. She felt nothing but contempt for him, but she had him well trained. Tonight, when he took her to the local disco, he would watch over her like a guard-

dog, and be content when he returned her to the door of her
home with a quick peck on the cheek . . . though doubtless
puzzled afterward that after doing so much for her he settled
for so little in return.

Today the lifts were working, which was a mercy, for she
had no idea where Kevin was at the moment and she wouldn't
have cared to carry her shopping up the stairs. The flat, of
course, was a mess, apart from her own room which she kept
meticulously tidy, but that was the way of things. Her mother
was pretty much of a mess, too—sitting around moping in a
soiled dressing gown, red-eyed and snappish. She spoke not a
word until she had seized the cigarettes, lit one, and poured
and drunk half a tumblerful of vodka.

Eventually she said in a dull voice, "Show me what you
got."

Stowing her purchases in the kitchen cupboard, Pepita
complied.

"All right, I suppose," her mother approved grudgingly,
and turned to retrieve her glass. Behind her back Pepita pulled
a rude face, implying:

You couldn't have done a tenth as well!

Which was true. Could anyone?

A little later, stretched out on her bed listening to her new
tapes—her player had been second-hand, but it was an expensive make and she took good care of it—that question
returned to haunt her as it had so often in the past.

Could anyone else do what she'd been doing this past couple of years? Not always, only when the aura was at its
height . . . but what she could get away with on days like today
still astonished her.

For the latest of countless times she reviewed what she
knew of her background. She had acquired the information in
garbled form, scrap by scrap, when her mother was in a particularly self-pitying mood.

And of course drunk, but that went without saying.

What she had pieced together went like this. After five
years of marriage her parents had still had no children, and
they both wanted at least one. According to Cynthia—but
who could tell how true the claim might be?—her husband,

whose name was Victor, was convinced the fault lay on her side, or at any rate maintained so. After one row too many she had decided to find out. And it wasn't.

He must have known all along, for the moment she became pregnant he called her a whoring bitch and walked out, never to be heard of again—quite a feat in modern computerized Britain.

Hence the squalid council flat. Hence the dependence on exiguous government grants, second-hand clothes from jumble sales, and—increasingly—the bottle. At one time, Pepita suspected, the authorities had threatened to take her away, and for long enough to satisfy them Cynthia had pulled herself together. Now, of course, no one seemed to care. Every other week in the papers or on the telly government spokesmen kept complaining about how much it cost to keep children in care, masking their true opinions behind a veneer of humanitarianism, mouthing respect for the "ties of blood" and the unique care and affection that only a natural parent could provide . . .

Load of bocky old canks!

The tape had played through and was starting afresh on the first side. She reached out a languid arm to change it for another of her new acquisitions. Before switching it on, she was afflicted by a sudden shiver. It was going to be such a long time before she could legally move out! She would have to be sixteen, free from the school that she dutifully attended —and where she was regarded as a first-rate student, for she had a keen mind. A term often applied to her was "sensible." Sometimes the teachers confided their surprise at how well she coped, having to act as her mother's deputy in almost everything.

Well, it was the easiest way . . .

But sometimes she was tempted, as now, simply to walk out. How long, though, could she survive if she did? She made a mental resolution. She must practice more with her aura, work out when the best times were to exploit it, and also establish whether she could make it act better on people who weren't as distracted and preoccupied as shop assistants. For instance, she ought to try a policeman, and maybe someone at the National Assistance office, and—come to that, why not a post office, or even a bank?

A dazzling vision of crisp new fifty-pound notes over-whelmed her for a moment. But at length, with a sigh, she lay back on the bed again.

No, better not. At least this way she had some degree of control over her life. Nonetheless, she felt a stir of shame at her own reluctance to cut loose.

Know something, Peppy? she said to herself, half aloud. *At bottom you're a bocky coward, aren't you?*

And, resigned to the fact, switched on the new tape and shut her eyes.

You're watching TV Plus. Time for Newsframe.

The source of the blue dye that caused thousands of liters of milk to be condemned in Yorkshire last week has been traced. The farmer added to his cows' regular feed a batch of out-of-time potato crisps from a local supermar-ket, without removing the blue salt-bags. A spokesman for the County Veterinary Inspectorate said the cows were none the worse, but declared that in view of the mounting potato shortage the crisps' expiry date should have been extended.

Six teenage boys have been remanded in custody in North London following allegations that they stripped a black girl of fifteen naked and painted her with red-white-and-blue stripes. Asked to comment at a news conference, General Sir Hampton Thrower said . . .

PETER STARED AT CLAUDIA FOR A LONG MOMENT. Then he gave a harsh laugh and took another swig of his drink.

"You seem to be implying," he said at last, "that you've

tracked down a group of hereditary criminals. Born to the trade, as it were."

Her eyes fixed on him, she nodded.

"But why shouldn't they, too, be accounted for by your theory? Pressure to conform to the ideal of the nuclear family, which you argue is obsolete, could just as well explain—"

"Oh, sure!" she cut in. "Don't you think I want it to? If only to spite the puky funders with their endless gabble about original sin! But these are the exceptions that are going to prove my rule in the proper sense, right?"

"I see," Peter murmured. And in fact he did. He wasn't used to meeting sociologists willing to apply strict scientific rigor to their work, and it made a refreshing change from those who preferred bombinating in a vacuum. He never expected to like this woman, but he was starting to respect her.

Claudia was going on.

"My sabbatical was due, and I needed a subject for a thesis. This looked like the ideal challenge. If I could show that my ideas held good even in cases of this kind, I'd have put the whole argument on a much firmer basis. I had a couple of other possibilities in reserve in case this one wasn't accepted, but in the upshot it was approved almost at once. Now, of course, I think I can guess why. The puky Dean just wanted me out of the way when he caved in to the bribes he was being offered . . . Did you ever hear the story of the student who received a record grant for his doctorate thesis? It was to be about the effect on academics and business executives of a series of extremely large bribes."

If she intended that to be funny, it didn't show in her face or voice.

"Next I was going to ask what you know about artinsem, but I think I can guess the answer. A lot. Because that was another of the subjects *Continuum* tackled."

Peter gave another short laugh. "No, oddly enough. I do know a lot about it, but from personal experience. Lord, I haven't thought about it in years!"

Claudia started upright. "Now I know I was right to change my mind about talking to you! Explain, explain!"

"You know, this is ridiculous," he answered slowly, staring at the carpet. "It was so minor an episode in my life, I've been thinking Ellen is my only child. In fact she's not. I must have kids scattered over half creation! Grief! I hope they don't all come home to roost!"

"How did this happen?"

He shrugged, leaning back. "Before I went into television I was studying medicine. Grants for people like me weren't exactly generous, though not as bad as they are now, so when one of my friends told me he was being paid five quid for donating semen I asked if I could—well, get in on the act."

"Which you did?"

"Why not? To be candid, I wasn't thinking so much about the money. I was rather hoping to be told I was sterile."

"That's an extraordinary attitude!"

"Not at the time it wasn't. We were out of the Swinging Sixties, but we hadn't yet reached the AIDS phase and a lot of the sixties' attitudes were lingering. Around then, though, people were starting to cast doubts on the Pill. A tolerably attractive guy with a certificate of sterility could have played the field . . . Claudia, I must be drunk!" He set his glass aside with a gesture of annoyance. "I never admitted that to anyone before!"

She let it pass. "Obviously you weren't," she prompted.

"Sterile? Of course not. My count fell square in the middle of the normal range. What was more, they happened to need someone of my physical type and coloration at the clinic. So, over the next year and a half, nearly two years, I dropped by every six or eight weeks and—ah—went through the motions, as and when they had a couple of similar appearance."

"There's a limit, isn't there?"

Peter nodded. "Ten times. So I made fifty quid. I hope they pay more nowadays—a fiver isn't much when tube and bus fares start at a pound!"

"Did you have to give any sort of undertaking?"

"Lord, yes. Apart from pledging myself to report any disease I might be suffering from, especially the STDs which were fairly rife around then, and any medication I might be taking—this of course was the reason practically all the donors were medical or dental students, who could be expected to understand the importance of keeping their word—apart from that, the main one was an undertaking never to attempt to trace the recipient. Frankly, though, I can't imagine how you'd set about that."

"Now that's something I need to investigate." Claudia leaned forward intently. "What can you tell me about the way donors' records were maintained?"

"Well, I can only speak for the one clinic that I know about," Peter countered. "Very little AID was done under the Health Service. About ninety percent was private."

"Because of the high cost?"

"Not at all. In my day the fee was around—oh—twenty or thirty pounds, plus of course the cost of preliminary consultations and examinations. A hundred quid would probably have covered the lot. Not excessive even then, for a couple desperate to have a child."

"And there are, or were, a lot of clinics undertaking such work?"

"'Were' is more like it. People grew so terrified of AIDS they wouldn't risk an unknown donor any more, so transplantation and *in vitro* fertilization have taken over almost completely . . . Well, I don't know what you mean by 'a lot.' But I've seen some figures. Just a second." He knitted his brows with the effort of memory. "Yes, that sounds right. In those days the annual rate of artificial insemination was between three and four thousand."

"Hmm!" Claudia sounded depressed. "You're talking about an average of ten per day, year in, year out, over quite a long period—and just in Britain, at that."

"Easily."

"I confess I hadn't realized it was quite so high. I'd been expecting to amass my data fairly quickly, write my first draft, take a couple of months off to explore Europe, and revise at leisure before going home . . . But you haven't answered my question about donors' records. I presume they had to be kept. Apart from—oh—not wanting a black kid to turn up in a white family, for instance, what if one of the donors proved to be carrying a deleterious gene and had to be traced and warned? Back then they couldn't have screened them in advance, could they?"

Peter shook his head, his expression still vaguely tinged with amazement.

"You know, I really hadn't given the matter a thought in years . . . Why do you need to find out about the records? Do you—?" He checked. "You don't honestly think you're looking for a common father in all these cases?"

"I sincerely hope not!" was Claudia's tart reply. "Can you imagine anything more destructive to my theory? No, what I want to do is prove that the whole notion is—is stupid!"

"Well, if some mental handicaps are known to be hereditary, like Down's syndrome and Alzheimer's disease, which depend on chromosome malformations—"

"Why can I not accept that the same may be true of inadequate criminal personalities?" she cut in. "Believe me, all your arguments have been thrown at me before. The answer to that one is that the kids I have data on are not inadequate. Absolutely the contrary. They are coping far better than almost anybody else. Think about the evidence. Didn't I say the second thing that connects them is that they get away with what they've done?"

Contrary to his former intention, Peter took another sip of whiskey. He said, "I'm going to have to ponder that. As to records of donors, though . . . Well, that was one of the points I raised when I first went to the clinic."

"You call it a clinic. Was it part of a hospital, a larger operation?"

"Not at all. It was the consulting rooms of two doctors in partnership, one man and one woman, an obstetrician and a gynecologist. They had premises in Wimpole Street. That's not quite as famous as Harley Street but it's just around the corner. I didn't get to know the woman at all—the friend who let me in on the act had some sort of contact with the man, I don't recall what—and I believe that not long afterward there was a bustup between them and the partnership was dissolved. But that was after I'd exhausted my quota."

"You keep harking back to your own experience," Claudia murmured. "Would you stick to generalities for a bit? I want to know how they kept their records!"

"Ah . . . Sorry." Peter licked his lips. "They were on regular index cards. Each donor was given a code known only to the doctor and his nurse. I wasn't even told what my code was. I didn't ask. It struck me as a good way of keeping the data confidential."

"What if, say, the doctor and his nurse were killed in a car crash? Wouldn't the other partner have been able to access the data?"

"I've no idea. Grief!"—with sudden force. "This all happened well over a decade ago. Besides, it's late. You expect me to remember minor details like that?"

"My turn to say sorry," Claudia sighed. "Didn't I say earlier that I'm becoming obsessed with this? I had so much hoped the data might be stored on a computer, because computers can be hacked . . . Well, you're right: it is late. I'd better be going. Want to copy that disk of mine before I leave?"

But Peter wasn't paying attention. He tensed and snapped his fingers. "Just a moment! It's coming back to me . . . Yes, that was part of what the row was about, the one that led to the breakup of the partnership. I was told about it afterward by another of my fellow students, who stayed the course and became a GP as I'd intended to. He'd been a donor as well. There must have been—oh—at least half a dozen from my hospital. We all vaguely knew who else was on the list, but it wasn't any reason for us to be friends, you see."

"Breakup . . . ?" Claudia prompted.

"Ah. Yes. Well, Dr. Chinn—the male doctor—felt the setup was becoming like an assembly line. At least that's what I was told. So when his female partner suggested going over to a computerized record system he tried to veto it because he felt it was too impersonal as well as less secure. But she had more clout than he did, or more money invested, or something, and in the end he quit."

"Is the clinic still in existence?"

"It's mutated into a general fertility clinic, with a pretty good reputation, I believe. But like I said, I can't speak for all the other similar operations there were in Britain. There must have been dozens—scores!"

"Some not quite as—ah—ethical as others?"

Claudia waited a long moment for an answer. None came. Peter's face had frozen into a mask of concentration.

At long last he said, "I think I know someone who might fund your research. I know you don't much care for the media, but if you want to reduce the load on Strugman . . ."

"I certainly don't want to abuse his generosity."

"Well, do you know a paper over here called the *Comet*?"

"You did a program about it," Claudia said. "One of your last. It was all alleged to possess the most technically advanced—Just a second! I think I see what you're aiming at. I need access to one hell of a lot of cheap computer capacity, don't I? Would they provide it?"

"It's worth trying. I know for a fact that Jake—the editor —is desperate for any sort of an exclusive."

Waiting for her reaction, he drained his glass, feeling the last fragments of ice chill against his lip.

"You're right," she said eventually. "I don't care too much for the media. But so long as we could sew up a good tight contract, so they didn't rush into print with some half-assed corruption of my findings . . . You know, I never thought I'd be driven into a corner like this! You think this—this Jake can be trusted?"

"About as far as I could throw a taxicab." Peter set his glass down with a slam. "But at least he's an honest rogue. The ones I can't stand are the ones who don't even know they're bent. He does. I'll give him that."

"Sounds like the best one can hope for in this day and age," Claudia grunted, retrieving her bag and rising. "Do you want to copy my disk or not? I have to get home."

"Sure!"—hastily. "Just a second while I find a scratch one."

And while the copy was being made (he noted it was auto-protected against copying the copy, but that was to be expected):

"Are you serious about taking over my old place?"

"Sure!" She raised her eyebrows. "Sounds like the ideal solution to my problem."

"In that case I'd better give you the address and the name of my bank." He seized pen and paper and wrote rapidly. Handing her the note, he added, "This has been kind of a constructive meeting. Thanks for changing your mind about me."

"You're still on probation," she retorted, reaching to reclaim her own disk as the copying process went to completion. "But . . . Okay, constructive I will grant. If I'd realized you had personal experience of artinsem, I'd have called you sooner."

"But it wasn't a personal experience. It was the opposite. It was just about the most totally *impersonal* experience of my entire life. That's why—like I said—I literally hadn't given it a thought in a good ten years."

"Were all the donors you met as detached as you?"

"I hope so. I sincerely hope so. Imagine getting hung up on biological paternity!"

"You're asking me to imagine it?" Her tone was oddly gentle, albeit mocking, as she scrutinized him with those strange artificial-looking irises. "Me, who can't even imagine being hung up on maternity? Or didn't you realize?"

For a second he was confused; then he caught on. Having spent so long in his company and alone, she was warning him not to try and kiss her good night, or the like. But this must surely be a reflex. He hadn't been aware she was gay, though now he had to assume she was, or wanted to be taken as such . . .

Grief! The shifts and makeshifts of our society!

"Shall I call you a cab?" he said at length, having decided the whole matter was too trivial to waste more breath on.

"No thanks. I guess I can find one myself."

Was that the tone of an offended feminist? Peter was too tired, and possibly also too drunk, to figure it out. He said with what cordiality he could muster, "I'm flattered that you shared your data with me. I'll be as helpful as I can."

"Fine. Just don't forget I still have the agreement you signed when we had dinner together."

"As though I would!"

When she had finally departed, Peter stole into the room that had become Ellen's. She was fast asleep, the phones of her stereo still on her head although the broadcast she had been listening to had gone off the air.

Detaching them with maximum gentleness, he stared around at what he had never expected to find in any of his homes: a teenager's bedroom. It was weird to see his old belongings in this novel context. In particular, he was impressed by the way she had taken to the computer he had given her. He had to admit that the teaching at her former school must have been pretty good, for she had got the knack of its more esoteric potential remarkably quickly, and it kept her occupied for hours on end.

He only hoped she wasn't going to start running up heavy bills due to interrogating distant data-bases.

The rest of the changes, though, were entirely hers: indefinably juvenile-plus-feminine touches that had made even the furniture look different . . .

It was no use. He couldn't define them. They were just *there*.

And he had better not be any longer, not after so much whiskey and such a weird conversation. Did Claudia really think she'd lucked into a genetic component of criminality? Against all her prior convictions, and everybody else's?

It was all too much to digest at a single sitting. Peter switched off the lights and stole as quietly as possible to bed.

By morning, however, he had reached a firm conclusion.

He was going to have to follow up Claudia's lead. He was going to have to con as much money as possible out of both Jake Lafarge and TV Plus, to fund his investigation.

There simply wasn't anything else in the offing that held out any promise whatsoever.

PART TWO

"But if God is love, why is there any bad at all? Is the world like a novel in which the villains are put in to make it more dramatic, and in which virtue triumphs only in the third volume? It is certain that the feelings of the created have in no way been considered. If indeed there were a judgment day, it would be for man to appear at the bar not as a criminal but as accuser."

—Winwood Reade:
The Martyrdom of Man

As it turned out, Harry Shay needed little persuading to sell his company and return to England. The alternative was to stay on but now as managing director of a wholly-owned subsidiary, and he was not of the temperament to work well in committee or by consensus, let alone submit his proposals for approval by higher authority. Alice was far more reluctant—she had become addicted to Californian weather—but David coaxed and wheedled and eventually she gave in. So there was no need to explain about the secret bank accounts in the Bahamas.

The company fetched an excellent price, much higher than the gloomy Goldfarb had predicted. But then, the prospective buyer had had the benefit of a business dinner at the Shays', during which David was able to soften his resistance. In short, everything went extremely well—or almost everything.

The exception was due to a man called Pedro Gui, one of the pushers who had been making handsome profits out of David's ingenuity. He had also, obviously, made a grievous mistake: he had sampled the product much too often.

Thanks to certain precautions he had taken after being visited by the FBI, David had imagined his identity secure. How Gui could have traced him he had no idea, but on the Saturday before the family's departure, when he was at home alone except for Bethsaida, who was in the kitchen, an unfamiliar car drew up and out got a black-haired, sallow-faced man in his late twenties. After a cursory glance around, he walked across to where David lay on dry grass, half his mind on a book and the other on a broadcast from Pacifica Radio.

There was a bulge under the newcomer's jacket; that was the first thing the boy spotted.

A great coldness invaded his mind as he rose to his feet. Imposing his will on his parents, whom he had known all his life, or on ignorant and timid Bethsaida, or on businessmen who could be manipulated by appealing to their greed, or even on an FBI agent, was very different from outwitting an armed stranger who, by the wild look in his eyes, was angled on one or several kinds of dope.

After surveying David head to toe, he said incredulously, "You? Goddamn. I didn't believe it when they said you were just a kid... You *are* David Shay?" he added with an access of suspicion. "The growser who figures out all those featly kinds of yeast?"

Feigning a boldness he did not command, David retorted, "Sure. And if you're anybody, you have to be Pedro Gui—am I right?" He made a point of checking out his dealers' credentials, discreetly.

"How the hell did you—? Ah, shit. So you know me, I know you. Puts us on level terms, I guess."

There was a canvas chair nearby. David gestured at it.

"By the sound of it, you have business to discuss. Normally I wouldn't consider it, but since you must have gone to a lot of trouble to find me, I presume it's urgent. Care to sit down while we talk?"

Gui shook his head as though fearing a trap. "I just got one thing to say to you. Don't quit."

"I don't understand," David prevaricated.

"I said *don't quit*! Word is, you're winding down the operation. I won't let you!"

He uttered the last sentence with such force that tiny drops of spittle flew from his lips, glinting in the sun.

David relaxed a trifle. Gui was clearly not in control of himself, and that ought to provide an opening. He needed one in a hurry, though; Harry and Alice were due back soon—in fact, on hearing the car he had glanced up, imagining it might be theirs.

For an instant he considered countering, "And how are you going to stop me?" But he was too aware of the presence of the gun. Instead he said, "Why not? There are other design-ers—"

"Ain't none like you!" Gui folded his thin hands and squeezed until the tendons stood up in ridges. "Man, you got any idea how *good* that shit is that you teach the bugs to make? No, I guess you don't use. Like the chef in the classy restaurant picks up a cheeseburger on his way home. But, oh *man* . . . Listen!" He approached David, dropping his voice to a confidential whisper.

"Listen, man, you're on the track of the Last with the capi-tal L. You know what I mean? You follow me?"

Mouth dry, David gave a nod. Where the legend had sprung from, no one could say, but within the past year the simple symbol of an L had been scrawled on walls from Baja to Nantucket, from Taos to Yellowknife—and maybe else-where, too. There had been a program on TV that he had watched out of professional interest. It stood for and defined the conviction among users that soon now, very soon, the Big L would be discovered, or rather invented—the ultimate drug that bestowed total enlightenment, comprehension of the pur-pose of the universe.

Perhaps, he remembered thinking as he watched the broad-cast, this was a counter-culture response to the teaching of the Rapture. When so many people were predicting the immi-nence of Judgment Day, it was hard not to be half-convinced if only by the sheer weight of repetition. The drug of drugs, the super-duper drug, was just as much a chimera, yet for the majority of poor or disappointed people far more credible.

But Gui was still talking. To be precise, he was saying, "—so I won't let you quit! Not when you're so close!"

David's sense of calm increased still more. This man only thought he had come here to threaten. In fact he had come to beg and plead.

In that case—!

He donned his most convincing smile.

"Well, hell. You know you're the first person to figure it out?"

Gui looked blank.

"Why do you think I'm quitting? Don't I have a sweet

racket? Don't you think it's made me a fortune? And like you said I am still only a kid—can't deny that, because it's true. So why do you think I'm winding up the operation if it's not because I reached my final goal?"

He waited for the bait to be taken. Gui's dope-slow mental processes could be read in his face as clearly as on the screen of a computer. At last, eyes round with wonder, he forced out, "You—you *got* it?"

"The L for Last," David solemnly confirmed. "And since like I said you're the only growser so far who's figured it out, I guess you deserve to sample it."

By this time Gui was practically drooling. Holding out both hands, palm up and shaking terribly, he whispered, "Oh man! I dreamed about this day so long . . . How much?"

Abruptly he was groping inside his jacket, heedless of the fact that the movement exposed his gun to view. He produced a wad of hundred-dollar bills, but David waved it away non-chalantly.

"The only reason for me to make money was so I could carry on my research. Now it's over . . . Wait here and I'll bring you a sample. No charge."

For an instant a ghost of rationality seemed to haunt Gui's deranged mind, bringing with it the possibility that this might all be a trick. But he wanted to believe too much.

"Yeah!" he said. *"Yeah!"*

On his return, carrying a test-tube wrapped in crumpled tissues that held about a quarter-teaspoonful of grayish-yellow crystals as fine as table salt, David half expected to find that Gui had fled after all. Since that would have engendered later complications, he was pleased to find him still there, trembling with anticipation.

"There you go," David said encouragingly.

Turning the glass tube around and around, unable to take his eyes off it, Gui husked, "How do you use it?"

"Shoot it, toot it, stuff it up your ass—doesn't matter. I'd say let it dissolve on your tongue. Reaches the brain faster that way, via the palatal route. But listen!" David's tone was abruptly stern.

"You need to take it in the right kind of surroundings, hear? Like don't get so eager you stop off in the nearest men's room! You go home, you make yourself comfortable—like on your bed, or in a good deep armchair, so you don't get all stiffened up while you're under. And maybe lock the door because you won't want to be disturbed."

"Sounds like a long trip," Gui ventured.

"The longest. The ultimate. And afterward you won't ever want to use anything else."

For an instant he feared that Gui was going to embrace and maybe kiss him. Instead he thrust the tube into his breast pocket and ran full pelt back to his car. He burned rubber on the driveway as he left for home.

Well, one thing at least was true, David thought as he resumed his book. Gui would never use a drug again. Not after ingesting five or six lethal doses of ricin. A year or so ago, out of curiosity, he had isolated a quantity of it from a castor-oil plant that grew right alongside the house. The rest of what the test-tube held was sugar tinted with tobacco-ash and turmeric.

So long as nothing worse interfered with what he had planned . . .

You're watching TV Plus. It's time for Newsframe.

Have you noticed any starlings lately? According to the Royal Society for the Protection of Birds, one of Britain's commonest and best-loved birds is in danger of dying out. A "Save the Starling" fund was launched today to try and preserve it. More follows in a moment.

Charges brought against supporters of General Thrower in Newcastle under the Race Relations Act, alleg-

*ing that they threw black members out of a multi-racial
club, were dismissed by magistrates today. One of the injured victims . . .*

FROM THE KITCHEN, WHENCE EMANATED A DISTINCT
smell of burning oil, Ellen bore a laden tray into the living
room. Setting it down on a table beside her father, who was
deep in argument with Claudia, she said anxiously, "Here you
are—I do hope it's okay!"

Peter suppressed a sigh. This was not the first time she had
attempted to reproduce her mother's Indian dishes for him, so
far without notable success, and he recognized what she had
brought them: rotis stuffed with yesterday's leftovers plus a
dash of curry powder.

*But when she's so desperate to please . . . And besides, ac-
cording to today's news, if this gene-tinkered rye-grass gets as
much of a grip on our farmland as the experts are predicting,
we'll soon be eating worse . . . !*

"Ellen, you're a sweetheart," Claudia said without even
glancing up. "Pop mine on a plate, hm? And bring a fork—
I'm not terribly good with my fingers."

Delighted that her efforts had met with approval, Ellen
made haste to comply, for Peter as well. Then, having topped
up their glasses—beer tonight—she took the last roti for herself and withdrew to an armchair in the corner to eat it.

As it turned out, this time her cooking had much surpassed
her previous endeavors. After his first bite Peter raised his
eyebrows.

"Ellen, darling, this is good!"

"Really?" Her eyes were instantly alight.

"Yes, really! Carry on like this and—" He had been about
to say she would become as good a cook as her mother, but
there was a tacit agreement between them not to refer to Kamala, even indirectly. He compromised: "And you'll have me
eating at home every night!"

After which he resumed his conversation with Claudia.
They were planning the pitch they intended to make to Jake
Lafarge tomorrow, noting and discarding dozens of possible
approaches. Jake was their only hope, TV Plus having decided

the story was too long-term, so they were determined to present it in the best possible guise.

Which was why Peter didn't notice when the brightness in his daughter's eyes overflowed and trickled down her cheeks.

When they had eaten, Ellen took the dishes to be washed and then, unusually, instead of withdrawing to her room, returned to her chair in the corner. By then Peter and Claudia were so engrossed they scarcely registered her presence, and she eavesdropped as though she were a shadow.

Peter was saying with a trace of anger, "Look, you haven't had as much to do with this kind of—"

And she was interrupting: "I won't kowtow to their damn commercial demands!"

"But if we're going to raise the wind—"

"Wind you know about, don't you? Every time you open your mouth a positive gale spills out!"

"Better to burp it up than play King Frog and burst with your own self-righteousness!"

For an instant they were glaring at each other across the paper-littered table. Then Ellen gave a tinkling laugh. The tension broken, they both turned to her.

"Excuse me," she said when she recovered. "I was just thinking . . ."

"What?"—curtly from Peter.

"You sound like a married couple. The way you're squabbling, I mean!"

For an instant they bridled; then her point sank home, and they sat back ruefully and in unison picked up their respective glasses of beer and took another sip, as though the simultaneity of the act had been rehearsed.

Peter said after a pause, "Well, I must admit I used sometimes to think of working on *Continuum* as though our team were a kind of enormous marriage, where everyone had to play along or else risk wrecking the current project. I suppose any kind of cooperative venture—"

"Is as difficult as marriage if without the legal bond," Claudia cut in. "Ellen's right. I'm sorry, Peter. I am being obstructive. You do have experience in selling a story to the media. All I know about is how to persuade my peers and my publishers, and I'm not even very good at that. You don't suppose Ellen could act as referee?"

"You can't be serious!" Peter started to retort—yet the phrase died halfway through. Turning, he stared at his daughter, who was gazing eagerly at them, and saw her as though for the first time. She was objectively taller than when she had arrived at his home, by two centimeters; she was growing at such a rate, the jeans he had bought her then seemed to expose more of her shins every day. (Memo to self: buy new, and soon.) Her smooth brown skin, her slender grace, her long sleek hair, had already attracted boys from her school and elsewhere in the neighborhood, wanting to take her out . . . and for some unfathomable reason he had let her go with them, convinced on a level below consciousness that she was not about to come to any harm. In a fit of uncharacteristic incertitude he had asked Claudia's opinion on the matter, and he remembered her brusque reply: "We all have to grow up some time, and she's grown up faster than most. She can take care of herself!"

It was a risk, admittedly, but it did save worrying about baby-sitters. (*Baby?* But Peter kept that to himself.)

He said after a moment for reflection, "You know, you have a point. If there's any truth in what the market survey people say—"

And could have bitten his tongue out as he realized what he had been about to utter. Covered in embarrassment, he reached for his beer glass again.

But Ellen repeated her tinkling laugh. Easing her chair forward—it was on casters—to make herself a member of their circle, she said, "I know, I know! The newspapers aim at a readership with a mental age of twelve, right?"

"Uh—"

"And I'm a bit older than that, but not by much, so I might serve as a sort of touchstone, right?"

Not for the first time, Peter had the impression that this accidental daughter of his was an extremely worthwhile acquisition. What would life with her be like a few more years from now, though? If she was this sharp and this alert at present, despite what she had been through, she was apt to turn into . . .

Something.

But he quelled that response by turning the "something" into the sense of the phrase "quite something!" And was able to say—to Claudia—"We'd have to do an awful lot of explaining first, wouldn't we?"

"I'm not so sure." Claudia was surveying Ellen with an inspectorial eye. "I think she's been paying a lot of attention to what we're talking about, because it's part of your job. Same as she watches the TV news and reads all the papers because of what you do for a living."

Peter started; he hadn't realized she was taking so keen an interest in his and Ellen's day-to-day existence.

Still, it was of a piece with her normal attitude. He could not envisage her failing to research a colleague . . .

He said with more gruffness than he had intended, "Well, all right. Let's try our presentation out on her, and see if it will click with Jake Lafarge. I don't suppose"—and this time the words were tinged with unintended bitterness—"his mental age is any higher than Ellen's!"

Dead silence, bar what sounds drifted in from the street (and how many fewer they were, Peter thought irrelevantly, than in the street where he had formerly lived and Claudia did now: how many fewer fire alarms, police cars, sounds of riot and commotion, breaking glass . . .)

And Ellen was on her feet, cheeks aglow and pouting.

"If you're just going to make fun of me—!"

He reached out an arm and caught her as she made to vanish into her own room, pulling her around to dump her on his lap.

"I'm sorry, I'm sorry! I wasn't thinking! I mean, I wasn't thinking about you, but about Jake! He— Never mind. You can get an impression of Jake from reading the paper he edits, okay?"

Of a sudden Ellen was smiling. He put an arm around to cuddle her and leaned his cheek against her smooth tresses.

"Actually it's a very good idea. That is, if you don't mind being treated as a one-person captive audience . . . ?"

She shook her head vigorously.

"Well, then," Peter said with a cock of one eyebrow at Claudia, "let's run it up the flagpole and see if Ellen can salute it."

"Sometimes," Claudia retorted caustically as she sorted through the mass of rough notes on the table, "I suspect you must be far older than you claim . . . Okay, here we go."

An hour later, when Ellen had dutifully retired to bed and Peter was seeing Claudia out the door, the latter said, "You know something?"

"What?"

"Getting back that daughter of yours is the best thing that could have happened to you. She's humanizing you."

"I don't quite . . ." With a lot of blinking.

"For pity's sake!" Had she been younger, Claudia would have stamped her foot. "Even if you don't notice, I do! A few weeks ago you were a go-getting self-serving so-and-so and totally unaware of it—even *proud* of it! Since the kid moved in, you've softened. Gotten nicer. More caring. Do I have to run through the entire thesaurus?"

The street door was ajar to what might be the last warm night of autumn; the hallway was in darkness because he hadn't switched the lights on—it had become a reflex since he realized how limited his budget was with a child to look after. But there was a diffuse glow from the streetlights. Around here they worked more often than not.

In the dimness he could read Claudia's expression, and it mingled admiration with frustration.

"Goddamn it!" she forced out at last. "I think I could even come to like you, Peter Levin! *Me*, who after I broke up with my husband swore I was going to hate men for ever!"

And she put a muscular arm around his neck and pulled his mouth down to meet hers.

She kissed delightfully. Her tongue on his hardened him on the instant. But she withdrew the instant he tried to cup her breast, and disappeared behind a slamming door.

"See you at the *Comet* office, ten tomorrow!" was the last he heard. "And say thanks to Ellen! Now I think we have a deal!"

▐█▌▐█▌ IN HIS NEW SANCTUM DAVID SHAY CHECKED HIS morning post. There was little of importance among it, bar one item. As nearly as he could make out from her semi-literate scrawl, Bethsaida was pregnant, and since she must have been fertilized at a time when her husband was away on the cruise liner he was threatening divorce. He authorized transfer to her of $50,000 from his Bahaman account, which ought to shut them both up for a fair while, and consigned her letter to the shredder beside his desk, along with most of his other mail. Then, leaning back, he yawned and stretched and looked about him.

The temporary home he had chosen for himself and his family was a large Victorian house within easy reach of London, in the Surrey district of Virginia Water. It was set well back from the main road among trees that were about to drop their leaves, but still afforded adequate privacy, since there was a winding driveway flanked with evergreen shrubs. It had stood empty for nearly a year, being too large for most people nowadays, with its twenty rooms, extensive outbuildings and enormous garden. Running it properly, the estate agent had said apologetically, would call for at least three live-in staff, and the seller was so greedy he had at first insisted on nothing less than an Arab millionaire as the new occupier. However, with the general decline in world trade no such buyer had appeared, and the Shays had leased it for twelve months at a most advantageous rate.

David's mouth quirked up at the corners. The rent had rather less to do with the owner losing patience than with the dinner he, Harry and Alice had invited the estate agent to at a fashionable local restaurant, during the course of which he had been able to turn the charm on full. Of course, he had had to work the same trick on the landlord as well, but that wasn't hard . . .

Hard.

Reminded, he rubbed his crotch. He must do something, and soon, about arranging for those live-in servants, and he wanted them all to be young and female. He made a mental note to mention it to Harry and Alice when they came home tonight—they were in London at the moment. He himself was far too busy setting up his new gear, the last of which had been delivered yesterday. He would have brought what he was used to from California, but the voltage difference might have caused problems and in any case most of it was two or even three years old. Better, therefore, to scrap it and acquire a whole new setup, even though there were bad reports about the competence of UK maintenance engineers.

Bad reports . . .

He glanced at the TV, that was playing the early evening news, and sighed aloud. Did there *have* to be another disaster every single day—or further horrors in the long-running dramas? Was the human race really composed of, or at any rate ruled by, total idiots? The evidence seemed incontrovertible. The Netherlands were under martial law because the Surinamese, inspired by the "heroic resistance" of the Sri Lankan Tamils, had decided to undertake a similar campaign of sabotage. The Sikhs in India had killed their tenth Congress Party MP, along with his entourage, by mining a road-bridge he was due to cross. Yet another attempt to launch an SDI "defense" satellite had ended up with the launcher crashing in the deep Atlantic, and people were starting to claim that communists must have hacked their way into the computers that designed either the launch vehicle itself or a key part of its control system. Right now the heavy betting was on a programmer who had quit in disgust after having created such a gang of indispensable software for the DoD that even the American government—read taxpayer—couldn't afford to scrap it and start over.

But that, of course, might be a red herring; a bit of "disinformation" put about to disguise the fact that the Soviets were able to tap into NORAD, the Pentagon, all the main defense contractors . . .

Which, in David's view, went without saying. Idly he keyed a code that interrogated the master launch computers at Cape Canaveral. Inside thirty seconds he was looking at the fault-diagnosis display from the just-crashed rocket. Without bothering to read it, he hit the cancel command. He had only done it in order to confirm that his new rig was status go.

Now, therefore, he could start work on the most important task that lay ahead of him. Who was his real—his biological —father? There was an obvious first line of approach: he must search the Police National Computer for gossip, slander, and any other malicious allegations about his mother. From that source, he was virtually certain to obtain clues to the clues that might reveal his paternity.

And if not, there were many other avenues to be explored.

He had mentally drafted the necessary program while traversing the North Pole on the way back to Britain. In odd moments since then he had found time to debug it. Now it was ready to run. It would certainly take hours, maybe days, but it was ready. He called it up and activated it, then rose from his chair and stretched and yawned again.

At that precise moment the sound of a car approaching up the driveway reached his ears. It halted; the engine was switched off. Shortly after, the front doorbell rang.

For a moment David considered pretending that the house was empty, but had to discard the idea as soon as formulated. Had it indeed been so, electronic devices would have interrogated all callers, recorded their replies, and fixed their images on tape. The security level here was *high*.

Annoyed that he hadn't thought of switching the machines on, he headed for the door.

"Good afternoon!" said a bright-faced young woman in a brown trouser-suit, a portable computer no larger than a camera slung over her left shoulder on a yellow strap. "I'm Gladys Winter! Are your parents at home?"

She had been alone in the car—or, at any rate, there was

no one else in it now. Of course, one or more fellow-passengers might have darted off to scour the grounds . . .

David realized he was beginning to feel paranoid. Why should she not have come here by herself? He said in as normal a tone as he could contrive, "I'm afraid they went up to town for the day. Can I help you?"

"Well, maybe you can." Gladys consulted her computer. "I gather you returned from the States after an absence of some years, and—well, for some reason your parents don't seem to have made arrangements for you to attend school this year. At any rate our records . . ."

She droned on for another couple of sentences, while David cursed himself yet again for overlooking an important point. But he kept control.

"Now this is something they would certainly wish to talk about if they were here," he said when he had the chance. "Won't you come in for a moment? And—excuse me, but are you on your own?"

Gladys blinked. "What makes you ask that? Who else can you see around here?"

"Well, I just thought that if you had a companion he might have—uh—vanished into the bushes . . ." With a winning smile.

An answering grin. "I see! Yes, men aren't so good at holding their water, are they? . . . May I come in?"

Didn't I just say so?

But David stepped aside politely and closed the door.

Guiding her into the newly—and lavishly—furnished drawing room, he bade her sit down and offered her a drink, which she refused. He didn't insist; he needed to exploit his charm for more important matters.

"Now what precisely can I do for you?" he murmured as he installed himself beside her on a chintz-covered sofa, donning as grave and adult an expression as he could contrive but seizing every chance to breathe toward her face and brush her with his arm or hand.

She explained about Acts of Parliament, local regulations, sundry by-laws and statutory instruments authorized by the Ministry of Education . . . growing more and more agitated as he found other opportunities to touch her: first her cheek, then her bust, then her waist and hips.

"So, you see—" she attempted to conclude, but he cut her utterance short, clasping and kissing her fingers.

"So *you* see, there's no need to worry about me. Regardless of English law, I don't have to go to school. Do I?"

"I—"

"I mean, you wouldn't think of reporting me and my parents as lawbreakers, would you?"

"I . . . Well, no. I suppose not." Gladys ran a finger around her collar as though it had grown unbearably tight, but made no attempt to release her other hand.

"Isn't that the part of your work that you hate most?"

"Frankly . . ." Of a sudden she relaxed and smiled. Her face, which was rather square and flat, underwent a transformation. "Yes, I do hate having to report people for neglecting their kids. How did you guess?"

David evaded an answer. Instead he parried, "And do you think I'm being neglected?"

"Goodness! The way you talk, the surroundings here . . ." A helpless gesture as though she was trying to seize a handful of air and mold it into meaning. "Of course not! It's just that your family's name cropped up on our main computer, so—"

"Which computer is that, by the way?" David inserted. By this time he had progressed from caressing her hand and wrist to stroking her nape.

"The Department of Education's."

Mm-hm. What was that traditional saying of the Jesuits? "Give me a child before he is seven and after that you may do with him what you will!"

A policy being as thoroughly exploited by the present British government as ever by the régime Franco visited on Spain when it too was a once-great nation mourning the loss of its overseas empire. One of these days, when he found time, David planned to analyze that parallel to see whether it stood up as well as he imagined.

Not, however, today.

Gladys was rising, albeit with visible reluctance, having punched an entry into her computer, and was saying, "Well, I won't delay you any longer. Obviously there's been a mistake.

Your parents are planning to send you to a private school, aren't they? Sometimes that sort of data takes a long time to find its way into our records."

Figures! The richer you are, the better you can elude Big Brother!

But since she was here, there was one thing she could do for him. David glanced at his watch and saw that over an hour remained before the earliest time he could expect Harry and Alice to return from London.

"What about blowing me before you go?" he said with his sweetest smile and most cajoling tone.

"Well, I wouldn't normally, but—"

"You like me, don't you?"

"Yes. Yes, as a matter of fact. Even though I don't know why." She was sweating and trembling, proof that his charm had worked as easily on her as on Bethsaida.

"But you do. And it isn't very much to ask, is it?"

"No . . . Oh well, all right." Swinging her computer behind her back, Gladys dropped to her knees as he unzipped, then checked with an apologetic expression, saying, "I—uh . . . I don't have an AIDS certificate, you know."

"I do."

"At your age?"

"I've been living in California, remember."

"All right."

She wasn't very skilled. He found himself wondering what Alice was like at this; then, whether it might be advisable to advertise for the people he was looking for; then—

Eventually he came, and thanked her. Conceivably she might prove useful, one of these days.

You're watching TV Plus. Now for Newsframe.

At an emergency meeting of the European Parliament, called to consider the catastrophic loss of tree-cover in Northern Europe, Britain again vetoed attempts to reduce atmospheric pollution on grounds of cost. The West German Green spokesman proposed that oxygen-counts should be added to all TV weather reports; this motion was defeated in spite of powerful scientific backing.

Supporters of General Thrower were today accused by an opposition MP of fomenting racial hate in schools. Asked to comment, the general said, "The purity of our heritage is precious to all right-thinking people. I myself . . ."

"PETER, GOOD TO SEE YOU! AND YOU MUST BE DR. Morris! Sit down, make yourselves comfortable! Laura love, bring us coffee, hm? Or would you prefer something stronger? Let me give you a preview of what we have lined up! It's going to *rock* the competition!"

They were in the wide low-ceilinged room that was the *Comet* office. It looked more like the set of a cheapo sixties science-fiction film than any place where ordinary people worked. Eight sub-editors were at work on display screens underlined by keyboards, flanked by microphones, for they were currently experimenting with voice-input of news-stories. So far, however, the technology worked only in Finnish, the language of the country where it had been developed, because it was phonetic and unambiguous.

Now and then one of the subs, assigned today to carry out a routine test, said something loudly and clearly to a micro-

163

phone, inspected what appeared on screen, swore, and recorded the nature of the fault before rectifying it by more conventional means.

Jake Lafarge was a ruddy man in his middle forties, with a moustache the shape and color of a worn brown bootbrush and a prominent pot belly, testimony to his weakness for drink. But he had kept the *Comet* afloat for a year longer than the pessimists had predicted, and the paper's backers were cautiously allotting more and still more money as he came up with neat new ideas that exploited its ultramodern technological equipment. Each in turn, though it might achieve little in the long run, prompted a flash of new interest among the public and a transient upturn in the sales graph. His latest coup had been to realize that the incredibly expensive computers his proprietor had bought allowed him to fake news pictures from what was already in store in the library, and this was what he wanted now to demonstrate to Claudia and Peter.

"Today's *Guardian* broke the capture of that opium-lord in Northern Burma!"

He was slumping into a swivel chair and feverishly hitting (mis-hitting and cursing) keys on a board before him.

"What they didn't get, because their photographer was shot in the kidneys and died on the way out, was—*this!*"

Triumphantly he pointed at the screen. In full color it showed the said opium-lord surrounded by Burmese troops holding him at gunpoint. Another touch on the board, and there he was being manacled; again, and he was being forced aboard a helicopter with a sack over his head.

"Sorry about the sack," Jake sighed. "But the machines weren't up to a convincing left-rear profile . . . The rest is spot-on, though, even the 'copter! Isn't it amazing?"

He wiped the screen and swung his chair through ninety degrees to confront them again, beaming exultantly.

There followed, fortunately, an interruption. The girl he had addressed as Laura arrived with cupfuls of coffee—real, at least, not assembled in a dispenser. Having issued it like field-rations, having offered capsules of milk and sachets of sugar, Jake leaned back and demanded of Claudia, "Well! Don't we have a breakthrough?"

"It's phony," she responded in a grumpy tone. "And not original."

Peter tensed so violently he almost spilled scalding liquid in his lap. Did she not realize how much depended on—?

But she was continuing.

"The first time a hoax of that kind was pulled, as I recall, was during the Spanish-American War. I think it may have been the Vitagraph company—the one O. Henry wrote scripts for—but I'm not certain. It was around then, anyhow. They faked newsreels in the studio using silhouettes and cut-outs, and audiences all over the States and even abroad were fooled to the point where they clapped and cheered. Later, during World War I—"

Jake's face darkened. Peter was framing a hasty apology, and at the same time planning what he was going to say to Claudia as soon as they got kicked out of here, when he realized abruptly that his reflex assumption had been wrong. Jake wasn't flushing with rage. He was . . . Yes! Incredibly, he was *blushing* at having been caught out!

"The sinking of the *Lusitania*! You—you—you . . . Oh, bloody *hell*! I'm sorry! It's just that I so seldom meet anyone who remembers further back than what was in this morning's paper, or on the news last night, and even that is stretching it these days."

Claudia leaned back and crossed her legs, neat as usual in one of her formal trouser-suits; she had five that Peter had managed to count, all in the autumn colors, old-gold, russet, sage-green, wine-red and plum-blue. Today she wore plum-blue.

She said composedly, "What all this boils down to is—"

Brass tacks? Peter recalled her comment from the night of their first meeting in London, and wondered how wrong he could have been.

But she was continuing:

"—you're trying to update a trick that's been tried before with earlier technology. It made the groundlings cheer in the old days when there wasn't anything else. Do you honestly think it's going to part them from their money when they all have color television, VCRs, hi-fi and CD rigs, and God knows what?"

There was a terrifying pause—for Peter, at least, who was envisaging the collapse of his Ellen-tested deal. (Why should he think of her at just this moment?)

Then Jake slapped his desk, open-palmed, and jumped to his feet. Pacing back and forth within the shoulder-high partitions that defined his territory, no larger than was Ellen's room at home (a second time!), he said:

"How the hell did you sus me out so fast—? Excuse me just a moment! Laura!"

"Yes?"—as it were from the air.

"Total privacy for the next ten minutes! And I don't care if it's his Ultraviolent Highness in person!"

"Sure, Jake. Right away!"

Privacy? In an open-plan office?

Then something happened to the air; it made Peter's ears feel numb, obliging him to yawn and release the pressure in his Eustachian tubes. Awed, he realized this was the effect of a technique he had read and heard about and never experienced before: a sonic barrier.

Undisturbed, as though it were no worse than what one felt as an airliner soared to altitude, Claudia fixed Jake with her implanted irises. Responding like a rabbit confronted by a snake, he halted in mid-stride and swung to face her.

"Blast you—*woman!*" The last word carried a load of venom. "For targeting my weakest point!"

It was too early for Jake to be drunk, Peter thought. And yet . . .

"All this fabulous technology! And here I am acting like Wenceslas's page!"

"'Mark my footsteps, good my page! Tread thou in them boldly! Thou shalt find—'"

Claudia got that far before Jake pounded fist into palm and stamped on the floor.

"Yes! Yes! *Yes!* I'm following up everyone else's stories because my stinking boss won't spend as much on decent correspondents overseas as he does on these damned machines! And you're bloody right! Dressing up second-hand material isn't going to keep the paper on its legs! I need an exclusive—a major break—something that nobody else can get at before I do! When Peter rang me up he promised he had found one. Tell me what it is."

He slumped back into his chair, breathing hard. "It had better be good," he concluded. "But if it is—well, you can count on all the help you need."

When Peter returned home he was in a daze. The outside world seemed distant and unreal. Claudia, despite all his misgivings, had sold the story brilliantly. Jake was over the moon about it, regardless of the long lead-time. Provided he had it before Christmas, he had said . . .

Which presumably was the deadline set by his proprietor for discontinuing the paper.

Moving stealthily, as though to make too loud a noise would wreck his mood, he let himself into the flat and hung up the coat he had donned against the increasing chill of autumn—and grew abruptly aware of a humming noise from the living room.

But there shouldn't be anybody here! Today was a school day, and Ellen ought still to be with the helpful minder—

Intruders?

In the hallway there was a stand that held two umbrellas and a heavy walking stick. He caught up the latter and rushed through the door, prepared to wield it like a club. But it was Ellen who turned to him, wide-eyed, alarmed. She was seated at his desk, silhouetted against the green-gleaming screen of his computer.

"Oh, Dad! It's you! You frightened me!"

"You're not supposed to be here," was his foolish reply. "Why aren't you at Jeannette's?"

Instead of answering him at once, she was wiping the display with slim and accurate fingers, not looking at the keyboard. Now she rose to embrace him.

For once he thrust her aside and held her at arm's length, searching her face suspiciously.

"What else have you been up to? I didn't tell you you could use my rig!"

"I know you didn't! But I haven't done any harm, I swear! It's just that . . ." Her eyes were filling with tears. "I did mean to tell you, I swear, only—"

"Come to the point! Please!"

She turned away glumly and sat down. Avoiding his harsh gaze, she said, "I couldn't stand the way the other kids were treating me because I'm not white."

"What? But I thought—"

"Oh, Jeannette's all right. She does her best to shut them up, but now that all their parents seem to be wearing Thrower ribbons . . .

"So I lied to Jeannette. Said you were going to be home earlier in future and it was all right if I came straight here after school."

"And she didn't check with me?"

"She left a message on your answering machine."

"I didn't find it!"

"No. I—uh . . ." Dreadfully embarrassed, Ellen licked her lips. "I called back and said it was all okay, and then I wiped the tape. I know I shouldn't have, but I simply couldn't take it any more. Honestly I couldn't!"

She twisted round to confront him defiantly. "And I haven't just been coming straight home and costing you a fortune in computer charges! I got myself a job. So if I have cost you anything, I can pay it back."

"A job?"

"Yes!"—defiantly. "Three afternoons a week for an hour. I clean house for an old lady! She gives me ten pounds! It isn't much, but at least it's pocket-money."

Pocket-money.

That brought Peter to a frozen halt. Harsh words died on the tip of his tongue. He was so totally unused to parenthood, he had *forgotten* about pocket-money. Here was this teenage girl who was his daughter, going out two or three evenings a week with boyfriends, and he wasn't even giving her enough to pay for a bus or taxi home if something went amiss!

And here he was standing, ridiculously, with a stick in his hand as though to fend off a burglar . . .

Swallowing hard, he replaced it in the hallway. Returning to the living room, he said, "Ellen darling, it's me who ought to apologize. I'm sorry about the pocket-money. Here!" He groped for his billfold. "Would a tenner a week do for starters? I'll see about a raise, soon as I can."

Instead of merely taking the money, she caught hold of his hand and kissed it. Her long sleek hair brushed his skin as she raised her head, all tears forgotten.

A sense of warmth pervaded his entire being as he smiled back.

"And that may be quite soon," he said after a pause.

"Was it useful, trying out your idea on me?"

"Useful! Grief! We have to go back to the *Comet* tomorrow. A high-powered lawyer will be there with a draft contract. That's in the morning. In the afternoon, if all goes well, we're scheduled to meet an ultra-super hacker, who Jake swears can get at practically any data anywhere, so long as the machine's on line . . . By the way, I suppose you checked my email."

Instantly crestfallen, Ellen bit her lip and gave a nod.

"I'm sorry. It was one of the things I thought would help me to figure out your system."

Let there not have been any more messages from women wanting to interface with me again . . .

Not, on reflection, that he imagined Ellen would have been upset by it . . .

"And was there anything?" he said after a pause.

"Some people called Shay, that you've been trying to reach in California."

"Oh!" His interest quickened. "What—?"

"They've moved. I think they're back in Britain. But they don't want their new address made public." She was all little girl at the moment; he could imagine her aged six, with her hair in a fluffy halo around her head. "I—uh—I hope you don't mind, but I tried to find it anyway. I thought you might be pleased if I tracked them down."

That, Peter thought, should have made him annoyed. But he couldn't summon even the ghost of anger. Instead he had to fake sternness as he said, "You've got to learn, young woman, that this kind of thing can be dangerous! Harry Shay is very,

very rich! If he finds out someone's attempting to invade his privacy he could easily afford to bribe a few policemen and have me locked up under the Data Protection Act!"

"Goodness!" Her eyes grew wider than ever. "Dad, I'm sorry! I had no idea!"

"All right, forget about it. Just bear in mind that for the foreseeable future all our—ah—dodgy operations must go by way of the computers at the *Comet* office."

Our? Why had he said that? The sense of unreality that he had felt on the way home was growing unaccountably stronger...

"Dad! Sit down!" Ellen urged, guiding him to a chair. "Let me fetch you a drink. What do you want? I think there's some whiskey left. Dinner can be ready in half an hour if you like!"

Well, it had been a hard day. A rest in a comfortable chair, a good stiff drink, a meal cooked and served for him—yes, that sounded like a well-deserved reward.

When she brought his drink, mixed precisely as he liked it, along with a glass of orange squash for herself, Ellen perched on the arm of his chair and after a moment, unexpectedly, leaned over to kiss the crown of his head...where, as the touch of her lips reminded him, he was starting to go bald.

"Dad," she whispered. "Dad!"

"What is it?" He reached up to stroke her neck. "Want me to tell you again how useful you were last night? You were, you know! While we were in Jake's office, I could have shut my eyes and sworn it wasn't Claudia but you doing that marvelous sales job!"

"No," she whispered, her mouth still close to his scalp. "No, I just wanted to say...Dad, I love you. After the awful thing that happened, I was so frightened of what might become of me! But you've been wonderfully kind!"

"I love you, too," Peter said sincerely. And only later realized it was the first time he had said that, save to various and half-forgotten mistresses, since he stopped saying it to his mother at about the age of eight.

He pulled her down on to his lap and for a long while held her close, glowing inwardly, not wanting to be the first to break the mood. Facing the chair they shared, the TV was playing, but the sound was turned down and without a commentary the images that filled the screen struck him as meaningless.

Then at last Ellen jumped to her feet.

"Dinner!" she exclaimed. "Country Captain! Frozen chicken pieces, I'm afraid, but I've done my best. I do hope it's good!"

Me, too. But at least I know one thing that is. Claudia was right, wasn't she? And I thought she was a shellbacked feminist who hated men. Until last night . . .

The recollected taste of her mouth mingled on his tongue with the sharp bite of whisky. Utterly relaxed for the first time in years, Peter awaited Ellen's call to join her at the table and try out her culinary masterpiece.

WITHIN A SHORT WHILE OF HIS FAMILY'S RETURN TO England, thanks to the computer search program he kept running night and day David Shay had established two facts for certain.

Harry had indeed had a vasectomy. It was in his medical records. And it had been done while he was still living with his former wife, very probably at her insistence. Right up to the time when he moved to California, there was no mention of the operation having been reversed.

So how had Alice become pregnant? For a while he considered the possibility she had had an affair with a friend, but eventually he dismissed it as out of keeping with Harry's attitude toward her. He might be proud of his wife's figure, and like her to show it off, but he was nonetheless possessive, sometimes downright jealous.

That left, essentially, one alternative: artinsem. In David's view Harry could have tolerated her having a baby by an anonymous stranger, particularly since the technique was adequately impersonal, and fourteen or fifteen years ago it was still pretty widespread.

Unfortunately, of course, that meant his search for his biological father was going to be even longer and harder than he had originally imagined. Still, he was getting far better at unearthing data intended to be private; he had, for instance, no business accessing Harry's medical records yet that had gone off smoothly enough.

And the second discovery he made was of almost equal importance. The faculty he thought of as his "charm" did almost beyond a doubt have a hereditary component. Perhaps it was even a mutation. There was scarcely anything in the formal literature concerning cases like his, but extensive—and expensive—searching turned up occasional news-items that sounded tantalizingly similar to his own case: reports of young people, all around the same age, who had the knack of getting their own way...

At first the prospect of meeting others like himself struck him as immensely exciting. On reflection, however, he decided it might be risky, too. He had no idea whether their "charm effect" might not be stronger than his. He was becoming well adjusted to the idea of controlling people; the risk of being controlled in his turn did not appeal. Nonetheless, if he did have siblings...

In the upshot he decided to go ahead, albeit with great circumspection, and in particular to follow up the idea of advertising that had come to him in a flash of inspiration.

This was how he made his third discovery, and his first breakthrough.

He had located an agency that offered maximal exposure for minimal outlay—not of course that cost was any object, and he paid at once, in full—by syndicating its insertions in English-language journals from Ireland to Greece. And, to his surprise, it was from Ireland that he received the first response to his cautiously worded inquiry.

Widowed, deprived of her only child, who had been perverted into the paths of evil thanks to the refusal of the teach-

ing nuns at her convent school to root out the true source of
the wickedness festering among their pupils, to expel instead
of her daughter that younger girl who must plainly be a monster despite her charm, Caitlin's mother was constantly on the
lookout for anyone who would believe her story and sympa-
thize—maybe take action. Of some kind . . .

For the latest of a dozen times she began to set forth the
details.

In green ink on pink and scented paper, with no signature.

Why David took the letter seriously, he could not quite
figure out. In the end he decided that he must believe in instinct, which he had previously and sometimes publicly de-
spised. At all events . . .

"We're going to Ireland tomorrow," he informed his parents at lunch, the day he received the letter.

"What?"—from Harry and Alice in astonished unison.

"You heard me!" As he grew more confident of the power
that he thought of as his "charm," David was also becoming
curter in his manner. "There's someone there I want to meet.
A girl."

They relaxed and exchanged smiles—predictably. He had
worked out that it was always better to provide a reason that
could be rationalized. In another day or two, they'd have convinced themselves that it was their idea all along.

Everything went as smoothly as he could reasonably hope.
Having met Dymphna, learned that she was an orphan, that
she had not been the daughter of her mother's husband—she
admitted as much within minutes, though unfortunately she
had no idea who her true father might have been and there was
no one left whom they could ask—she agreed instantly to his
suggestion that she come and live with him.

But traces of residual resistance endured.

Harry and Alice raised no overt objection to the removal of
Dymphna Clancy from her school, any more than did the
nuns—though some of her fellow pupils broke down in tears
and insisted that she keep in touch by letter. His charm wasn't
quite up to coping with so many nubile girls all at one time,
and for a brief moment he wished he could have brought them

all to England with him. That would have been so much better than hiring servants . . . !

He was sure, however, that he had been right in his decision to come here. Simply by looking at her he could tell that he and Dymphna had more in common than their mere appearance: the same dark hair, the same dark eyes, the same slightly tawny, slightly sallow skin . . . He was on the right track at last!

And his charm went on working, at least so far as Harry and Alice were concerned. Indeed, though they were visibly puzzled about the fact that their son ("their"!) had insisted on traveling to Ireland, and now and then remembered that during the trip they had been—well—*charmed* into signing papers whose content they could no longer clearly recall, but which satisfied both the Mother Superior of the convent and the lawyer whom she brought in to advise her (what had his name been?)—in spite of that, they made no bones about Dymphna sharing David's room. The rest of the house was huge and echoing, unfurnished save for odds and ends; she could have had her choice of half a dozen.

But despite the shift in moral attitudes that had followed AIDS, they somehow felt it unobjectionable that she and he should sleep together . . .

That first night, Dymphna wept herself to sleep on David's shoulder, not out of misery, but from pleasure mingled with relief. David himself, less inclined to tears, kept shuddering with joy till nearly dawn.

There was a scent on her skin that he had dreamed of without knowing, that he had never known existed in reality, but held out a terrifying promise . . .

A trace or two of resistance:

"Dammit, boy!" Harry boomed when he was told there were to be other recruits to the "family." "You've got what you wanted, haven't you? Dymphna's lovely! Wish I'd had a girl like her when I was your age!"

Beyond the windows she was dancing for pure joy, though it was raining—dancing on the lawn in shift and panties, feet bare, legs bare, delighting in the world.

"A part," David sighed, leaning back from the breakfast

table. "By no means all. And there are so many empty rooms in this great house . . ."

"You want to cram them with orphans?" Alice cried.

David's charm was not at its maximum. Concentrating, he raised it to a peak. (What was it? How did it work? That was the next question that he needed to investigate . . .)

In his severest tone: "Is it not right and moral for those who are well off to help others that are not, by no fault of their own?"

To that, Harry and Alice found no answer. At least, none before he clinched the argument, leaning forward with his elbows on the table and switching his blazing gaze from one to the other.

"You know I've kept search programs running on my computers since we got here?"

"Well"—disconcertedly—"of course. You said so."

"Among the things I've found out is that you are worth eighty-seven million dollars. At current rates of interest the income from that would be enough to support a dozen kids, at least, along with you two and myself, at a very high standard of living."

"David!" Alice began, but he cut her short.

"How do you feel about children who are starving in a world of plenty?"

"Well—uh . . ."

"Uncomfortable?"

"Yes. Yes, I suppose so." She snatched at her coffee cup and took a gulp.

"You, Harry?"

It was the first time he had addressed his putative father so directly; until now he had maintained the polite fiction of calling him "dad."

"The same, I suppose"—in an uncertain tone. "But do you honestly mean you want us to fill the house with—?"

"Riff-raff? Rubbish? Guttersnipes? Heavens, no!" David tipped back his head and let go a healthy laugh. "I want to share my home with brilliant kids, underprivileged but capable of learning—fast! Tell me straight: what better use do you have in mind for your fortune?"

Abruptly he was earnest, gazing into Harry's eyes and reaching out to grasp his hand.

"Well—ah . . ."

"Nothing better?" David challenged.

"In the moral sense, the absolute sense . . . I suppose not."

"There you are!" David crowed. "So the matter's settled. Excuse me. I think it's about time for my program to throw up more news."

Later, Alice said to Harry, "Are you sure—?"

And he retorted, "No! But I can't find any reason to object! Can you?"

After a pause: "Well . . . no!"

All, then, was as it should be. David, who was listening because he had bugged as many of the rooms as were in current use, allowed himself a chuckle and went back to investigating the data his computer search program had turned up. There was, according to the machine, a very interesting means to access PNC, thanks to a policeman who had done something highly unofficial for an American sociologist. There was a filter in the way, but British filters were as nothing to the ones he had tackled in the States when confirming that the FBI's agents had given up on the idea of prosecuting him for drug-designing.

Soaking wet, Dymphna came running into his—no, now it was their—room just as he was reviewing the fresh data that his program had unearthed.

"Let's make love again!" she whispered in his ear with all the enthusiasm of a girl who had often dreamed of bedding boys and been denied the chance for much too long.

"In a moment," David sighed, punching commands into his board. "I've finally got the breakthrough that I wanted into PNC . . . Yes! Look!"

The screen display, though, meant nothing to Dymphna, so he gave up and yielded to her importunities. As he stripped her and rolled her into bed, David wondered how long he could stand the company of his peers.

She was one. There was no doubt about it. Though she used a different term, he had seen her charm at work on Harry, and Alice, and the nuns. Possibly he had just experienced a trace of it himself . . . Without it, any or all of them might have balked at her being brought here from Ireland. For the first time, David felt genuinely afraid of the phenomenon that he was letting loose, as though he had unbarred a tiger from its cage.

But it was already too late to worry about that.

You're watching TV Plus. Newsframe follows.

The Japanese government has blamed the recent mass outbreaks of arson in Tokyo and other large cities on the disaffected Korean minority, despite claims by left-wing MPs that this is an attempt to find scapegoats. The true reason, they argue, is the high cost of housing, which has already led to rioting among students who object to their future earning capacity being mortgaged by parents and even grandparents in order to purchase over-priced apartments.

However, General Sir Hampton Thrower, currently in Japan on a "goodwill mission to another island nation," has come out strongly in support of the government line. Quote: "Any discontented alien group . . ."

AT CLAUDIA'S INSISTENCE A COPY OF THE CONTRACT Jake Lafarge proposed had been faxed to New York for vetting by her friend the lawyer, the one Peter had met by chance. His name, it turned out, was Walter Stine.

He proposed relatively few changes, and the *Comet's* lawyer accepted them after only token objections. Well pleased with the success of their negotiations, Jake left his deputy in charge and took them to a hurried lunch. All three were eager to rush back to the office, but for different reasons: Jake because a major story was breaking—Peter was dismayed to learn that once again the arrest of a black drug-pusher threatened to entail rioting—and the other two because they were anxious to meet the hacker.

On their return he was waiting for them: a blond, untidy man in anorak, jeans and boots, overdue for both a shave and a haircut, wearing heavy horn-rim glasses—almost a caricature of the popular concept of his kind, too interested in computers to worry about his appearance. Jake had time only to introduce him as Bernie before being called away to make a decision about which of two stories should be followed up first.

Bernie had been assigned an alcove in one corner of the office, equipped with a computer terminal. Temporary screens had been placed around it, and as soon as he sat down he turned on another sonic barrier. Inside the protected area there was barely room for three chairs.

"Right!" he said. "What exactly is it that you want from me?"

Peter left the explanations to Claudia. She had brought a copy of the disk she had shown him before. Loading it, she ran through almost exactly the same exposition. Bernie listened attentively, asking a question now and then. When she had finished, he pondered in silence for a while, and finally gave a brisk nod.

"Should be possible," he said. "The first thing you need, I take it, is the name of the clinic that these women went to—assuming they all went to the same one. Matter of fact, though, I'm a bit surprised you haven't got at that already."

"I told you," Claudia began. "There's a filter—"

A dismissive wave; his fingernails were edged with black.

"No problem. It just so happens I know what sort of filter you're talking about. I was one of the team that designed it. My mates and I left a couple of loopholes, thinking they'd come in handy some day. Looks like the day has arrived . . . I can probably also get you some personal names, maybe not the lot but a good few, if they can be cross-referred to newsreports. And the next thing will be the identity of the donor. I can't promise that, though."

"Obviously not," Peter said. "Not if they still keep their records manually."

"Precisely. I'll do my best, though. I should find the name

of the clinic fairly quickly—or clinics. Beyond that point, like I say, no promises. Can I hang on to this disk?"

"Yes, of course."

"Well, that's as far as we can go for the moment." He slapped the top of the terminal and rose, switching off the sonic barrier. "I'll be in touch in a few days."

Leaving the office, Claudia said anxiously, "What do you think?"

Peter shrugged. "Too soon to be sure. But at least he grasped what you told him right away."

"Mm-hm...How are you going to kill the time until he comes up with something useful?"

"Me? I have a weird story to follow up—the weirdest. Did you hear that AIDS has been found in pigs?"

"I thought that was just a silly rumor!"

"I'm afraid not. They think they've traced the source: a mentally subnormal farmhand in Essex...You?"

"I'm going to take a weekend off. I feel haunted by this damned idea. I need to think about something else for a while. A trip to Paris strikes me as a good idea."

"Enjoy yourself."

"I'll try. Give my regards to Ellen. Remember what I said about the good effect she's having on you. Treat her well."

"I will."

ROGER CRAY WILSON HAD HAD THE MOST MARVEL-ous summer holidays imaginable. During the previous term he had learned that for the whole of August and the first half of September the school's Victorian-Gothic buildings were to be rented to a film company. An idea had sprung to his mind at once . . . and, crazy though it was, he'd brought it off. He had scarcely had to see his bocky parents—

Well, just for the first few days after summer term ended, long enough to convince them that he ought to return to Hopstanton. He couldn't employ his powers of persuasion over a telephone; he had to be physically present. One of these days he intended to try and find out how his trick worked, but being lazy and self-indulgent he had never put the plan into effect.

Why should he bother, when he could twist anyone—boy or girl or adult—round his proverbial little finger? (Or as he often thought and sometimes said, another organ?)

He had proved the fact in spectacular style.

In a terraced row of cottages adjacent to his school boardinghouse he had met Mildred, a pretty young widow whose husband had been killed in an accident at the factory where he worked, leaving her with a daughter of sixteen even prettier than herself, called June. His sympathy with their plight had led to a close—well, maybe not friendship, because Mildred was, to be candid, a bit of a dimwit, and June wasn't much brighter. Say a functional and profitable relationship.

It had been no trouble at all to suggest that the three of them provide an attractive service for the people working on the film. They had, admittedly, been doubtful at the start, but once they realized how much they could make, even after deduction of Roger's commission . . .

Of course, he had been meticulous about ensuring that every client had an AIDS certificate.

And as a result he had met people who were internationally famous: a major director, his producer, four of his stars and countless players in the minor rôles. Roger himself had been in several crowd scenes as an extra, and had even been offered a speaking part when the Equity member who should have played it turned up with laryngitis. But he had had the sense to decline. He was aware of the need to keep a low profile.

Already, on this first day of the new term, gossip was spreading about his coup. It wasn't to his housemaster's taste, but that was a minor problem; he simply needed to cajole Mrs. Brock for a few minutes and she was, as usual, firmly on his side. If only he didn't have to stay on at this horrible place . . . !

It was too soon, though, to break loose and follow up the valuable contacts he had made in the film world. It wasn't that he preferred to remain here and endure the boredom of the daily classes, the obligatory chapel services, the petty authority of the prefects; rather, it was that he felt unready to strike out completely on his own. Using his power of persuasion was, after all, quite hard work in certain cases—Mr. Brock, for instance, and above all the Headmaster, who had taken a certain interest in him but was rarely available to be exposed to the "effect."

The chaplain, fortunately, had proved instantly pliable, and had already supported Roger more than once. He did have doubts about the pleasure he obtained from their intimacy, but so far he'd managed to keep his sense of sin under control. Oh, yes! Things were going fine!

It was no special surprise when, on the first evening of the winter term, he was summoned to the housemaster. He was in fact whistling as he approached the latter's office—until, through an open window, he spotted a parked car.

It was his parents' Rover. And next to it was a Rolls Royce that he didn't recognize and was certain he had never seen around the place before.

Abruptly worried, he honed his power to a sharp edge and entered warily into Mr. Brock's sanctum.

His parents were indeed present, and he greeted them with convincing enthusiasm, going so far as to kiss his mother's cheek—which she usually liked, though he hated, because her face was always crusted with makeup.

This time, however, she flinched away. And he had never seen his father's face so stern . . .

Moreover they weren't the only ones in here with Mr. Brock (no sign of Mrs., as though he suspected his wife of being a weak point in his defenses).

No, there were two other adults present, both of whom showed traces of what must have been a deep tan, fading now, plus a girl and a boy of roughly his own age, alike enough to himself to be—well, not his siblings, but at least his cousins.

And his attention focused instantly on them. He knew in less than a heartbeat that they were the ones that mattered. He could sense it from their relaxed, assured attitudes, the gazes that they bent on him, the very air . . . !

It had been a long while since he found himself at a total loss. Now he blindly fumbled his way to a chair at Mr. Brock's bidding as though he were ten years old again, transported back to helpless and dependent childhood before the onset of adolescence gave him his new sense of confident control.

He strove to master his reactions, and failed. He felt a sense of dreadful weakness, and prepared himself in dismay for the worst news he had ever heard.

Luckily, it wasn't all that bad . . .

"Well, Cray Wilson!" Mr. Brock snapped, seeming to have been lent far more than his usual degree of confidence—no doubt by the two young strangers. "I suppose you know why I've called you here!"

"No, sir." The words emerged in a mumble. "My people didn't even tell me they were coming—"

The housemaster disregarded him. "Some alarming reports of your activities during the holidays have come to my notice! I'm prepared to accept they may stem from your—ah—unfortunate association with a woman of loose character, and a daughter whom she appears to be bringing up in the same tradition, but I would have thought better of any boy in my care than that he fall victim to such allurement!"

His parents looked downcast; his father shifted his feet noisily under his hard and upright chair.

"I was surprised," Mr. Brock went on, staring at them under his untidy eyebrows, "that you permitted your son to pass the holidays here, given that the morals of people in the—ah—entertainment industry are always questionable. As a consequence of what has transpired, as a consequence of events that have created a considerable scandal, that have indeed come close to drawing the attention of the police, I am gravely disturbed, as are your parents!"

What does he mean, "come close"? I could name four bent coppers . . . !

But there was no time to complete the thought.

"Fortunately," Mr. Brock rumbled on, "it looks as though a

way out has been found, that will save both your family and this school from involvement in a public uproar. Mr. and Mrs. Shay, it seems, are in process of founding a sort of refuge for children like yourself, those who have been regrettably corrupted by exposure to the sleazier side of adult life. Mr. Shay?"

But it was the boy who leaned forward and spoke in a clear firm voice that struck Roger as astonishingly like his own.

"I think I might get through to Roger more easily than my father would—sir." The last word sounded like an afterthought. "May I—?"

"Go ahead." Mr. Brock sat back and mopped his forehead with a none-too-clean handkerchief. "God knows, all I want is to see this dreadful affair resolved! I can't believe half of what I've heard, and yet I must!"

No wonder you didn't want your wife in here! Roger said cynically to himself. But at least what lay in store for him didn't sound as bad as he had briefly feared. He said in a cautious tone, "May I hear more?"

Afterward he could never accurately recall what had been said. He only retained the impression that for the first time he had been in the presence of someone with the same talent as himself, but infinitely more developed. He remembered being ashamed at the brilliance with which the other boy—whose name, he learned, was David—deployed not merely his naked power but also reasoned lines of argument, expressed in a voice whose very tone and pitch compelled agreement. After a while he felt he was living a dream, and could only comply passively with what he was told he ought to say and do.

In the upshot, he was in the Rolls along with the Shay family, and the girl who—he had vaguely gathered—was like him an adoptee, and all his belongings in the big old trunk his parents had given him to take to school, and they were gone. Vanished. Their car was hurtling down the road . . . and they hadn't even said good-bye!

The only person who did before he left was Mrs. Brock, who appeared with tears streaming down her cheeks and gave him a wordless hug before turning back and slamming the door, an act that said as clear as speech, "I'll miss you! But because of what you've done—!"

In the wide soft back seat of the purring car, Roger, too, broke down and wept. David and the girl put their arms around him until he got over it; then they did other things that made him feel better yet.

Up front, Harry and Alice pretended not to notice what was going on.

That made him feel the best of all.

You're watching TV Plus. Time for Newsframe.

It's not only in Europe that deforestation is approaching the disaster level, according to a United Nations report published today. In countries south of the Sahara, patches of desert are breaking out, in the words of the report's compilers, like an epidemic. More in a moment.

On his way home from Japan, General Thrower has praised the Pamyat movement in the Soviet Union, as a model of patriotic enthusiasm which, quote, "Britain would do well to imitate . . ."

DAYS PASSED WITHOUT NEWS FROM BERNIE. Now and then Peter rang Claudia, or she him, and they exchanged sour words of frustration, but it was worse for her. He did at least have plenty to keep him occupied. The pigs-with-AIDS story duly broke, provoking the usual outcry from religious extremists about the Judgment of God, plus a practically universal boycott of pork and bacon. Given that the reason for the current shortage of potato crisps and frozen chips was traceable to that imported virus which despite originating in the

Mediterranean had found the British climate vastly to its liking, Peter couldn't help wondering sourly as he contemplated his exiguous fee for securing the scoop:

Is God's judgment being visited on spuds, as well?

Eventually the signal came for him to rendezvous with Claudia at the *Comet* office—Jake had insisted that no details of the story ever be discussed by phone. Arriving late after being delayed by a pro- versus anti-dog riot—rabies had indeed been confirmed in Kent and a muzzling order had been issued—he found the famous Dr. Morris waiting in the foyer for a lift, her expression downcast.

Foolishly he tried to cheer her up with bantering chit-chat. She cut him short with a glare.

"That's the last thing I need!" she snapped.

"I'm sorry," he said with the best approximation of contriteness he could achieve. "But I expected you to be glad that Bernie has finally—"

She wasn't listening. She was saying, "Remember the policeman who fixed for me to access PNC?"

"Of course!"

"He's dead."

"What?" Peter took half a step toward her.

A grim nod. "He died yesterday. He'd been in the hospital since those riots up north. What's the city called?"

"You mean where they tried to drag that drug-pusher out of the police station?"

"Mm-hm." She passed a weary hand through her hair. "As I heard the story, half his skin was melted off with a gas bomb, and he inhaled the flames . . . Well, I guess we'd better head upstairs and hear what Bernie has found out."

The lift arrived. She entered. Following, Peter folded his hands into fists and muttered curses that though inaudible were vehement.

Behind the now-familiar sonic barrier Bernie was already in conversation—or argument—with Jake. As Peter and Claudia approached, the editor swung around in his chair and snapped, "I don't know why I bothered to call you here! This bastard's let us down!"

Flushing, Bernie banged the corner of Jake's desk. "Now you shut up, hear me? I've told you already—I've done my utmost, but someone's caught on to the loopholes me and my mates left in that sort of filter, and . . ." He paused, drew a deep breath, and continued to Claudia instead.

"Look, maybe I can get you to listen! Jake won't! On the basis of what you gave me, I started interrogating PNC and got considerably further than you had. I—"

"How much further?" Claudia stabbed.

"For starters I established that all the kids on your list were indeed born to clients of the same clinic."

Bernie sat back with a triumphant grin. The response he had hoped for, though, was not forthcoming. Eventually Peter said, "After this long, all you've found out is 'for starters'?"

And Claudia chimed in: "So what's its name?"

The grin became a scowl. "I told you—I'm working under a handicap! Someone caught on about the loopholes in the filter! Not surprising, I suppose; after all, the design is five or six years old. But what's done can be undone. All I need is a little more time—"

"And no doubt a lot more money!" Jake rasped. "What about the names you were going to trace, through correlating Claudia's data with news-reports?"

"Christ, I can't do that in just a few days! I admit this rig of yours is the most advanced I've ever worked with, but sifting through literally thousands of—"

"You're stalling!" Jake broke in. "I've used our setup since it was commissioned. I know how fast it can trace a cross-reference! Maybe I should have assigned one of my own people instead of swallowing your load of bock!"

Peter winced. That image of ingesting someone else's vomit had always revolted him, no matter how often he heard it casually used.

"I want the truth!" Jake roared on. "You've run into a problem you can't solve—isn't that the way it is?"

For a moment Bernie seemed inclined to shout back. Then the bluster leaked out of him and he slumped back in his chair.

"I haven't solved it *yet*," he said with a final trace of defiance, and then, with reluctant candor: "But you're right. I am bogged down."

"Why?"—from Claudia.

A helpless shrug. "It's as though someone else is in there ahead of me, guessing what approaches I might try and blocking them off. Like I said, it's not altogether surprising. Once they found out the weaknesses in the filter, the rest would have followed logically. I'll keep on trying, of course, but . . ." He spread his hands.

"Sounds to me," Jake said cynically, "as though once again we have to forget about the marvels of modern technology, and revert to tried and trusted methods."

"Such as?" Bernie flared.

Jake curled his lip. "Bribery and blackmail, if all else fails! Never forget you're talking to a veteran of the Wapping Wars! Back then I sold my honor and my self-respect for the sake of a fat salary, and my sense of morality took a beating that it's never recovered from. I quote a growser who hates me very much . . . Ah, what the hell? The important point is this."

He folded the fingers of his left hand around his right fist, staring down as though into a crystal ball.

"All these kids—with the couple of exceptions you've told me about—have turned out to be from the same clinic. That much I grant you've accomplished. The fact that you haven't yet managed to correlate any news-reports with the details Claudia supplied may be due to the whole lot being juveniles, so one wouldn't be allowed to print their names. It follows—"

"Think I'm an idiot?" Bernie interrupted. "I've been running my search-pattern on a basis of related events and backgrounds. I don't have any names I could search for, do I?"

"You said you expected to find at least a few—" Peter began.

"And I've explained why I can't!" Bernie barked.

As though the sonic barrier were letting out at least his peak loudness, some of the subs at work in the vast open-plan office glanced uneasily in their direction before continuing with their assignments. Jake forced himself to calm down.

"I was saying," he gritted, "it could take a very long time to complete a search-pattern on that basis, so it makes sense to supplement what you're doing."

"How?"—from Claudia.

"In the good old-fashioned way." Jake leaned back and

reached for a tissue to wipe his forehead; it was pearled with sweat. "I suppose I should have recommended this at the start, run the two in parallel . . . Peter, are you busy at the moment? I mean, with other stories?"

"Yes. There are three or four leads I should be chasing up this minute."

"Does that mean you've lost interest?" Claudia demanded, rounding on him.

"Stop that before it starts!" Jake ordered. "I've worked with Peter often enough to know he doesn't drop a promising story until it's past hope. No doubt he'll spare what time he can . . . Meanwhile, though, this is your baby, Claudia!"

For an instant it seemed she was about to erupt at his use of what she might have held to be a sexist metaphor. With vast effort she overcame the impulse.

"So what exactly do you suggest?" she sighed.

"A bit of legwork. Good traditional legwork. Start by calling on this friend of yours in the police, this chief superintendent—"

"Scratch that!" She repeated what she had told Peter in the foyer. In conclusion: "What other bright ideas do you have?"

Momentarily disconcerted, Jake said, "Ah . . ." And found the thread again.

"Well, too bad. So move on to the next possibility. On a purely statistical basis, the largest and best-known of the old AID clinics would be the likeliest. Make a list of those that are still operating, call on them, see whom you can chat up, find out whether any former staff are still around who are down on their luck and might take cash in hand for information. Like I said, good old-fashioned stuff. You might begin with the clinic Peter went to."

For an instant Peter tensed. He had never mentioned his experience as a semen-donor to Jake, so how—?

Then he remembered: following their initial heart-to-heart Claudia had updated the information on her master disk with reference to "an acquaintance in London" who at some unspecified past time had—and so forth. It couldn't have been too hard for Jake to figure out who the acquaintance must be.

Swallowing his annoyance, he muttered, "It's gone."

"What?"

"I looked it up in the phone book." With a glance at Claudia: "You didn't think I'd just been sitting on my backside, did you? It isn't where it used to be—it isn't anywhere. Dr. Chinn is dead. His partner, Dr. Wilson . . . Sorry, not Wilson; her name was Wilkinson. Anyhow, she's retired. I tried asking the BMA whether anybody bought the operation, because it must have accumulated a load of goodwill by the time it folded, but they refused to answer on grounds of confidentiality."

"That sounds like something I could dig into," Bernie ventured. He had been sitting in discomfited silence, but had not lost track of what was being said.

"Go ahead, why not? We need all the help we can get. But . . ." He broke off.

"But what?" Jake urged.

Peter shook his head as though he had briefly fallen asleep. "Nothing. Just a sense of—of connection: the clinic, the doctors who ran it, the donors, the mention of computerizing their records . . ."

They waited expectantly, but he disappointed them.

"Sorry, I can't pin it down. I'll think about it again, though. Jake, I think you were going to say something else, weren't you?"

Calmer now, Jake shrugged. "I think I've spelt out my messages. What about it, Claudia? This is strictly your pigeon, you know."

She hesitated. He went on, "I can read your mind! You think you might be a trifle—shall we say notorious?"

Relieved, she gave a nod.

"But your face hasn't exactly been plastered all over the telly. I can furnish you with fake ID, in either the name of the *Comet* or that of the agency that syndicates our stuff in the States, to account for your accent. Well?"

After a pause: "I don't see any alternative. Okay. I don't imagine I'll be much good at the game, but—yes, it is my pigeon. Funniest kind of research I ever undertook!"

"Funniest kind of subject," Peter said, and he wasn't joking, "that I ever found a scientist researching."

"That's settled, then," Jake said, and rose. The others did the same. "Bernie, I'm sorry I bit your head off—"

"Forget it. Just believe me when I say the data I imagined I could find for Claudia have turned out to be shellbacked to the *n*th degree. Talk about turtle inside tortoise inside terrapin . . . Still, I'll keep on hacking."

"You do that," said Jake. "You, too, do that."

Waiting for the lift—Bernie had remained behind—Claudia said anxiously to Peter, "You seemed to be having some kind of insight, even inspiration. Have you figured out what it was?"

He shook his head. "No, damn it. It was on the tip of my tongue and wouldn't come out. Still won't. Like trying to recapture a dream, know what I mean? But at least I do recall what brought it on: Dr. Wilkinson, the people who were donors at the clinic, the connection with computers, the row that led to her and Dr. Chinn dissolving their partnership . . . I'll work it out sooner or later. Put the computer on the job, maybe. Or get Ellen to."

"Ellen?"

"Didn't I tell you? No, I don't suppose I did. We haven't talked much recently . . . Well, she's turning into an absolute whiz. Got herself email friends all over the place! I had to put my foot down, of course, when I found out she was interrogating boards as far away as Australia. Even though—would you believe?—instead of going to the minder her school recommended after classes, she's found herself a part-time job cleaning house for an old lady! This, in order to be able to pay her own way on my rig!"

"I told you she was a bright one, didn't I?" Claudia murmured.

"Oh, sure! No doubt of it! So I've told her: provided she confines herself to Europe and doesn't mind moving over when I have work to do, she can play around as much as she likes."

"You're not letting her become—well, agoraphobic?"

"On the contrary." Peter shook his head vigorously. "Her teachers say that because she's learning so much so quickly it's doing wonders for her confidence. Being at a new school where there are relatively few kids of—ah—mixed extraction, she was having trouble for a week or two. In fact, that's what turned her off going to the minder. Now, it seems, the other kids are appealing to her for help and information. You're right: she *is* bright."

"And nice with it," Claudia confirmed. "Give her my regards."

The lift arrived. Neither of them spoke again until they reached the foyer. Then Claudia said musingly, "I never expected to turn into an investigative journalist. I don't expect I'll be much good at it . . . May I call you up for advice?"

"Any time, lady. Any time. But it may be Ellen who answers."

"Don't worry. I'll be polite . . ." They'd reached the entrance; the pavement outside was littered with hysterical anti-pet leaflets, bearing photographs of rabies victims. At hazard she said, "Aren't you glad you don't own a dog?"

"As a matter of fact I've been thinking about getting one. It'd be company for Ellen when I'm out. But given what's going on . . ."

"It'll blow over. We have rabies in the States. We live with it."

"I know, I know. Given the frenzy we're working ourselves into, though, I could imagine the poor kid finding it crucified on the front door when she got home from school. She's had enough to put up with. I don't want to add that as well."

"What do you predict concerning pigs?" she countered with Jewish causticity, and without waiting for an answer swung on her heel and headed for the nearest bus stop.

Good question. The Animal Liberation Front . . .

Peter snapped his fingers. That was the fresh angle he needed to follow up the pigs-with-AIDS story. During the next two days he didn't spare a thought to Claudia's.

Unfortunately, though, the second pig item didn't sell.

Nor did the others he had had high hopes for.

Growing more and more depressed, he began to wonder about being blacklisted. Of course there was no proof, but when so many hot leads died . . .

Perhaps it was as well he couldn't afford hard liquor any more.

REACHING FOR AN ADMISSION FORM, NOT LOOKING up, the hospital's night receptionist said in a weary tone, "Cash or charity?"

So low had been reduced the once-noble concept of Britain's National Health Service.

From this lobby three passageways extended like the branches of a T. The one on the right was noticeably cleaner than that on the left, and far less shabby, with carpet on the floor instead of vinyl tarnished by the passage of uncountable feet. The one between was scarcely even lighted; there were fluorescent tubes, but half were dark.

Then, roused by the sound of sobbing, the receptionist lifted her head and realized that Crystal stood between two women constables, hands 'cuffed behind her back.

"Oh," she said, and jerked a thumb to indicate: behind me. "Criminal. That way."

Twilit, the third corridor was full of screams and moans.

When she wasn't overcome by tears, Crystal was purely and simply furious with herself: *I should have had more sense, I should have had more sense . . . !*

Yet how could she have foreseen that a punter would accuse her of infecting him with not AIDS but syphilis? And, although neither had learned the other's name (she used invented names with her clients and changed them from day to day) would enable the police to trace her because he was a computer-graphics artist and arrived at the station equipped with a near-flawless likeness of her.

And—this was where sobs racked her anew—that the Bill would come searching for her while she was briefly deprived of the Shadow's "power to cloud men's minds".

She'd been amused by that term; she owed it to a client who had sought her out six or eight times, wanting as much to talk about the fads and fancies of his teenage years as to get it on with her. He'd shown her prizes from his valuable collection of old comics, and in one . . .

But that was then and she was here and now, sullenly ignoring questions, hearing them answered for her by the butch policewomen, gazing with hate-filled eyes at her surroundings: cracked tiles on floor and walls, a row of dirty chairs, a wired-glass door whose pane was held together with crossed strips of tape . . . As well as screams, this area was full of stinks.

". . . and he's prepared to swear she was his only contact in over three months, so it must have been her who infected him."

"Right"—in a bored tone. "I'll take a blood sample straight away. Our automatic Wassermann machine is working for once. You'll have the evidence before she goes before the magistrate."

"Not magistrate. Juvenile."

"Christ. Isn't it hard to tell these days? When I was young, kids looked like kids . . . Does she have a smart lawyer on tap to turn her loose?"

The policewomen exchanged first glances, then grins. The older of them said, "We won't go into that—hmm?"

"Suits me. What time is she due in court, anyway?"

One of the policewomen punched keys on a belt-slung computer and fed the result to her radio. After scant seconds the reply came back in an unconvincing synthetic voice. A slot had been assigned her on the juvenile court schedule at about ten next morning.

"Pick her up around nine, then." Crystal hadn't even looked at who was speaking; she only knew the tone was harsh and male, a jailer's. "We'll have the proof for you."

Making up your mind a little prematurely, aren't you?

But she had more sense than to speak aloud. She had been beaten up on the way here, and she ached already; she had no wish to make herself feel worse.

And after that there was a cell. Blank walls. No food or

drink, nor even anything to lie down on or wrap around herself: just a china toilet in the corner, with no seat. It was against AIDS regulations—but since when did this puky government obey the laws it passed? And they were riddled with holes, anyhow. Under age, she should have had a responsible adult with her throughout this agony, but when she tried to insist . . .

She managed sleep, somehow; drank a mug of sour tea by way of breakfast; appeared in court an hour and a half later than predicted by the *wonderful* computers at New Scotland Yard; was fined ten thousand pounds which she couldn't pay, with the alternative of jail, for "biological assault" upon the punter (that was a relic of the panicky days when AIDS victims sometimes deliberately passed it on and left lipstick messages to say so on the bathroom mirror); and by three P.M. was in the infirmary of a young offenders' prison for compulsory treatment of a notifiable disease.

Detachedly she began to wonder what weapons she could lay her hands on—broken glass, for instance, or discarded hypodermics. Then she calmed, remembering that within a few more days she would be able to talk her way out of here without violence.

The waiting wasn't going to be easy. But she could stand it. Meantime: low profile.

Low.

Even when a bocky chaplain with a high whinnying voice came round to declare that she was an instrument of Satan and deserved her punishment.

"Knight!"

She started and swung round.

"Go to the chaplain's office! You've got visitors!"

Her heart sank. *Oh, no! Just as I'm feeling the power again! Tomorrow I'll be able to use it properly! I'll bet he's mustered missionaries to save my soul!*

But she complied meekly enough. Even during her period she seemed to retain enough of her talent to elude the worst that others had in view for her, though she could not impose direct commands.

* * *

What she encountered, however, was nothing like what she'd expected. The chaplain, certainly, was in the room, thin and bent-shouldered at his desk. But Crystal spared him scarcely a glance. Also present were two adult strangers . . . and a boy about her age.

He had the Power.

She had never imagined it could be so strong.

Nor, indeed, that anybody else possessed it.

For the space of five accelerated heartbeats she was both terrified and disappointed: the former, because she felt as though something private to herself had been put on public sale like auction goods, to be pried at by greedy questing hands; the latter, because if this meeting had to happen she would have wished it to occur when she was at her peak, so there might be a just and equal contest.

And then she realized it had always been impossible.

No, more than impossible. Unnecessary.

For he was on her side . . .

She gasped and tilted forward, fainting.

Though they revived her swiftly, only fragments of what transpired thereafter endured in memory. She recalled words in the chaplain's horrible voice, and would rather not have thought about the Houyhnhnms . . . yet, there having been so many Yahoos in her life, she couldn't help it. Consequently: fragments.

"—seems that Mr. Shay has set up a refuge for you pitiable creatures—sad that it's not a religious foundation—nonetheless in present circumstances what with overcrowding in all jails—paid the fine and sworn to have you treated—sign this and we can go before the governor . . ."

(Later she found herself unable to distinguish between what the chaplain had said, what David Shay had said, what if anything the governor had said, and what her own drug-distorted mind had supplied to fill the gaps. To cure her syphilis, which was resistant, strangers had stabbed her over and over, some relishing the pain they were inflicting with the needles. And she had only been here two days. So how—? So why—?)

* * *

She was still babbling those questions when she found herself in the back seat of a Rolls Royce, a bag containing her
meager possessions on her lap. David, beside her, told his
parents in the front to open the windows, which they did although it was cool and rain was threatening. He said it was to
ensure that Crystal didn't pass out again. His tone sounded
sympathetic, and she felt reassured.

But when she tried to hug him out of gratitude he thrust her
away with a scowl.

"You," he stated crudely, "are a twat."

And with fastidious grip he lifted clear her clutching hands.

"What . . . ? *What?*" Crystal was on the verge of tears
again.

"A twat! A damnfool version of a female person! I hoped
for better when I started hunting—Never mind! But given the
talent that I know you share with me, should you have wasted
it on *prostitution?*"

It was as though all air was emptied from her lungs—as
though she were aboard a spaceship punctured by a meteor.
She tried to fall, moaning, across David's lap; he shoved her
roughly aside.

"Don't touch me!" he ordered. "Or any of us! Not until
you're cured of all your STDs!"

And withdrew to his corner of the seat to attend to other
and more urgent business. Cowering, Crystal tried to make
sense of what he was doing. The Rolls was fitted with not just
a phone, but also the facility to access remote computers,
which was what David was exploiting at the moment. She
blinked away tears and suffered the return of memory. The last
car she had seen so lavishly equipped had been Winston
Farmer's Jaguar—and even in that case she hadn't known
how rich he was until he came to court.

When, luckily, she had not had to testify. The fact that he'd
been caught in possession of two k's of crack had been
enough—

For a moment she was frantic, reflex superseding rationality. Could these weird people be ex-customers, their sights set
on taking over his business?

As though he had sensed her reaction, David snapped,
"Shut up!"

But she hadn't said anything . . . Maybe she ought to listen for a change. She did her best to concentrate, and heard:

"What name? . . . Yes, I got the surname. But the first one? . . . Ah, I got you! Garth!"

Whereupon he produced a pocket organizer and entered a memo to self, then posted it to a remote computer.

Passive, Crystal leaned back against the soft, absorbing cushions of the car, not noticing the route that it was following but savoring the contrast between this setting and the chill harsh building she had left. She waited until David had finished, then ventured timidly, "How did you track me down?"

"Through PNC, of course," he sighed. And added cruelly, "Given that you were jailed for spreading syph I'm not so sure it was a good idea!"

She was instantly in tears. No one had spoken to her with such authority since her parents died. Her aunt and uncle had been brusquer, but earned none of her respect. This boy, however, from the very start . . .

She forced out, "It was my only hope!"

"Of wiping out the whenzies?"—cynically.

"No! To survive!"

There was a pause.

During it, up front, Mr. Shay kept on driving and Mrs. Shay kept on pretending that she didn't give a damn about whatever happened. That was a fact. Crystal knew it, didn't have to guess. Her period having drawn to its close, her talent —her power—was being bit by bit restored.

Though she never expected to match David's.

At last David, uttering a sigh, reached out to pat her hand, if only for a moment.

"Welcome, sister," he said half-inaudibly.

"What do you mean?" She jolted upright.

"You must have believed you were the only one."

"I don't understand!"

Seeming to ignore her words, he carried on. "I did for a long while, and so did . . . Never mind. You'll meet them in a little while. I only wish you hadn't declared biological warfare on the whenzies, given the risk to yourself—"

"I didn't!" Crystal's voice was half a scream.

He searched her face with dark intense eyes while she fought to make him believe what she had said.

And won. Perhaps her magic was returning. For he let his face relax toward a smile.

However, what he said was not what she'd expected . . .

"Ah, what the hell? We couldn't all be lucky, I suppose. Statistically there was apt to be at least one who went on the streets and didn't care about disease—"

"I did *so*!"—erupting. "Got my AIDS certificate! *And* I paid a mint for the inoculation!"

He fixed her with his stern dark gaze.

"And had room for only one disease in your mind? Forgot about syphilis and gonorrhea and soft chancre and NSU and the fungal conditions that you could have been transmitting and quite likely were?"

Crystal was crying; she didn't quite know why, but it might have been because this strange boy sounded so much more like her father than her unwillingly adoptive uncle. She forced out, "What the hell else was I supposed to do to stay alive?"

"For the first time," said David Shay, and sounded strangely old—one could have invoked the term patriarchal —as he spoke the words, "you have the chance to *be* alive. And so do . . . . No, that has to wait. You'll find out in a little while."

The car was whirring along a motorway, dispersing lesser vehicles like a fast launch dismissing rowboats.

"We'll get properly acquainted when you're cured," David went on eventually. "Meantime, my search program appears to have turned up another of our siblings."

What?

But she didn't dare ask for a more detailed explanation. His power . . . Oh, Lord! She'd never guessed the magic could be strong! Convincing, yes—persuasive, yes! But never *strong*!

And yet . . .

For the first time in months she confronted the fact, so long and so often pushed to the back of her mind, of the difference between herself and other people. Sometimes she had been frightened by her talent, even when she was using it to maximum advantage. But at bottom what she really feared was being *unique*—an exception, a mutant, a monster.

At least she wasn't that. Here was David for proof. And he'd mentioned the possibility of yet another...

Little by little, as the car hummed onward, she started to relax, and when they reached their destination she was able to laugh and clap her hands with unalloyed delight.

You're watching TV Plus. It's time for Newsframe.

Thousands of acres of crops in the basin of America's Colorado River are under threat following an irruption of salt water from a natural underground reservoir. Water-engineers believed the reservoir to contain fresh water. This may have been true ten years ago when test-wells were last sunk to it, but subsequently salt water appears to have leaked in through a rock-fault. More details later.

Speaking in West Germany at a rally organized by descendants of servicemen who died in World War II, General Sir Hampton Thrower praised the valiant spirit of the fallen...

"Miss Morris? From the *Comet*? Do come in, do sit down."

Got it!

In memory Claudia could still hear Peter's excited voice on the phone when his vague recollection ceased to be vague after two days of striving. And here was the person it had led her to: Dr. Ada Grant, who had been on the staff of the Chinn-Wilkinson, though not a partner, at the time Peter was donating semen, and who was now director of possibly the best-known fertility clinic in London. Long-faced, long-boned, with short dark hair, she wore a severe white coat and narrow black skirt. A red-white-and-blue ribbon was pinned to the breast of the coat—but one saw the emblem everywhere nowadays. (Even Peter . . .)

Now she was waiting expectantly for Claudia to explain her business.

She was nervous, naturally, but Jake Lafarge had given her an extensive and extremely useful briefing, and she felt her anxiety fade as she sat down, produced her pocket recorder, and reviewed her surroundings prior to conducting the planned interview. An incongruous hi-tech office had been implanted behind the Georgian façade of this building—in Marylebone, about half a mile from the traditional "doctors' area" of Harley Street and Wimpole Street where Peter had fathered his ten anonymous children, but that, so she had been informed, was because the rents there now precluded occupation by any doctor whose patients were less than millionaires.

Admittedly, with the falling value of money, it was much easier to be a millionaire nowadays . . .

She forced her mind back to more important matters.

"I ought to start by thanking you for sparing time for me," she said, switching on the recorder and placing it on the doctor's desk. "Oh—do you mind?"

A single headshake, and: "Not at all."

"Thank you. Well, I'm sure you must be very busy, so I won't waste more time on preliminaries than I have to, but I'm afraid I shall need to give you a bit of background before I start asking questions."

The lies, honed and polished under Jake's expert guidance, slid easily off her tongue.

"You see, my editor recently received a letter from a woman who bore a child through artinsem—AID, of course, before the coincidence of initials. Frankly, I think she should have addressed it to the Agony Aunt of one of the women's magazines, but she's a *Comet* reader, so . . .

"I don't of course have all the details, but what it seems to boil down to is this. Her son is now in his teens. She and her husband originally intended to tell him the truth when he got to about his present age, but apparently things haven't worked out too well, and she's afraid that if they do, he might become obsessed with finding out who his—ah—biological father

was. Since people no longer know very much about artinsem
. . . Excuse me: I'm a complete layperson when it comes to
matters like these, but I have the impression that it went out of
fashion virtually overnight when AIDS appeared on the scene.
Is that so?"

Dr. Grant leaned back, her expression thoughtful, and set
her fingertips together.

"It's certainly true that AIDS had a marked effect. Largely
thanks to the media, if you'll excuse my saying so, there was
a lot of panic, and prospective parents became very reluctant
to accept an anonymous donation. On the other hand, there
were a lot of additional factors. The chief, naturally, was the
development of *in vitro* fertilization. Unless the husband has
no viable sperm at all, we can now take one of the wife's own
eggs and literally create an embryo which is the natural offspring of both parents. Then it's implanted and with luck proceeds normally to term."

"But this is all comparatively recent?"

"How recent is 'recent,' these days?" Dr. Grant countered
with a thin-lipped smile. "It's a good decade or so since we
reached the stage where it was obvious artinsem was bound to
be superseded. Not, you realize, that it wasn't invaluable in its
day. For instance, when I first came into the field, working at
the then-famous Chinn-Wilkinson clinic, AID was undoubt-
edly providing a very useful service to the community. Well
over three thousand impregnations were performed successfully each year, in Britain alone. At Chinn-Wilkinson alone
we carried out, on average, four or five hundred annually.
That meant nearly a thousand contented new parents."

"Due just to the one clinic? That's most impressive." Claudia hoped her tone carried conviction. "Tell me, as a matter of
interest: did you have what you might call typical clients?
Obviously every case must have been different, but can you
make any generalizations?"

"Yes!" Dr. Grant said immediately, with emphasis. "The
people who came to Chinn-Wilkinson then were exactly like
those who come here now: stable couples, married at least five
years and often as long as ten. They've tried for a baby the
ordinary way; they've been to infertility consultants but tend
to distrust fertility drugs owing to the risk of multiple births—

we do sometimes use them, but only rarely, for precisely that reason—and they've tried the alternatives, such as mineral supplements. Quite often they've gone the whole alternative route, from acupuncture and even moxa—I ask you!—to herbal remedies and homeopathy. They're determined, that's the word. They want a child! In some cases I can recall . . . Well, I suppose I shouldn't say this about people who I'm sure are perfectly sincere, but it's a sad fact that a lot of them don't know what they're about. To be blunt, some of the people who finally apply to us turn out to have spent twice as much on techniques that didn't help as it would have cost to come here in the first place."

"You mean it's a field in which the ethics of some practitioners are—shall we say not of the highest?"

"I won't say anything of the kind," Dr. Grant smiled. "I prefer to leave it at that. But aren't we rather straying from the point?"

"Yes, of course. Excuse me." Claudia dragged her mind back to the fictitious mother worried about her artinsem son. "Obviously what I chiefly need to find out is how donor records were kept. How was it done at the Chinn-Wilkinson, for instance? Were the records computerized?"

Dr. Grant gazed at her visitor for a long moment, her thin fingers still steepled together. Eventually she said, "Let me make a guess. You, or your editor, aren't totally convinced by this woman's letter. You suspect she may be spinning a colorable yarn. The true reason for her anxiety is far more likely to be that she's afraid her son's biological father may become obsessed with the notion that he has offspring he has never met, and attempt to track down the recipient of his genes. Am I right?"

"Why, we were thinking along precisely those lines," Claudia murmured, striving to conceal her jubilation. A matter she had expected to have to work up to by a roundabout route was being broached after barely more than a hint. "Of course, one respects the confidentiality of your profession, but when so much of people's private lives is on computers now, and there are constant stories in the news about how secrets have been unearthed by hackers and used for—well—even blackmail... And since, no doubt, the records *were* kept on computer..." She let the sentence trail away.

"Well, there did have to be records, obviously," Dr. Grant said after a moment. "For instance, one wouldn't have wanted a black baby to turn up in a white family, or *vice versa*. And yes, in the last few years at least we did keep them on computer. But they were never on-line to anywhere else. They were solely for use within the clinic." Lowering her arms, Dr. Grant gazed challengingly across her desk.

"So that if the clinic had caught on fire, say, or been— well, bombed by some extremist religious group—there would have been no other copy?"

Claudia waited tensely for the answer.

"Ah..." The doctor suddenly seemed uncomfortable. "Well, to be perfectly frank, we did use to copy our data to a commercial storage center, one that specializes in medical records, and they're still on file there in case I ever need to consult them. But—"

The nape of Claudia's neck was tingling. She leaned forward. "Excuse my interrupting! But I deduce from what you just said that you inherited the goodwill of the Chinn-Wilkinson?"

"I—ah... Yes, as a matter of fact, I did take over when the original partnership was dissolved. It's public knowledge. It was a question of new specializations, more than anything ... May I finish?"

"Please!"

"As I was saying, the data center—which we still use— has an excellent reputation. Most fertility clinics in this country, and indeed a good few from overseas, patronize it, because it's extremely well defended, and there is no way anyone could hack into it given the complexity of its password system. Take my own case by way of example. Someone would have to burgle my home, or that of my head nurse, and steal the password list, then decode it—we both keep it in cipher and we each invented our own and neither of us knows what the other's is—and *then* try and convince the data-bank that he or she was myself or my head nurse. Which would not be easy. Besides, the traffic is strictly one-way. No one even at the data-bank can access our computers from outside...

Hmm! I just remembered something! I wonder whether I can lay hands on it. It used to live in that file cabinet over there."

Rising, she pulled open the cabinet's bottom drawer. Claudia waited eagerly. In a moment the doctor exclaimed in satisfaction, producing an oblong box.

"That's it! The videotape we used at Chinn-Wilkinson to convince doubtful would-be clients. You can play it before you leave. Of course it's out of date to some extent, but the principles remain the same."

"That would be most interesting!" Claudia breathed.

"And if your correspondent needs any further reassurance about the security of our records," the doctor went on, turning to a shelf on which rested two keyboards and a shared monitor, "this will give you some idea of the standard we subscribe to." She entered a quick command and the monitor lit. "It's the ethical code of the International Association of Fertility Services, or 'Yafs' as we call it. Every reputable clinic in the field, not only in Europe but in North and South America, Australia, New Zealand, too—every reputable clinic adheres to it, and you can see how strict it is just by looking."

Indeed it was both lengthy and detailed, and Claudia would not have dared to question its integrity. After watching it scroll slowly through three screenfuls, she murmured, "Again I have to say: most impressive. And reassuring, too. May I have a printout, or is it confidential?"

"Oh, the only confidential part is the one I'm not going to show you," Dr. Grant said with a faint chuckle. "That's the actual instructions to member clinics explaining how best to protect their records. By all means you can have a copy of the rest."

"And is there a directory of the member clinics?"

"Of course. Would you like that as well? I'm sure you won't want to limit your inquiries to one clinic, but I'm sufficiently proud of our services to imagine that you'll want to feature us rather than the competition. However, I suspect you may want to visit one or two agencies that don't belong to Yafs and don't conduct themselves in such a—well—professional manner."

"The directory would be invaluable," Claudia said. "And if

I hear of an agency that isn't on the list I'll treat it with due suspicion."

"Precisely. Is there enough paper?"—glancing at a printer which reposed on a steel-framed stand at her right. "Oh yes, that should be plenty. This will only take a moment."

The printer sprang into silent action, and the printout was ready within seconds. Dr. Grant handed it over with a smile.

"And now, if you'll excuse me, I have business to attend to. But do watch this tape before you go. There's a VCR in the waiting room—on the left of the front door—and there's no one in there at the moment. If you have any further questions, feel free to get in touch again."

Accepting the tape, Claudia asked, not without a trace of malice, "Might I inquire, doctor, whether you have children of your own?"

"I carry the gene for cystic fibrosis," was the answer.

"Oh! I'm sorry!"

"Don't be. I've had years to resign myself to it. And I have an awful lot of godchildren, as it were. More than a hundred couples send me pictures of their kids every Christmas. They don't half clutter up the drawing room . . . When the tape is over, my receptionist will show you out. Good afternoon!"

Later, it came as a severe blow to Claudia's pride when Bernie dismissed the "Yafs" directory as something he had thought of accessing right at the beginning. At least, though, he was pleased to be told about the medical data-bank patronized by so many British fertility clinics, and promised to start hacking at it right away.

WITHOUT WARNING, THE OFFERINGS AT THE GATE had ceased . . .

In desperation Roy Crowder bought a couple of piglets and reared them on what sparse fodder his fields afforded, plus household scraps that would ordinarily have gone for compost. The dream he had once had of self-sufficiency, which he had spelt out spellbindingly to Tilly, had vanished under the impact of Garth's never-ceasing demands. The boy seemed not to understand how much sheer *time* it took to scrape a living from this unforgiving land. Night and day he was avid for information, tools, materials, more information! A second mortgage had provided him with a computer and a phone line to link it with the outside world; now it looked as though it was going to take a third—impossible—to pay for the use he was making of it . . .

But his parents dared not refuse, for when he grew angry—! For the past week Tilly had been hobbling around with one leg wrapped in bandages from hip to knee because, dissatisfied with his evening meal, Garth had ordered her to spill a bowlful of boiling soup into her lap.

No. Not "ordered." That was what, in the intervals of lucidity Roy achieved by driving to the nearby market-town, seemed so terrible. His son seldom descended now to overt commands. He merely suggested, in persuasive tones, and suddenly it seemed right to do as he requested, obligatory, unavoidable.

As today. The piglets were not nearly fat enough to fetch the price that Roy had had in mind, but Garth had declared that he must have more money, now. If he had come to town and worked his incomprehensible power of persuasion on intending buyers, things would have been far different.

But as it had turned out . . .

On his way home Roy found that he was crying. So blinded was he by his tears, he ran the ancient Citroën off the road at a sharp bend, and because there had been rain the night before and there was a heavy load in the back, the wheels sank into soft mud. Frantically he tried to dig them out and failed, and in the end realized he must trudge up the last few hundred yards of the track and face whatever horrors his son would conjure up as punishment.

"I would rather be dead," he said to the air. "I would rather cut my throat and join my pigs."

But he didn't. Even though he carried a pocket-knife. He couldn't bear the thought of what Garth might do to Tilly afterward.

"How much did you get for the pigs?" the boy demanded, not glancing away from his computer screen.

"They're in the back of the car."

"I told you to sell them!" Now Garth did swing around, his face a mask of fury. "Why the hell didn't you?"

"Nobody would touch 'em. Nobody wants pork since they found AIDS in—"

"You bloody fool! Who the hell could possibly imagine you buggering them? I don't suppose you can bloody get it up any more, not even for a pig!"

"Not me," Roy said, slumping into a wooden chair. Of a sudden he seemed to have discovered fresh inner resources. Perhaps they were due to absolute despair. "You."

"What?" Garth erupted from his seat and advanced threateningly.

Cheeks still wet with tears, Roy Crowder raised his head and looked his son straight in the eyes. "You heard what I said," he forced out. "When I found no one would buy them I was going to put them back in the car so even if we had to sacrifice our principles we might at least eat the meat off them, and maybe use the skin. They say you can use all a pig except the squeal . . ."

"And—?" Garth was leaning over him now, teeth bared.

"Half a dozen men came after me. I didn't recognize any of them. They had nylon stockings over their faces, coats made of old sacks to hide their clothes. They cut their throats. Flooded the road with blood. Told me not to come to market any more. Said they've found out how you get your power— by fucking animals! It's one of the things witches and magicians do, one of the ancient rites!"

He was on his feet without intention, face whiter than paper and gleaming with sweat. In that instant he would cheerfully have killed his son.

"Roy?" Tilly called anxiously; she had been in the kitchen garden trying to scrabble up enough potatoes for their supper. Basket under her arm, she limped in through the back door, and halted in terror on the threshold.

There was a dead pause. Then, making a gallant attempt to maintain her usual pretense that all was normal, she said, "I didn't hear you drive up."

"I didn't. Car's stuck in mud, halfway down the lane."

"So, you stupid son-of-a-bitch, you've cost us our car as well as our pigs!" Garth was beside himself with fury now. "What I ought to do to you—"

"Hello?"

The voice was the familiar one of Mr. Youngman. With an oath the boy swung to face the door.

I thought I'd cured the bastard of his habit of calling here without warning or permission!

Lately it had seemed unimportant to persuade the authorities that he was being properly educated. Besides, it wasted a lot of time and effort.

Here he was, though, advancing into the kitchen. His face was wax-pale and his hands were tightly locked in front of him as though to stop them shaking. His posture communicated, clear as words: *I know you don't want me to come in, but I must.*

Garth felt a dreadful tightening in his chest. By what means had this ineffectual frustrated teacher summoned up such courage? After so long, he must be aware of the risk he was running. He might never have admitted it to himself, but he must realize what power Garth exerted over adults—

And then another boy appeared in the frame of the door.

Not as tall as Garth, but exuding confidence. Expensively dressed, his fashionable—American—shoes stained with mud, but otherwise as smart as though he had been walking city pavement, not a puddly lane.

The tightness in Garth's chest became agonizing. He had to fumble his way to a chair and sit down. From the corner of his eye he saw his parents exchanging glances pregnant with wild hope.

"Hello, Garth," he heard. "My name is David. We've come to take you away."

"I don't want—"

"Garth, in fact you do." David drew closer, eyes alert. There was a breadknife on the clumsy wooden table in the middle of the kitchen; one heartbeat before Garth thought of snatching at it, the newcomer had already knocked it over the far edge and out of reach.

"Stay away from me!"

But he didn't. Smiling, he reached out a hand and patted Garth's wrist.

"Save your trouble," he advised. "I know who we are and you don't—yet."

The turn of phrase penetrated Garth's resentful mind. He said after a moment, "We . . . ?"

"Yes, Garth. On the way here I've been talking with Mr. Youngman. He didn't want to come back—said the last time was too terrible—but in the end he did agree, so I'm indebted to him. You are as well, of course."

Mr. Youngman didn't seem to understand the words. He had withdrawn to a corner, visibly shaking now. But one point at least had got across to Roy, for he forced out, "You said you'd come to take Garth away?"

"Yes." Not looking round. "Whether or not he wants to come."

"Thank God," said Roy. And, an instant later, Tilly was in his arms and weeping her heart out for relief.

"Right!" David said briskly. "Move! Don't bother to bring anything. I have everything you have, and more."

A final flare of resentment. "Who the hell do you think you are, ordering me about this way?"

"I don't *think*. I *know*."

There was a tense electric silence. At last Garth rose unsteadily to his feet.

"All right. Whatever the hell you have in mind for me, it can't be worse than living here. I'm coming."

You're watching TV Plus. Now for Newsframe.

British radioactive waste on its way to burial in China's Gobi Desert has allegedly been hijacked by Tibetan revolutionaries. Hundreds of refugees are fleeing the area for fear of contamination. Both the British and Chinese governments are denying that there is any danger, but an antiterrorism specialist in London was today quoted as saying, "This is something we have long feared. Set it on a hilltop to windward of any large city, blow it up, and you'd have a disaster compared to which Chernobyl and Three Mile Island were as nothing." More in a moment.

The first "Thrower" candidates, standing for the British Patriotic Party in next week's local elections . . .

TIRED, PETER SAT BESIDE ELLEN WATCHING THE mid-evening TV news. As ever most of it concerned disasters or the activities of the royal family and cabinet ministers. Recently the subservient BBC had taken to signing its bulletins on and off with snatches of the national anthem. Today the prime minister had mentioned the fact approvingly in Parliament, and much play was made of that.

More interesting to him, however, was a story with a medical bias. There had been an outbreak of botulism in Greater Manchester among people who had eaten frozen chicken, with twenty dead so far and more than a hundred ill. Now a radical vegan group was claiming to have poisoned the chickens and threatening a repeat.

The name they had adopted was The Hitler Youth.

"Hitler was a vegetarian, wasn't he?" Ellen said.

Taken aback that she should know such an odd fact, he did his best to answer in the same calm tone.

"Yes, and a teetotaller. But he wasn't immune from addiction. Apart from the drugs his doctor dosed him with, and most of his entourage, he was a chocaholic. He—"

The phone rang, and with a grunt of annoyance he rose to answer. Just as he was picking it up, the doorbell rang.

"I'll go," Ellen sighed, switching off the TV sound.

"Check the monitor!" Peter cried, but she brushed aside his warning.

"It's all right—I saw through the window. It's only Claudia."

And it was. He heard her greeting Ellen in the hall as he said to the phone, "Levin!"

"This is Bernie."

Instantly he was all ears. He barely contrived a smile as Claudia entered and sat down.

"Yes? What have you got for us?"

"Some good news, some bad. Can you meet me?"

Peter hesitated. "Well, my partner just arrived."

"I'll come to you, then. Soon as I can."

"Okay."

Though he didn't think it was at all a good idea . . .

Playing hostess, Ellen brought Claudia her usual whiskey on the rocks with a splash of water. Accepting with a word of thanks, she asked who had rung up.

"Bernie. He's coming round."

Instantly she was alert. "With news for us?"

"Some good, some bad, he says. What news from you?"

Claudia hesitated a moment before replying. As though taking a hint, Ellen rose with a muttered, "Excuse me."

"I don't want to drive you out!" Claudia exclaimed.

"You aren't," Ellen said firmly. "But I have a lot of homework."

Yet she left behind a definite atmosphere . . .

Looking concerned, Claudia set her glass aside untasted. She said, "You having problems? I thought, after we—what was that featly old-fashioned phrase you used?—ran our project up the flagpole and got her to salute it, everything was smooth."

"I don't think she's in the mood for company just now. She's upset because she was due to spend the evening with a school-friend. Only the other girl's father has decided he doesn't want his children mixing with niggers."

"Oh, no!"

"Oh, yes." Face grim, Peter dropped ice-cubes, *crash-crash*, into a glass for himself. "I swear I don't know what's going to happen to this country." He splashed a generous double measure of whisky over the ice. That left only a drop in the bottle, which he drained into Claudia's glass before dumping the empty in a waste-bin. It was likely to be the last for some while . . .

Sitting down, he concluded bitterly, "One thing's for certain, though. Next winter, if the power-workers try to strike, they'll be driven back to work by the army."

"Who says so?"

Peter gestured at his computer. "Ellen lucked into that one yesterday. She's getting better than I am at finding where the moles leave their droppings. This one turned up on a board I didn't even know existed—let alone that you could access it free of charge."

"And you believe this rumor?"

"More and more civil servants are getting so disgusted with the government, they're risking their jobs and even jail to leak the bosses' plans. This is just the latest of several similar cases. You can judge how seriously to take them by the vehemence of the denials that follow. This is already being denied in a hysterical shriek, so—yes, I do believe it."

He tossed back a gulp of whisky that nearly choked him.

"However, it hasn't happened yet," he resumed when he could. "How are you getting on?"

"Well, I've been to the Grant clinic, as you know, and another that's on the register, and a couple that aren't and don't seem to be any less efficient even though they're cheaper. And in *no* case does there seem to be any way of accessing their records from outside. They simply don't allow them to go on line, except for blip-style transfer to a commercial data-bank. I thought I was going to find myself knee-deep in puky sleaze—you know, corrupt quacks exploiting the vulnerable public—but in fact they seem to be decent honorable people providing a valuable service."

"Hmm!" Peter stared at her. "And I thought you were too hard-boiled to swallow a PR job!"

"Fold it and stow it," she sighed, sipping her drink. "What I'm driving at is that Jake was right. We're going to have to fall back on traditional methods."

"Bribery and blackmail, you mean."

"He said that, I didn't. And he's a cynical cank, isn't he? No, I think the right approach might be to track down someone—say a retired employee—and interview them about their recollections. Elderly people, out of touch, are often more willing to talk informally than those who are still working in the field. After all, the past decade with its monstrous expansion of computerized records has made younger people that much more paranoid . . . You don't agree?"—in a frosty tone, for he was signalling with his free hand.

"No, no, no! It's just that you seem to be taking something far too much for granted."

"For example?"

"You said 'a' retired employee. From every fertility clinic in this country? Do you think they'd all prove malleable if you could track them down? What if they aren't?"

There was a dead pause. Claudia passed a hand through her hair, which was overdue for a trim. She had become neglectful of her appearance lately, and sometimes—as now—her face looked like that of a far older woman.

"You're right," she said dully. "Talk about wishful thinking . . . I guess I haven't really gotten over losing my helpful friend the policeman. Especially since they seem to have wised up to the PNC access he arranged. Do you imagine that's what Bernie wants to discuss?"

By reflex Peter's eyes had darted to the TV monitor that surveyed the entrance. Setting down his glass, he rose.

"We'll know soon enough. He's walking up the path."

* * *

Not so much walking as swaying, with a black eye, a swollen lip, and his clothes smudged with dirt. All of them, including an aroused Ellen, rushed to help: wiped his face, brushed his trousers, took his coat to be sponged, then sat him down with a good stiff drink.

Peter's and Claudia's, since there wasn't any more.

"Who attacked you?" Claudia demanded.

"Who knows? I noticed they wore Thrower ribbons, but . . . Oh, most likely Special Branch's bully-boys. At any rate they were fast enough on the job, and accurate with it." He winced as whisky burned his injured lip.

"But why?"

"They don't like the *Comet*, for a start. Because it's dared to criticize the government, they'd like to see it fail. And they don't like you"—a glance at Peter—"because of the fuss you kicked up over the Heathrow tragedy."

Somehow, in spite of the reference, none of them thought of suggesting that Ellen retreat again to her own room.

"You think they knew you were coming here—"

"Peter, you weren't born yesterday!"

Not waiting for an answer, Bernie glanced around. "My coat?"

"I took it in the kitchen to wash off the mud," Ellen exclaimed. "I'll fetch it, but it is rather wet—"

"No need! Just bring me the package in the right-hand pocket. Wrapped in a white plastic bag."

And, a moment later: "Here!"

"Thanks. Peter, you know what this is?" Bernie opened the bag and produced a palm-sized, battery-powered device bearing red and green lights.

"A bug-hunter," Peter said, nodding.

"Better. An exterminator. Want me to run it around?"

"No, I'll do it." Suddenly feeling—like Claudia—far older than his years, Peter forced himself to his feet. "All I can say is, I hope it doesn't spot anything."

"Clean. Rather to my surprise." He switched off the gadget and tossed it into Bernie's lap.

"Mine too." The hacker frowned. "I hope it's working. I'd have expected at least a passive tap on your phone—"

"Oh, I have a service that takes care of that. And my modem is protected, too. Lord, the shifts we're driven to if we're to think in private nowadays!"

"Not to mention the money," Claudia put in. "You know it cost me a week's rent to have your old place swept and garnished? There were bugs there, all right. Four."

Peter started. "New?"

"By the look of them, installed after you moved out of the place. Usual bureaucratic screw-up, I guess."

"Or aimed at you," Peter riposted.

She paled. "I hadn't thought of that! You're right, of course. I'll call the exterminators again tomorrow. I hate to squander Strugman money, but needs must . . . Well, Bernie!" Briskening, she turned. "What have you found?"

"Well, I'd better tell you the bad news first." He sipped his drink and grimaced again. "It doesn't look, after all, as though the Bill spotted the loopholes in our filter design."

They looked at him uncomprehendingly. At length Claudia ventured, "How can that be bad news?"

"Because if it's not the Bill, who else can it be?"

"You said before," Peter muttered, frowning, "though I didn't take you very seriously, that it was as though someone were getting to all your leads ahead of you."

Bernie gave a solemn nod. "*And* closing off the routes to them afterward."

"That does sound bad," Claudia conceded.

"Not as bad as you might think," Bernie countered. "I'm finding alternative pathways. They're slow, they're complicated, but they're starting to pay off. That's how come I also have some good news. It may not be as much as you were hoping for, but . . . Well, stuff the modesty bit. I suspect you don't think too much of me, but I swear I've dug up more than almost anybody else could!"

Soothingly, Claudia smiled at him. "I'm sure you've done wonders. All we want is to find out what they are."

Mollified, Bernie leaned back and gazed at the far wall.

"When I started looking for alternative approaches, I concentrated on the fertility clinic. There's no longer any means of finding out its name directly, but I'd already established that all the kids came from the same clinic, right? So I tried trawling for low-level associations. That paid off."

Claudia tensed. "Which one?"

"There's a ninety percent chance it was in the Harley Street-Wimpole Street area."

Bernie looked as though he expected lavish praise. He was let down. Claudia and Peter exchanged glances. Eventually the latter said, "But, Bernie, at the time there were five such clinics within a square mile, and another three or four a bit further off. What led you to this Earth-shaking conclusion?"

"If you're going to make fun of all my hard work—!"

"Calm down, calm down," Claudia broke in. "Peter, that was tactless. It's a start, it's a clue, if nothing else. And there's probably more, isn't there? I mean, you didn't risk being beaten up just to tell us that?"

"Damned right," Bernie grunted. Draining his glass, he held it out in hope of a refill. When Ellen displayed the empty bottle he sighed and set it by. "Yes, there is more. The confidence level is poor, but given the vagueness of the data it's as good as you can expect. I wish I could 'port you all the stages I've been through, so you could see how thorough I've been, but . . . Well, you said you didn't want it on-line to anywhere until it was rock-solid. That's why I came to tell you myself."

"When you get around to the actual telling . . ." Peter hinted.

"Oh, bock! What d'you think I'm doing?" Bernie rasped.

With a frown Claudia signalled a warning. Peter subsided. She was right. The poor growser must be suffering delayed shock. No wonder he was taking a long time to make himself clear.

"What's turned up *is*," the hacker continued at length, "one of the points your average flatfoot wouldn't think of. At that stage, you see, I still imagined that it was the Bill who had forestalled me. I decided to try sneaking in from the medical statistics direction."

Abruptly both Peter and Claudia were leaning forward tensely on their chairs.

"I searched for children reported born by artinsem during the relevant period—sharing the physical characteristics you described—subsequently involved in court proceedings as juveniles—and back-tracked from there to see whether there was any link between them that might indicate which clinic they derived from.

"Which there was. And what is more, there were enough physical descriptions, albeit in sketchy form with very low confidence, to hint at a common donor for them all."

"That's fantastic—" Claudia began. Bernie cut her short with an upraised hand.

"Just one problem. There are too many of 'em."

After a long pause Claudia said, "I'm not with you."

"Okay, okay, I'll spell it out. The clinic that the evidence points to is the Chinn-Wilkinson. But wasn't it among the most reputable of the lot?"

"Absolutely!"

"One of the clinics whose code of practice evolved into guidelines that are now internationally accepted?"

"I believe Dr. Chinn helped to draft them."

"In that case, like I said: there are too many of these kids. If they all stemmed from a single donor, there ought to be a maximum of ten. But we know of that many already. I just can't make myself believe that by this stage we've traced the lot. Can you?"

Pale, Claudia said, "I left a program running in the States to look for others. I haven't interrogated it lately, but it's meant to signal me if anything turns up. So maybe—"

"Maybe you have found them all? Sounds like negative evidence to me. What if the donor was servicing several clinics? I could imagine this kind of payment for a cheap thrill turning sort of addictive . . . Hello!" Bernie tensed, leaning forward on his chair. "Peter! Is something wrong?"

He had closed his eyes and was swaying. Alarmed, Ellen dropped to her knees at his side and clasped his hand.

But he waved her aside. "No, I'm all right," he said in a thin voice. "It's just that I suddenly realized who it is we're talking about."

And, with abrupt force, thumping fist into palm and staring around the room as though he had never seen it or them before: "Yes, of course! That's the growser I've been trying to remember! *Louis Parker!*"

*   *   *

For a long uneasy moment there was silence. Just as Claudia was about to speak up, however, Peter relaxed and gave a short laugh.

"Sorry about that. But—well, you remember I had a sort of association-fit the other day at the *Comet* office? I had something on the tip of my tongue and it wouldn't come out?"

Claudia gave a cautious nod.

"Remembering Dr. Grant was only half of what was on my mind. Bernie just added the missing bit of the puzzle."

"Did I?"—from the hacker. "What? *I* don't know."

"Too many kids!" Peter was chuckling with excitement by now. "You see . . . No, I'd better start at the beginning."

"You do that," Claudia instructed, and he drew a deep breath before continuing.

"It was this way. Most of the other donors at the clinic were medical or dental students like me, as I've already explained. But there was one who was a complete exception. He was older than we were, for one thing—must have been in his thirties, at least—and very un-English: tall, slim, elegant, dark-haired, olive-skinned with a neat black moustache at a time when they were out of fashion . . . I suppose if someone had asked I'd have guessed him to be Turkish, but in fact he was Armenian. Parker wasn't his original name, but I forget what—No, I don't, for someone told me! *Parikian!* Lord, it's coming back as though it were last week, and I swear I haven't thought about the guy in ten years!"

"Point!" said Bernie firmly.

"Point? Oh! Yes, I'm afraid I'm not making myself terribly clear, am I? Well, you see, when the partnership between Dr. Chinn and Dr. Wilkinson broke up, rumor had it that among the reasons was the fact that Dr. Wilkinson had allowed this guy to donate umpteen times. It was said that Louis was always broke, in spite of always being smartly dressed, or maybe because, so he'd charmed Dr. Wilkinson into letting him father more than his official ration, at five pounds a time or possibly more. It was also hinted that they were having an affair."

He leaned back in his chair, looking smug. "Well, there you have it."

"A suspicion," Claudia said after a pause.

"Yes, but— Grief, doesn't it fit? Bernie, you talked about these physical characteristics, right? Among the kids, I mean. Dark hair?"

"Yes, and darkish skin, or at any rate sallow. It does sound rather promising."

"Well, there you are!"—triumphantly. "Don't you realize the implications? If I'm right, there's one man out there who could have fathered all these children who can do terrible things and get away with them, and now I've hung a name on him!"

Soberly, Claudia ventured, "Peter, that goes without saying. But on the one hand you may be grasping at straws, and on the other—"

"A straw is better than nothing, isn't it?" Peter cut in. And, mastering his annoyance with an effort, added, "Sorry. Finish what you were going to say."

"Well . . . Well, what exactly are you expecting?"

"Grief, isn't it obvious?"

"Peter! *Shut up!*" Abruptly she was on her feet. "All right, I grant you this much—I have been talking as if there might be a common father for these kids I'm trying to investigate, and you think you've spotted the ideal candidate. As a result you're forcing me to confront the implications. First of all, assuming you're right about this Louis Parker, what do we do when we catch up with him? Compel him to undergo a gene-test? Interrogate him about the number of times he donated semen? If he was doing it through the Chinn-Wilkinson clinic, he presumably had no idea who the recipients were. We've satisfied ourselves that their records are shellbacked."

"Of course, of course, but . . ." Peter drew a deep breath. "Look, the point is—"

"The point," Bernie interjected unexpectedly, "is that this may be the first piece of concrete evidence we've acquired except via the PNC tap."

"Precisely!"

"Okay, I'll follow it up in the morning. Tonight I'm too tired. How can I trace this growser? Anything else you can tell me about him?"

"He was in computers," Peter said slowly. "It's coming back to me, more and more. In fact that must have been how he met Dr. Wilkinson. It was his company that she called in for a quote about computerizing the clinic, and Dr. Chinn took such a dogmatic stand against the idea that . . ." The words tailed away.

"That everyone assumed it was because he suspected she wanted to let the contract to her lover?" Claudia's tone was harsh.

"More or less."

"I see. Well, there's one step we can take right away. Let's find out whether he's on the phone."

"What? And ring him up?"

"I don't imagine he'd talk freely to strangers about his murky past, if it is murky." She shifted from harsh to caustic. "But it'd be a start."

"Let me!" offered Ellen, and was hitting the phone-directory code on Peter's computer keyboard before she had even sat down in the chair. Seconds later she reported, "No, there are lots of 'Parker L' but no entry for a 'Parker Louis.'"

"That's okay," Bernie grunted. "There are more efficient ways of tracing him—which I propose to do because if he's in computers he could well be the growser who's ahead of me at every step."

"If so," Claudia said slowly, "that means he knows who he is. He knows about his—well—uniqueness."

They contemplated that dismaying possibility for several seconds. At length, shrugging, Bernie pushed himself to his feet, saying, "That's for tomorrow. I'm worn out."

"Just a second!" Peter exclaimed.

"Yes?"

"Didn't you have something else to tell us?"

"Oh. Oh, so I did. I almost forgot. Assuming the kid in Italy that Claudia listed was in fact one of the cases we've been—ah—considering . . ."

It finally seemed to dawn on him that Ellen had been listening to the whole of the recent conversation, and maybe she hadn't been supposed to. His face was eloquent of anxiety.

But, with instant tact, the girl exclaimed, "Don't forget your coat! It should be dry by now!" And vanished.

"I like that kid of yours," Bernie murmured, sinking into his chair again. "Bright!"

"Never mind her!" Peter said impatiently. "We want to hear the rest."

"Where was I . . . ? Oh, of course. Yes, assuming the boy in Italy is one of the—*your* cases, then the association with the Chinn-Wilkinson clinic is virtually definite."

"How?"

"During the relevant period the clinic had exactly one Italian client, and the match is excellent."

Claudia blinked. "How can you be so sure?"

"Because—" Bernie broke off, looking surprised at himself. "Grief, I keep thinking I'd already told you, and I haven't, have I? Maybe being banged on the head sent my wits woolgathering." He touched his nape gingerly. "I located the medical data-bank the Chinn-Wilkinson used to use—security wasn't so tight when they were among its customers—and set a program to mouse around it on the assumption it's the one Dr. Grant told you about. And it is."

"Why didn't you say so earlier?" Peter exclaimed.

"Peter, for pity's sake!" Claudia reproached him. "The poor growser is still in shock! You ever been beaten up on the street?"

"Ah—well, yes, once or twice," Peter admitted, and subsided with what could have been meant for an apology.

"As far as I'm concerned," Claudia declared, "that's the best news we've had so far, and Bernie deserves our congratulations. Are you expecting any more revelations?"

"I'll do my best," the hacker sighed. "Ellen mentioned my coat—?"

She rushed back from the kitchen carrying it, still damp but otherwise spotless. Thanking her, he rose to put it on, and she turned to Peter.

"Dad, I have to get up for school, you know. Do you need me for anything else?"

Earlier she was eager to make herself scarce . . . Am I ever going to understand the female mind? Oh—sexist!

"Goodness, of course not!" he exclaimed, embracing her. She turned politely to Bernie and shook his hand, saying it was nice to have met him, gave Claudia a peck on the cheek, and disappeared.

As the door closed, Claudia said, "Bernie, want to share a cab?"

"No thanks. It isn't raining. I can walk."

"And risk another beating-up?"

"I don't expect them to attack me twice. That's not Special Branch's style."

"And if it wasn't Special Branch that did it—? Come along. I'll pay. Good night, Peter."

"Good night."

It took Peter a long time to get to sleep. When he eventually dropped off, he found his dreams haunted by a tall suave Armenian, offensively well dressed and reeking of expensive aftershave.

HELLO. I'M DAVID SHAY. YOU'RE SHEILA HUBBARD, aren't you?

Oh, featly! You know my name! But you don't know who I am.

At least I know what you've done. And I can guess a little about how you feel.

Featlier and featlier! All right, put it in one word.

Haunted?

You—you bocky . . . How the hell—? Cancel that! I don't believe in ghosts, I don't believe in hauntings, I don't believe in life beyond the grave! I'm a good agnostic, like I was brought up to be.

In which case, what makes you react so violently?

None of your bocky business!

Nonetheless what I suspect is this. Your victim was, after all, a highly trained professional killer, a Marine Commando.

You disposed of him with absolutely no trouble. Ever since, it's been as though some element of him has entered into your subconscious—not in any physical sense, but purely because after what you did the temptation to repeat your achievement has sometimes become more than you could bear—

Stop it! STOP IT! Or I'll—I'll—

You can't, Sheila. Not to me. Haven't you realized yet?

I . . . Oh, this is ridiculous!

Don't try and run away when you hear the truth. It won't work. You've got to face it sooner or later. How many times have you given in?

What?

I said: how many times have you given in? To the temptation. I know you have.

If you're so sure, why ask?

As I said, you've got to face the truth instead of running away. You thought keeping it a secret would suffice. But it isn't a secret.

Yes it is!

You can say that now I'm here, talking to you?

I . . . I suppose not. But how the hell did you find me?

Like finds like, one way or another. I'll explain later—that is, if you decide to be frank.

If I don't?

Look inside yourself for the answer. You know what becomes of those who oppose us.

. . . Us?

Precisely. Now will you tell me?

All—all right. After the first one, the one everybody heard about, I was terrified. I mean, I couldn't tell anybody, because obviously they would think I was insane, but I knew what I'd done, and . . . and I simply couldn't believe it. So I started to suspect myself of being crazy. In the end . . .

In the end, the only way of proving that you weren't was to use the power again?

Yes. Yes, exactly.

On—?

He was a reporter. A nasty, greedy, foul-mouthed slob of a reporter, working for the local paper, dreaming of making it into the big time, television maybe. He'd made up his mind that I'd murdered the—the one you know about. I think he was married to the growser's cousin—something like that. Anyway he felt he had a personal stake in the affair. What's more he hated my school and everything it stood for. He'd have liked to see it burned down and all the kids and teachers.

A ribbon on his coat?

Oh, yes! Soon as everybody else took to wearing them!

So—?

In the end it just got too much. I filched a bottle of gin and got a message to him to meet me—made him think he was going to get the inside track at last, the lowdown on the scandal of the school—and . . .

Persuaded?

Good word. Persuaded him to drink the lot and then drive home as fast as possible.

What did he hit?

Nothing. Ran his car off at a bend in the road beside the river, flat out, and sank in ten feet of water.

How did you feel after that?

I'd be lying if I said anything but "better!"

And how long was it before the next time?

What makes you so sure there was one?

You still didn't have anyone to tell.

No, that's true . . . All right. The next one was a missionary. Female type. She'd convinced herself that I must be a vessel of evil. And you know something? By that stage I was coming to the same conclusion. It was either that, or insanity, or—

Or?

Or nothing. I didn't mean to say that. I meant to say that actually at first I welcomed her arrival in my life. If I could find—well—sanctuary from my fears about myself by converting to a religion, adopting some system of belief that would make sense of what I was and what I'd done, I felt I'd be all right again, able to face myself, able to cope . . . Do you understand?

Perfectly. And I'm the only person you've ever met who might. She didn't—the woman missionary.

You don't make that a question.

No.

You're right anyway. I never met many religious people before, you know. Oh, for the sake of appearances there's a chaplain at the school, but he only comes when sent for, to—heh!—we say "service" the kids whose families insist. There aren't many of those . . . But this one was thick, know what I mean? She knew the answer—her mind was made up—and her entire goal in life was to make me swallow her preaching.

You didn't.

How could I take her seriously after I discovered that she honestly thought the Bible was written in English?

Mm-hm.

Doesn't that surprise you?

Not at all. I've run across lots of similar cases, particularly in the States.

Don't be so bocky patronizing!

I'm not going to apologize for having had a more varied and interesting life than you so far. What did you do to the missionary?

Oh . . . In the end I—I persuaded her to put the love of God to the test. Wasn't hard.

And—?

They found her hanging in the old stables behind the school.

After which you felt better again?

No!

Explain why not.

I don't know why I'm telling you all this. I mean, I never met you before.

You do know why. You knew from the moment I entered the room.

Yes. Yes, I suppose I did, really. Just didn't want to—well, like you said, face the truth. I still don't want to.

But you're going to.

. . . Yes.

So explain why this time you didn't feel better.

Because . . . Because of the responsibility.

What sort of responsibility?

If you don't know, who does? Didn't you see the TV news

today? This crazy kid who shot the archbishop? You couldn't hear what he was shouting, but it wasn't hard to read it off his lips.

"I'm a fucking Christian, aren't I? And I'm sick of you making out that wogs and niggers are as good as me!"

You did watch.

Of course.

And was yesterday's news any better, or the day before's? Do you expect anything better tomorrow?

This is what you mean when you talk about responsibility?

What else?

"The time is out of joint. Oh curséd spite—"

"That ever I was born to put it right." Yes. Of course the idea's completely crazy. Yet I can't escape from it. I seem to have some sort of—of power, and everybody says I'm more intelligent than average, and . . . Well, what the hell else am I to do with my life? Now tell me I'm off my rocker. Tell me I'm a megalomaniac.

Not at all.

Stop messing about. I can't put the world to rights on my bocky tod.

True. But you aren't on your tod. Not any more. Coming?

Wait a moment! What about Ingrid—my mother? What'll Joe say? He pays my fees here. Douglas, come to that. He'll raise hell!

It's all taken care of.

No, I don't believe it. You can't possibly want to be lumbered with me! I mean, I've told you—God knows why, but I suppose you've been pulling the trick on me that I can work on other people, and you knew enough to track me down during my period when it doesn't function properly—I've told you what I've done! I've killed three people, don't you understand?

I've killed, too. And I think it won't have been the only time. Now come along. There's a car waiting.

Where are you taking me?

The only place in all the world where you can stop pretending.

You're watching TV Plus. Time for Newsframe.

Once again a computer-driven crash on the world's major stock exchanges has led to a record number of bankruptcies. Recently the commonest cause of them in Britain has been inability to meet mortgage repayments following redundancy; however, last month private bankruptcies were exceeded by commercial ones, which averaged fourteen per working day.

Returning from his triumphal world tour, General Sir Hampton Thrower told a cheering crowd at Heathrow, quote: "Since an Englishman's home is his castle, he needs a home, and any system that doesn't guarantee him one but hands out cheap accommodation to lazy, irresponsible aliens . . ."

FOOD SHORTAGES THIS WINTER, PARTICULARLY IN view of the potato blight, were certain to be even worse than last year, but the government-approved news on radio, BBC-TV and ITV disguised the truth according to orders. Only TV Plus was still making a pretense of objectivity. The first deaths from starvation had followed an unseasonable cold snap, but although the *Comet* risked describing them for what they were, the rest of the media concentrated on the usual pabulum. Jake, Peter felt, was doing his best, even though he resorted more and more often to the bottle, while his backers were among the few people who still cared about the once-vaunted freedom of the press, being prepared to lavish money on defending their correspondents from prosecutions ordered by the government. How long, though, could they hold out? It had become an offense, as of the present parliamentary session, to publish "anti-patriotic" news. When Peter rang TV

Plus to ask why he wasn't receiving any more assignments, he was told apologetically that they no longer dared to hire him. However, if he had any leads their own staff could follow up, they would guarantee a finder's fee, if he didn't mind being paid in cash . . .

A pittance. But he had to grab it.

Despite its apparent political neutrality, Jake seemed to have given up on the story of the criminal children. Without putting it into so many words, he appeared to have decided that the project was a waste of time. When the criminals had taken power, what point was there in worrying about a bunch of kids?

"And can you blame him?" Peter said bitterly to Claudia and Bernie when they next met. Ellen had invited them all for dinner; she was turning into an excellent and ambitious cook, capable of conjuring tasty dishes out of unpromising ingredients. Thank goodness, as Bernie said, for those who remembered what to do with odds and ends, because they had inherited the tradition of peasant poverty and didn't insist on being fed from cans and freezer packs.

The cost of which was soaring as North Sea oil ran out ahead of the predicted schedule.

"Jake, you mean?" Claudia sighed, reaching for her glass. It held beer: homemade. Anything more expensive was now beyond Peter's means. Last week he had offered TV Plus a promising scandal concerning sausages made from AIDS-infected pork supplied to public hospitals by a prominent supporter of the government, but it had been scotched under the Official Secrets Act. So his fee had been withheld.

Sometimes he had considered discarding the red-white-and-blue ribbon he still wore, but it was too risky now to go without one—at least, if you were white. Watching Ellen as she cleared away the dishes, humming to herself, he wondered how much longer she would be able to wear hers at school, before it was torn away on the grounds that she wasn't British.

Correction: English. Here in London schoolyard gangs of self-styled "Cockneys" were starting to attack the Scots, Welsh and Irish, along with the—what had that fanatic said

who shot the archbishop?—the "wogs and niggers" who were
inferior to him, a *white* Christian . . .

He roused on realizing that someone had spoken: Bernie?
Yes.

"At least Jake seems determined to go down with flying
colors. You heard about the petrol-bomb attack?"

"What?"

"This afternoon. The *Comet* has this display window at
street-level, right? Some yobbos in a stolen car threw a fire-
bomb at it. No damage worth mentioning, luckily. But still
what you might call a less than healthy trend."

Smiling broadly at the success of her meal, Ellen returned
from the kitchen and sat down on the sofa next to Peter. She
had become a part of their group, and there was no longer any
question of her retreating to her room.

"Sometimes I'm tempted to emigrate," Bernie went on.
"But where on earth could I go? Xenophobia in the States is
peaking again and in any case the country's due to go bust,
same as Britain—Canada's in the throes of another fit of
Francophilia—Australia's trying to turn itself into an anti-Jap-
anese bulwark and inside a generation it's liable to be as racist
as South Africa . . . As for the rest of Europe, they're on such
an anti-American kick they don't want to know people who
speak only English. Even the Dutch and Danes are going back
to German as a foreign language."

"Keep going," Claudia said tartly. "You've left out the
Arab world, for starters—"

"And Asia!" Ellen chimed in. "Who'd want to live in India
when there's practically a civil war going on?"

Peter started. It was the first time, to his recollection, that
she had voluntarily mentioned her mother's country of origin.
But all he could read on her pretty face was simple sadness, as
though at far too early an age she had grown resigned to the
waywardness of humanity.

What an inheritance for a teenage kid!

After that, for a long while, there seemed little left to say.
It was only after Ellen had re-adopted her hostess role and
topped up their glasses that they reverted to the topic they
were supposed to be discussing. Typically, and in a typically

caustic tone, it was Claudia who set the ball rolling.

"What I can't help wondering," she said, addressing Bernie, "is why, since you've gotten so far, you can't get any further, especially with the tracing of Louis Parker. If you see what I mean."

Sourly he replied, "I do, and I wish I could explain. You'll have to take my word for it, I'm afraid. My best guess is that this growser caught on before you did."

Peter leaned forward. "So you agree that he's the likeliest candidate?"

"Are there any others? But—okay, I have to grant that on the basis of what you told me he seems like a prime suspect. Physical appearance—the fact that he was working in computers—and the fact that he's either dead or in hiding—yes, it does add up to a fair case."

"In hiding?" Claudia stabbed.

"Or, I suppose, out of the country. But I've run a program to search every accessible phone directory and now I'm following up with one to search every postal reference. I do mean *every*. It's costing an arm, a leg and a prick, and the balls come next! Jake isn't going to be at all happy when he sees the final bill—Oh, excuse me, Ellen."

She gave a crowing laugh, leaning back and crossing her legs. Of late, as though out of defiance, she had taken to wearing traditional Indian garb, and the sari she had on, bought second-hand at a Saturday jumble-sale, was of shiny lavender fabric that caught reflections from the wall-lights.

"Never mind! I hear far worse things at school!"

Peter put his arm around her and drew her close. He was becoming more and more attached to this unwanted daughter.

"In spite of all," he said, addressing Bernie, "there's no trace?"

"Louis Parker might as well have dug himself a hole, climbed in and pulled it after him."

"So that blocks off one approach. Claudia, what about you? You suggested contacting ex-employees of fertility clinics. Did you get anywhere?"

She looked at him steadily.

"You told me it was hopeless. Remember? You said there were too many and there was no reason to expect—"

"Grief!" Peter burst out. "I was only pointing out the difficulties—"

"You didn't give *me* that impression," Claudia cut in coldly.

Bernie uttered a loud sigh, setting by his empty tankard. "Sometimes," he muttered, "I wonder what you lot are up to. When you hit on an idea, why the hell don't you try it out? *I* did!"

Embarrassed, Peter and Claudia looked a question at him.

"Aren't the former staff of the Chinn-Wilkinson among the first people you should have talked to? Frankly, I thought you had done!"

Peter said defensively, "It was a long time ago, and I don't remember many of their names—"

"Oh, shit," Bernie muttered. "They're on record. For instance, who was Dr. Chinn's head nurse?"

"Ah . . ." For a moment Peter hesitated. Abruptly he snapped his fingers. "Sister Higgins! Thank you for reminding me! And why the hell didn't I think of her before? She was getting on, but she could still be alive!"

"And you didn't tell *me*?" Claudia burst out. "Why, I've been sitting around chewing my nails! I could have—"

"Do you remember Sister Higgins's first name?" Ellen put in, just in time to defuse a full-blown quarrel. She had risen from her seat and stood with one hand poised above the computer keyboard.

Calming himself with an effort, Peter said, "Uh—yes! Marian! I'm not sure whether it's Mari-*an* or Mari-*on*, but I do remember that's what Dr. Chinn used to call her."

Dropping into the chair before the board, Ellen called up the telephone directory. They all waited in silence until she said, "Sorry. Nothing for Higgins Marian spelt either way."

"Not to worry!" Bernie cut in. "If you—"

"I know!"—with abrupt annoyance, swinging to face him. "What?"

"What you were going to say."

"That being—?"

"You can access out-of-date directories. If she ever had a phone in her own name in the London area, even if she was entered as plain 'Higgins M,' the exchange still knew she was

Marian. If she's moved elsewhere, there's a contact facility for emergency use, for instance if she's been taken ill and relatives are trying to get in touch. Isn't that what you were going to explain?"

Bernie froze for a moment, disconcerted, half in and half out of his chair. At length he subsided with a grunt.

"Keep at it, lady. You have the makings of a hacker. Did you write the search program yourself?"

"No, I didn't bother. I found it in real time. I don't have too much to do in the evenings nowadays."

Which was true, Peter reminded himself ruefully. Even those of her boyfriends who had seemed most enthusiastic a few weeks ago had now abandoned her. The—infection? Yes! The *infection* of what was suddenly being called "Throwerism" had struck that deep that fast, like a surgeon's lance releasing a flood of pus from an ulcer. Even the "nice" kids that the friendly minder Jeannette took care of after school had imitated their parents' hardening intolerance. Had it not been for Ellen's thrice-a-week cleaning job . . .

Overwhelmed with dismay, he was all set to reproach himself in public for neglecting his daughter when she cried, "Gotcha!"

Just in time . . . !

They crowded around the machine, staring. There it was:

"HIGGINS Marian Martha. Sex: F. UK citizen with right of residence. Marital status: S. Birthplace: Huyton, Lancs. Parents: HIGGINS William Brian; HIGGINS Karen née Thwaites. Age last b'day: 73. Profession: nursing sister (ret'd). PNC status—"

"*She* had a police record?" Peter burst out. "I can't believe it!"

Claudia hushed him as the display scrolled upward.

"—suspected involvement in unauthorized abortion/s. No confirmation. Latest reported domicile—"

"That's what we want!" Peter rasped, but Ellen was ahead of him, and had already dumped the data into local memory, wiped the screen, and ordered the address to be printed.

"You do have the makings of a hacker!" Bernie said approvingly. "Peter, does that sound like her?"

"Absolutely," Peter murmured as he looked at the printout. "Just one problem."

"What?"

"I happen to recognize this address. It was one—"

"Don't tell me!"—from Claudia. "One that you went to while you were working for *Continuum*?"

"Yes, dammit!"

"So?"

"It's a hospice for people suffering from Alzheimer's. If that's where she's wound up, we don't stand much chance of getting any data out of Sister Higgins."

"Maybe she's on the staff—"

"At seventy-three?"

"Okay. 'Six impossible things before breakfast . . .' But I'll look into it, anyway. I only wish you'd thought of it before!"

Peter bridled, prepared to blame her for his own oversight. Once more, in the nick of time, Ellen intervened, offering the last of the homemade beer, and the atmosphere calmed.

When the others had left, Peter so far recovered his self-possession as to knock on Ellen's door and, on her invitation, enter. Rising drowsily from her pillow, she looked a question.

"I'm sorry," he muttered, brushing her cheek with his fingers. "I'm going through a bad patch."

"Oh, I know," was her reply. "But I am doing what I can to make it easier, aren't I?"

"Yes!"

"That's all right, then. Good night . . . Hey, just a moment!"

He had already turned toward the door. Checking, he glanced back.

"You heard what Bernie said? I have the makings of a hacker?"

"Yes, of course."

"What do you think?"

Peter hesitated. Was it good or bad to be a hacker in this strange and changing world? He opted for good.

"I'm sure he meant it as a compliment. What's more, I think he was absolutely right."

"That's what I hoped you'd say. G'night . . ."

Her words dissolved into a sigh, and before he closed the door again she was asleep.

WITH THE ONSET OF AUTUMN, NIGHT BY NIGHT THE mist grew denser that drifted up from the stagnant, filthy river. Older folk, imprisoned at home with nothing but TV for company, abandoned the city's streets to youngsters like Terry Owens and his mates—except, of course, that there was in fact no one like Terry—sporting their pro-Thrower ribbons. A few had had their foreheads tattooed with Union Jacks in token of patriotic fervor. Rio had considered that, but Terry had dissuaded him.

Nightly, in consequence, black families huddled in fear of the bricks and petrol-bombs that might be hurled into their living rooms; Indian and Pakistani shopkeepers replaced their windows with armor-glass—if they could afford to, and if they could find someone willing to sell it to them; otherwise they boarded up with corrugated iron—and the proprietors of Chinese takeaways installed closed-circuit video-cameras recording images every ten seconds on a VCR secure behind a solid wall.

Not, of course, that the police gave an ounce of dogshit for that sort of evidence. But there was a brotherhood now, that had learned to tell Europeans apart, and on occasion even the cowed BBC managed to mention—at least hint at—the way the Chinese community had come to admire their mainland cousins, rather than their families in or from Hong Kong. As for their opinion of their former overlords, who had so cheaply sold their homeland . . . !

In addition, the smouldering warlets of the subcontinent were finding an outlet in most British cities. Sikhs and Tamils and Bengalis and Pakistanis and members of other groups known beforehand only to specialists were venting bitter grudges in this foreign land, and woe betide whoever stood in their way.

As for the Cypriots, whether Greek or Turkish, scarcely a day went by without another murder, save when they united against the British if they tried to interfere. By now the police had given them up for lost, as they had the black areas of most post-industrial towns.

All that was the background to the arrival on Terry's manor of the gray Rolls Royce.

When he first heard about the silent, splendid car, as gray and glistening as the mists through which it prowled, his reaction had been one of scorn.

"Lose it, you bocky cank! Who'd bring a Roller into streets like these?"

Rio ventured, "After cunt, maybe?"

"Shit! You can afford a Roller, you can afford a better class of slag!"

"They do say," Taff murmured, "there are growsers who can only get turned on by dirty scrubbers."

"Hah!" Terry exclaimed. "Didn't know you were a psychologist!"

That made Taff blush and turn away. Briefly Terry exulted in his power to control these older, stronger boys.

Then Barney said obstinately, "I don't like it, Terry."

"Who's asking you to?"

"I don't like it!" he repeated. "No one knows who's in it, get me? It's loaded with these very heavy tints, like the cars the Mafia use in America. Like on TV."

"I don't watch TV too much. You know that."

"Yeah, I know. But"—with increasing confidence—"maybe you should. Sometimes, at any rate."

"Look," Terry said with forced patience, "if the tints are that heavy, how can the driver see in the dark?"

"Got these infrared lights," Taff countered. "You put on these special glasses——"

"But the tints on a Roller are supposed to keep out both infrared and ultraviolet," Terry cut in.

His oppos looked at him doubtfully for a long moment. At last Rio said, "Been checking 'em out, have you, Terry? Thinking of buying one?"

Taff supplied, "And hiring one of us to drive it?"

Terry was shaken. Was his grip on these three slipping? If so, how? Why? He blustered, "Look, all I said was that I don't reckon a Roller would keep coming back here!"

"Well, there it is," Rio grunted, pointing to the corner of the next street. And, as Terry swung around, added, "I'm for home."

"Me too!"

"Me too!"

And they were gone, leaving Terry to confront the car alone amid the swirling mist.

It did nothing, save purr past him at a walking pace. And duly vanished into mist again.

Yet it left him with a sense of terrible anxiety.

Half the night he lay awake wondering who could have sent it. Obviously its purpose was to frighten him—by now, his universe revolved so totally about himself he could not have envisaged any other possibility.

But why a Roller—? No, that question answered itself, and instantly. Air-conditioned. Sealed against the outer world, its occupants might also be immune to his personal magnetism. (That was the latest of several terms he had found applicable, and the one he preferred, inasmuch as it sounded solid, physical, concrete.)

And behind the dark glass . . . who? Agents of a tong, summoned via the grapevine by long-suffering Mr. Lee at the Chinese takeaway—or, more likely, by his wife? Or distant relatives of Mr. Lal the newsagent, expert killers who owed some kind of vendetta-style loyalty to his family? Or someone local, furious because he, Terry, unawares, had trespassed on the turf of an adult gang already running a protection racket in the area?

On the whole it was the last possibility that scared him worst. He had only a vague impression of what a tong did to those who offended one of its members, and a longstanding if now rather faint belief, acquired at school, that brown-skinned people such as Indians and Pakistanis and Bangladeshis lacked bottle and were consequently soft. But as to his own kind . . .

Well, notoriously, in this town they used cut-throat razors, and with skill.

Matters grew worse when Rio disappeared.

"Where *is* the bocky cank?"

"Last I heard," Taff said, having glanced nervously up and down the street from their usual meeting-place, "he was—uh —seen talking to the growser in the Roller."

"You're shooting me!"

"Straight as I stand here!" Taff asserted. "Last night when you wouldn't come the pub with us. Barney got in a barney" —it was a stale joke but good for a grin—"and Rio slid when someone bust a bottle. After, this slag touting on the next corner said she'd seen him."

"Doing—?" The tension in Terry's gut was unbearable.

"The Roller stopped and someone in it talked to him. I told you!"

"And—?"

"Today he's not around."

"We better go turn over his drum!"

Rio's home was in a refurbished but still detested high-rise block. His mother having walked out a year or two ago, his father was living with a younger woman, pretty but stupid. Despite Terry's best efforts the couple were evasive. All they were willing to say was that the boy had gone south—maybe to London.

Waiting for the lift after they quit the flat, Terry grew aware that his "mates" were looking at him in a new way. Never before had they shown such open distrust.

His confidence began to evaporate, and they sensed it.

"I think Rio had the right idea," Taff said as the lift arrived. Getting in, Terry tried to counter, with a forced laugh.

"Think he hitched a ride in the Roller? Think he's gone for rent in Park Lane?"

Ordinarily, among youths who sported the red-white-and-blue, reference to being kept by a rich homosexual would provoke instant fury. Terry had relied on that reflex. This time, to his dismay, it didn't work. Taff and Barney merely exchanged glances and gave a simultaneous shrug. Terry's heart sank into his traditional lace-up boots.

The lift arrived, and he relaxed a little. In a confined and airless space—he didn't know why—his personal magnetism seemed to work the best. Wheedling, he said, "I didn't mean what I just said about Rio. I know as well as you, he'd never go for rent in London!"

And made the mistake of reaching out for Taff's hand.

"No, he wouldn't! But you would, wouldn't you?" Taff blasted, and kicked him on the right shin just as the lift reached the ground floor. Barney, ever glad of the chance, added a second kick, accurately beneath the kneecap, and the two of them ran off laughing into the foggy night.

"Wait! Wait . . . !"

But it was no use. They were out of earshot, and there was no one else around save a tired, middle-aged woman, clinging to a half-filled shopping bag and afraid to risk the lift unless she was alone.

Cursing, Terry staggered past her and out into the dim of evening. The sky was cloudy, most of the streetlamps, as usual, were broken, and the only response to his shouting of Taff's and Barney's names was alarm among those other local residents brave enough to be abroad after dark.

No. Not the only response.

For, as he hobbled to the edge of the roadway, staring left and right for any sign of the mates he had so long relied on, a huge gray silent car whispered out of mist, and stopped.

A rear door opened. A voice spoke to him—only a few syllables: "Get in! We'll take you home."

But that was enough to convey a mass of alarming information. For one thing, the words were in an American accent. Among the chimeras that had haunted Terry since he first heard about the mysterious Rolls Royce, persecution by the Stateside Mafia was the least—yet, on the instant, thanks to years of conditioning by the American programs on TV that he affected to despise, he was prepared to believe it and feel powerless. For another, the voice was that of a boy not much older than himself, but it was going to be an authoritative baritone when its owner became adult, whereas Terry's—as he had realized after listening to recordings that his "friends" had made—would remain a light tenor.

A snatch recalled from a news bulletin abruptly came to dominate his mind: *The American occupation forces in Libya* . . . With all that that implied regarding war!

Terry was on the verge of screaming when his hand was grasped and he was drawn into the womblike car.

"So, you see, Mr. Owens—Mrs. Owens—there is no real alternative, is there?"

Where am I? What's going on? Blurrily, as though lost in the river-mist that enveloped the street outside, Terry strove to recover his self-possession. He was in his parents' living room; the first clue he had, before he managed to open his eyes, was the smell of over-brewed tea, which his mother would reflexively have offered. When he looked around, he saw that cupfuls of the precious liquid were cooling and growing a skin. Shameful waste, when tea cost so much, was such a luxury, was due—so rumor held—to be rationed, along with other oriental goods like rice.

But that was somewhere else, and in another time. Terry anchored himself to here and now, and found a boy his own age talking to his parents, backed up (on the two-seat sofa near the window) by an incredibly well-dressed couple both tanned to a degree even Rio couldn't achieve, using the best artificial creams . . . It dawned of a sudden: they must be the owners of the Roller.

I'm trapped. I don't know how. I can only admire who did it!

He listened again. The boy was saying:

"Of course, if it were to become known that a kid your Terry's age had been masterminding a protection racket, the consequences would be terrible. Your competence as parents would be called in question, to begin with. Our present government, as you are well aware"—as though by reflex, he stroked the red-white-blue ribbon he wore in his lapel—"lays great stress on parental responsibility, even though they make certain allowances for disadvantaged citizens . . ."

His parents were nodding, even though—no! Because they understood the police-type code: *It's all right for our sort to go around smashing windows, stuffing shit through letterboxes and burning kids in bed, but as soon as the bocky blacks and wogs hit back the Bill comes down like a landslide . . . and good luck to them!*

This was Terry's language, the one he had been brought up to. He nodded vigorous approval.

And yet, at the same time, was aware of something very wrong indeed. The air in this room—and it wasn't the smell of stewed tea . . .

No good. He couldn't work it out. He could only sit back and go on nodding.

"So, for the benefit of your neighbors, shopkeepers like yourself, such as your newsagent Mr. Lal, and Mr. Lee at the takeaway, who provide such valuable services for the community—"

Just a moment!

Those being precisely the people Terry, with help from Barney and Taff and Rio, had been struggling to force into line, he felt impelled to jump up and yell!

And found he couldn't.

With the sweetest possible smile, the boy-stranger (at some stage Terry had registered that he was called David) took his arm. He said, "Oh, don't be so scared! Come along—the car's outside."

Me? Scared? I've had the widest boys on the manor eating out of my hand since the year dot!

And yet he was. He was shaking, head to foot. He was crying, and afraid he might—well—wet his pants!

How? Why?

But as to crying, he saw as he cast a last glance over his shoulder that both his parents were in tears.

Yet at the same time laughing. Laughing with sheer relief!

For the first time the question crossed his mind:

Who am I? What kind of person?

* * *

In the incredibly comfortable back seat of the Roller, like all the three-piece suits in local shops that he had thought of conning into his home except that the living room was too small, he tried to frame the question.

But could not. He could only say, "What happened to Rio and my other friends?"

The boy beside him, the one called David, said, "They weren't your friends. They were your tools."

Terry could not avoid a giggle, which David froze with a glare.

"You've had your fun," he said. "Now you have to do your duty."

"What?"—trying not to laugh again.

"Shut up! There's not much time!"

You're watching TV Plus. Newsframe follows.

Car-bombs this morning exploded outside five Malaysian embassies in Western European capitals including London, causing extensive damage and many casualties. In telephone calls to newspapers, TV and radio stations, a group using the name Free Singapore Army claimed responsibility. More in a moment.

In a radio interview, General Thrower said, quote, "It's intolerable that a petty squabble half a world away should be made the excuse for destroying British lives and British property." Asked what countermeasures he could suggest . . .

THE CLOCKS HAD GONE BACK AN HOUR OVER THE weekend, so this evening it was dark when Ellen returned home from her cleaning job under the suspicious gaze of those who still belonged to the Neighborhood Watch. Lately such organizations had again been condemned by the government as a plot to obstruct the police in the execution of their duty, and their signs had vanished from all save a few defiant windows. (The other day Peter had confessed to being ashamed of not having joined the Watch in this street, as he had intended when he moved here, but he wasn't going to now.)

Moreover it had begun to drizzle. She was eager to get indoors. As she was fumbling for her door-key, however, she heard a faint mew. Glancing around in the gloom, she spotted a small tabby cat, very thin, sheltering under a bush beside the path.

"Poor thing!" she exclaimed, slinging her shoulder-bag behind her and dropping to a crouch. "Here, kitty! Here, kitty!"

It would have liked to flee, but it was too weak. Resignedly it let her carry it indoors.

Peter came home fuming, having spent another fruitless day in vain attempts to interest someone in yet another disaster story—the only sort of lead, it seemed, that he was picking up these days. This time it concerned a painkiller banned in the United States and several Western European countries but freely available in Britain and the Third World. (Nowadays he was often tempted to say, "The rest of the Third World . . .") The evidence that pregnant women who took it bore deformed and mentally handicapped babies was almost at the thalidomide level, but nobody would pay him to investigate. Even Jake had shrugged and said it was out of the question.

In addition, on the way home he had counted five fish-and-chip shops displaying hopeful "For Sale" signs. Driven out of business, of course, by the potato shortage. What with one thing and another, therefore, he was in a pretty bloody mood.

"What's that?" he rasped as he entered the kitchen and saw the scrawny cat lying on a scrap of old carpet near the stove.

"It's a cat, of course," Ellen answered, not looking up from her attempts to feed it. Tonight they were having liver and onions for dinner, offal still being comparatively cheap. She had cut a few shreds of the liver and was offering them in her fingers. Also she had put down a dish of milk.

"I think it's hurt," she added.

"More likely ill," Peter grunted, taking the jug of home-made beer from the fridge. "And probably alive with fleas! Did you have to bring it into the house?"

For an instant she seemed on the verge of exploding. Then she changed her mind, as the cat accepted a mouthful of the liver and essayed a feeble purr by way of thanks.

Rising, wiping her hands, she turned to her father. "Dad, don't be like that!" she pleaded. "Let me try and rescue the poor thing! If I can, it'll be company for me when I'm home alone."

You don't have to be ...

But the words died. Didn't have to be? That wasn't true. Fewer and fewer of her friends from school, boys or girls, were willing to be seen in her company, for fear of reprisals from the Throwers ...

Pressure, of course. But encouraged from the top.

And, speaking of pressure—

"All right," he sighed. "You can keep it overnight, but tomorrow it goes to the vet for a thorough check, okay?"

Somehow, when she turned her melting eyes on him, he found it impossible to resist her. Which wasn't too surprising. All his life he'd been a sucker for beautiful sad girls. Just so had Kamala attracted his attention, having been cruelly jilted by a former lover. It looked as though Ellen had inherited at least one of her mother's traits ...

She kissed him smackingly on the cheek. "Thank you so much!" she cried. "Dinner will be ready in half an hour! What's more, I found some potatoes. Do you want chips or mash?"

"With—?"

"I told you this morning! Liver and onions!"

"So you did ... All right, mash."

"Right. Got to keep down the intake of fried food, hm? Eat better, live longer..." And her face changed magically to a mask of misery. "Not that I know why anyone should want to."

"Ellen darling, what in the world—?"

For suddenly tears were flowing down her cheeks.

"It *is* the world," she forced out, turning away to seize a tissue. "All the bad things that are on the news every day, worse than my most awful nightmares! Did you hear about the train crash?"

"What train crash?"

"At Manchester this afternoon. It was on the radio—I heard it when I first came in. No, don't turn on the telly"—as by reflex he moved to do so. "I don't want to see the pictures. People were crushed alive, squashed into pulp! They said something went wrong with the computer that controls the signals . . ."

She was recovering. After a final dab at her eyes she discarded the tissue.

"Sorry," she mumbled at last. "It's just that it made me think of what must have happened in the plane crash that—that burned down my old home."

It was the first time in weeks that she had made direct reference to her mother's death. Peter put a comforting arm around her, at a loss for anything to say.

"And there's a message from Claudia," Ellen went on after a pause. "She's ill. In hospital."

"Oh, no! What's wrong?" He remembered that she had complained of feeling unwell recently, but since the story that had seemed so promising was completely stagnant he had allowed himself to drift out of touch for several days.

"Codworm."

"What—? Oh. No, don't tell me." Peter felt his mouth set in a grim line. "I know about codworm. And it's nasty."

"Yes, it sounds awful. I looked it up. Its medical name is anisakiasis and you catch it from eating raw fish."

"Or cheap fish improperly prepared."

"It said that, too."

"Will she have to have an operation?"

"I don't think so. They're giving her a—a vermifuge, is that right?"

"Yes, quite right. But is she going to be in hospital for long?"

"A week at least, she said. I don't mean she actually said. She didn't phone up, just left an email message."

"Then I'd better send a get-well card in the morning. I don't suppose she has an email terminal beside her bed."

A faint whimpering noise emanated from the cat. Turning, they saw it trying to rise and head for the door.

"I suppose I'd better let it out," Ellen said after a moment. "I hope it doesn't run away..."

It didn't, but came gratefully back into the warm and dry. And, just as it returned, the phone rang.

"Bernie. Can I drop around? I need to talk."

How can I say no?

But what Peter mainly wanted to say—only he couldn't find the proper words—was this, to Ellen: *Yes, you poor kid! We've messed up the world for you, haven't we? Me, I envied the generation just before mine, who had all the fun of the permissive society, when you could shrug off a dose of the clap or even pox and carry right on screwing. Then came AIDS... And now there's a sense of universal doom. What if those Tibetan terrorists really have captured a load of nuclear waste? It's been denied, but who believes governments any more? If some crazy dictator in the Third World gets hold of nuclear weapons, and they keep talking about India and Pakistan and the Malaysians, not to mention the South Americans —or if it's true about the ozone layer being destroyed, and I suspect it is—or if the loss of the Amazon rain-forests really means we're running short of oxygen—or if poisons in the food we eat are really due to cut our life-expectancy—or if the tailored bacteria we're releasing to the environment are as imperfect as our computer programs, another of which just broke down and ruined a major Japanese bank—or if our squandering of fossil fuel is really going to melt the icecaps ...then all we can say to our children is, "We're very sorry!"*

And a fat lot of good that will do!

Meditatively, as Ellen busied herself at the stove, he said, "You know, years ago I read about a mother who cured her daughter of making a mess. The kid was careless and kept knocking things over, and thought it was enough to say, 'I'm sorry!'"

Ellen glanced around with large dark puzzled eyes. Suddenly Peter felt it very important to complete the story and put its point across.

"So one day when she knocked a jugful of milk all over the table and the carpet, her mother handed her a tea towel—tied it around her head like a turban—and also a stick. She said 'Right, now you're a magician, and you've got a wand. Wave it over the spilt milk and say the magic word "sorry"!' And, of course . . ."

"Of course the mess was still there," Ellen said in a brisk tone. "So?"

"So that's what I'd like to do to all the politicians and economists and businessmen and—*all* those bocky canks! Because it's not enough to say sorry to you kids that we're leaving to clear up the mess."

"Don't worry," she answered, piling richly scented fried onions on to plates, adding the grilled liver, scraping every trace of the precious mashed potatoes from the saucepan, producing cutlery and mustard to go with the food.

He blinked at her. "What on earth do you mean? How can I help worrying?"

"We kids may not be as willing as they think," she answered enigmatically. "I mean, to sort out other people's mess . . . Shall we eat? If Bernie's coming, we don't have much time."

At least this time the hacker arrived without muddy smears and a black eye, though the drizzle had turned to rain and the rain was, as ever, filthy. Accepting a beer, he sat down in what had become his customary chair.

"You heard about Claudia?" he said.

"Yes."

"Selling fish that contains live anisakiais larvae is illegal in all EEC countries."

"Maybe she contracted it in America—"

"The symptoms, including vomit tinged with blood, come on within a few hours. I've been checking."

"Then she must have lunched at a sushi bar with sloppy standards of hygiene! Lord, do I have to tell you how the government has cut back on food inspectors? If there had been another series of *Continuum* that would have been one of the subjects we tackled."

"Then I shouldn't have to repeat what I just said. It is *illegal* to sell fish containing live anisakiais larvae."

Peter stood rock-still for a second. Then he whistled.

"Got my point, have you?" Bernie grunted. "Even if she did catch it in a Japanese restaurant—and we dare not of course risk offending the Japanese, not so long as we're begging to be readmitted to their economic sphere—the owner should nonetheless have received a call from the Bill and been ordered to prove his premises were not the source of the infection. It's a notifiable condition. The hospital should have reported it immediately."

"And they didn't?"

Bernie shook his head. "Security on police reports from hospitals is so lax, they're practically public domain. It wasn't done."

"Well, they are terribly overworked," Peter murmured. "I suppose someone forgot."

"Or else Claudia doesn't have codworm at all."

There was a pause. Eventually Peter said in a cold, thin voice, "Go on. Spell it out. I don't think I'm going to like it, but—well, spell it out."

From the inside pocket of his jacket the hacker produced a slip of paper, a computer printout. "Here. Take a look at this. I'm not supposed to have it, of course, but . . . Hey, did Claudia get to see Sister Higgins?"

Scrutinizing the printout and having to move it closer to a lamp, remembering that he had promised himself glasses some time soon—only until he found more work he couldn't pay for a pair, since they were no longer available free on the National Health Service—Peter grunted, "Yes, and she is a patient at the hospice, not a member of staff. What's more she's completely gaga and not expected to live more than a few months . . . Grief! Is this for real?"

Crumpling the paper in his agitation, he stared at Bernie.

"Far as I know," the hacker sighed. "At least I picked it up from an authentic source."

"So she doesn't have codworm!"

Ellen had been in the kitchen washing up. Returning in time to catch the last words, she demanded an explanation.

Summing up briefly, Peter rushed on, "But why? And how?"

Bernie spread his hands. "It's a standard technique for losing unwelcome investigators for a while. MI5 and MI6 are fond of it, the CIA and the KGB both use similar methods . . . The idea is, you give someone a temporary ulcer—there are all kinds of local irritants you can slip into their food, in a capsule that will dissolve at the right point in the digestive tract—and then arrange a false diagnosis so they get the wrong treatment, ideally something that will make matters worse. After a week or two—"

Peter was on his feet. "For heaven's sake! We've got to tell her!"

"Have you forgotten that she's a foreigner, being treated in an NHS hospital, which is a rare privilege for anyone from outside the EEC, and—?"

"And she's ill and in pain!"

"You're going to march in and tell her doctor that he's either a fool or a dupe?"

"But how could a doctor—?"

"People can be bent," Bernie said succinctly, and emptied his mug of beer.

"You honestly mean—"

"Oh, grow up, will you? I'm only a few years younger than you, but I feel a sight older, I'm telling you! *You* ought to know what kind of a country this is turning into!"

Peter subsided slowly, clutching his own beer.

"Yes, I think I do," he muttered, glancing at Ellen. "I was . . . Well, I was thinking along those lines before dinner. What do we do?"

"You must visit Claudia in the morning," Ellen said in a positive tone. "And insist on talking to her doctor."

"Ellen, dear," Bernie said, rising to refill his mug, "it's wonderful to be young and idealistic. But I'm afraid that if our home-brewed version of the Gestapo have got to that grow-ser—"

"*Why?*" Peter burst out.

"That's what I don't know. But it's what I mainly came to talk to you about." Having topped up his mug and taken a long draught, Bernie fixed him with a glare.

"I'm quitting."

"But—"

"Don't say I can't! I sure as hell can, and you're holding the last scrap of data I produce for you! Call me a coward if you like, but I'm telling you straight: the fact that the heavy mob are trying to stop her from digging any deeper makes me worry about my own hide. Sorry. I'll tell Jake in the morning —no point in depressing him while he's trying to put an edition to bed."

After a further gulp of beer he added mildly, "Besides, I think I'm up against a brick wall. Louis Parker is too smart for me."

"I was going to ask—"

"And I was going to tell you. Sorry, the paper in your hand isn't quite the last bit of data that I owe you."

"Well, for God's sake give me the rest!" Peter barked. "You've been looking for Louis Parker for bocky weeks, and never found a trace of him!"

"Nor have I now. But I've reached a conclusion."

Peter felt his nails biting painfully into his palms. "Out with it!" he gritted.

"It is my considered opinion," Bernie said, avoiding the others' eyes, "that you are right about Louis Parker. And he knows it, and he knows you're after him, and he's—well— taken the appropriate precautions."

"You mean the bastard has Special Branch in his pocket, not to mention NHS doctors?"

"It seems all too likely. Look!" He hunched forward in his chair. "I've run that immense search I told you about—run it as far and as long as the money would stretch. I do not find *any* trace of Louis Parker. You told me a bit about his background, his family being Armenian and so on, and you said he donated semen and he worked for a computer firm and—and so forth. I've cross-checked every reference I can, and he's not there. You saw how Ellen located Sister Higgins by tapping into obsolete phone directories. If you try that for Louis Parker, you don't find him. But you said he was a swinging man-about-town type; can you imagine him not being on the phone?"

Cold sweat was pearling on Peter's brow. He was about to speak, but before he found the right words Bernie had charged onward.

"And don't talk about ex-directory! If you know how to go about it, you can get *anybody's* phone number, alive or dead!

Or at least anybody's who was around after they computerized the system. Also the passport office doesn't know about him. Social Security doesn't know about him. None of the major clearing banks ever kept an account in his name. I said before, and I say it again: he's dug a hole, jumped in, and pulled it after him. And that spells trouble on a scale I don't want to get involved with!"

Draining his beer anew, he rose to leave. On the way to the door, however, he hesitated. He had become aware that Ellen was staring at him.

"Is something wrong?" he demanded.

"Yes. You." The girl rose from the couch and held herself very upright.

"How do you mean?"

"You've taken money from the *Comet* to investigate this story that Claudia brought you. You didn't treat it seriously at first. Now it's turned out to be real news. You ought to be excited, you ought to want to push through to the end. Instead, you're sliming out!"

Small face eloquent of disgust, she marched back into the kitchen and addressed herself loudly to the cat.

On the doorstep Peter said, "Ellen's right, you know."

"Maybe so. But I'm going to—to cover my ass, as the Americans would say."

"And I'm going to put mine on the line!" Peter flared. "Tomorrow I'm going to do exactly as Ellen suggested!"

"What? Try and make Claudia's doctor admit—?"

"Exactly!"

"Well, all I can say is I hope you survive! 'Night!"

Next morning Peter had no trouble gaining admittance to Claudia's ward. Pale, reclining against a heap of shabby pillows, she smiled appreciation of his visit—and stopped smiling when he surreptitiously showed her the computer printout that Bernie had forgotten to reclaim.

"Oh my God," she whispered when its import sank in. "I've stumbled on to something even bigger than I first imagined."

"Very big," Peter muttered, glancing around to make sure no one was in a position to overhear—but an orderly was pushing an electric polisher across the floor, and that much noise ought to take care of eavesdroppers. "I've been thinking about it half the night because of what Bernie told me about Louis Parker." He summarized rapidly.

"And if he is the father of all these children," Claudia said slowly, "then—"

"Then what more likely than that he possesses at least some of their 'talent'? No wonder he can dig a hole and climb in, as Bernie says, and still influence people like the doctor in charge of your case!"

"I still find it hard to believe," Claudia sighed. "I could have sworn I'd been given an honest diagnosis . . ."

"Not according to that printout—which, by the way, I had better reclaim." Peter suited action to the words. "I think you'd better get yourself transferred to a private hospital, and never mind how much of Strugman's money it will cost. And you might well phone your lawyer friend, Mr. Stine, and— Well, you probably have a code, don't you?"

Claudia nodded dully. "I don't know how secure it is, but we change it pretty regularly."

"I can imagine what Bernie would say about that . . . Ah, never mind. You get in touch. The Strugfolk must have a good many contacts."

"Yes, of course."

"Time to start using them." Peter hesitated before adding, "Claudia, I hope you'll forgive me, but—"

"Ah, shit. What for this time?"

"Well"—uneasily—"not treating this theory of yours as seriously as I now realize it deserved."

"And I guess I ought to thank you, as well. After all, you aren't exactly going to make international headlines with the story, are you?"

"Not until it breaks on the grand scale."

"And now you know what we're up against, that doesn't seem likely— Oh, oh."

A portly nurse was approaching like a ship under full sail, expression stern.

"Mr. Levin! You've been here longer than the regulation time. You mustn't tire our patient."

"Going, going, gone . . ." Peter tucked the printout back in his pocket, hoping it had not been noticed. But this was a "charity"—i.e. NHS—ward, and only in wards reserved for private, paying patients were there expensive luxuries like TV cameras to monitor their progress. He bent to kiss Claudia's forehead.

Reaching up to embrace him, she whispered close to his ear, "If Bernie's right, you know, it means that Louis Parker knows about his children—who they are, and where."

"Oh my God!" Peter stepped back in horror.

"Now, Mr. Levin, you mustn't upset—"

"She's just upset me!" Peter snapped. "I hadn't thought of that . . . I know who would have, though!"

"Who?"

"Ellen! She's developing just the kind of paranoia I often wish I could have cultivated, because it's perfect for a reporter!"

"Talk to her when she gets home from school, then," Claudia said composedly. "And—nurse!"

"Yes?"

"Bring me a phone. At once. I believe my condition to have been misdiagnosed and I want to call in a second opinion. After that I plan to call my lawyer in New York with a view to filing suit for medical malpractice."

The nurse looked blank. Peter donned a false smile.

"Do as she says," he told her. "If not, you could be liable for damages, as I'm a witness to this sad affair."

She strove for a moment to avoid compliance. Then she crumpled. But, as she turned away, the movement of her lips could be clearly read:

Bocky American!

"Cancer," said the vet to whom Peter and Ellen took the cat that evening.

"But he's so young!" Ellen exclaimed.

"Yes, about nine months, I'd say. But last week I delivered a litter of kittens that were riddled with tumors in the womb. I sometimes wonder, if we're doing this to our pets, what we're doing to ourselves and one another—"

He caught himself. He wore a red-white-and-blue ribbon

on his white coat, and his hand flew to it as to a talisman, as to a crucifix.

"Well, I'm sure the government is doing all it can!" he concluded heartily. "But it would be kindest to have your cat put down. One wouldn't want to prolong its suffering. Please sign this form . . . Thank you. That will be £25. We accept all major credit cards; please tell the receptionist which you prefer. Next!"

THIS FAR SOUTH IT WAS STILL WARM, ALTHOUGH THE business of summer was long over. The grapes and olives had been harvested and pressed; the tobacco—still grown around here—had been sold, along with the maize, whether for *polenta* or for oil. Almost the only touch of color in the gray-sandy landscape was to be found where families had retained tomatoes to dry or cook down into paste.

There was something old and dusty about the view David stared at from the passenger seat of the Alfa Harry had rented at Foggia airport. It was like entering one of the paintings he had been instructed to admire at school. When he was still obliged to attend one.

For the first time since their brief encounter he remembered the education inspector he had seduced (much in the manner of Garth or Roger, he could now think) after ensuring that he would never again be distracted by dull-witted teachers.

Now, though, he was distracted by far worse problems. One was simply physical: the food he had risked eating on the plane had given him a belly-ache, and with vast embarrassment he had twice had to ask Harry to stop the car, so he might crouch behind dry-leaved autumn bushes and void his bowel.

David did not enjoy being reminded of his base humanity.

Prompted by thoughts of Garth, he started worrying about another problem. He had assumed his siblings would be on his side, so it would be safe to leave Alice in charge of them and the house while he and Harry made this trip to Italy—based on a mere suspicion, yet one that struck a chord in his imagination . . .

No! It must have been worthwhile! My program said . . .

Distrust, abrupt distrust, fought in his mind with tattered hope. He strove to sort the data he was processing. (How long before he himself started to think like a computer?)

First—!

He compelled himself to face the fact that his siblings were not automatically his allies. The worst of his early fears were being borne out. They had, as he was learning, spent too long on their own, with no conception of partnership and cooperation.

Maybe I shouldn't have risked leaving them . . .

His guts ached, his eyes were sore, he felt at his absolutely worst. The car trundled on, down potholed roads, while dust rose in their wake and sometimes ahead, when a tractor or a lorry was preceding them. The Alfa had no air-conditioning, and it was too hot to keep the windows shut. When he licked his lips, he tasted grit.

It dawned on him that when he planned this trip and *persuaded* Harry and Alice to arrange it, he had been visualizing this rented car as identical to the Rolls Royce he was accustomed to. His hand kept groping for the keyboard and modem that would have allowed him to interrogate the programs he had left running when he came away.

And he wanted to know their outcome. Needed to! If this mysterious Louis Parker was indeed his natural father—!

"Left or right?" Harry demanded in a rasping tone. They had come to a T-junction.

"What?"

"Damn it, you're supposed to be navigating!"

How dare you talk to me like that?

But David's fury flared and vanished like the fuel in a pizza oven. He hadn't bargained for a pain in his belly, or the debilitation due to constant diarrhea . . .

Mastering himself with vast effort, he glanced around. To the right, in the direction of the sunset, he spotted stone pillars framing the entrance to a driveway flanked by olive trees. Pointing, he muttered, "That looks like it."

"It had better be! I swear I don't know why I agreed to bring you here! Christ, I haven't felt so ill in years!"

Oh, no. If I lose control over my "father," what's left for me to look forward to . . . ?

But, summoning all his force, David laid a reassuring hand on Harry's right wrist, not so hard as to delay him turning the steering wheel. When simple speech and presence didn't work, contact tended to, as he had learned.

"Please, for me, drive to the house. You'll understand some day, I promise!"

If Louis Parker is real. If he's still alive. If I can track him down. If I can make him make me understand before I have to do my own explaining . . .

But if he's dead, rather than in hiding? Or even—?

The alternatives were too terrible to think of. David said aloud, to quiet his mind, "Handsome old place, isn't it? Shame it isn't kept in better repair . . . Look, there's someone we can ask."

"In Italian?" Harry grunted. But he slowed the car.

A portly middle-aged man was snipping off dead flower-heads in what must once have been a splendid formal garden with fountains, steps, and marble urns. Now the urns and steps were cracked, and none of the fountains played.

"Buon giorno!" David shouted, having remembered in time to turn the handle that rolled down the car window. (In the Rolls, of course, one pressed a switch.) *"Il signor Tessolari?"*

A vigorous headshake.

"Per favore, dov'é il signore?"

Which was about the point at which David's command of Italian ran out. Before leaving home he had reviewed a supposed "instant course" on videodisc, but even though he had only arrived in the country a few hours before he had already discovered its limitations.

However, a stroke of luck followed.

In English, the portly man said, "Are you American?"

"No, British!"

"Hmm! What business do you have with Renato?"

That, David recalled, was the name of GianMarco's "father." He debated with himself a moment, then settled for an empty phrase.

"We have a personal matter to discuss."

There was a pause. Eventually the man sighed.

"Very well, but you will have to wait. I am Fabio Bonni, GianMarco's uncle, and also his tutor." He hesitated, then gave a sudden, rather unpleasant laugh. "That is, I am supposed to be his tutor. I cannot make him express a simple sentence in either French or English. Yet he is not stupid. Already, at his age, he is more in control of the family's affairs than is Renato . . . Oh, park your car and get out. I don't know how long before they return, but we can take refreshment on the terrace. You are British, so you will want tea, of course. Well, we can still afford tea."

There was mockery in his tone and his expression. The hairs on David's nape prickled and he wished himself a thousand miles away.

I've seen people like this before. Only when I had done with them!

The possibility that GianMarco might be a rival such as he had never yet faced began to frighten him. Yet in the upshot, surely, with his experience in California he must be better informed, better adapted, *stronger* than someone living in a more-or-less peasant community in the *Mezzogiorno* . . .

The man who had identified himself as Fabio Bonni was shouting for a servant as he led them around the house to the promised terrace, overlooking dry pools and withering shrubs. The servant appeared, an elderly short-sighted woman, curtseying on sight of the visitors.

"Tea!" Fabio commanded. "In the English style!"

And when it came it was revolting . . .

I shouldn't have done this! Why am I here? I've dug a pitfall and I'm trapped in it!

* * *

They had to make forced conversation for nearly an hour. Fabio proved to be an archetypal whenzie. He complained endlessly about the state of Italy, the arrogance of the peasants, the local priest who sided with them as though he were a communist instead of a Christian, and the declining fortunes of the old landed families, including his.

David thought he might have gone on till midnight but the sound of an approaching car interrupted him. He tried to relax, forget his nervousness . . . but it was hard.

The first glimpse he had of GianMarco convinced him, on grounds of appearance alone, that here was yet another of his siblings, and after the first few politenesses had been exchanged he was satisfied on another, rather peculiar, score. He was certain Renato Tessolari believed the boy to be his own child, whereas his mother and uncle were under no such misapprehension.

Odd! But maybe, if necessary, I can play that card . . .

He cancelled the notion at once as dismal visions filled his head: the gradual establishment of intimate acquaintance, many exchanges of letters—it was unlikely that the Tessolaris possessed email facilities—in short, a slow and painstaking siege . . .

But there isn't time for all that mucking about!

Yet it was already clear that, whether he suspected what he owed it to or not, GianMarco was in full command of his talent, and enjoying his position of precocious power too much to want to give it up on the say-so of a stranger. He spoke no English, as his uncle had warned, but the latter acted as interpreter while he recited a lively account of the way in which he and his parents had just sorted out a recalcitrant tenant-farmer, who to his own amazement had this afternoon agreed to leave, along with his family, and take his chances in the north.

"So we can put in someone who isn't infected with these radical left-wing ideas, but shows proper respect for his superiors!" Fabio wound up. David's knowledge of Italian was too limited for him to be sure whether this was something GianMarco himself had said, or Renato, or just a footnote expressing Fabio's own opinion.

Then, of course, there had to be an explanation for the

foreigners' visit, unheralded as it was. And this was where David had made his worst mistake. So sure had he been that when he arrived he would be able to persuade the other boy to come to Britain, and his family to let him go—for it had been so easy in so many previous cases, and he had grown so used to Harry and Alice bending to his every whim—he hadn't bothered to work out a credible story.

And Harry was no help. Extremely tired, perhaps suffering from the same digestive upset, he only muttered, "My son wanted to come here, so I brought him."

At that GianMarco stiffened in his chair and gave a nod.

He's caught on, David realized sickly. *And he's well, and speaking his own language, and I'm ill and having to rely on an interpreter. This mess is getting worse by the minute.*

So, even as the thought passed through his mind, did the griping in his belly. He rose, wondering how to ask for a toilet, and didn't have to. As though reading his mind across the barrier of language, GianMarco called the maid.

He stayed out of sight for what felt like ages, striving to conjure up a credible reason for the visit, and failing. When at length he dared not remain in hiding any longer, he returned sullenly to the company . . . only to discover that the necessary story had been invented in his absence. He knew it, the moment GianMarco rose to clasp his hand and express, in the slow and well-articulated tones of one who feels he has to contend with a simpleton, the hope that his *malattia* was not too severe.

What's happened? Why is everyone smiling—Renato and his wife, Fabio, even Harry?

He had been outsmarted. For the first time he had met his match, and more than his match. GianMarco was indeed one of his siblings, and for whatever reason he had attained greater control, if not a fuller understanding, of his powers.

"Well, we must be on our way!" Harry said heartily. "If you're okay again, son?"

God, how I hate it when he calls me "son"!

But David forced a smile, and uttered a few words of thanks in his rudimentary Italian. They had such impact that GianMarco's mother Constanza embraced him, kissing him on both cheeks.

And, before he fully realized what was happening, they were back in the Alfa and he was cradling in his lap a bag containing bottles of wine made on the Tessolari estate.

"Remarkable boy, that GianMarco," Harry said as he dexterously negotiated bends and potholes on the way to the *autostrada* that would lead them back to Foggia and the airport. "Come to that, you're pretty remarkable yourself."

What? Abruptly David was alert. And Harry was continuing:

"I'd never have thought of importing wine guaranteed to be produced by chemical-free methods! But it's an obvious winner, isn't it? I only wish you'd told me beforehand. I literally didn't realize what was going through your head until GianMarco spelt it out. Next time, do me the favor of remembering that your old man can't read your mind!"

He waved at the surrounding vineyards and olive groves.

"It's not exactly my regular line, but with the contacts I have, not to mention the spare capital, I can just see it working. Yes, I can see it very well . . . Are you okay?"

"Frankly, no," David gritted.

"Then I'll stop hurrying. We don't have to fly home tonight. I'll call the airline and change our booking to the morning. Look, there's an *albergo* sign. I don't suppose it will be luxy accommodation, but if at least the beds are clean and the food fit to eat . . ."

David uttered a moan, at which Harry looked alarmed.

"Maybe I should get them to call a doctor—"

"No, no!" The boy forced himself to calm. "I'll be fine in the morning. But . . . Well, damn all bocky airline food!"

"I'm sorry." Harry sounded concerned. "It used to be okay in first-class. Nowadays, I suppose, what with the chemicals that have contaminated so much agricultural land . . . Next time we'll bring a packed lunch, hm?"

He clapped his "son" on the shoulder and turned the car off the road, under a red neon sign.

Behaving more like a father than at any time David could recall, Harry marched him into the hotel and, using a mix of bastard Spanish, half-remembered French and vigorous gestures, secured a twin room with its own bath and toilet. He insisted on David getting into bed at once, and arranged for a plain, easily digestible meal: boiled pasta with scrambled egg instead of a sauce. When he saw it David thought it was sure to make him gag, but for once he let Harry override his own opinion, and in fact he managed to eat almost all of it.

Much relieved, Harry went downstairs for his own meal. When he returned, David was dozing, but Harry roused him, proffering a glass that held a syrupy green liquid.

"The people here say this is what you need. It's a liqueur called *Centerba*, 'hundred herbs.' I tried a drop. Watch out— it's pretty strong. But it seems to help. If it does nothing else, it ought to give you a night's rest."

Too weak and weary to resist, David swallowed it like unwelcome medicine. It exploded in his guts like a fireball, but in a little while he felt a sense of warmth and comfort. Leaning back, he closed his eyes. Harry, who had been sitting anxiously on the other bed, smiled and rose.

"Looks as though they were right! I'll return your dinner tray. In case you drop off before I get back—sleep well!"

Which David did. But, before he fell asleep, one thought came to dominate his mind.

Grief! What power that GianMarco has! Not just to have explained away our arrival on the spur of the moment—to have wrought such a change in Harry!

Something must be done about GianMarco . . .

And blackout.

The opportunity to "do something" about GianMarco arose fortuitously the next morning.

David, feeling much better after nine hours' sleep, was breakfasting with Harry in the bar, off excellent coffee and rather disappointing bread and jam, when a police patrol car drew up. At some stage in yesterday's conversation with the Tessolaris it had been mentioned that they were on intimate terms with the local *Maresciallo*, and David felt a spasm of alarm. But it proved to be unwarranted; the driver and his companion merely ordered two espressos and stood at the counter drinking them.

Harry, who was still clearly taken by the idea of wine-importing (yet more testimony to GianMarco's power!), was enthusiastically outlining what he planned to do about it. Overhearing, the junior policeman, who carried a carbine on a sling, approached to inquire whether they were British or American, and what brought them to the area. Again David grew uneasy, but the man seemed merely curious, and eager to practice his English.

Harry said, shrugging, "We visited Signor Tessolari. We had a business deal to discuss."

At the mention of that name, the policeman's face darkened. Glancing around to make sure his superior was not listening—he wasn't, being engaged in chat with the proprietor's wife—he leaned forward and spoke in a low and confidential tone.

"You don't trust him, sir. He is very bad man. He is *murderer*."

"What?" Harry blinked in astonishment.

"Yes, sir. I swear. He killed my cousin with a—a . . ." At a loss for the word he touched his carbine, and David, suddenly all ears, supplied the word "gun."

"Gun, yes! But he is rich and powersome, and was our mayor. He lied to say it was one of the people that live on his land, and paid him money to go to the north and hide in a big city with a different name."

Miracles will never cease.

David seized his opportunity. He could feel that his talent was back to normal. Hoping against hope that he would have sufficient time to exploit it, he caught the policeman's hand, leaning close.

"This is terrible! Was he never arrested? No? But it's a scandal that such people should go free when people who commit much lesser crimes are sent to jail! Such villains are unfit to live—don't you agree?"

For another two or three minutes he continued in the same persuasive strain. By the time the senior policeman called his subordinate back to the car, he was virtually certain he had planted seeds for action in the young man's mind. Into the bargain, when Harry inquired with puzzlement what all that had been about, he was able to brush the matter aside with a request that it not be mentioned again.

At the very least, he thought grimly, *I've wished a major headache on GianMarco—enough to stop him meddling in my affairs until I've had time to make plans! And if I could deal with a tearaway like Gui, I ought to be able to cope with a boy my own age!*

Owing to a computer failure at the Rome air traffic control center their flight was delayed for ten hours. Fuming, Harry tried to charter a private plane, but failed; all non-scheduled flights were grounded until the computer was repaired. He tried to switch to Alitalia, the national airline being the only one still operating, but there were no vacant seats. Losing his temper, he demanded of David why he was so unconcerned.

But the boy only smiled.

On their return home, David claimed the bottles of wine not to drink but to analyze. Meantime he set one of his computers to monitor the news-services out of Southern Italy, keyed to the name Tessolari. The following morning his search was rewarded. Even his rudimentary knowledge of the language sufficed to inform him that Signor Renato Tessolari, together with his wife Constanza, brother-in-law Fabio Bonni, son GianMarco and an unnamed servant, had died in a fire that broke out at their home during the small hours.

He printed out the data, ripped the paper from the machine and bore it to the dining room where Harry, Alice and the other children were assembling for breakfast.

"You can forget about that wine-importing deal," he grunted as he dropped into his chair and helped himself to cornflakes.

Harry read the printout with dismay, and swore under his breath.

"Don't worry," David sighed. "'Chemical-free wine'! It contained the maximum allowed under EEC law of just about every additive you can name. Bunch of puky liars, the Tessolaris. And if that policeman was to be believed, they only got what was coming to them . . . Will you canks stop hogging the milk and sugar? Alice, where's my tea?"

Even as he stirred it, though, he shivered to think how close his project had trespassed toward the verge of disaster.

You're watching TV Plus. Now for Newsframe.

Allegations that the disastrous flooding of the Norfolk Broads during the past week might be due to subsidence of the bed of the North Sea following the extraction of so much oil and gas were officially dismissed as "unfounded" this morning. Police have been called out to control refugees swelling the ranks of farmers quitting the so-called East Anglian dustbowl, now a sea of mud after heavy rain. More in a moment.

A group of self-styled "Throwers" today threatened to close down TV Plus, if necessary by force. Contacted at home, the general dissociated himself from what he termed "such precipitate action," but added that he fully supports the official ban on "anti-patriotic" news . . .

AT LAST PETER HAD HAD A BREAKTHROUGH, AND HE owed it to Ellen. The revelation that their beloved cats and dogs were dying *en masse* of premature cancer had stirred the normally cowed and docile British public in a way that scarcely anything else could. When he was able to prove that several of the royal racehorses had gone the same way, not only the *Comet* but even TV Plus remembered him and sent him off on a joint fact-finding mission.

Bernie's withdrawal from the search for Louis Parker had seemed like a stop sign, and with Claudia still convalescing from her illness (which was, as Bernie had predicted, not after all due to codworm, the X-rays supposed to be hers having been "mixed up" with someone else's), he had given little thought recently to the criminal-children story.

Nonetheless, he remembered to mention it when Jake rang

up to confirm his assignment, though he was not at all surprised by the disillusioned answer:

"What you've given me so far won't make page ten, let alone page one!"

Curiously, however, it still engaged Ellen's interest. Peter had let himself be cajoled into explaining what few details she didn't yet know on the way back from visiting Claudia in hospital, and since then she had taken over what inquiries could be made using the equipment they had at home. So far she had reported little or no progress (was it surprising, given that Bernie the expert hacker had run into a dead end?) but at least it kept her occupied. The mood of the country was darkening as autumn dragged on, rainy and misty and cold, and the news that did not reach the papers or TV—the news that Peter had access to as a journalist—was full of racial attacks, unsolved arson and random violence in the streets. Even when those of her schoolfriends' families who were standing out against the pervading atmosphere invited Ellen to tea or to attend a birthday party, she declined, and none of her former boyfriends had taken her out in weeks.

What sort of a life is that for a teenage kid? I wish I knew what to do . . . but I can't abandon her to "her own kind," as so many pundits tell me I should. What is her own kind? Isn't she as British as I am?

For a while he compromised, increasing her pocket-money and buying her presents he could ill afford. After a week or two, however, he noticed she was simply putting them away in a cupboard, so that wasn't the right approach. The only positive step open to him lay in spending more time with her. But if he was to keep up his payments on their home, he must accept any job going, no matter how long it took or how often he was obliged to break the promise he had made to himself about not leaving her alone overnight.

It was a trap. He fretted over it. Yet Ellen herself seemed resigned and not unhappy. He postponed a solution, and again, and again.

And again.

He made a killing on the racehorse story, even though he had to lay out nearly as much as his own fee in bribes. But then, that was the way of things nowadays. All the newspapers and commercial TV companies maintained so-called contingency accounts in foreign tax-havens from which they could allot such "inducements"... One of the chief reasons why the money-starved BBC was turning more and more into an organ of official propaganda was because it had no such supplementary resources and had to lick the government's boots in order to survive.

Knowing that he had earned enough to support himself and his daughter for at least three months, if he didn't overspend (and there was less and less to buy, anyhow, so that should not be hard, though he had taken advantage of his temporary affluence and was carrying a heavy bagful of groceries) Peter was humming as he approached his home. At least the windows were intact—recently gangs of children had taken to smashing the glass of any house or flat round here where "colored" people lived—and when he slipped his key into the lock it turned easily, so it had not been dosed with superglue.

Ellen, whom he had phoned to warn of his return, emerged from the kitchen to give him a kiss. As she relieved him of his load of shopping he inquired, "Anything been happening around here?"

"Mm-hm." She tossed back her long dark hair. "They used a chunk of your horse-cancer story on the early evening news. I only hope that doesn't provoke anyone to find out where you live and do what they did to Bernie...Oh! Speaking of Bernie: there's a message from Claudia. She wants us to go round this evening."

He had been looking forward to a quiet evening at home; his assignment, though profitable, had been tiring.

"Any special reason?" he said at length.

"She wouldn't say. But it sounded urgent."

"Hmm! Convince me."

"Well, she did say something new has turned up." Ellen caught his hand in hers and adopted her usual melting-eyed expression. "Can't we? I'd go by myself except—"

Except dark-skinned people like me can't walk a British street alone any more.

She didn't have to finish the sentence.

"All right," he sighed. "But after I've had a drink and a

decent meal . . . Know something? I'm getting addicted to Indian food. Haven't eaten anything else all the time I've been away, apart from breakfast."

She beamed at him. When he produced whiskey from the bag he had brought she seized it, told him to sit down, and brought him a drink mixed exactly to his taste.

How strange it was to return to his old home . . . Peter found himself clutching Ellen's hand as they walked from the bus stop. They were arriving much later than he had told Claudia on the phone; the bus had been re-routed owing to a fight between a white gang and a group of Pakistani vigilantes which the police had broken up with tear gas.

More of the streetlights out than when I lived here . . . More windows boarded up, not only shops now but the ground floors of homes— Grief, what is this country coming to?

Also the Neighborhood Watch signs had vanished. It looked as though the windows that displayed them had become prime targets.

They were approaching the house door when two young men emerged from shadow, wearing Thrower brassards and balaclavas drawn up like masks. Dazzling them with a flashlight, the taller of the pair demanded what they were up to.

Feeling Ellen shrink back into shelter behind him, remembering what had happened to Bernie, Peter fought down the sick sensation that rose in his belly and strove to snap back in a properly defiant tone.

"I used to live here! On the top floor! I've come to call on the person who took over my old flat!"

"More likely looking for a quiet spot to take his black scrubber," said the second man.

"Don't you call my daughter a scrubber!" Peter blurted before he could stop himself.

"Ah! Another bocky nigger-lover! Well, we'll show you what we think of *your* sort! Right, Ted?"

"Right," said the tall one, switching off and pocketing the flashlight.

Oh, no! Let this not be real!

But, even as Peter was preparing to offer what resistance he could, Ellen darted away from him, up the steps to the house. It was divided into eight flats and each had an answer-phone. She planted her hands on all the bell-pushes at once and held them down.

"Why, the bocky cunt!" the shorter youth burst out.

Amazed and indescribably relieved at her presence of mind, Peter shouted, "Tell them to call the police!"

"Ah, shit!" Ted muttered. "All right, better get out of here. But"—with a final flare of defiance—"if we ever catch sight of you again we'll leave our mark on you, hear?"

And they were gone.

After explaining and apologizing to the other tenants—who recalled him from his time here and were willing enough to believe him, though some of those who emerged into the hall or on to the staircase bestowed harsh glances on Ellen—they were finally able to ascend to what was now Claudia's flat. Pale, obviously still weak, but improving, she made them sit down at once. She was drinking Gibsons from a chrome-plated cocktail shaker veiled in condensation, and insisted on pouring for them both.

"Should I?" Ellen asked nervously.

"I don't think one will do you any harm," Peter replied. "Claudia, you know I have a genius for a daughter? I never saw anything so quick-witted!" And he recounted in detail how Ellen had saved their skins, while she sipped nervously —once—and then ate her onion, nibbling it layer by layer off the stick as she gazed around.

The moment Peter finished, as though to forestall more praise, she said, "You couldn't have put me up here."

Briefly confused, thinking Ellen was addressing her, Claudia said, "You need somewhere to stay for a while? I could always—"

"No, no! I meant if the police had dumped me on Dad while he was still here, there wouldn't have been room."

"We'd have managed somehow," Peter said. "On the trip I just got back from I saw far worse crowding than two people in three rooms. You know there are places in Britain where houses are literally falling down because the owners can't af-ford repairs? In some streets you find whole families forced to live in a single ground-floor room because the rest of the house is uninhabitable. I'd have squeezed you in, don't worry."

Ellen caught his hand and gave him a brilliant smile.

After a pause Claudia said dryly, "I admit, young lady, I was wondering why you'd want to stay in an area that made you so unwelcome. By the way, I think I know the thugs who accosted you. I'm surprised the threat of the police drove them away. They were only planning to do what the fuzz around here make a habit of when they run across a mixed-race couple."

"Have things got that much worse since I moved?" Peter demanded. "Or is it simply that I didn't attract that kind of attention while I was here?"

"I suspect the latter," Claudia sighed. "But it's over, and you're both okay, though when you leave you'd better call a cab and wait till it's at the door . . . Don't you want to know why I asked you to call by?"

The powerful drink had calmed Peter's nerves. Leaning back in his chair, he invited her to go ahead.

"Bernie's turned up something new."

"But he told me he was quitting!"

"He changed his mind. He came to see me when I got back from the hospital—brought me a bouquet that must have cost a fortune—and after I talked at him for a while he promised he'd keep at least one search program running. And today this turned up."

She tossed him a sheet of email printout. For Ellen's benefit he read it aloud.

"'Nothing on LP'—has he suddenly taken to music?"

"If that's a joke it's a pretty bad one," Claudia said tartly. "Louis Parker, of course!"

"I know, I know. Sorry. 'But another possible kid. Check North of England juvenile court reports for last Thursday.'"

"Which I did." Claudia passed over another sheet of paper. "I think this must be what he meant."

"Hmm!" Suddenly Peter's interest in the matter was rekindled. "It says here that a girl—the right kind of age—was caught when store-detectives investigating thefts from a supermarket checkout discovered that she was conning the assistants into giving her not only her change but also the money she'd originally handed them. In spite of which she was found not guilty and allowed to go free."

"Bernie's promised to track her down," Claudia said. "But he thinks it's going to be difficult. Juvenile court records are kind of shellbacked."

"Good to know something is," Peter grunted, emptying his glass. As though they were at home, Ellen was prompt to refill it, and Claudia's. Her own was barely touched.

While she was at it, he went on somewhat shamefacedly, "I must confess I haven't been working much on the story. And I don't expect I can in the near future, either. While I was away I found something else. I don't know whether you heard about it, but last summer an awful lot of plants died over here, or didn't set seed. Was that reported in the States?"

"I don't think so," Claudia answered. "Oh—wait! I think I heard some reference to it after I arrived. Wasn't there some sort of blight, like the one on potatoes?"

"That's what they tried to make people think. I just found out it was nothing of the kind. It was due to a new insecticide called Thanataph, a bestseller because it's supposed to provide complete control of aphids all summer with a single application."

"Does it?"

"Yes. Unfortunately it also kills bees. I didn't make the connection, but you can't buy British honey any more. *I* thought it was just another matter of economics—Greek honey in particular has been flooding the market because it's still cheap. I was wrong. Bees have been dying by the tens of millions. They're trying to make out that was due to a disease, too, but I have proof that it was not."

"Think it'll make page one?" Claudia countered in a cynical tone. Harking back to Jake's comment of the other day, Peter answered:

"Maybe not. But it could make page ten."

A drab silence followed. For the first time Peter realized that there wasn't even a radio in the room, let alone a TV or stereo. He was framing an embarrassed question about Claudia's finances when she shifted in her chair and heaved a sigh.

"Sometimes I wish I'd never started on this project, you

know. Half the time I can't believe my evidence. All the time I can't lick it into shape. I can't concentrate. I keep wondering whether whatever I was given was meant to affect my mind."

Peter offered awkward consolation, but she brushed it aside. They both knew that governments the world around now routinely used drugs to derange or handicap those who opposed them. She went on.

"Things are pretty bad at home, too. The Strugfolk are under mass attack from the right. Cecil may not be able to underwrite my lawsuit—maybe not even be able to keep on funding my research."

"I was going to ask about that," Peter muttered, feeling guiltier by the moment.

With a shrug: "Well, he does have—what's the phrase?— other calls on his purse. It looks as though Walter may finally have put together a case against the funders that will stand up all the way to the Supreme Court, but that won't be cheap even though the lawyers involved are donating their services. Just to complicate matters, there's a movement in the various legal associations to have free representation declared unprofessional."

Peter whistled. "We really do live in an age that worships Mammon!"

A harsh laugh. "You noticed? Amazing!"

Diffidently, having taken another sip of her drink as if to garner courage, Ellen spoke up.

"Claudia, I don't know whether Dad told you, but I'm keeping on with the research, as well as Bernie. I—uh—I hope you don't mind."

"Mind?" Claudia echoed, reaching out to pat her on the shoulder. *"Mind?* Why, that's the best news I've had in weeks."

"Really?" Of a sudden Ellen was eager. "I was worried in case you felt I was sort of intruding."

"On the contrary. The way I feel right now, I'd welcome help from the devil himself . . . Excuse me: bad choice of phrase."

Ellen smiled mechanically.

"Of course, I wouldn't want you to think I'm being much help, because I'm not. But if—" She broke off, biting her lip.

"If what?"

"Well . . ." Encouraged, she sat forward on her chair. "If I could ask about a few things that still aren't quite clear, maybe I could do better."

"Ask away!"

"Really?"

"Really really really! What do you want to know first?"

It was almost midnight when they finally called their cab. On the way home, Peter found himself marveling at Ellen all over again, this time for the grasp she had displayed of the problem that was baffling Claudia, and him, and even Bernie. When she came in pajamas to kiss him good night, he hugged her close.

"I was right," he said. "I do have a genius for a daughter. I'm sorry I didn't find out sooner."

"So am I," she murmured, head against his shoulder. "I wish . . . But it's no good wishing about the past, is it? You can only wish about the future."

"You're wise," he said. "You're very wise."

"But am I smart?" Drawing back, she pulled a face. "If I can find Louis Parker, will you think I am?"

"If you can, I'll think you can work miracles!"

"One miracle coming up! Good night!"

THE BIG HOUSE IN SURREY THAT HAD FELT SO EMPTY was now crowded. Every week, or so it seemed, David added another to the roster of its occupants. But when the burden of cooking, cleaning and washing became too much for Harry and Alice, he simply walked out one morning and returned with two middle-aged women from a nearby village, with time on their hands now their children were grown, prepared to work long hours for a pittance. Similarly, when the roof needed emergency repairs, he made himself popular with the landlord by finding a local builder who quoted a ridiculously low price—"as a favor for the young gentleman"—but did a sound, fast job.

By now Harry was talking about buying the property when their twelve-month lease expired.

And the very atmosphere of the house seemed to change. At the time of the first arrivals it had been tense, charged with mutual suspicion, and Harry and Alice had tried to argue against what he was doing. Now, however, they were relaxed, even content. So was Sheila who had been withdrawn and spiteful; so was Terry, who had at first been afraid of living in isolation, away from his familiar city streets.

One chill, foggy evening after supper, when—as had become the usual practice—the kids had withdrawn into the biggest of the reception rooms to hold some kind of council or discussion, Harry heard Alice humming to herself as she loaded the dishwasher.

"You sound cheerful," he observed.

"Do I?" she countered in surprise, and then added after a moment's reflection: "Yes, I suppose I do. I think we're doing something—well, worthwhile. Don't you?"

"As a matter of fact," Harry answered slowly, "yes. At first I was very doubtful, same as you. But—well, the last time I lost my temper with David was in Italy, and that was only because I was feeling so unwell. And it wasn't his fault that the growser we went to see turned out to be a rogue."

The last plate duly racked, Alice shut the machine and turned it on. Wiping her hands, she said, "Let's sit down for a bit and have a drink. It's been a long day."

"All days around here are long," Harry sighed. "Grief! I never expected to find myself surrogate father to such a mixed-up bunch of mixed-up kids! But I can't."

"What?"

"Can't take time off for a drink, I mean. I have a pile of forms to complete. Apparently a government education inspector called some time ago, while we were out—"

"I don't remember David mentioning that!" Alice exclaimed.

"He didn't tell me, either . . . but he seems to have done a splendid PR job. We can apply for this house to be recognized as a fit alternative to a regular school. The only trouble is that stack of bocky forms. The inspector's coming to collect them any day now. They've become much tougher about this sort of thing recently. So many child-abuse scandals at unlicensed residential homes."

"You worry too much," Alice said, taking his arm. "You don't have to fill in the forms this very minute."

"I suppose you're right, but it's a matter of showing willing, isn't it?"

"They can wait until the morning," his wife insisted. "Come on."

And, a moment later, as they passed the closed door of the room where the kids were in conclave, she murmured, "I wonder what they're getting up to."

"What kids that age always get up to, I imagine, when they're allowed to."

"If you mean what I think you mean—" she began in sudden alarm. He cut short her reaction.

"I'm sure there's no need to worry. David's a sensible boy. As a matter of fact, when we brought Crystal here"—He hesitated for a second—"I think he must have guessed what I was bothered about, because he contrived to let it drop that she had a valid AIDS certificate. And you remember how scathing he was about the way she'd been behaving."

"Yes, and I think that was a bit unfair. After all, what alternative did the poor girl have?"

"Until she was brought here."

"Yes, of course . . . We really *are* doing something worthwhile, aren't we?"

"Absolutely. Even though I don't know how or why we drifted into it."

"I think it must be because . . . " The words trailed away.

"Go on!"

In a defiant tone, as though expecting to be contradicted, or mocked, she said, "I think it must be out of love."

He raised his eyebrows. "Hmm! Now you put it like that . . ."

"I know it sounds rather sententious, but—"

"But me no buts. I think you're right. I didn't realize until now, but—yes. I've always loved David, naturally, in spite of him not actually being mine. Now I'm coming to feel the same sort of affection for them all. And—" He hesitated, then concluded, "And I'm glad to be out of the commercial rat-race. I've cut a few corners in my time, I admit, but the people in charge of the world's economy nowadays act as though they'd learned their business in the drug trade."

"Maybe they did."

"As a matter of fact, I wasn't entirely joking . . . No, I feel we're well out of it."

"What better reason for a drink?"

After the second snifter of brandy they were becoming amorous for the first time in several weeks, when the kids' meeting broke up with a noisy clatter of feet on the hall parquet and David walked in. As ever, his expression was neutral; he looked neither happy nor downcast, merely purposeful.

"We have to make another trip tomorrow," he announced.

"What if the education inspector calls?" Harry objected.

"Oh, her!" David said dismissively. "She's a soft touch. Provided the forms have been filled in, Alice can cope."

Dismay showed on her face. "I honestly don't think—"

"Or the other kids can." He brushed the objection aside with an impatient wave. "I'll brief them on what to say. But I've found another possible recruit."

They knew, though didn't understand, how. It had to do with the efficiency of his computers, that included some of the world's most advanced models. Compared to what the British were using—even the British government—they were five years ahead, and he was exploiting this fact to unearth data from supposedly shellbacked sources. However, they sensed it would not do to inquire over-closely into that side of David's affairs.

He concluded, not expecting opposition, "I'd like to leave directly after breakfast."

And was gone.

Tracy Coward had enjoyed a grim moment of triumph in court, when the girls who had attacked her were punished while she herself received back all the possessions they were trying to reclaim.

But that had been the last time she felt remotely happy or satisfied.

Her decline began when she was warned that the scars inflicted during her beating were not going to disappear without long and expensive cosmetic surgery. Now she had to smear herself with makeup, privately in her room, before showing herself even to her parents, and even that didn't entirely hide the marks—especially when the sight of her own face in the mirror made her weep and mar her cheeks. In addition she had to comb and spray her hair so that it covered the place where a patch of scalp had been torn away.

Furious, vengeful, she took to brooding alone every evening and weekend, poring over her jewelry like a miser counting coins. At school she refused to work, but found entertainment in provoking fights between the other girls— she hadn't lost her talent for that—in the hope they too might wind up scarred for life. The teaching staff were helpless to control her.

Until one of them, smarter than the rest, took advantage of her monthly "window of vulnerability."

Thanks to that, she had been suspended and was awaiting an order that would transfer her compulsorily to a special school for disturbed children.

Me, a mental case! I'll get my own back on that bitch! I swear I'll see all these canks rotting from the arse up before I'm through with them!

Inevitably her parents bore the brunt of her rage. She forced them to behave like her fellow pupils, bent them to her every whim: buy me this, take me there . . .

She would lie awake at night and listen to her mother weeping in the next room, and think:

It's no more than she deserves. It's no more than all of them deserve who landed me in this bocky mess!

"Well—hello!"

It had become Tracy's custom, every lunch hour, to walk from her home and pass the school playground, wearing her most fashionable clothes and sporting her finest regalia. In her mind was the idea that the other girls would see and envy her, free to go about where and when she chose instead of being shut up for hours on end in bocky classrooms listening to bocky stupid teachers.

But this encounter, practically on her doorstep, she had not been expecting.

Here was a good-looking boy, dark-haired, with an olive complexion not unlike her own (she still remembered the gibes from primary school, years ago, when she had been called "blackie" and "coon") and extremely but *extremely* well-dressed; indeed, his gear was of a kind she had only seen hitherto in American magazines.

And he was looking her up and down appraisingly, and nodding.

"Hmm! You're a bright sight on a gloomy day! I'm David —who are you?"

All of a sudden her mind was a jumble of possibilities, a torrent of optimistic visions.

Suppose I play up to him—maybe take his arm—walk with him past the school . . .

As though he had read her thoughts, he smiled.

"Going anywhere in particular?"

"Just—just for a stroll."

"I'm at a loose end, too. Shall we make it together? And you still haven't told me your name."

Feeling as though she had been caught up in a dream, she whispered, "Tracy . . ." She had never liked her surname, Coward. That too had caused her persecution.

"That's a pretty name. To suit a pretty girl."

Can he truly not see through the makeup? Or . . .

The dream intensified.

Or does he simply not care? After all, I do have a fairly good figure . . .

By this time the chaotic images at the back of her mind had already extended to the point of showing off her body rather than her face, her flawless unmarked skin beneath the hampering clothes of chilly autumn. They focused into a climactic phrase:

I heard of love at first sight. Do you suppose . . . ?

But he had linked his arm in hers, companionably, and was asking, "Well, which way? Oh, just a second."

And he waved toward the corner of the street.

Glancing to find out why, she saw an improbable Rolls Royce, such a car as never normally intruded into areas like this.

"Excuse me," he was saying. "I just had to tell my driver I'm okay."

"Your"—faintly—"driver?"

"Mm-hm. I get bored sitting on those bocky cushions. So insulating! Riding in a Roller cuts you off from the real world, you know? I simply had to stretch my legs. He'll follow us, of course, but don't worry."

To walk to the school with this David—to wave at the girls I used to call my friends—then to let them watch me getting in a Roller with him . . . !

The plan was complete in an instant, bar some petty details about maybe kissing him, too, where they could watch and hate her. She let a slow smile spread across her face.

"This way," she said.

All went precisely as she had planned—at first. They arrived just at the right moment, when her former fellow pupils were turned out for a few minutes prior to the commencement of afternoon classes. She waved to them, not letting go of David for an instant, saw the envy on their faces—or interpreted it as such, though it could equally have been hate—and, even as they were recalled indoors, the Rolls arrived. They were too far away to hear her whisper, "I've never ridden in a Roller. May I—?"

"Jump in!"

He held the door for her.

And then, almost at once, things went terribly and fearfully awry.

Why did the car immediately head toward her home? Why was she being taken inside, still clinging to David's hand as to a life-raft in a rough sea? Who was this strange, grave adult discussing her future with her parents?

I've been drugged! I'm going to be kidnapped!

But such wild notions culled from television vanished. She grew calmer, recognizing key words from the conversation: "special school"—"many similar children" . . .

And realized with a flash of insight: *He's a liar! He didn't just chance on me in the street! Because—!*

Here came the most exciting news of all.

Because he has the power, too. I'm not alone.

She buried her face in her hands and started to cry.

During the long trip to Virginia Water she snuggled into a corner of the car's luxurious back seat and enjoyed her soundest sleep in months.

You're watching TV Plus. Now for Newsframe.

Three hundred people were rendered homeless in Staffordshire today when methane escaping from a forgotten rubbish dump caught fire. Fire engines and ambulances on their way to the disaster were stoned by youths wearing pro-Thrower armbands. One of them, who declined to be identified, claimed that the gas had been fired deliberately because the area is largely occupied by blacks. More in a moment.

General Thrower himself, addressing a rally in West London this afternoon, said, quote, "The abandonment of medium-range nuclear missiles was the greatest act of treachery in living memory. We British deserve to wield the most modern weapons in defense of freedom and democracy..."

TURNING AWAY FROM HIS COMPUTER, PETER SWORE under his breath. From the couch facing the TV, whose sound she had turned down for a commercial break, Ellen inquired what was wrong. The air was full of spicy scent from the vegetable curry she was cooking. Later, she'd said, she would make chapattis; the cost of rice had risen from astronomical to prohibitive in the past few weeks.

Peter slumped down beside her, wiping his forehead with the back of his hand.

"Someone very high up indeed owns shares in the company that manufactures Thanataph—the stuff that killed the bees. Jake daren't touch the story, nor the TV people. I thought I had another certain winner. We're going to be surviving on vegetables for the foreseeable future."

"Never mind," she said consolingly, pressing his hand. "Something else will turn up. I've made some more beer and it should be about ready. Like me to bring you some?"

"Yes, please—Goodness, I didn't realize what time it was!" He reached for the remote control to turn up the TV sound again. "I wonder what news *is* making it to the screen these days."

The answer was, in a word, bad. He jolted upright at the first item. During a storm in the North Sea, a Dutch freighter had been driven against a drill-rig and torn it loose. The resulting oil slick was already ten miles long and spreading, with no hope—said a miserable-looking company spokesman —of capping the broken pipe until the weather improved ... which the forecasters warned might not be for a week.

"Oh, kid," Peter said in a broken voice. "What a world we have bequeathed to you! When I think what could have been done with the profits from that oil—from all the oil! Unemployment is up to five million now, you know."

"I didn't see that on telly!" she exclaimed as she handed him his glass of beer.

"You wouldn't. Officially it's less than four, but they're running out of ways to drag the total down. What that means, of course, is that the profit from North Sea oil has been squandered on paying people to do nothing, instead of repairing the infrastructure ... Sorry, I've told you this before, haven't I?"

She nodded, frowning. "But how could they be so stupid? I mean, surely even Cabinet ministers and businessmen need clean water, proper drains, safe bridges and all the rest."

"I don't think the trouble is so much that they're stupid. I think it's simply that they're greedy. I remember reading years ago—probably when I was about your age—about a rich American who said, when he was tackled by an environmentalist worried about pollution and asked what sort of a world his children would be living in—he said he didn't care because he'd bought land for them in Canada, away from all the mess."

"That's stupid," Ellen said with authority, her eyes still on the screen. It now showed a map of the North Sea with the prevailing winds and currents. "Oh dear, that looks bad, doesn't it?"

Peter forced his mind back to the present. After a moment he said, "Very bad. I'd hate to be a trawlerman in the northeast, to start with. And when the bills come in from Scandinavia . . ."

"Why don't you ring Jake and offer him a piece about the consequences?"

"Darling, you *are* a genius. I don't know what's come over me lately!" Gulping his beer, he headed for the phone. Over his shoulder he added, "Call up a North Sea weather map, please!"

"Sure!" She was seated before the computer instantly. "What do I key?"

"021-METEORO. My user code is PETREL." He was already punching the number of the *Comet*.

"Hmm? Dad, you did say petrol, didn't you? The system won't recognize it."

"What—? Oh, sorry. Petrel with two e's. The stormbird."

"Ah! . . . Okay, got it. North Sea . . . What do you want added?"

"Same as they had on the telly—winds, currents—plus commercial activities around the coast, economic values, income from tourism . . . Anything else you can think of?"

"What about the value of the lost oil?"

"Good idea!"

The *Comet*'s lines were of course busy. Peter left the phone on automatic re-dial—though plenty of other people had most likely done the same, which meant the lines would be tied up indefinitely—and came over to study the map when it was complete.

"That's really bad," he muttered. "File that for the moment, though, and try something else that's just occurred to me. You heard that rumor about the flooding in the Norfolk Broads being due to subsidence of the sea-bed? They denied it, and they might be right—after all, there have been lots of floods in the area before—but this time there's a lot of gas coming out as well as the oil. Normally, to stabilize the sea-floor, they pump water in as the oil and gas are drawn off, and this time they aren't going to have a chance, are they? See if you can find your way to a geological profile of the area—there's a data-base in Oslo called SEADRILL that ought to have one on call—and figure out what might happen if the sea-bed suddenly collapses."

Ellen's hands, poised above the keyboard, abruptly froze.

"Tidal wave?" she said in a shaky voice.

"Oh, I doubt there'll actually be a tsunami. I was more thinking of what might happen to the people trying to cap the pipe."

The phone rang. He seized it, leaving her to get on with the search.

Which she did to such effect that the data were already on screen before Jake had agreed to take his usual 800 words. Peter had been intending to dictate; seeing the diagram Ellen had constructed, he changed his mind and promised to file via modem within the hour. He added that he might need a thousand words. Jake sighed, but since this was bound to be the biggest story of the day conceded the request, subject to editing.

As her father sat down to the computer again, Ellen slipped into the kitchen to turn off the dinner. In the end they didn't eat until nearly ten.

It was good, anyway.

Strictly Ellen should have turned in directly after the meal, it being past her bedtime, but lately they had fallen into the habit of winding up the evening with a quiet chat, companionably side by side on the sofa. A sub from the *Comet* had called back to say she needed to lose a few lines from the story, but at least she'd had the sense to ask before she cut, which was reassuring. Pleased with this unexpected windfall, Peter smiled sidewise at his daughter.

"At the risk of repeating myself," he murmured, "I do more and more regret that things didn't work out between Kamala and me. I could have been eating meals as good as yours for years!"

She dug him playfully in the ribs.

And then grew serious.

"Dad," she ventured after a moment, "why *did* you and Mum break up? I would like to know. And before you answer"—she laid a slim brown finger on his lips to forestall an immediate reaction—"please remember that I'm quite grown up now. It happened years and years ago, and there can't be any harm in telling the truth after so long. Which is what I want to hear."

He pondered a long while. In the end her appealing eyes decided him. Sighing, leaning back and gazing into nowhere, he explained.

"It was because of a girl called Sindy . . . I suppose I ought to say woman. I met her at a party when I was still studying medicine. She was older than me, married for several years, but constantly quarrelling with her husband because they both wanted children and she had never conceived. But he wouldn't go for a check to see if it was his fault—insisted that it must be hers."

He had poured more beer to drink with his meal; there was a little left, and he sipped it.

"So . . . Well, I was a bit drunk by then, or I wouldn't have talked so freely. I mentioned the Chinn-Wilkinson, said she ought to go there while she was in London—she came from somewhere in the provinces but she never said exactly where —and she said she'd thought about artinsem but the idea didn't appeal to her because it was much too impersonal. So . . ."

An embarrassed shrug.

"You have to understand that I'd been a donor for several months by then, and it was coming home to me that by now I very likely had a child somewhere, with more to follow. I'd meant to be detached and cynical about it—like Louis Parker, if I have to be absolutely frank. He didn't seem as though he could give a hoot. Probably had by-blows already in half a dozen countries. I think I told you he was devastatingly handsome?"

Ellen gave a wry grin. "You said something about women swarming round him like flies on a rotting carcass."

"I must have been in a particularly grumpy mood . . . But anyhow: I'd realized my detachment wasn't up to his, so the idea crossed my mind that I ought to know what happened to at least one of my—ah—offspring. I imagine you can guess the rest."

"You seduced her?" Ellen suggested.

"I don't know which of us seduced the other. But—yes, we had a brief affair. Two weeks."

"Was it her husband's fault?"

Peter nodded. "Presumably. But I never saw her again. So much for my original idea! As soon as she knew she was pregnant she rang me up and said good-bye. I hadn't even learned her surname, let alone her address."

"Really?"—eyes wide in disbelief.

"Really! She was much better off than me, used to pick me up from the hospital in a taxi, take us for a meal, go home with me, and then leave after a couple of hours. She and I never spent a whole night together . . . I hope you don't mind my being so frank."

"No, it's what I asked for." Ellen hesitated. At length she went on, "You didn't know I was on the way?"

"Of course not! I'm not sure your mother did, even. At any rate she didn't tell me until my involvement with Sindy was all over."

"So how did she find out? That was what broke you up, wasn't it?"

Peter thought carefully before replying. Now he had gone so far, though, he was bound to admit the rest.

"It was one thing to know I'd fathered a child that was going to be accepted by a married couple, brought up as their own. That's what I sincerely believed was going to happen, because Sindy had laid so much stress on the fact that her marriage would have been fine except for not having kids. But it was something else to take on responsibility for one of my own when I was so poor during my studies that I'd had to donate semen for extra income. I . . ."

"Did you try to talk her into an abortion?" Ellen suggested.

Her tone was utterly devoid of emotion. He tried to read clues in her face, but it showed no more than apparently casual interest.

Well, she did say it all happened years and years ago . . .

Gruffly, he confessed the truth.

"And that upset her?"

"Yes."

"And that was why you broke up?"

"I think she might have seen sense and we could have got back together but for what happened a little later on, a few weeks." Peter licked his lips. His belly was tense of a sudden. He always hated recalling what he now had to describe, and had never told anyone about it before.

"Go on."

Were those words chill and reproachful, or merely curious? He hoped for the latter, and plunged ahead.

"I said just now Sindy's inability to conceive was 'apparently' her husband's fault. In fact it was incontestably his fault, and it turned out that he knew all along. He was sterile, but he couldn't face the fact. When Sindy became pregnant he knew it had to be someone else's baby and he threw her out. She had my phone number and one evening in a fit of hysterics she rang up to tell me what he'd done.

"Only I wasn't there."

"Kamala was?"

"Kamala was. Not for very long, though. I never found out exactly what Sindy said, but I can imagine. After that it was all over between us. We scarcely even talked again. Saw each other once or twice when the dust had settled, but—well, that was that. And now you know."

He finished his beer in a single angry draught.

While he was still wondering what Ellen's reaction would be to the naked truth, there was a shrill beep from her own computer in the next room. Jumping up, she ran to see what had provoked it, and shortly returned, holding a page of print-out but looking downcast.

"Is something wrong?" Peter demanded.

"Oh, I just turned up another Louis Parker."

He almost choked. "What do you mean, another?" he exploded.

"This is the fourth. None of them any good to us." She thrust the paper into his hands and slumped back on the sofa, disconsolate. He read rapidly. It was true; she'd found four people of that name. But one of them was over sixty, living in retirement near Harrogate, and in any case his full name was Christopher Louis Parker-Haines; another was Louis X. Parker, an American citizen on the staff of the embassy in Grosvenor Square; and the third was an actor who had taken Louis as a stage name because his baptismal name was Lewis and Equity already had a Lewis Parker on its register. As for the fourth, whose details had just emerged, Louis Alan Parker had been born in Sydenham three months ago to a Frenchwoman named Suzette Legrand, and one Alan Raymond Parker, who was British, had acknowledged paternity.

Nonetheless, it was an astonishing achievement. Marveling, Peter demanded, "How in the world did you come up with this lot? Bernie hasn't produced a single candidate so far!"

Stifling a yawn, Ellen hoisted her slim body off the sofa, supporting herself with feet and shoulders, until she was sufficiently stretched.

"Trade secret," she said with a mocking grin as soon as her yawn permitted. "But at least it's a step in the right direction, hm? Well, I'd better turn in. I have to go to school tomorrow, remember."

"Yes. Yes, of course. Good night. And thanks again for another delicious meal."

"Any time," she said. "Any time."

Peter himself was too wound up to sleep. Pacing up and down, wondering whether or not to check the late-night TV news, he was struck by a sudden inspiration. Perhaps Louis

Parker had reverted to his family's original name. If it was in
fact Parikian...

But though there were nearly ninety subscribers of that
name in the national phone directory, none bore the initial L.

What the hell could have become of him?

LEAD US NOT INTO TEMPTATION...

The phrase echoed and echoed in David's mind as the Rolls
purred through the desolate hop-fields of Kent under a drift of
rain. Now and then the cone-shaped roof of an oast-house
appeared and vanished as the road curved and wound. There
was something very curious about the next of his siblings that
he hoped to recruit. From all the available evidence it seemed
she had exercised her power once, and on one person.

But once you've realized you have the talent...

After the salutary lesson of his encounter with GianMarco,
he was constantly worried about his precarious dominance of
the group. Either this Mary Gall did not properly understand
what she was capable of, and the way she got rid of her father
had been the result of an instinctual reaction, never repeated
because never comprehended, or (and David felt this was the
more likely) she must have remarkable subtlety and self-
control—or, putting it another way, the ability to resist the
temptation implied by possession of absolute power over other
people.

David Shay not only did not possess that ability, but didn't
want to. There wasn't enough time for luxuries like having a
conscience...

Which was why he had brought Crystal with him. Despite
his initial contempt, he had come to like her much the best of
his half-siblings. Her experience on the streets of London had

made her cynical, admittedly, but beneath her shellbacked veneer she seemed to hunger, as he did, after an ideal. In effect, she had a vision of a better world.

It was she, during the group's endless arguments, who most quickly and most clearly grasped the import of his proposals, and more than once it had been her alliance with him that turned the mood of the meeting against Sheila's sullenness, Terry's crude desire for material belongings, Garth's bitter detestation of all adults.

He hoped Mary Gall would prove another ally. Outwitting the others, coaxing them around to his point of view, was draining his strength. He *knew* what must be done, and how little time was left to do it. But among the rest only Crystal seemed to have any inkling of urgency...

If Mary Gall turns out to be another opponent—

But he didn't want to think about that possibility. By way of distraction he lifted the armrest concealing the car's computer keyboard and tapped out the code that interrogated the search-program hunting for Louis Parker. The screen mounted on the back of the driver's seat informed him there was still no joy. With a sigh he switched to a map display tracking their progress.

"Fork left at the next junction," he told Harry. "We should be there in five or six minutes."

Both his guesses about Mary, as it happened, were quite wrong.

She and her mother had left Marshmere in the end, unable to bear the pressure of gossip. The house had sold for a handsome profit, and their new home at Poppy Cottage was quite as luxurious if not so large, with a splendid garden. Neither of them wanted to keep the Jaguar, so that and the Citroën had been disposed of, but a medium-sized Volvo stood in the garage. A long time still remained before Richard completed his jail sentence; nonetheless Mary had insisted on Edna obtaining an injunction to prevent him from contacting them when he was let out. Everything should have been fine.

Except it wasn't.

Despite her daughter's reproaches, backed up by the use of her magic touch, Edna had grown more and more morose. She began to drink heavily, and avoided company. Often she would stay at home for days on end. When she had to go shopping, she bought at random, stocking the freezer with packages of food that later had to be thrown away unopened. Mary, who now attended a local school within cycling distance, took to playing truant purely in order to keep her mother under control. When teachers came to find out what was wrong, she of course had no trouble sending them away placated, but the task was a strain, and sometimes she found herself exhausted from the exercise of her powers.

On top of which, little by little she started worrying about what she had done. Had Richard truly deserved his fate? She had, after all, only her mother's word for it. Admittedly he had put his wife through a most unpleasant experience, but if he hadn't, then Mary herself would not be here . . .

Guiltily, she wrote letters in which she begged him to set her mind at rest, to say that he forgave her—and tore them up and flushed them down the toilet for fear Edna might find the scraps in the wastebasket and piece them together. Now and then, when she went to school, she reacted to taunts from the other pupils who had discovered (the tongue of scandal being long, long) that her father was in prison, and engaged in pointless, futile fights. Why, she wondered, did she never remember to use her magic instead?

But when she was in a calm, normal mood, the idea never crossed her mind. When she had been provoked into a rage, she couldn't take advantage. Sometimes, late at night, she would lie staring at the ceiling of her bedroom, planning the vengeance she was going to wreak on those who worst tormented her, and went to sleep chuckling. In the morning, though, she was always too preoccupied to recall her schemes, and they vanished as irretrievably as dreams.

Now winter was drawing on, and the isolation of the house was preying on her mind. She hadn't been to school for a full week; indeed it was that long since she last forced herself out of doors any further than the front gate. Edna hadn't bathed in at least as long, and spent most of the day in her dressing gown, that was overdue for laundering. Formerly she had smoked little, if at all, but now she was burning up forty a day, and the air smelt permanently stale. To compound the problem, Mary's period had started. She had lost her magic again.

She always wept a lot during the few days it lasted. Now and then she cursed herself.

The doorbell rang.

"I'm not at home," Edna snapped, reaching for another cigarette. Rain was beating a dreary rhythm on the leaded-glass windows that were supposed to add "period charm" to the cottage, but served chiefly to reduce the amount of daylight. She was pretending to read a book, but her gaze kept wandering away to watch a rerun TV game show. Why, Mary could not imagine; the sound was off.

The bell rang a second time, longer and louder.

"All right," Mary sighed, hauling herself to her feet as though she were suddenly carrying twice her usual weight. Nervous, Edna's eyes followed her out of the room.

In the narrow hallway of the cottage, alongside a window next to the front door, hung a mirror intended for checking one's appearance before venturing forth. Viewed from the proper angle, it showed anyone standing beyond the window. Mary paused at exactly the right spot, and was rewarded with a glimpse of a girl about her own age, and—so far as the window could show, which was only head and shoulders—not unlike herself in appearance.

The bell rang a third time, impatiently.

She had vaguely expected yet another caller complaining about her non-attendance at school, and as a second bet one of her fellow pupils—not that she had made many friends, and few who cared to visit her home more than once, a major reason why she had become so depressed of late. The idea of a stranger dropping in made her unaccountably excited. She hastened to open the door.

And found not the girl she had glimpsed, but a boy. Who said, "You're Mary Gall. I can tell. I'm David Shay. This is Crystal Knight."

Crystal advanced into the shelter of the porch. Short-haired, she wore an X-rated jacket, on whose front a red elasticated saltire cross framed and emphasized her bust, and tight black trousers splashed with yellow blobs: fashionable gear that Mary had envied but not dared to indulge, already being sufficiently persecuted at school. She said, not to Mary but to David, "No problem. No power."

What?

Dizzied, baffled, by that matter-of-fact comment, Mary felt her jaw fall ajar, and would have shut the door in reflexive panic but that David caught her hand and said smoothly, "Aren't you going to ask us in out of the rain?"

Rain?

Suddenly the world was a different place, and rain was far too ordinary to be real.

"Whoever it is, tell the buggers to go away!" Edna shouted from the living room. The words were underlined by a familiar chinking-splashing noise: ice-cubes being dumped in a glass, then covered with gin and not nearly enough tonic. (Tonic water was becoming very expensive. No one had yet marketed a synthetic quinine cheap enough to be incorporated in drink mixers, and the authentic kind was disappearing with the rain-forests.)

"We can handle her," Crystal said assuredly, and marched past Mary. David put his arm around her and urged her to follow.

Glancing back—they hadn't bothered to close the door— Mary saw a car at the end of the path, and a man with a worried face staring toward the cottage.

But she had no time to think about that.

Indeed, for the next several minutes it seemed she had no time to think about anything.

The rain had let up by the time David and Crystal led Mary out to the car, each carrying a suitcase full of her belongings. The man behind the wheel got out to open the rear door for them. David said, "Mary, this is Harry."

Harry nodded a sketch for a greeting. "Papers?" he muttered nervously.

"All signed. Here." David thrust a sheaf of documents into his hand, and he tucked them inside his jacket.

"What about—uh—Mrs. Gall?"

"The hell with her. She'll drink herself to death. Or set the house on fire when she's sozzled. She smokes like a chimney."

"David, don't you think you ought to—?"

"There's no 'ought' about it!" the boy flashed back. "I told you already. You had the chance to think of 'ought' before— and passed it up! So all that's left is *must*! Get in and take us home!"

You're watching TV Plus. Newsframe follows.

Half a million people in the Midlands have been warned not to drink the public water supply without boiling. Tailored bacteria from an experimental biological laboratory were accidentally spilled down a drain last week and have allegedly survived normal treatment at a sewage plant.

General Thrower today told a rally of his supporters in Surrey that Britain needs another war, quote, "to stiffen the moral fiber of this spineless generation," and brought the audience to its feet by quoting Rupert Brooke's poem about the outbreak of the 1914 war, "Now God be thanked Who has matched us with His hour . . ."

WHAT WAS ON THE MENU FOR TODAY?

Drearily Peter installed himself, as he did each morning after Ellen had left for school, in front of his computer, sipping now and then at a mugful of the latest horrid substitute for coffee. The real stuff was beyond his means these days— and, indeed, anyone's except the super-rich. Tea was about to go the same way, according to rumors that the government would not permit on radio or TV.

If only they had heeded warnings about the deforestation of Northern India . . .

Did the air in here smell bad? He sniffed, and decided: no worse than usual. He had a headache, but that was most likely due to over-indulgence last night in Ellen's homemade liquor —this time, red wine. So . . .

First, his email, in the faint hope that someone might need his talent for a story with a medical bias, despite the fury his story about the royal horses had entrained in official circles.

So strong had his reflexes become during weeks of boredom and frustration, at first he was about to dump the lot as not worth noticing. Just in time he checked his fingers on the way to wiping out the sort of message he had been dreaming of. It was from the *Comet*, and it was in caps emboldened and underscored.

COME AT ONCE!

When had the message been sent . . . ? Foggily, for this ersatz coffee had none of the arousal effect he had been used to (how long ago? When Britain could still afford to buy crops from the world's primary producers!) he scrolled back the screen display in search of the data he needed. They shocked him.

0535? Jake, at work at that hour? It can't be—must be a hoax! He wraps up the national editions at one or one-thirty and goes home to sleep . . .

At which moment the phone rang. He snatched it up.

"Jake," said a distant voice. "Thank God you finally woke up! I've been trying to get hold of you for hours! Get your arse over here, dammit!"

Peter bit his tongue to stop himself from uttering a whole bunch of profit-losing comments. When he recovered, he said, "Jake, please—why?"

"I may have been up all night, I may still be boozing at breakfast time, but I have more sense than to answer a stupid question like that over the phone!"

Oh. This sounds big. I don't want to comply, but I suppose I'd better . . .

Wishing, oddly enough, that Ellen were here to counsel him, Peter heaved a deep sigh.

"All right. I'm on my way . . . Oh, just a sec!"

"What?"—in a tone bordering on explosion.

"If I call a cab, will you—?"

"Call a bocky helicopter if you must! Just get here—and bocky well move!"

Peter rang for a cab at once, but it took half an hour to arrive, and then it was detoured by the police to avoid a procession of fishermen from the northeast, driven out of business by the ever-widening oil slick in the North Sea, marching on Whitehall to present a petition of protest.

They would not, of course, be allowed to get there. No one without a government pass had entered the zone around Parliament Square and Downing Street for eighteen months.

On reaching the building where the *Comet* office was located, he had to walk up from the ground floor. Yet another power failure had put the lifts out of operation. A battery radio that he heard when passing, exhausted, a dangerously open door on the floor below, was informing London in a cheery voice that the saboteurs responsible were known to the police and someone would shortly be "assisting Scotland Yard with their inquiries."

Why do I have the feeling that I've heard that before?

Most of the business of the editorial office was proceeding normally—after all, there was tomorrow's edition to prepare —but there was an air of tension that struck Peter immediately he entered. He noticed with surprise that Bernie was installed in his usual corner; from their by-now long acquaintance he was aware that the hacker preferred to get up around midday. Had he, like Jake, been here all night?

Red-eyed, unshaven, his jacket hung on the back of his chair, his shirt-cuffs grimy and his tie-knot halfway to his navel, the editor broke off from intense discussion with a woman Peter didn't know, and let out a cry of mingled annoyance and relief.

"Finally you made it! Don't bother explaining—I've heard all the excuses and the trouble is most of them are true. Come here! By the way, this is Sally Gough, our crime-reporter."

A long-faced woman with heavy glasses, she offered a firm handshake.

"Sit down, sit down," Jake invited around a yawn. On his

desk ice-cubes were melting in a glass, and he took an absent-minded sip. Then he leaned forward intently.

"Peter, you've got to keep this under your hat, because I finally have the beat I've been dreaming of. But I dare not publish until it's rock-solid. I have all my top people working on the story, but Bernie thinks I need you as well. And Claudia."

Peter started. "Don't tell me you found Louis Parker!"

"Who—? Oh, him! No, no, no! But what's happened may just possibly tie in with this red herring you spent so much of the paper's money on . . . General Thrower has apparently been kidnapped. Emphasis on *kid*."

"I can't believe it! How? When?"

Reaching into a drawer of his desk in search of the bottle he was drinking from, Jake indicated with a nod that Sally Gough should take over. In a few crisp sentences she explained what they believed to have happened.

"He addressed a public meeting at Sandhurst last night—Sandhurst in Surrey, near the officers' training college. It's all army country around there, solid pro-government with a strong admixture of pro-Thrower. Among the audience were a bunch of kids in their early teens. After the meeting they came up and asked him for autographs. Somehow the organizers' attention was distracted, and when they came back to look for him he was nowhere to be found. The police are working on the theory that he's been abducted by a left-wing group who used the kids for cover."

Peter whistled soundlessly. "That's incredible," he muttered.

"My reaction precisely," Jake concurred, having taken a gulp of his fresh drink. He was beginning to show the extreme caution in speech and movement of someone who knows he is on the brink of complete intoxication. "He never moves a step without a bodyguard. Anywhere he goes, he can count on scores of disenchanted unemployed as volunteers."

"This time—maybe not genuine volunteers?"

"Hmm!" Jake raised his eyebrows. "Good thinking. Sally, have we anyone who could check out the stewards at the meeting?"

Overhearing, Bernie said without looking around, "The police have already interrogated them. So far all of them have turned out to be long-term British Movement, National Front or whatever. Dyed-in-the-wool types."

"Sorry, Peter," Jake said with a shrug. "Unless the left-wingers planted them years ago, which I suppose isn't inconceivable, that knocks your notion on the head."

"Well, it was just a thought . . . But what is it exactly that you want me and Claudia to do?"

"Grief, man! Isn't it obvious?" Jake was abruptly on the verge of alcoholic rage. "A gang of kids! Making off with a national celebrity under the noses of his private army!"

"You mean you think it could have been the kids' own idea?"

"Any lead is worth following up," Sally said. "So far, you see, we appear to be the only national paper that's picked up the story. There were three other stringers at the meeting, all from right-wing tabloids, and according to what we can deduce from the grapevine they accepted the official yarn that General Thrower was too tired after his speech to answer any more questions and had decided to turn in early. Ours was the only one who bothered to sneak around the back door of his hotel and bribe the porter. General Thrower did not sleep in his own bed last night."

"He'll get a bonus for that," Jake said blurrily. "If we are the first to break the story."

"Hang on," Peter said in confusion. "I'm still not sure what exactly you want me to do."

"Oh my God." Jake leaned his elbows on his desk and rested his head in his hands. In a muffled voice, as though his patience were at its uttermost limit, he said, "Look, what I want is eight hundred words on cases where kids have broken the law and got away with it in spite of the best that adults could do to stop them. Okay? I don't want anything down-market and cheaply sensational. I want something sober, reasoned and convincing. It doesn't have to be right, but it has to be *convincing*."

"And you want it by nine tonight."

"Six would be better."

"Okay. Can I use your phone?"

Jake raised his head sharply. "To call Claudia? No way! Use a public phone, or just go straight there! The chance exists that some police nark may have noticed our reporter at the meeting, or one of the other people I've assigned to the story this morning, and started eavesdropping on us again."

"Again? I didn't know they'd stopped."

"Not funny," Jake said wearily. "Last month the Bill decided we didn't pose any sort of threat because we'd be bankrupt by Christmas. It's no secret that our sales have plummeted. But by God, if I do have to go under, I'd like it to be in a blaze of glory!"

The force of his last phrase was undermined by another uncontrollable yawn.

"Okay," Peter grunted, rising. "Claudia has an interesting theory about this phenomenon—this control over other people—going back to Neolithic times. Says it could account for Stonehenge. What about something for expenses?"

"Hm? Oh. All right." Jake fumbled for an intercom switch and issued the necessary instructions.

"Stop by on the way out. The cash will be waiting for you. And do a good job, won't you—please?"

The public phones that Peter passed on his way to the only bus route he knew still to be running in the direction of his former home had all been vandalized; some, to judge by the state they were in, several weeks or even months ago. Catching sight of a bus—far too precious to miss—he abandoned the idea of ringing to warn Claudia of his arrival, and hoped against hope that she would be in.

She was. But by the look of the flat, not for much longer. She had added only a few personal touches to it, chiefly books, posters, and a few pictures. Now she was taking them down and packing them into cardboard cartons.

"What's going on?" demanded Peter, aghast.

"I'm going to have to go home," she answered with a shrug, closing and triple-locking the door.

"When?"

"Before Christmas. Come in, sit down. Want a drink?"

"Much too early," Peter said reflexively, and thought of the state of Jake's liver. "But why?"

"Oh, the funders won. I no longer have tenure, I can no longer look forward to a salary, and Cecil Strugman has been driven to the verge of bankruptcy by a bunch of smart financial operators who call themselves Eye of the Needle. Reportedly they include the head of the Federal Reserve Board. They don't care for Cecil's political views, so they decided to force down the value of his investments. Rumor has it that they bribed the broker who handles his affairs. Cecil himself is pretty unworldly, you know."

"This is awful," Peter said, sinking slowly into a chair. "Can't your lawyer friend do anything—Walter?"

"Walter's dead."

"*What?*"

"Yesterday." Claudia passed a tired hand through her hair. "Car crash. Early snow—slight thaw—hard frost the following day . . . I suppose one has to believe it. Especially since he'd been drinking. Funny, though . . ."

"Go on!"

"I've never known him to drive after drinking. He'd leave his car on the street and risk it being stolen rather than drive himself. In fact two of his cars were stolen for just that reason. One of them turned up in Mexico."

"So you're abandoning your research," Peter said after a pause.

"I can't see any way of staying on." She glanced despondently at a pile of printout on a nearby table: he recognized it as the draft of her thesis.

"So what will you do? Couldn't you—well, if you can't keep up the payments on the flat, couldn't you go back to stay with your friend, where you were before?"

"No, she's in the hospital. Hepatitis. Could be fatal."

Peter clenched his fists. "It can't be true, but I keep getting the feeling that everybody's dying!"

"Life expectancy in Western Europe and North America has gone down each year for the past three years. Ask any actuary. Not, of course, for the very rich—mainly for people on the poverty-line, or in manual work like farming, street-cleaning, that sort of thing. And they don't buy much insurance, so . . . Didn't you know about that?"

Peter shook his head, licking dry lips. "If only *Continuum*—"

"You'd have made a program about it," Claudia cut in. "Let's skip that, shall we? What brings you here, and will it take long?"

He recalled himself to duty with an effort, and outlined the story Jake and Sally Gough had told him. Her dull expression changed as she listened.

"Lord! It's too much to hope for, but it's a remarkable coincidence, isn't it? Not that I can stick around and follow it up, of course. But—well, say again what Jake actually wants from us."

He repeated the editor's specifications, and concluded, "I thought particularly of that point you made about Stone Age culture. I'm afraid I don't recall the exact details, though."

"Stone Age . . . ? Oh! Yes, I know what you mean. My idea that this kind of control over other people might not be new after all."

"I think you said"—frowning with the effort of recollection—"it would account for Stonehenge."

"Mm-hm. Which called for an immense communal effort at a time before there were kings or armies, let alone police forces, and in a culture where there wasn't even a hierocracy of the kind that resulted in the Pyramids."

"A what?"

"Ruling class of priests, controlling people through religion. In spite of the lack of any obvious means to compel them, thousands of people worked sometimes for years to create these gigantic structures. Someone must have had a silver tongue, at least."

"That's good for a couple of paras," Peter said with satisfaction. "Can you spare the time to help me with a rough draft? I'll make sure you get your fair share of the fee."

Rising, he turned toward her computer.

"No power," she said.

He blinked in startlement. He had noticed that despite the gloom of the day no lights were on, despite the damp chill there seemed to be no heating, but had forborne to comment, assuming that her lack of funds meant she was economizing.

"No power!" she said again, standing up angrily. "It went off around nine, when everybody else in the house had left for work—or to look for some. I'm the only one here during the day, did you know?"

"Have you phoned the electricity board?"

"They claim to be working on it."

"Well, then, I suppose we'd better go to my place. Jake gave me plenty for expenses, so we can afford a taxi . . . Can you spare the time?"

She was already in the hallway, donning a coat. Over her shoulder she said, "Who am I kidding? All the gear I have I can pack in a couple of hours. I don't have to prolong the agony. Besides, I'm cold."

By tacit agreement they drafted the story as though it were the definitive epitaph for Claudia's original project. The hard part, of course, was condensing the material into the allotted space. More than once they started snapping at each other, Claudia insisting that a particular point was indispensable, Peter countering that this time Jake's limit of 800 words must absolutely be adhered to. Having broken off only to make and eat some sandwiches with stale bread and cheese they had to scrape clean of mold, they were still at it when Ellen returned from school. She seemed subdued, but refused to talk and insisted they must go on working, and disappeared into her own room. Shortly they heard the hum of her computer.

At long last they reached a compromise, and when Peter called for a word count, it came up at 799. He leaned back, stretched and yawned.

"Can't ask for fairer than that," he grunted. "And—grief, it's not yet six. Well, this ought to make a good impression on Jake. Fire up the modem, would you?"

And within moments the text was on its way.

Rising, bending back and forth to alleviate stiffness, he went on, "Lord, I wish we had something better to drink than Ellen's homemade! Still, it is improving—"

"What's wrong with my homemade wine?" Ellen demanded from the doorway.

"Sorry, sorry! I did say it's improving, didn't I—? Say, you look excited about something."

"I am." Flushed, eyes sparkling, she advanced into the room. "You want to know where Louis Parker is? Somewhere in Surrey!"

"Surrey!" Peter exclaimed. And looked at Claudia, his expression saying as clearly as words: *That's just too much of a coincidence!*

Visions of a fantastic conspiracy came and went in a flash.

But Ellen was continuing in a more apologetic tone, "I'm afraid I can't narrow it down any closer, not yet. I only know that the age fits, and the physical appearance. But the program I'm running ought to find some clue to his actual address, or at least a phone number he's been using. With luck we should have it some time this evening . . . Claudia, excuse me, but you don't look very pleased."

Claudia shrugged, leaning back and stretching as Peter had done, and explained.

"That's terrible!" Ellen cried. "But—well, goodness! After getting so close, don't you want to find out whether it really was Louis Parker who—who fathered these kids? You said you don't have to be home until Christmas, and that's still a long time off."

"Two weeks, to be exact," Claudia muttered. "Though you wouldn't think it was that long, the way everybody's hyping it this year. The shopkeepers must be desperate to make people part with their money . . . By the way, Peter, one of the investments Cecil was backing, one of those that have just been bankrupted, was a chain of stores selling organic produce and additive-free foods."

"But I thought—"

"You thought they were booming? They were. Until the slump."

"Are they actually saying slump now?" Ellen put in. "Not recession?"

"The people on the receiving end are."

Then, with an unexpected access of briskness, Claudia pushed herself to her feet.

"Ellen dear, you must forgive me, but I still find it kind of hard to believe that you managed to trace this Louis Parker when Bernie failed. Mind showing me what kind of program you're running?"

Ellen flushed again. She said diffidently, "Well, I shouldn't be running it, not really. I came by it sort of unofficially. I did honestly mean to tell Bernie about it, but—well, he seemed to have lost interest. I hope it wasn't wrong of me to go ahead on my own?"

"Wrong?" Peter echoed. "Not at all. You're a marvel! But I'd like to see it, too."

"Well . . ." She hesitated. "The trouble is, if you want me to show how it works, I'll have to interrupt the run, won't I?"

"You don't have a copy?" Claudia demanded. "One you can show us in here?" She gestured at Peter's computer.

Ellen shook her head. Today she was wearing her hair neatly braided and coiled around her small shapely head. "I'm afraid not. It's the kind that only allows any user to copy it from the master once. If you try and copy the copy, it corrupts itself. I haven't tried it, but there's a warning."

"Sounds like a high-security job," Peter said slowly. "How in the world did you come by it?"

Ellen put her hand to her mouth and bit her knuckle, giggling. Suddenly she seemed all child again.

"By trying to get a bit of my own back. I moused into PNC looking for the data they keep on brown and black people, not because they've done anything but because of their color—I wanted to find out what they had about my family, you see. Suddenly I found I'd accessed a national search program, that can trace literally anybody who's ever been mentioned on any data-base, and it mistook me for an authorized user because until I came along nobody else had ever lucked into it."

Claudia looked worried. She said after a pause, "But won't they notice? I mean, if someone who isn't really an authorized user stays on-line to the program for this long—"

"Oh, I figured that one out. Thanks to Dad."

Peter blinked, and she amplified.

"Remember all those papers you collected at the computer security conference, just a few days before I—uh—turned up? Well, you didn't seem to be using them, so I borrowed them, and reading between the lines I found the dodge I needed to fool PNC!"

She started to chuckle. But the chuckles turned into a hysterical laugh and then into tears. Claudia rushed forward, caught her in her arms, and whispered reassurance in her ear until she calmed.

When she drew away with a wan smile—but a smile—Claudia glanced at Peter.

"Know something? You do have a genius for a daughter."

Before Peter could reply, the phone shrilled. He caught it up.

"Jake here," said the familiar voice. It sounded as though he must have caught up on his sleep during the day. "Featly stuff, just what I wanted. Your fee has been sent to the bank."

"That's wonderful," Peter said. "Any—ah—progress?"

Jake hesitated, obviously asking himself what he might safely say. In the end: "So far, no sign. We're going to risk it."

"Good luck!"

Setting down the phone, he turned to the others. "He likes it and the money's been paid. And there's still no sign of Thrower. I suggest we celebrate. Let's go out for dinner."

"No," Ellen said promptly.

"Why not? Might as well take advantage of the *Comet*'s money."

"I want to be around to hear that beep," Ellen said obstinately. "I don't want to come in late and find the data has been sitting on screen long enough for someone to trace and wipe it."

"She has a point," Claudia put in. "And the way that kind of program runs through data, you don't want to waste print-out paper."

"Ah, I suppose not," Peter sighed.

"Don't look so miserable, Dad," Ellen reproved, patting his arm. "I'm going to make stuffed pancakes, and you always like those. But if you really can't stand my homemade wine . . ."

"Okay, I'll compromise. I'll go and buy a decent bottle—won't be long. Red or white?" he added to Claudia.

"I don't mind. I can't afford either, myself."

During the meal they watched the mid-evening news. There was still no mention of Thrower's disappearance, which was good from their and Jake Lafarge's point of view, but that fact was outweighed by a number of other depressing items, most notably a report from Bonn that agreement had been reached with East Germany, Czechoslovakia and Austria to monitor and announce daily on TV the declining oxygen levels in those areas that had within living memory been forested. Moreover there was still no bleep from the search program, though Ellen assured them it was still running. "It's bound to be much slower on my machine, isn't it?" she added at one point, as though growing worried. And they had to agree. In fact, Peter was privately wondering how she had got it to run at all.

But one mustn't look gift horses in the mouth . . . Given that even the royal racehorses are dying of cancer, how long before people forget what horses used to look like?

Gradually conversation died. There was another news-bulletin at ten, and since tomorrow was Saturday and there was no school Peter was prepared to let Ellen stay up for it, but a few minutes before it was due she rose despondently and announced her intention of turning in. Perhaps, she muttered, the program wasn't working properly. So long after narrowing Louis Parker's location down to a single county, it ought to have come up with more precise data.

Claudia voiced the suspicion that was dawning on them all.

"Unless he, or someone protecting him, has covered his tracks. After all, Bernie had no luck, did he? And you told us, Peter: this Parker was a computer expert."

"I wouldn't have thought of him as an expert," Peter muttered. "But it's true he did work for a computer company."

"Well, it was a brave try," Claudia told Ellen comfortingly, and gave her a good night hug. After kissing her father, she returned downcast to her room.

Where, within seconds, they heard the rattle of her printer.

"Got it!" she shouted. "The bocky thing just didn't beep! Come and see!"

Peter and Claudia exchanged glances of disbelief, and rushed after her.

"There!" she said proudly, holding out a sheet of paper. "It did work! It must have found its way to a phone line the name of Louis Parker had been spoken on, and taken ages to locate the right address. But it's done it." She was almost shaking with excitement at her success.

Taking the paper, Peter studied the address. "That's only a mile or two from Sandhurst," he murmured.

"Peter..." Claudia drew a deep breath. "I think I know what's in your mind. You're assuming something like this.

"Louis Parker found out, somehow, that he was fathering children with a gift of—of supernatural persuasiveness. He decided to exploit their power. He's raised a whole bunch of kids of his own, taught them complete obedience, and is now —what? Planning to hold General Thrower to ransom, for God's sake?"

"You were the one who came up with the idea in the first place," Peter retorted sourly.

"I did nothing of the kind! I don't make crazy intuitive leaps like that! You just forget about Thrower's disappearance. The fact that Parker turns out to be in the neighborhood doesn't necessarily have any connection with what happened after his meeting last night. The kids may have come from anywhere, a local private school for instance. The more I think about Jake's theories, and yours, the less I want to take them seriously."

"My theories? You just put words in my mouth! I—"

He realized abruptly that Ellen was turning away with lowered head.

"Darling, what's wrong?" he demanded.

Repressing a sob, she mumbled, "I thought you'd be pleased. It took a long time, and lots of hard work, and I probably broke the law by doing it... I did think you'd be pleased!"

"Of course we are!"

"You bocky well don't sound like it!" she flared. Spinning round, she revealed that her cheeks were wet.

Seeing her tears, Peter felt an appalling pang of guilt. To judge by Claudia's expression, she was reacting the same way. Finding words as best he could, he said, "Darling, I am sorry! But we are both very tired, and—and anyhow, what can we do about it right this minute?"

"Not much," she sighed. "We can go there in the morning,

though, can't we? I mean, it's Saturday and I don't have to go to school."

"Yes, of course. And I'm sure Claudia would like to find out whether her theory is correct. We'll have to figure out how to get to this place. We could take a bus, I suppose, or even a train—I think there are still trains around there. And then find a taxi, or rent a car, though on a Saturday that might be difficult, because it's a wealthy area and they're probably booked in advance . . . Ellen love, I'm doing my best to work it out!"

"All right," she said after a pause. "Claudia, you'll come too, won't you?"

"Yes, of course. What time do you want me to be here?"

"You're going home? At this hour? Don't be silly." There was a hint of peremptoriness in her tone.

Peter hesitated. "Yes, I think it might be simpler if you stay over. I can kip on the living room couch—I have a sleeping bag."

"Don't be *silly!*" Ellen said again, more forcefully.

Claudia shrugged and turned toward the door. "Okay," she said. "Good night."

"Good night! And—Dad!" Ellen had closed the gap between them with a single long stride, and thrown her arms around him. "Dad, I'm sorry I snapped at you. I do love you, you know."

"I love you," he said sincerely, and squeezed her hard.

The unexpected details of an unexpected encounter . . .
Claudia had to clean her teeth with his toothpaste on her forefinger. He didn't have a spare brush, and with the advent of AIDS sharing toothbrushes had become uncustomary. They undressed by the light of a single shaded lamp, not looking at each other. Having removed her jacket and trousers, she hesitated a moment, then discarded her bra and panties as well. He had been intending to don the pajamas lately bought—he said facetiously—in case he, too, had to go to hospital, but on seeing her naked he changed his mind. When he joined her in the bed, she embraced and welcomed him without a word.

To his surprise, their love-making was excellent.

* * *

Afterward, while he snuggled against her shoulder, she said thoughtfully, "You know, I have a peculiar feeling that I've been conned."

But Peter was already fast asleep.

HARRY SHAY FELT UNEASY AS HE SLOWED THE Rolls at the speed limit of the run-down northern town to which David had directed him.

Directed, in the sense of given orders . . .

During the long drive from Surrey, the longest time—come to think of it—that he had been away from David since returning to Britain, he had started to have second thoughts about the course he and Alice had adopted. The way the American economy was collapsing, of course, they had in one sense been lucky; they had pulled out in time to take a considerable fortune with them.

On the other hand, if anyone ever gets to hear about the way we allow these underage kids to carry on . . . !

One of them was beside him, and he kept casting worried glances at her. She looked positively demure in her dark jacket, mid-calf skirt, neat low-heeled shoes, innocent of either makeup or jewelry save for a silver watch. But she had been a prostitute since she ran away from home at twelve—she had somehow caused one of her customers to cut his own throat—she already had a police computer-record longer than his own, who had sailed financially close to the wind before he left for that land of opportunity which now was turning into a disaster zone . . .

Grief! Who'd have thought that a few tons of solvents leaking over such a large area could lead to such a crisis? But it's

*happening. It's going to be like Texas when the oil bubble
burst. For the first time in living memory California has
shown a net annual loss of population . . .*

He'd learned that by phone from Goldfarb, whom he had
rung last week. He hadn't seen it in the papers, nor on the
news services he subscribed to via computer.

Where have they gone? They surely can't have died!

As though sensing his mood, Crystal laid her hand on his
and smiled.

"You're worried, aren't you? Why?"

He was obliged to answer, though he didn't want to.

"Well—for one thing, David usually comes on these trips,
and I don't know why he didn't want to this time."

Reassuringly: "Something else has come up—very important. But until now he didn't really feel he could depute the job to
someone else. I'm flattered that he feels I can take care of this
one . . . In any case, it's the least promising lead so far."

"Lead?"

"To—another of us," Crystal replied enigmatically.

"Yes, that's been bothering me." Harry drew the car to a
halt. "How does he choose our—our recruits?"

"Through his computers, how else? The same ones that
generated this map." It was a four-color printout showing the
town down to house numbers. Leaning close despite the re-
straint of her seat belt, she spread it before him on the steering
wheel, and put her arm around his neck so that she was
speaking close to his cheek—so close, he could feel her
breath on his skin. "The Hallams live where you see the red
star. We have to take the second right, the third left, and the
first right. Okay?"

"Okay!"

She gave him a hug and resumed her place. After that he
forgot the doubts that had been plaguing him.

Pepita Hallam looked about her nervously as she dragged
her wheeled shopping bag toward the entrance of the tower-
block where she lived. There was going to be trouble when
Cynthia found out how much less than usual she had brought
home: one carton of cigarettes instead of two, no vodka,
barely enough food to keep them going over the weekend . . .

But since the detectives had arrested her at the supermarket, since she had actually been taken to court—even though, of course, she had been found not guilty—she had grown terribly uncertain of her own talent. There had always been gaps in it, naturally, and she had made allowances for them. What she hadn't bargained for was that people out of range of her influence—plus, inevitably, their computers— would be able to work out what she was doing, and pounce.

I'm going to have to get out of here. Why should I lay my neck on the block for my sick whenzie of a mother?

The sound of a car made her check and turn. Around here most cars were abandoned wrecks, either because their engines had seized up for lack of oil or because their owners could no longer afford a road-fund license or the annual roadworthiness check, or simply because of the price of petrol. For whatever reason, they served chiefly as shelters for the exploding army of the homeless unemployed.

But this one was a Rolls Royce.

And it was drawing up beside her.

And a girl her own age was first looking at her, then getting out.

A girl enough like her to be, if not her sister, then at least her cousin.

Pepita's mouth was dry, her limbs were frozen. She could only stare.

"You must be Pepita," the stranger said with total confidence. Behind her, leaning across to the open passenger door, a serious-faced man was also gazing her way.

She forced out an admission of identity. She had feared the police, of course, and was at a loss on finding that assumption irrelevant.

"Was your mother ever known as Sindy?"

"What?"

Patiently the girl from the car repeated the question.

"Well—yes! But how did you know? How do you know me?"

"All in good time. I'm Crystal. This is Harry."

Mumbled: "How do you do?"

Now Harry too emerged from the car and came to stand at

the side of his—daughter? Not very likely; there was a resemblance, but also something about the girl's manner and attitude . . .

"Harry," she said, and her tone was one of authority.

"Yes?"

"Ring David and tell him he was right. Then we'll help Pepita take this stuff upstairs."

Bitterly: "Upstairs is right! Unless they've fixed the lifts! Just as well I have a light load today, isn't it?"

Why am I saying this? I don't know these people! I don't talk to strangers about my problems!

Crystal came forward and clasped her hand, smiling. A sense of confidence invaded her mind during the brief time it took for Harry to place a call via the phone in the car. In fact it wasn't really a call, not a spoken one at any rate. What he did was convert the phone buttons into a computer keyboard and punch in a brief code. Pepita had read about that sort of thing, but of course no one in her personal world . . .

"Now," said Crystal encouragingly, "let's go up."

It isn't happening. It can't be.

Where were the howls, the screams, the drunken tantrums? What had made Cynthia remember and revert to the person she must once have been, the polite and gracious girl who made visitors welcome with cups of tea and biscuits? What had made her vanish in order to put on a dress instead of her housecoat, wash her face, comb her hair, apply lipstick? The transformation was incredible!

Gradually the truth began to dawn.

This Crystal: she can do what I can. Only better.

Pepita began to tremble with excitement. Barely an hour after the arrival of the visitors, she was packing her gear into paper bags and plastic sacks. Cynthia was sighing as though she felt it expected of her, but her eyes were shining on her daughter's behalf, thanks to the vivid word-picture of the future she could look forward to in the wealthy south . . .

Yet no one has actually put it in so many words!

It didn't matter. It was real. What she had been dreaming of had come about.

When she hugged her mother at the door, she knew it was
—if so she chose—for the last time.

Drowsy beside Crystal in the back seat of the Rolls, she
whispered, "How did you find me?"

"Ask David," Crystal answered. Overhearing, Harry spoke
over his shoulder.

"Yes, ask David! He's a phenomenon, my son! Half the
time even I can't figure out what he's doing, but it always
seems to turn out right!"

A dead pause, during which they listened to the purr of the
car's engine and the hush of its tires on the roadway and the
wind of its high-speed passage.

Son?

Unspoken, the question could be read on Pepita's face.
Sensing what she meant, Crystal donned a wry smile and
shook her head. Shaping words in a less-than-whisper, drawing back so Harry could not glimpse her in the rearview mirror, she communicated:

He'll catch on. All in good time. All in good time . . .

You're watching TV Plus. Time for Newsframe.

*In South Korea the air force has destroyed a pharma-
ceutical factory and the surrounding area with incendiary
bombs. According to the Ministry of Public Health the
operation was necessitated by the escape of organisms
containing cancer-causing oncogenes. Two hundred people are reported dead and hundreds more in hospital.
Rioting has broken out in several nearby towns. More in a
moment.*

Here at home, concern over the disappearance of General Sir Hampton Thrower . . .

"DAD! CLAUDIA!" ELLEN, IN PAJAMAS, RUSHED into the sitting room regardless of the fact that they were still in bed, and switched on the TV. "Jake got his beat!"

Forcing himself up on one elbow, bleary-eyed, Peter said, "What the—? Damn it, girl, it's barely seven!"

"Don't you want to see what's happening?" she countered, and stood aside from the screen. The early news had just begun, and the lead story was the Thrower kidnapping, broken exclusively by the *Comet*. It was mentioned that Jake had gambled on printing an extra half-million copies, and they were already sold out.

Swinging his legs to the floor, heedless of the fact that he was naked, Peter said sourly, "How long before Special Branch closes the paper down?"

"Oh, Dad!" Ellen would have stamped, but she was barefoot. "Just watch, why don't you?"

"Yes, I certainly want to," Claudia said, rising and pressing herself against his back with one arm over his shoulder for want of other concealment of her nudity. And indeed the news was worth watching. Almost half the ten-minute bulletin was given over to the subject, and it was the lead item in the talk show that followed. When that came on, Peter said soberly, "I apologize. They wouldn't dare. Not with this level of exposure."

"I bet it's on all the channels!" Ellen cried, pressing the remote control. And, indeed, it was.

"I think I'd better find out whether they want me on the box," Peter muttered. "Sling me my dressing gown, there's a love."

Moving reflexively to comply, she let her face fall.

"But we're supposed to be going to see Louis Parker!"

Peter was about to say, "It'll have to wait!"—when she darted toward the bed and dropped on her knees, gazing up earnestly at him.

"Please?" she whispered. "I have worked very hard to find him. And you did promise."

Tugged two ways, he hesitated. At length he appealed to
Claudia, who pondered for long moments, but said eventually,
"You know, I think she's right. You could probably pick up
some quick cash because you had that piece in the *Comet* and
thousands of people who never heard of you before must be
reading it right this minute. On the other hand, if while Jake is
in a good mood we confront him with the first really hard
evidence concerning the kids you wrote about . . . It could be a
long-term benefit."

Jumping up, Ellen hugged her and her father both. "Just
what I was hoping you would say!" she exclaimed. "Right!
I'll make some breakfast. You can have first turn in the
bathroom."

Since many wealthy commuters lived in the area, there
were still frequent trains to Camberley. Despite the cost—
British Rail having "rationed" its passengers by raising prices
since the late 1980's, rather than providing additional trains—
Peter and Claudia decided to travel that way. It would be a
treat for Ellen. She had never gone by train, apart from the
London tube.

It being Saturday, the train was packed, and since they
could only afford the second-class fare Ellen, at half-rate, had
to sit on their knees by turns. Watching her leaning back
against Peter, vaguely eavesdropping on the conversation of
their fellow passengers—which, inevitably, centered on General Thrower's disappearance, and reflected the scores of in-
compatible theories already circulating—Claudia wondered
about their fondness for each other. From what she knew or
guessed about him, she felt certain Peter must have been in-
furiated when his long-neglected daughter was dumped into
his life. Moreover, given that he had abandoned her mother
when she was pregnant, and shown virtually no interest in his
own child until they were thrown together, one might have
assumed that Ellen would resent her natural father. Yet now
they seemed to be on the best of terms. It was almost as
though she had seduced him into accepting her. Certainly she
had charmed him . . .

In the long run, might not such a relationship become—
well—unhealthy?

However, all such thoughts evaporated when Ellen, to give her father a break, came and sat on Claudia's lap instead. No, she was just a normal if unusually intelligent girl making the best of a bad situation, and doing so with mature competence.

You, Claudia chided herself, *have paid too much attention to too much scandal. Not every single male parent has sinister designs on his nubile offspring . . .*

With a wry private smile at her own suspicions, she turned to gaze out of the window. The glass was streaked with rain, growing heavier by the minute.

An almost constant series of FOR SALE signs met her eyes, mainly on empty factories. The economic crash that had begun in the States was taking its toll here as well—that, and competition from more efficient countries elsewhere in the EEC. She recognized the name of one firm; a recent news report had mentioned that it was moving lock, stock and barrel to Spain. A wan-looking group of former employees, sodden by the downpour, were holding up banners for the passengers to read, but the windows were too smeared for them to be legible.

Whenever the train stopped, groups of hopeful beggars darted up to the alighting passengers, whining after alms. Armed police dragged them aside, cuffed them about the head, pushed them back against the wall, saluted their intended prey. By Camberley, however, it was no longer the police but the army that was on patrol.

"You think this is because of Thrower?" Claudia murmured to Peter as they prepared to get out. Face strained, he nodded.

"Something wrong?"

"Yes." He bit his lower lip, glancing sidelong at Ellen.

"We can brazen it out. Come on."

She caught his hand—and, on the instant, froze. His answering squeeze reminded her how skilled that hand had been last night . . . and also that she had made love unprotected.

Am I insane?

It was his turn to ask what was amiss. But before she could answer—before she had even had time to reason through what she was alarmed about—Ellen was urging them onward, toward the khaki-clad men and women guarding the exit from the platform, some of whom were already curling their lips at the sight of someone with dark skin. With a sick sense of foreboding, Claudia noticed that they were all wearing red-white-and-blue ribbons.

Then the miracle happened. A clear voice called, "Peter! Peter Levin!"

They halted and swung around. Approaching was a tall man, extremely well-dressed, who had just emerged from one of the first-class compartments.

"Peter, don't you remember me?" he demanded.

"My God, of course!" Peter caught his hand and shook it warmly. "Harry Shay! I've been trying to get hold of you for ages! What made you leave California—? Oh, by the way, this is my friend Dr. Morris, Claudia Morris, and this is my daughter Ellen. Harry Shay, formerly of Shaytronix Inc.! What are you doing back in Britain?"

Flourishing a season ticket, Harry led them to the exit, brushing aside the suspicious soldiery with such authority that they simply turned their attention elsewhere. They were outside in no time, sheltered against the rain by an awning. From a gray Rolls Royce waiting illegally in the roadway a hand waved and the engine started.

"Got out while the going was good, shall we say?" Harry replied at length. "More to the point, what brings you here—? Ah, don't tell me. Let me guess. I saw that piece of yours in the *Comet*—dreadful rag, don't normally waste money on it, but when they got this incredible scoop . . . Your editor has sent you down to follow through?"

"Well, not exactly," Peter admitted. "We're on the track of something different—"

Ellen butted in unexpectedly. "Mr. Shay, do you know anyone around here called Louis Parker?"

Harry repeated the name, frowning. "No, I don't think I do. Where does he live?"

Before the adults could answer she produced a slip of paper from the pocket of her jeans.

"Oh, I know where that is. I'm going past it, in fact." The Rolls drew up level with them, and a bright pretty face smiled from the driver's window. "You remember Alice, I'm sure! Alice, look who I've bumped into! They're going to call on

someone who lives nearby—let's give them a ride! We can't
make them walk, and they'll never get a cab on a day like
this!"

"Featly!" Ellen exclaimed, and clasped her hands.

Claudia murmured something under her breath. Peter
glanced at her.

"I missed that?"

"I said: if all our problems could be solved so easily...
Thanks a million, Mr. Shay!"

It was infinitely relaxing to ride in this luxurious car, protected against the chill and damp. Even the empty shops
masked with tattered posters, the groups of workless youths
shivering in their doorways, the police in yellow plastic capes
chaining up abandoned cars to be dragged away for scrap,
could not erode their sudden joint mood of optimism. It was
as though they were aware of reaching journey's end. Claudia
tried to think about what they had to expect—what they were
going to say to this mysterious Louis Parker when at long last
they encountered him—but laziness like the effect of good pot
pervaded her mind, and she was content to relax and let things
happen.

The town gave way to suburban roads lined with gaunt
trees. The leaves they had shed, sodden with wet, barely
stirred in the gusting wind. Here and there they saw optimistic
youngsters gathering them up in wheelbarrows; they would
make compost from them during the winter, and sell the result
next spring to fertilize the gardens of wealthy local residents.
It was one of the employment schemes fostered by the government. Of course, it didn't provide a living wage, but it was
supposed to keep them out of mischief, and it assuaged the
demands of the Greens...

All of a sudden they were turning off the road down a
winding driveway. Peter became suddenly alert. Tensing, he
glanced from side to side.

"This is the address your daughter showed me," Harry said
in a reassuring tone.

"But should we just turn up like this, unannounced?"

It was obvious what he was worrying about. At the mouth
of every driveway for the past three miles there had been signs

warning of security patrols. In the aftermath of the Thrower kidnapping, were they not bound to have been redoubled?

"Don't worry, Dad," Ellen said, laying a hand on his. And, miraculously, he didn't.

The car halted outside a large Victorian house: not a mansion, but immense. Peter whistled.

"Did all right for himself, didn't he—old Louis? Well, all I can say is thanks very much, Harry. And hope the guy's at home. Otherwise we've come on a wild-goose chase."

A disturbing point crossed Claudia's mind:

Why didn't we phone to say we were coming?

However, a second later she had thought of reasons why not—*mustn't alarm him, if he's warned he may run away...*

And was distracted because both Harry and Alice were getting out of the car.

Following uncertainly, Peter said, "But..."

"You go ahead," Harry smiled. "Go ring the bell."

In fact, though, that was unnecessary. The front door swung wide and here came a boy bearing a huge umbrella. He hurried over to the car with a broad grin.

"Mr. Levin! Remember me? I don't suppose you do—I was only about eight or nine when we last met. I'm David. And you're Ellen, aren't you? Great to meet you!"

To Peter and Claudia's vast astonishment, the two children embraced like long-lost friends.

"Quickly! Inside!" Alice cried. "It's pelting down!"

And long before objections could be formulated, they had been rushed into the hallway. It was dry in here, and warm, and there was a pervasive pleasant smell of roasting meat: lunch being cooked rather early?

That was the first thing that struck Peter and Claudia. The second was a series of indications that the house must be full of children: bicycles propped against the foot of a balustraded staircase, a dozen pairs of small rubber boots untidily against the wall, discarded anoraks waiting to be hung up...

No toys. But definitely children's belongings.

Peter blurted, "Does Louis Parker live here?"

Harry shook his head.

"Then why have you brought us here?"

"This is the address you asked to be brought to. It just so happens that it's ours."

"I don't understand!" Clenching his fists, Peter rounded on his unexpected—and suddenly unwelcome—hosts.

"Don't blame him, Mr. Levin," David said softly, taking his arm. "It wasn't his idea to bring you here. It was mine. You see, I have something to show you. And you too, Dr. Morris. If you would kindly come this way...?"

Moving as though in a dream, Peter and Claudia allowed themselves to be led across the wide tiled hallway to a door at the far side. Opened, it revealed a high-ceilinged room with immense windows giving on to a neglected garden. Children, all about David and Ellen's age, all with the same dark hair, the same slightly olive complexion, the same general build, were standing around a long oak table. At once the smell of roast meat became intense.

As though they had been rehearsed in their movements, they parted to let be seen what lay on the table: a naked human figure, seared and blistered and blind, its hair scorched off, its limbs contorting in pain but restrained by plastic straps. Hanging from the ceiling, the impersonal eye of a TV camera, whose field of view the children carefully avoided, was recording the victim's agony.

"Mr. Levin, you're a reporter," David said. "Among other things. Allow me to present General Sir Hampton Thrower. He has been exposed to precisely the degree of heat—we couldn't imitate the blast effect, but the heat was easy—that would be suffered by someone standing unprotected on a clear day five miles from the ground zero of a one-megaton hydrogen bomb exploded at ten thousand feet. In other words, the typical yield of one of the missiles that would inevitably be used in the war he claimed would be so good for the people of Britain."

Claudia doubled over, striving not to vomit.

"But—"

Peter managed to force out the single word despite his own violent nausea.

"You wish to know how we could be sure?" David murmured. "Well, the data are available . . . But to be on the safe side, we had our calculations checked by someone you know."

Overlooked until now, a familiar figure emerged from an alcove, untidy, shabbily dressed . . .

"Bernie!" Peter burst out.

"I couldn't help it," the hacker muttered, his eyes roving everywhere save toward the ruined figure on the table. And then, with a hint of defiance: "I think it serves him bocky right, anyhow!"

"A taste of the medicine he wanted to prescribe for others," David confirmed. "By the way, he'll live. Long enough to be shown on television, heard describing the agony he's suffered, making his apologies on the grounds of ignorance . . . Of course, as the old legal principle has it, *ignoratio legis nihil excusat*—saying you didn't know it was against the law is no defense. We rely on you to organize that for us—*Dad!*"

Harry, who had been hanging back beside the door, said uncertainly, "Well, I'll do what I can, of course. But—"

The children suddenly burst out laughing, except for David, though it cost him a visible effort to control himself. A hint of amusement nonetheless colored his voice as he said, "No, Harry, not you. Nor Louis Parker either, though I confess that for a long time I, too, imagined he was the person we were looking for. In case you're interested, he wasn't having an affair with Dr. What's-her-name. She must just have been a bit of a fag-hag, as they used to say, because he's homosexual. We've traced him to a villa near Malaga. He made a fortune peddling amyl nitrite to the gay community in London, enough to retire on before he was forty. So that leaves . . ." And he cocked one eyebrow.

"Oh my God," Peter said brokenly, clenching his fists.

David looked at him steadily. So did the other children. So—and this was the worst—did Ellen.

"I think you finally caught on," David murmured.

But instead of answering Peter began to groan.

"Come now," David said comfortingly, and took his arm. "We'll adjourn to another room and sit down, and Alice will bring you a drink, and we can all talk about it. Then you'll understand."

▓▓▓ ▐▐▐ *I DON'T UNDERSTAND, I DON'T UNDERSTAND . . .*

Peter came slowly back to himself. He was in a drawing room, huge, handsomely furnished with armchairs and settees covered in floral chintz, its windows half concealed by matching curtains drawn together at the top, held apart lower down by braided ropes. It was approaching noon, but the light outside was gray and dismal.

Yet I don't feel as awful as I should!

And that couldn't simply be due to the fact that the chair assigned to him was so comfortable, nor even the warming impact of the glass of brandy—traditional restorative—which Alice had handed him, its aroma running ahead of its hot taste. He glanced at Claudia. She was paper-white and shaking.

So should I be. I've just seen a human being reduced to a condition worse than . . . I don't know what it could be worse than. Is there anything worse? Except maybe to have live maggots dining on your flesh!

And then, unbidden: *If someone did let off those bombs, the victims would be food for maggots, wouldn't they, long before they died?*

All of which, contrary to his will, seemed distant, veiled and far away.

It's as though, the moment I crossed the threshold of this house, everything I've worried about lately, everything I've been afraid of, has—well—receded.

"It has," David Shay assured him, kneeling on a cushion at his side. Until that moment Peter hadn't been aware of speaking aloud. Yet he must have been—either that, or these children could read his mind . . .

319

Briefly distracted, he gazed from one to other of them in search of clues. Obviously these were the kids Claudia had come to Europe in search of, the ones that Bernie had failed to trace despite his mastery of hacking—

Just a moment!

As usual, Bernie was staying in the background. Peter might have overlooked his presence in the dimness but for the fact that Alice was offering him too a glass of brandy, and he had eagerly accepted. He found himself staring in that direction.

"Bernie, you lied to us," he said.

The hacker shrugged. "You try doing anything else when this lot are around," he sighed, and sank half his brandy at a single gulp. And then, as though relenting, as though inclined to apologize, he added, "My fault, I suppose. I thought if I could track them down before you and Claudia did I could get the fee from the *Comet*. I'm broke, aren't I? Same as virtually everybody in this poor sick country! And I have kids of my own!"

Peter jolted upright, but before he could speak Claudia had whispered, "We didn't know."

"Why should you?"—with contempt. "My bitch of a wife took them away from me. All I do nowadays is pay for them . . ."

He finished the brandy and held out his glass for more. Silently, one of the boys brought the decanter. Peter wondered which of them it was and what crimes he had been guilty of. The more he looked at these children, the more they seemed to resemble one another. He hadn't noticed until now, but they were all wearing the same kind of clothes, girls as well as boys being clad in jeans and sweaters. It was as though the fashion-clock had stopped somewhere in his own teens. He had worn precisely similar garb . . .

This is distracting me!

Foggily, perhaps more than ever because of the brandy, Peter strove to make sense of what was happening. He forced out, "There's something in the air! Is it a drug?"

Claudia glanced up at that, and a trace of color returned to her cheeks. Perhaps that was something she too had thought of, and been unable to express in words.

But Harry said with prudish sternness, "Peter! Do you really think Alice and I would let these kids use drugs while they're in our charge?"

Our—charge . . . ?

Once again Peter felt a sense of total bafflement. But David touched his knee with a gentle hand.

"Don't bother trying to work it out. We've brought you here for explanations, and as soon as you're ready—"

"Ready?" Peter exploded. "Bocky starving for them!"

"Very well." David sat back composedly on his cushion, folding his hands in his lap. "You're right: there is something in the air. But not a drug. Bernie?"

At first the hacker was reluctant to respond, but a stern unison glare from the children seemed to compel him. Noticing, Claudia feebly tried to push her chair closer to Peter's, but though it was on casters, the carpet was deep-piled and she couldn't manage it. At a signal from David, however, Harry was prompt to assist her, and she and Peter were able to link fingers across the abutting chair-arms.

Meantime Bernie had found words.

"I suspected this from the start," he muttered. "In fact I'm surprised Claudia didn't spot it before I did."

Nettled, she retorted, "You saw my analysis!"

"Yes, but you were asking the wrong questions . . . Oh, the hell with it. *I* don't want to talk about it. Leave it to David."

And he subsided into private misery.

Summoning all his concentration, Peter rose to his feet. He said, "Now you look here! Apparently you brought—you *lured*—us here because you want me to tell the world that what you've done to General Thrower is right and justified! If that's the case, I tell you right this moment, you are barking up the wrong bocky tree!"

"That's only secondary," David said with a trace of weariness. "More importantly: we wanted to meet our father."

"But there are too many of you!" Peter blurted.

For a second he imagined he had scored a masterly point. David, however, was patiently shaking his head.

"Clever of you to think of that, but you're wrong. In fact, we aren't too many. We are actually one too few. Now tell us:

what was the name of the woman you made pregnant while keeping company with Ellen's mother?"

"I never knew her name!"

"You said she was called Sindy, didn't you?"

"Y-yes." Uncertainly he licked his lips.

"In full, her name was Cynthia Hallam," said one of the interchangeable girls. "I'm Pepita Hallam, her daughter. And yours."

For a terrifying instant Peter had imagined her to be Ellen. The rest of what he had intended to say died in his throat.

Another of the girls, who had been standing against the wall, stepped into the middle of the floor. She said, "You were right, Dave. It does work the way you said... By the way: hello, Dad! I'm Crystal—Crystal Knight."

"I don't understand—"

"You keep saying that! Save your bocky breath, will you? David claimed that our talent can stop people asking the wrong kind of questions before they agree to do as we want. Most of us were pretty doubtful, even though we'd seen what we can do to Harry and Alice, not to mention the people who come in to clean up and help around the house. But he called you Dad already, and you didn't seem to catch on, so I guess he's proved his point. Either that, or you must be so shell-backed the computer people would like to know your secret... Ah! It looks as though Dr. Morris has finally logged on!"

Snap. It was the sound of Claudia's brandy glass breaking between her fingers. Blood ran down. There was an interval of mopping up and finding sticking-plaster. During that whole time Peter stood as fixedly as a statue. It didn't seem to him as though he had been petrified; it didn't seem as though he had been ordered to stand still. It was just that so many hints and clues and odds-and-ends of data had clashed together, so belatedly, that he had no energy to spare to move a finger. He barely retained the ability to breathe.

And kept thinking, over and over: *What am I actually breathing?*

Claudia's cut fingers being dressed, as though he had read Peter's mind David threw over his shoulder, "Not drugs—I speak with authority on that subject, I may say—but pheromones. That's what I hoped Bernie would have the guts to tell you. But as usual he's chickened out. So you're going to have to take it straight from me. Alice—Harry—I'm sorry. It's not going to be much fun for you, either. But it sure as hell isn't going to be as bad as it has been for most of us kids. I'm the lucky one, and I thank you for it. The others..." He shrugged, and resumed his cushion. "Well, we aren't going to ask you to pass judgment. We already did, especially on General Sir *Hateful* Thrower. Your function now—your only remaining function—is to shut up and do as you're told."

Where's Ellen?

The question sprang unbidden to Peter's mind as he sank slowly back into his chair. He needed his daughter's love and affection at this moment, to help him combat the terrible accusation he did not dare confront alone: the charge that these were *his* children, not those of Louis Parker...

But the midday light in here was so dim he could not distinguish Ellen from the other children. She too, he remembered, had donned sweater and jeans this morning, plus an anorak that now lay discarded in the hall...

I can't recognize my own daughter any more!

The taste of defeat was sour in his mouth. He tried to wash it away with another sip of brandy, but that didn't work. In the end, he husked, "Damn you! Go on!"

"Precisely as I predicted," said David Shay. "Your response on meeting your family for the first time is to say—*damn you!*"

And suddenly the air was full of menace. Gone was the sense of diffuse calm, of relaxation, of protection against the sight of Thrower burned halfway to death. Now there were eyes in the twilight like the eyes of wolves, watching and waiting for the moment to pounce...

Peter wanted to scream, but even that surcease was denied him.

"It's time," David said, and his voice seemed to have grown deeper and more resonant, like the tolling of a funeral bell, "for you to meet your children, and be told what they have suffered because you wanted a few more pounds to spend."

It wasn't like that! But Peter couldn't frame the words. The room had turned into a court of justice, and there seemed to be no jury, only judges. Even Harry, even Alice ... Even Ellen! Which of them *was* she?

"I'll start with myself," David said. "My ostensible father Harry had himself vasectomized because he wasn't interested in his first family and indeed was glad to say good-bye to them when he acquired a younger and more beautiful new wife. Only he still retained the macho image of a Man's Man as one who had to have offspring around, and in this view Alice heartily concurred. She wanted to be a Mother, capital M, as well as the partner of a successful businessman who could provide her with the sort of lifestyle to which she had always hoped to grow accustomed. Since Harry wasn't willing to risk an attempt to reverse his operation, the answer was the Chinn-Wilkinson clinic.

"Where you, Peter Levin, were the provider. Invoking Louis Parker was a clever attempt to evade the responsibility, but—well, the story goes that they had to supply him with ramrod porn before he could make his donations. As for Dr. Wilkinson, one assumes she was afraid of her femininity and obliged to sublimate it via the fertility clinic ..."

He snapped his fingers. "Oh, yes! A point I've been meaning to mention. According to Ellen you tell people that Levin means 'love-friend'! But did you know it also means thunderbolt? That makes us the children of the thunder, doesn't it? The Boanerges of our day! And the storm is due to break ..."

In the gloom his eyes seemed to glow, as though they were looking far beyond the here-and-now. Peter strove to speak and could not. Nor, as he saw when he glanced at her in desperation, could Claudia; she was in as piteous a plight as he.

And David was holding forth anew.

"Now let me introduce you to the rest of these children whom you just damned—and explain why we were already damned without exception, including me. Did I want to be a necessary status symbol rather than a proper son? I think I know what that means. Harry doesn't."

From the corner of his eye Peter saw Harry cringe. He wondered whether this was the first time the accusation had been brought against him so publicly, so nakedly . . . and had no time to complete the thought, for the inexorable words were flowing onward like an unstoppable river.

I'm being put on trial. For something I didn't even realize I'd done . . .

Once more it was as though David had read his inmost thoughts. He said, "Before I go on, perhaps I should cite another legal principle. I admire the law, and wish more people paid attention to it . . . Not knowing something is against the law is no defense, as I mentioned. But it has been held for centuries that a reasonable person is responsible for the foreseeable consequences of his actions."

"Foreseeable!" Peter managed to blurt out.

"Foreseeing is a duty," David countered in a dead voice. "How often did you, Peter Levin, consider the outcome of what you were doing when you donated sperm?"

"I—I hoped I would be making childless couples happy!"

"Very good!"—in a tone of surprise. "You have, as it were, entered a plea of not guilty. But these, here now assembled, are all your children. It is their verdict you must face."

"Children I've never met before?"

"We'll come to that. Right now, what concerns us is not your intentions but their outcome."

"I'm to be condemned because half a score of kids I knew nothing about were badly treated by their—?"

"No! No! *No!*" David was on his feet in a single swift motion. "You still don't understand!

"We are humanity's only hope of salvation."

With a sense of indescribable despair Peter realized:

He's a megalomaniac, and he's infected the others with his beliefs. And given that they have this power . . . !

He buried his head in his hands.

SUDDENLY PETER FELT HIS CHEEK BEING STROKED, and within seconds the future seemed less terrible. Of course, he could not reconcile the fact that he was calming down, even relaxing, while in the power—Power? Yes, that was the only word for it—*in the power* of these children who had demonstrated their willingness to submit another human being to indescribable agony...

Another human being? But even if they are my offspring, are they human?

Such thoughts evaporated as a hand sought his. It was Ellen's (yes, really, this time it was Ellen beside him) and he clasped it gratefully. Claudia was clinging to her other hand, jaw clamped tight to stop her teeth from chattering with terror.

"Now let me introduce the rest of us and tell you their life stories so far," David was saying in a didactic tone, rather like a lecturer conscious of teaching an unpopular subject. Peter couldn't help being reminded of Jim Spurman. "Then I'll explain how we got together, and deal with any questions you may have. It shouldn't take more than an hour or so, and afterward we can have lunch. In passing, Dr. Morris, let me compliment you on having traced us all, even though of course as soon as I realized how close you were I took steps to prevent you contacting any of us directly. For the fact that you were misled into believing it was Louis Parker who was always one jump ahead of you I have Bernie to thank, he being already predisposed to blame someone else even before Peter offered him a scapegoat—and of course Ellen, who has proved immensely helpful."

Loosing her hand from Peter's, Claudia bit her knuckles to

suppress a hysterical giggle. David favored her with a patronizing smile, and resumed.

"I thought of introducing us in order of age, but I think it might be easier to do it in the order in which we got together. As it happens I am the oldest, but we're all pretty close, naturally."

Naturally? A sick joke sprang to Peter's tongue, but it remained unspoken, surviving only as a bitter taste.

"I've told you about my own background. So we might as well carry on with Dymphna—Dymphna Clancy, from Ireland. Her mother, living under a régime that forbade divorce, was married to a man who treated her abominably for not producing children. In the end he drove her insane. One of the first signs, no doubt, of her impending breakdown was that she flew to London where such treatment was legal and, using a forged letter of authority purporting to be from her husband, had herself inseminated at the Chinn-Wilkinson clinic. That establishment was not run on quite the impeccable principles to which its directors claimed to aspire . . . Dymphna eventually wound up in a Catholic orphanage where, after reaching puberty, she delighted in committing supposedly mortal sins and getting away with them."

Peter could recognize Dymphna by her broad grin. Though she was paler, and freckled, and there was a tinge of red in her hair, she was unmistakably Ellen's half-sister . . .

"The blame, though, does not lie with her—nor with any of us. A sick society, that made her mother's husband so cruel to his wife, is what's at fault . . . And now to Roger, whose offenses were not dissimilar.

"Born to a mother who agreed with her husband that, while it was their duty to produce a child, that child should be sent away as soon as possible for at least three-quarters of the year to boarding school, Roger discovered when he entered puberty that he had certain tastes and certain talents. At the ripe old age of thirteen he was successfully operating a service for pedophiles, from which, by the way, he accumulated a considerable sum of money. Nothing like as much as I derived from selling my designer drugs, of course, but—"

Despite the restraining grasp of Ellen's hand Peter could

contain himself no longer. He burst out, "You sold drugs? You dealt in narcotics?"

David gazed at him blandly. "No. I designed them. Others manufactured them and sold them. I simply took a commission. Why not? None of *us* would ever be stupid enough to use them."

It was the first time he had so blatantly implied that he and the other children regarded themselves as different.

How different? A different species? Do they think of themselves as "the man after man"?

Ellen released her fingers and began to soothe the back of his neck, easing away tension with every stroke. Peter had intended to continue, but was forestalled. Claudia, regaining at least a modicum of self-control, was leaning forward.

"You keep referring to puberty," she whispered.

David nodded.

"Like most human pheromones, ours is hormone-related, more so in the case of the girls. In them secretion ceases for a short time once a month. In compensatory fashion, when it's at its peak it's far more powerful, and more effective against both men and women."

Against? The terrifying possibilities implicit in that single word made Peter shiver—but once again he had no chance to speak, for David had resumed his exposition. Apart from the occasional sound of a vehicle passing on the distant roadway, the silence was virtually total, as though the children were waiting to hear what he said about them and prepared to issue their own verdict afterward.

Or—and this thought was absolutely chilling—*do these pheromones knit them together into a superorganism, so that they will inevitably agree with their leader because they can't do otherwise . . . ?*

The implications almost prevented him from hearing what David said next.

"After Roger, I got in touch with Crystal. She's had a very bad time indeed. Her legal parents died in an epidemic of meningitis. A cure was found, but too late. If a fraction of what this country spends every day on armaments had been invested in a vaccine they would almost certainly have survived. Crystal would not have been committed to the care of a couple of religious bigots—would not have been beaten for petty offenses until she was driven to run away and seek a living as a prostitute, having to sell her body for the first time to the doctor who vaccinated her against AIDS."

Peter, appalled, could tell which Crystal was. She was nodding slowly, back and forth, with the measured rhythm of a mandarin statuette.

"Compared to her—though he might not agree—Garth had things easy. Trapped on an isolated farm by parents whose convictions about 'going back to the land' deprived him of most of the ordinary experiences young people should be able to look forward to, he did at least find it possible to turn the tables so that he wound up in control of them, and not *vice versa*. Correct, Garth?"

It was the first time he had appealed to one of the others for approval. Peter tensed, hoping for a contradiction. On the contrary. Garth gave a sour chuckle.

"They scared easy. Once I'd killed our bocky neighbors' prize sheepdog, and particularly after I'd drowned their son in our brook, they were amazingly pliant."

A girl spoke up, sitting in the darkest corner where Peter could not see her face. Her voice, though, was so like Ellen's . . . ! Bar a slightly different accent, it could have been his daughter's—

It is my daughter's.

Slowly, sickly, awareness of the truth was penetrating his mind.

What was she saying? He forced himself to recapture her first words, which he had nearly missed.

"I made my first kill before you did, Garth. I'm Sheila Hubbard, Dad . . . Dave, I want to speak for myself."

"Go ahead," David invited with an expansive gesture, and added by way of footnote, "Since joining us, Sheila has changed her mind about the way she looks at her plight."

"True," the girl acknowledged, hunching forward with elbows on knees. "I used to think it was my fault that soldier died—"

"The one who drowned in the river?" Claudia exclaimed.

"Yes, him." Sheila's tone was as dead as the soldier. "But I only killed him. My mother was responsible, because she wanted a child and her first husband didn't, but she went ahead anyway—"

"How?" Peter forced out.

"Let her finish!" David reprimanded sharply. "I told you— the Chinn-Wilkinson wasn't nearly as ethical as its owners claimed, at least when thousands of pounds were at stake . . . Go on, Sheila."

She shrugged and spread her hands. Still in the same dull tone, she muttered, "Well, she left him and got married again, this time to a rich old growser with a mess of money. But for a long time I didn't know I wasn't my official father's kid. I was lied to. I think it was knowing that my mother had lied to me that drove me to do—well, what I did."

"That," David prompted, "and the discovery of your power?"

"Shit, we've all been that route, haven't we?" Sheila sighed, and leaned back into darkness.

"Yes," David said. "It's a temptation. Just as well we got together before any of us yielded to it on the grandest scale, hmm?"

There was a pause, as though some of the children were still not convinced, but eventually there followed a murmur of agreement. Peter's view of what was going on kept shifting; he was no longer so sure that all the kids were under David's sway, even though Harry and Alice obviously were. So there might be some hope of escape . . .

He hadn't realized until now that escape would be necessary.

"Next I got in touch with Terry," David resumed. "You won't know his name, any more than you knew the others', but if I say he was running a neat little protection racket with a handful of older boys . . . ?"

A suppressed chuckle. The room was growing ever darker, yet Peter's watch confirmed that only as much time had passed as he had guessed. The rain, then, was due to redouble as the clouds densened—and here came the clatter of waterdrops as fierce as bullets. Raising his voice to compensate, David said, "Well, what else would you expect? A kid raised by a family of loyal government supporters, persuaded that if they didn't make their pile out of their little local shop they were somehow betraying Britain as the traditional nation of shop-keepers... Small wonder their son—excuse me: their boy—took to what is customarily called a life of crime."

Terry stirred. Until now he had been as motionless as he was silent. Now he said, "Some people call it private enter-prise, you know."

There was a general chuckle. Clutching at straws, Peter thought: *Well, at least they have a sense of humor.*

Already his background in medicine, biology and the media was reinforcing his suspicion that these children might regard themselves as superhuman...

"The next of us that I met was Tracy Coward, who made the silly mistake of trying to take away an engagement ring from one of her former school-fellows, and—"

"No, it wasn't!"

Everyone turned to see who had spoken, in a rough harsh voice. It was Bernie, emboldened by brandy. He was having difficulty hauling himself out of the armchair assigned to him, as though he had put on a vast amount of weight.

"No, it wasn't!" he barked again, and tried to set his glass down on a nearby table. A hand snatched it from him seconds before it would have crashed to the floor.

Steadying himself with an effort, he plunged on.

"The next was the one in Italy—the one whose mother wanted him because unless she had a kid expresso bongo she and her be-lov-ed brother would have lost her husband's fam-ily estates! The one who turned out better than the lot of you! The one you burnt alive because he would have been your rival!"

There was a sense of chill in the room, not due to the wintry weather outside.

Then David rose to his feet. "Bernie," he said softly, "you're sailing dangerously close to the wind."

There followed a chorus of agreement, while the children shifted menacingly on their chairs and cushions.

"I was planning to tell the story of GianMarco in due time. You think it should be now. Very well. What do you have to say about him?"

Defiantly: "That you got rid of him and his family in case he proved to be too much for you to cope with! Peter—Claudia—he arranged for the family's home to be burnt down!" Bernie rounded on them. "And this was a kid, a teenage kid, and his own half-brother! Not a whenzie cank like Thrower! A kid, the age of my own eldest son!"

He was shaking with passion, hands curled like claws before his chest.

"Crystal," David said softly, but not too softly to be heard, "make a note. Alcohol can minimize the impact."

"After continued exposure," Crystal suggested.

"Good point. Something to bear in mind. I wonder whether the invention of the still has something to do with the historical pattern. Mark that for further investigation."

"Will do."

For the first time Peter, still transfixed by the conflict between what he was hearing and how he was feeling, noticed that Crystal was wearing a computer-remote around her left wrist, like a calculator watch. She tapped several keys in rapid sequence, and there was a click from what until this moment had looked like a Louis XVI bureau.

Illusions, deceptions! Let this whole situation be un-unreal!

"However, in fact"—David turned commandingly to Bernie—"GianMarco was a failure because he had fallen beyond hope into the trap of the past. A born whenzie, as you might say. He had become convinced that the land his family owned belonged to his family. It does not! We—all of us—belong to the planet, and not the other way around!"

For the first time Peter felt a glimmering of the—the ideology? Perhaps the faith might be a better term?—that inspired this terrifying boy. If he was concerned to preserve the resources of the Earth, that was at least rational . . .

Rational? Or rationalized?

The question obtruded, because he remembered seeing a TV report: a family trapped in a burning house in Italy, their only son's name being GianMarco . . .

But he must compose himself to listen yet again. Ellen's caressing hand on his nape conveyed as much.

"I know Tracy doesn't want me to talk about her," David said. His voice had become suddenly light and clear, more like that of an ordinary teenage boy. "But, Trace, we all have to face the consequences of our actions! Sheila's managing it—"

For the first time one of the other children dared to interrupt. Again, had he not known that Ellen was perched on the arm of his chair, Peter could have imagined that the words were hers.

"I'm the only one who was such a bocky fool! And won't I wear the scars to prove it all my life?"

"Engagement ring," Claudia said softly. Unexpectedly, she seemed to have regained more of her self-possession than Peter. But then, she hadn't been hit with such a load of unwanted responsibility... During the next few seconds Peter hated her.

The emotion didn't last. It wasn't allowed to.

"I don't suppose I need to go into detail," David murmured. "For Tracy's sake, though, I ought to mention that it was because she was brought up by a couple who cared so much for trivial possessions, who indeed regarded her as a possession—"

"Dave, you're making her cry! Stop it!"

Peter could not tell who uttered the exclamation, but it was a boy, not a girl, who dropped at Tracy's side on the floor and put a comforting arm around her shoulders. David hesitated.

Ah! So he doesn't have total control! There is still hope!

The hope, though, was faint—and growing fainter...

David said, "Those responsible will be called to account. That's a promise, Trace. And there won't be any more scars."

"Except the ones the bocky canks have left where they don't show!"

The other children, even David, nodded in total unison. Peter could no longer see their eyes, so dark was the room as the storm beat at the windows, but he knew they were fixed on him—and Claudia—and Harry—and Alice...? No, there was no sign of Alice. She seemed to have left the room, doubtless to prepare the lunch reference to which had so amused Claudia.

"Nonetheless," David said gratingly, "they will be called to account. If they are not, we shan't survive."

■■■ ■■■ BEFORE PETER HAD TIME TO DO MORE THAN START worrying about that ominous statement, David resumed.

"Next I tracked down Mary, who is also still in two minds about what she did—she had her father sent to jail. However, she is gradually coming around to the majority view."

"Which is—?" Claudia demanded. Peter envied her relative self-control, achieved without the reassuring caresses Ellen was bestowing on his own nape.

"We cannot afford the luxury known as a conscience. The enemy we are up against certainly doesn't have one, so we are obliged to be absolutely rational. Cruel, if you like. People of good will, tolerant, liberal, whatever term you care to use, have always labored under a disadvantage. Those in power, those who want to hold on to power whatever the cost, have one ultimate recourse. If all else fails, they are prepared to kill. This is not available to pacifists. Mary, is there anything you want to add?"

The girl nodded. "Dad brought it on himself. I thought so in the first place; then I stopped being so sure; then I realized I'd been right the first time. Maybe it was rough justice, but it was justice. The bocky hypocrite!"

"That brings us to Pepita," David continued. "Our newest recruit. Daughter, as I mentioned, of Cynthia Hallam whom you knew only as Sindy, whose husband realized at once her child could not be his—he was yet another hypocrite—and threw her out. She became an alcoholic. It is a very sick society you brought us into, isn't it?"

Peter ignored the gibe. He was foggily trying to solve a mystery that had just occurred to him.

If Pepita is the latest recruit . . . I assumed Ellen! She can't ever have been here before! Does this mean that she isn't actually one of—of them? If she is, of course, it would explain a million things, up to and including Claudia and me last night . . .

"He's wondering why you haven't mentioned me yet," Ellen said.

Grief! Perhaps she really can read my mind!

"There's a reason for that," David said with a wry smile. "I found all the others. Ellen is the only one who found me. Though we'd never actually met before today. Isn't email wonderful?"

Peter, jerking forward on his chair, twisted around to stare accusingly at Ellen.

"Does this mean you knew these were"—he had to force the words out, had to hear his own voice shaping them—"my children? So what was all that taradiddle about four Louis Parkers? Why didn't you tell me the truth? If you had—"

"If I had," she cut in, "you'd have turned us into a newspaper story and a TV show, wouldn't you? And maybe a scientific article or two"—with a nod at Claudia. "That had to be prevented. By the way, we're obliged to you for recalling Louis Parker, even though you misled me and even David for a while. He turned out to be an invaluable red herring."

Awareness of the burden he carried in his genes was affecting Peter much as might the news that he had cancer. He wrung his hands.

"But, Ellen, I thought you—you loved me. You've told me you do, often enough."

Rising, withdrawing a pace, she gazed down at him. Seeing the iciness of her expression, he felt a pang as though something within his chest had been ripped apart.

"Love you?" she said. "After the way you treated my mother—after the years when you never bothered to get in touch, never sent me so much as a birthday card? Don't make me laugh! But what counts is that you love me. I know! You can't help it."

"I . . ."

Abruptly Peter was dumbstruck again, overwhelmed by the impact of fresh revelation. Watching keenly, David nodded.

"I was wondering how long it would take you to work out

the nature of our gift. It's a very old one. It may have been quite widespread at one time—Dr. Morris, you had some thoughts about that, I gather, in connection with the way ancient peoples were drawn to work together on colossal projects like Stonehenge before there were kings and armies and police. It's an interesting suggestion, worth looking into.

"But of course it's always cropped out in certain individuals, and nowadays it's usually called charisma. The commonest of its manifestations, though, is when one person falls in love with another, and can't escape the attraction even when he or she is totally mismatched.

"Putting it bluntly: we have the power to make people love us. They can't avoid it. It deprives them of reason and judgment, it makes it impossible for them to accept that we are guilty of any kind of crime—at least so long as we are nearby and preferably able to touch them now and then. The pheromone seems to be absorbed quite efficiently through the skin, as well as the nasal passages.

"And, naturally, possessing such power, we intend to use it. Because we want to live. Do you understand? We don't want to be burned in a nuclear war—we don't want to be poisoned by the food we eat and the water we drink and the very air we breathe!"

His voice rose to a pitch of passionate intensity.

"We want to survive! And we aren't going to let anybody stop us!"

You're watching TV Plus. Now for Newsframe.
Dr. Wallace Custer, who claimed to have evidence that the plastic from which most soft-drink bottles are made contains solvents that affect the intelligence and sanity of children, was found shot at his home in Berkshire this

morning. Reports that he had committed suicide were discounted by his wife and family. However, the police—

(All sets tuned to that channel went dead. Later it transpired that the Throwers had made good their threat to close the station down. With a bomb.)

THERE FOLLOWED A PAUSE MORE DREADFUL THAN any that had gone before. Peter's tongue felt like a blanket in his mouth, but somehow he contrived to speak.

"Use your power? For things like what you did to General Thrower?"

David shrugged. "They should not be necessary too often —though it went off very well for a first attempt, hmm?"

"But—"

Suddenly the boy was stern. "Don't tell us we should have been more merciful! He's been eager to consign people to that sort of hell all his life. He resigned as deputy C-in-C of NATO because he didn't like his precious nuclear toys being taken away. *You* know that. If he'd been allowed to carry on, the chances are excellent that he'd have become a dictator, Hitler-style. I've modelled it. All it would take is a fifty percent increase in crime, unemployment and bankruptcies. And the trends are there."

"But what else are you planning to do?" Peter whimpered. "You said something about salvation—"

"I'm glad you noticed." Now David's tone was ironical.

"I don't see—"

Abruptly the boy jumped to his feet and walked across the room to stare out of one of the tall half-curtained windows at the teeming rain.

He said over his shoulder, "Tell me, Mr. Levin, when did you last open a newspaper or switch on the TV news without being told about a political crisis, or an economic collapse, or an ecological disaster? Or a war, or starvation, or people being driven from their lands and homes?"

"Well, of course the news—"

"The news has been too bad for far too long!" David spun on his heel and pounded fist into palm. "We're going to do something about it! Nobody else can, so it's up to us. I told you: we have the power and we intend to use it. It'll take a while to bring it under fully conscious control, but some of us are pretty good at that already, so there's no doubt it can be done."

"Just you kids?" Claudia said incredulously. "Just you dozen kids?"

"Don't underestimate us. In a group, we're irresistible. We've proved that. General Thrower took about five minutes to decide that the thing he wanted most, right now, was to dismiss his bodyguards and come with us."

He hesitated, then added with a renewal of his wry smile, "Besides, it won't always be 'just a dozen.' Peter made you pregnant last night."

"What?" Claudia leapt to her feet. "How in hell's name can you possibly know that?"

"I've been keeping track of the dates when you visited us during your period," Ellen said composedly. "The timing is precisely right. And Peter fucked you twice. I was listening."

"I'll get an abortion! Or the 'morning-after' pill!"

"Oh no you won't," David said. "You already love your child. As much as you love us. Because it will be one of us."

Of a sudden the odor that had mingled with the smell of roasted meat when they first arrived in the house, which they had stopped noticing thanks to olfactory overload, redoubled in intensity. Peter shivered anew, and this time found he could not stop. He went on shaking, *shaking*.

"I . . ." Closing her eyes, pressing her hands against her temples, Claudia swayed. One of the boys helped her to resume her seat.

"Are you still in any doubt, Dad?" David murmured. "Oh, I called you 'Mr. Levin' just now, didn't I? Well, I think we ought to forget about that, and even about the use of Dad. After all, very shortly half of us are going to be on extremely intimate terms with you."

Peter's mind had wandered down an alleyway of the imagination, at the ends of whose forking branches stood small but menacing bands of children, his children, waiting to waylay the VIP he and other reporters were accompanying: a cabinet minister, an ambassador, the chairman of a bank, the managing director of an arms company, the spokesman for a government-in-exile . . . No. Not menacing. Welcoming. Ready, and able, to change their minds.

Or burn them alive.

Surely some people must be immune . . . ?

"Didn't you hear what I said?" David snapped.

What did I miss? Something about "intimate terms"—Oh, my God. He can't mean it. How can he possibly mean it?

Frantic counterarguments sprang to mind—*inbreeding, imbecility, why me and not the boys?*—but he was unable to utter them. David's words were inexorable.

"It has to be you to start with. I haven't yet pinned down the gene or genes involved, though I'm working on it, of course. The power is fully expressed in us, yet you don't seem to possess more than a slight trace, a commonplace sort of personal charm, so one can only assume a connection with your inheritance on your mother's side. I plan to look into that later. But since every last one of us has the power, and we need to increase our numbers as fast as possible, we'll have to start with you. Meantime, of course, we boys will play our part. There won't be any lack of willing women, as I can personally testify... Speaking of which," he added maliciously, "doesn't it turn you on, the prospect of making love with so many under-age girls? They're all pretty, they're all healthy, they all have lovely figures—"

"Shut up!" Peter exploded. "I won't have any part of it!"

"That's where you're wrong," Ellen said, rising from beside him. Stepping to the center of the floor with the slinky elegance of a professional stripper, she writhed her sweater from around her torso, tugged it clear of her hair, tossed it aside. Cupping her small bare shapely breasts, firming her nipples between forefinger and thumb, she leaned first one and then the other toward what was suddenly her father's eager mouth. A fraction of an inch from his lips, she snatched herself out of range.

But Peter had hardened on the instant. How quickly was conspicuous from his discomfort. The other children burst into cruel laughter.

Yet at the same time he felt as though, at long last, he had met the woman of his youthful dreams, the one whose name he had used as a key to his computer passwords . . .

Sharing the general mirth at least to the extent of a broad grin, David said, "I thought so . . . Well, in fact, of course, you won't have the chance to actually screw your daughters. They're not inclined to get next to anyone who cares as little as you did about the fate of his offspring. Still, in a sense it will be quite like old times, won't it? I don't know what they used to arouse you at Chinn-Wilkinson, but given the impact Ellen just demonstrated it shouldn't be too hard for the girls to make you—what did they say in the Bible about Onan? Ah, yes—'spill your seed' as often as we require it!"

Indeed, to Peter's shame and sick dismay, his penis was throbbing in his pants against his will . . .

With indescribable horror he looked from each to other of his children.

And felt wave on wave of uncontrollable, intolerable *love*.

Launching one last desperate appeal for help, he turned to Claudia. Tears were trickling down her cheeks. Nonetheless she managed to force out defiant words.

"Have you asked the girls how they like the idea of being turned into baby-minders at their age?"

"That doesn't enter into it," David sighed. "Thanks to Bernie, we've found an expert willing to transplant fetuses as soon as they're viable—including yours, of course; you won't have to carry it to term. So the girls can start again every eight weeks, which they welcome because it means their power won't be weakened by having periods. I believe you've met the person I'm talking about: Dr. Ada Grant? She says there'll be plenty of takers because so many men are infertile nowadays owing to environmental poisons . . . You might say that we plan to reproduce like cuckoos, if at a faster rate. I only hope it may be fast *enough*!"

For some reason that reference to cuckoos struck Peter as incredibly funny. He strove to master his reaction, and failed as completely as he had failed to control his—now cold, now sticky-wet—ejaculation.

The door of the drawing room swung wide. Alice entered. "If you lot have finished," she said brightly, "lunch is ready —Why, what on earth is wrong?"

And stood there, baffled, at a loss to understand why one of their guests was weeping silently and the other lost in paroxysm after paroxysm of hysterical laughter.

—South Petherton
February—June 1987

ABOUT THE AUTHOR

John Brunner was born in England in 1934 and educated at Cheltenham College. He sold his first novel in 1951 and has been publishing sf steadily since then. His books have won him international acclaim from both mainstream and genre audiences. His most famous novel, the classic *Stand on Zanzibar*, won the Hugo Award for Best Novel in 1969, the British Science Fiction Award, and the Prix Apollo in France. Mr. Brunner lives in Somerset, England.

Winner of the
Hugo Award
and
international
acclaim...

JOHN BRUNNER